fire in the veins

Genesis of the End

Graham Davidson

Published by Rack and Rune Publishing
rackandrune.com

Preface

After twelve years and countless drafts, here it is! Fire in the Veins: Genesis of the End had its actual genesis in 2010 when I was hired to develop a proposal for an animated television series. *The Protectors* never did find a buyer, but there was something about the twenty-page back story that beckoned to be pursued.

The first book in a series, it was also my first venture into writing outside of my professional work as an illustrator/animation designer in the advertising industry. As such, when I finished the first draft back in 2014, I made the same 'rookie author' mistake as others before me: I thought the book was ready and released it for a short time, online. Needless to say, it didn't take long before I realised it needed more work, and lots of it.

But the bones were always there. And in the years since that premature launch, much of what, at the time, were outlandish 'predictions', proved prescient. Beta-readers declared that no plague would ever lead to the grounding of global air traffic. "Far too fanciful to have any credibility," they said. Then, in 2020, COVID hit. In keeping with this, some of the futuristic technology featured in the book is well and truly on its way to becoming reality, and some of the political concepts that appeared improbable, are now more than possible (the United States may, indeed, split in two!).

By contrast, the prospect of generative AI was already being mooted in technical fields. As such, while there has been absolutely no use of AI within the writing process, it seems fitting that generative AI has been among the many tools used in creating the cover design, in the same way that I, and most other designers, have manipulated stock photography in the past. As a professional designer who has ridden the technology wave since 1978, AI is now an indispensable part of my everyday design workflow.

In the years since that early first draft, I've had several short stories published, written and self-published a junior novel and three middle grade/YA novels, illustrated eight books (including six children's picture books), founded and directed a Writers & Arts festival, established an author services company that to date has produced over one hundred titles, ghostwritten a memoir, facilitated several critiquing groups, and run numerous self-publishing workshops. On the back of what I've learned through these experiences, my career has shifted from being primarily focused on visual creativity to the wonderful world of literature. It also led me to recognise it was time to deep-dive once again, into my debut novel, which had sat idle in the drawer for so long.

You'll find a glossary at the back of the book to clarify some of the terminology used within the story.

I hope you enjoy the ride. I can assure you, it's a wild one.

Graham Davidson.

For eveyone who dares
to dream of the future

Prologue

"Sometimes, I feel…" Ron's hands trembled as he struggled to get the words out. "I feel like I wish it would all just blow up." He took a deep breath, held it in for several seconds, then slowly released it. His voice lowered to be little more than a whisper. "Everything, the whole fucking lot."

Doctor Petra Chan sat in an ornate high-backed chair with red lining and detailed gold trim, reminiscent of a fairytale throne. She held a notepad in one hand while holding an old-fashioned clutch pencil between the slender fingers of the other as it cradled her chin. "Oh? How so?" she asked, her face framed by the shiny black hair that flowed past her shoulders.

"*How so?*" asked Ron from where he sat on the plush, blue velvet couch. "What's that question even meant to mean?" He preferred to sit during these sessions, loathing the stereotypical image of the patient lying on their therapist's couch.

"You've brought this up before," Petra rolled her eyes mockingly, "this idea of blowing it all up." She leaned forward. "Is it something you've fantasised about? Something you've contemplated actually doing yourself? Have you gone as far as planning it out in these fantasies?"

"Planning? You just don't get it, do you? Like I've told you before, I'm not *serious* when I have those thoughts… it's unthinkable! The consequences…"

"And yet, as unthinkable as it may be, you *have* fantasised about it, haven't you? Could it be that a part of you sees it as your only hope of achieving some kind of inner peace? The peace that you've always been denied?"

"It's not like that," he replied.

Petra responded with brutal silence, an accusation apparent in her cold stare.

"Well, maybe," Ron fidgeted as he continued, "I am. I'm still angry. Really angry. Is that what you wanted to hear?"

Petra held her gaze.

"And you..." He raised a finger to point at her, an attempt at pushing back on the intensity emanating from the deep pools of her dark brown eyes. "You told me just last week." His own eyes darted back and forth while trying to avoid direct contact. It was a losing battle. He met her gaze, his voice shaking as the words spilled out. "You told me that's pretty normal after what I've been through."

"Of course, but you still need to tell me more about these bizarre fantasies, so we can both understand more about these supposed global consequences you've talked about." She paused before asking, "What exactly would they be? Do you imagine them in any sort of detail?"

"Why? Why would you *want* to know that? Why would *anyone* want to know that?"

"It's my *job* to know. Don't you see? Your anger, it still underlies everything you think of or contemplate. It's evolved into a deep-seated passion, a seeming lust for revenge that drives your innermost thoughts. I can help you take back control of those thoughts. But first, I need to ascertain just how extreme your passion for retribution really is... how far you're willing to let your imagination take you in a quest for cathartic release."

Ron's jaw trembled, betraying his growing frustration. "You're wrong. There's no valid link between the two."

"Oh?" Petra's eyes continued to tear at the fabric of his self-esteem as she leaned forward.

"They're just fantasies, nothing more. When I remember them, it helps me hold it together."

Petra still didn't respond.

"Isn't that normal?" he asked. "Don't you ever have thoughts of getting your own back on someone?"

"What I might have thoughts about isn't relevant here. My job is to ensure you're in a fit and proper mental state to control a major part of the single most important research project ever, one that could give humanity control of its destiny. It's what's happening in *your* head that matters. Not mine, or anyone else's for that matter." Petra sat back and hung an arm over the back of her chair. "And now, it's come up again. This recurring theme: fantasies where billions of innocent people suffer some kind of extreme consequence. And it's all because of your grievances with Alicia and your brother, Ben."

A tear trickled down his cheek. "Please, don't bring him up again."

"But isn't that what this is all about?" She brought her face as close to his as the distance between them allowed. "Just a fortnight ago, you told me about how you'd visualised strangling both of them. And the first time you found yourself imagining that? Why, it was a mere two or three weeks *before* Ben's mutilated body was found."

"They, everyone... they... they thought it was me."

"But you were working, doing your regular shift at the lab. The police know that. The Global Intelligence Agency knows that. The media reported that. Everybody knows, it couldn't have been you."

Ron's whispered response was barely audible. "If I'm truly honest, in a way, I wished at the time that it *had* been me."

"What, that you'd been the one to swing the axe?" asked Petra.

"Sometimes I—"

"Is it that you imagine yourself swinging it into your brother's back?" She flicked her wrists from left to right, making light of the gruesome scenario they were discussing. "Or, do you imagine Alicia killing *you* instead of him? Which is it? Do you wish you were the one doing the killing or the one being brutally slaughtered? Either way, it's not a pretty picture, is it?"

"She killed me long ago," he held a hand up to his chest, "in here."

"So, you *do* wish it had been you rather than her? Have you ever thought about what the ramifications of *that* would have been?"

"Ramifications? She hasn't had to face any."

"Maybe,' Petra shrugged her shoulders, "or maybe she just left the country."

"No. She's still here. I know she is. We're still connected, on our wristbands. I still message her." He cast his eyes downward. "But she never responds."

"If there's no response, how can you be so sure you're still connected, or that she's still here? And besides, don't you think that's a bit reckless?"

He shrugged his shoulders. "I guess if she did respond, the GIA would seize control of my wristband to track her down. But you know what? I don't care."

"No, that won't happen. Your work is too important. The last thing the project needs is a search warrant interfering in your affairs. And that's been made clear to all GIA operatives aware of your situation. Nothing is to interfere with your work—or our therapy sessions."

"Is that right?" replied Ron. "Well, perhaps it would be better if I got a *new* therapist. Someone who's not quite so aggressive in their approach."

"Come now, Ron. Do you remember what happened the last time you tried that one? Another therapist? That's not happening. Besides, no one but me has the required security clearance. You know that as well as I do. We're in this together for the duration." She paused for a moment. "But this isn't about me. It's about you and your anger management. And yet, here you are, going out of your way to protect her. Why? Is it about the boy? Are you protecting him?"

"I couldn't care less what happens to him. He's their son, not mine."

"So, why protect her?"

"I've told you all this before. How she said she'd tell them. My colleagues, my mother—everyone."

"Why should that worry you?" Petra shrugged her shoulders. "Nobody particularly cares what you get up to in your spare time."

"I do. I care."

"Why?"

"You're just not getting it, are you? It might change how they see me."

"I've met your mother. It wouldn't worry her. And Jardine, your boss? He's gay anyway. Why would he care about you getting it on with some dude? It wouldn't matter to your other colleagues either; the whole campus has a pretty normal spread of sexual preferences. Why would you worry about what any of them think?"

"Because, I feel like I've failed—like I've failed everyone. Alicia had said, she'd said she wanted me—that she loved me—more than anything. My mother and siblings? They all wanted to see us together. The 'perfect couple,' or so everyone said. And me? You know what I wanted? I wanted a family. A family of my own." Petra's blank stare compelled him to continue validating himself. "My father? He'd failed us all. I wanted to show that I was different—that I could do it right; to be that perfect husband—that perfect father. I liked her. I liked her a lot. And yes, I did genuinely *love* her when we were first married. I felt so sure that she loved me too."

"But it wasn't enough?"

"What do you think?"

An uncomfortable silence followed as Petra strained her neck forward, peering into his eyes, urging him to continue.

"It took a while, but after she fell pregnant, that's when I started to get a glimpse of who my wife *really* was. We'd lived together for two whole years before that, and there'd been no warning signs."

"Well, she *was* pregnant," replied Petra. "That changes things: needs, expectations, moods."

"But it was more than that."

"Oh, Ron. You're so used to being Mister Perfect, aren't you? The archetypal overachiever. School captain and dux of the school, athletics champion, swimming champion, flying through degree after degree, one of the country's youngest recipients of a doctorate. An amazing job: heading up research into groundbreaking technology. Technology that will change the future." She paused as if trying to process all that Ron had accomplished. "And yet, here you are, you're still so very angry about her having a bit of an affair with your brother... even after she'd found you in bed with *your own* lover."

"That's *not* what made me so angry."

"Oh?"

"It was discovering I wasn't Merrick's father, that his real father was *my own brother...*"

"Do you really want to go through this again?"

"The boy *I'd* helped deliver." Petra stared out the window as Ron rolled into a familiar diatribe. "My perfect son, who turned out to not be *my* son at all. Alicia and Ben... they'd been going at it for years behind my back! You *know* that. I was unfaithful just that *one* time... and I got caught." He paused. "I don't even know how that happened."

Petra lowered her notepad and tapped her chin with the clutch pencil before asking, "Are you perhaps just scared that maybe you're gay? Is that what this is about? Is that why you're so angry?"

"To be honest, I don't really know. Maybe that's why I didn't want Alicia to tell anyone." He leaned forward himself, bringing them even closer together, then buried his head in his hands, tears streaming down his cheeks. "I don't know who I am anymore."

"Did you enjoy it more than being with your wife? Could that be why it troubles you so much? From what you say, Alicia didn't seem too troubled by your infidelity. Could it be that you were simply evening the score a bit? Maybe you would have been better off pursuing an open relationship."

Silence.

A small smile escaped Petra's lips. This was a woman who took great pride in her work, pride in how skillfully she was able to manipulate a man who, to her, was little more than a puppet in a far grander scheme. "Don't you see? You're the same person you've always been and always will be. But the thing is, you've been thrust into a position with *huge* responsibility at a very young age."

"I'm not up to it. I just can't do it anymore."

"It's my role to decide whether or not you're up to it... and to help you navigate through this difficult time." She put her pencil down and leaned back in her chair. "But right now, I want to hear you tell me again... what *would* happen if you blew it up? If you blew up the Infinity Campus? What would these global consequences be? I want to know every gory detail of how you envision this calamity."

***

Petra closed the front door behind her as she arrived at her home in the leafy outskirts of New Haven. She put her bag down on the kitchen bench and kicked off her shoes. It'd been a good day. Although the session with Ron had run longer than usual, she felt her nearly decade-old plan was about to reach fruition.

She swiped her wristband to activate her lensview, then glanced up to the call icon in the upper left corner of her field of vision. She tapped her index finger against her leg before swiping the same finger to scroll through her contacts. Having found the right one, she tapped again and waited for the call to go through. "Alicia?" she asked when the icon indicated the call had been accepted.

"Yes?" The voice at the other end of the line was tentative.

"It's me, Petra. It won't be much longer now. He's just about ready. You'll be able to come out of hiding soon. Then we'll fly away from here. I can't see it being more than another month or two."

"Thank God for that. Has the idiot cottoned on to what's going on yet?"

Idiot? Who's calling who an idiot? thought Petra. "No, the poor boy doesn't have a—" The conversation was interrupted when a notification came up that someone was approaching the front door. Petra smiled when the camera revealed the visitor's identity. "Sorry. Something's come up," she said. "I'll have to call back tomorrow." She terminated the call then flicked her hair back and straightened her dress as she walked down the corridor and opened the door.

"Sorry, I'm early. Have I caught you at a bad time?"

"Your timing couldn't have been better. Come on in, before someone sees you."

He strode in, loosening his tie as he made himself at home. "Should it seem so unusual that someone pays their one-time therapist a home visit?"

Petra couldn't see that such a stupid question warranted an answer. "Do you have it?"

"Oh, yeah," he said as he handed her a tiny vial with a few drops of syrupy liquid. "There's well over a million nanobots in there. They're concentrated in a liquid form due to the vacuum in the container."

"No problems with security?"

"It was easy. Jardine's so trusting. He'd never think to question one of his hand-chosen team leaders. Especially not someone with my level of security clearance." As Petra slipped the flask into a pocket inside her handbag, he asked, "You *are* going to make sure that doesn't get released into the environment, aren't you?"

"I told you before, my client's looking at this from a purely economic point of view. If Infinity is the only corporation with this technology, their monopoly would give it far too much power."

He nodded, his expression betraying his uncertainty. "You do know that—"

Petra pressed a finger against his lips. "No more questions. Your job is done." She took his hand. "Now it's time to discuss your terms of payment." Leading him into the main body of the house, she thought, *Come, Judas, come collect your 40 pieces of silver.*

***

Emily Lucas pulled the ring box from her pocket. She opened it and pulled out the old coin cradled within its worn padding. Barely a centimetre in diameter, it had been a gift from her husband, Adrian, not long after they'd started dating.

He'd said to her, "I want to show you something special." Then, he'd pulled the little box from his pocket and opened it to reveal the small and battered coin.

"Where's it from?" she'd asked.

"From the ancient city of Ionia," he'd replied as he removed the coin from the box, "the birthplace of science as we know it. It's well over two thousand years old."

"So, I'm looking at a piece of history?"

"Perhaps it was used by an Ionian philosopher to buy a drink in a tavern, by the tavern owner to pay a carpenter... who then maybe used it to buy food from a market gardener. On and on." She remembered how his eyes had lit up as he'd held it up between their faces and asked, "Who knows what wondrous stories this little coin could share?" He'd then taken hold of her hand and drawn her close as he explained, "My father gave it to me when I started working for the UN. Now, I want you to have it." She'd felt a warm glow envelope her as her future husband placed it in the palm of her hand and folded her fingers over it before declaring, "I want you to keep this as a token, a reminder, of when humanity turned to reason above emotion to answer the big questions. You're a remarkable woman. You *can*, and you *will* make a difference. I believe in you."

That was Adrian all over. Flowers? Jewelry? No, he'd been too deep a thinker for that.

Why did you have to go and board that flight? Why aren't you here with me now... now when I need you more than ever? She rolled the coin once more in her fingers. *Why did it have to be that flight?*

Without his inspiration—without his steadfast belief in her, she never would have considered a life in politics.

A tiny drop of moisture trickled down her cheek as she held up the coin and stared at the image of the griffin stamped on the back of the cold silver disc. Here she was, almost twenty years later, watching the final count come in on her re-election. It was humbling to win with such an overwhelming majority. And yet impostor syndrome still consumed her. Despite everything she'd achieved in her first term, the same thought continued running through her head. *I'm not cut out for this.* She stared at the coin as she continued rolling it over in her fingers.

Adrian had always told her it was the fact that she didn't crave power, the fact that she didn't consider herself presidential material... those were the very reasons she was the right choice. "You've got the best judgement of anyone I know," he used to tell her.

It'd be so different if you were here. Everything seemed easy when you were around. Damn those jihadists... damn them to hell!

A knock on the door brought her attention back to the reality of the moment.

She slipped the coin back in its box, returning it to her pocket as she said, "Come in."

The door opened halfway, just enough for Daniel, her chief of staff, to stick his head in the room. "They're getting impatient for you out there. Are you just about ready?"

"Yeah, I'm good now. Let's go do this." She strode out of the room with deliberate confidence in her stride, an act of defiance against the emotions and doubts plaguing her.

The crowd chanted as she entered the auditorium, "Em – i – ly! Em – i – ly!" Her apprehension dissipated, and a smile exploded across her face as the crowd's chant was overtaken by their rapturous applause. Emily approached the lectern, both hands raised in a victory salute. Then, she leaned toward the microphone, the cheers subsiding as the crowd pushed close to the stage to hear what their freshly re-elected president had to say.

"Four more years! Four more years of sane, compassionate government. Government that puts people before technology and profits." The crowd erupted in a roar of approval. Emily stood back, absorbing the strength that came from the enthusiasm of her supporters. *I really can do this,* she thought. *Yes, I can do it for them.*

1

Gordon's stomach churned in agonising pain with each breath he took as his eyelids made an abortive attempt to lift. At first, it felt as though they were glued shut. But on his second attempt, he willed them to remain half open while they adjusted to the light. His mouth was parched, filled with the taste of dust and metal. He raised a trembling hand and held it against his forehead, trying to settle the throbbing pain in his skull while he struggled to focus. Gazing through the swirling dust, he took in the scene of utter carnage and destruction that surrounded him.

A burst of lightning flashed over the distant town as he pulled a sliver of glass from between his bloodied fingers. He stared at the distorted reflection of his face, hoping it might reveal some clue as to where he was and what had happened.

The lab—it had to be the lab—or what was left of it. From what he could tell, the whole campus was in ruins.

Tossing the glass aside, he turned his attention to the lack of information coming up on his lensview, the contact lenses that interfaced with his wristband. There were no icons, no text prompts; nothing. He lifted his wrist and inspected the band's cracked screen. Raising it higher, he swiped it and, in a rasping voice, issued a command to the broken device. "Security." After a few moments of silence, he called out louder, "Security! For fuck's sake—is there anyone—is there any goddammed bastard out there?"

He heard no response other than the persistent ringing in his ears as his earbuds received a faulty signal from his wristband. *Holy shit,* he thought, *there's no releasing those without a working wristband.*

Someone *had* to be out there, surely. With grim resignation, he accepted that, with his wristband and lensview out of action, there was no alternative but to rely only on what he could see, hear, touch, and smell.

"Guess I'm on my own for the time being," he mumbled. He felt impotent without his conduit to the rest of the world. And there was no way of knowing how long it might take the devices to self-repair, or if they were even salvageable.

The sting of the dust in his eyes brought his attention back to the immediate situation.

What's happened? Was it an explosion... an earthquake?

He slumped back into the rubble and twisted remnants of what had once been his place of work, the dust making every breath painful. Overwhelmed by anxiety, he feared he'd never live to experience the joy of another sunrise. *Is this it? Is this how it ends?*

Jumbled thoughts haemorrhaged as quickly as they appeared, becoming meaningless, like a surreal and contorted dream.

As he lay there, he continued breathing in the swirling dust, his mouth now even drier than before. Again, he tried raising his head, triggering awareness of more excruciating pain, this time in his left leg and ribs.

Grimacing with agony, he mumbled, "Bad idea, Gordy, better to just relax for a bit." He surveyed the debris around him once more. *This is different*, he thought, *I've moved. I'm sure of it.*

From out of the haze, a figure emerged from the mess of tangled metal, bricks and concrete rubble, moving toward him. A pair of familiar, worn brown shoes was all he could make out at first, the man's face obscured by the haze of floating dust.

The ringing in his ears had subsided somewhat, suggesting at least that his earbuds were still capable of self-repair. Distant sirens reverberated through his head as he felt his consciousness slipping away once more.

Is this real? Or is this just a really, really bad dream? His meandering thoughts were interrupted by another jolt of pain through his chest as he was rolled onto his back.

A muffled voice he was familiar with gently wound its way through the dark fog in his brain. "Gordon?"

He looked up, relaxing somewhat as the face of his companion became more recognisable.

"Gordy, hey! Are you alright?"

A groan escaped his dried and cracked lips before a single word slipped through them. "Craig?" Then, as the first drops of rain fell, he opened his mouth wide to the wetness of the rain, oblivious to his companion.

Craig brought his head down lower, allowing him to look into Gordon's eyes. "I thought you were a goner, like the rest of them. Then I heard you calling out for security. How bad are you hurt?"

Gordon lay there for a minute, letting the question sink in. *How bad are you hurt?* It seemed like the most ridiculous query he'd ever heard. "What do you reckon?" he croaked, his question followed by a guttural groan.

"I guess you've seen better days." Craig shrugged. "But hey, you're alive. That's more than I can say for everyone else." He looked off toward the approaching sirens. The Infinity campus was a long way from town, and there was still at least a minute, or maybe two, before the emergency vehicles would arrive. "Sorry to be the bearer of bad news, but we need to get out of here."

Gordon managed to lift himself enough to prop up on an elbow and face Craig without craning his neck too much. "Why, what the hell happened?"

"Suffice to say, there was a bomb... and it went off in a big way."

Gordon strained his head to take in what he could as he looked through the swirling dust to the ruined building and the remains of its surrounding parkland. Broken bodies were strewn randomly throughout. "It must have been damn big to cause this."

Craig looked away for a moment, then turned back to face Gordon, the effort to look him in the eyes quite apparent. How would he deliver the full news of their predicament? He spoke in a slow, deliberate manner, rain dripping off his face. "Gordon, what's happened to you and I, and everyone else for that matter, that's not..." He was struggling to find the words. "What I'm trying to say is, all this... it was no accident." He looked away again, his eyes scanning the area around them. "You need to know the containment chamber. It's been..." He took a deep breath to compose himself. "It's compromised."

It was the last thing Gordon wanted to hear. The consequences of a containment breach were too much to comprehend in that moment. *How could that happen?* The containment area was several floors underground, specifically to avoid any risk of a breach if the building were damaged. "It must have been one hell of a blast. I mean, even just the concrete surrounding that whole area..." He needed time to sit with the reality; to get his head around the ramifications. "What about everyone else? Jardine, Tanya, Lloyd, the rest of the team?"

Craig hesitated for what seemed an eternity before his voice dropped to a whisper, his foot tapping fast, "I've walked right around all of what's left of the campus." Tears traced wavy lines through the dust on his cheeks, his voice faltering as his shaking hands wrapped around his forehead. "As far as I can tell, we're it... the only survivors." He stared up into the rumbling storm clouds and took another breath to steady himself.

Gordon's head spun as he tried to grasp their situation. "And the chamber... any idea how badly it was compromised?"

"Completely destroyed. The floors above were blown to pieces... obliterated. The main blast was *in* the containment chamber."

Gordon sat for a moment longer, digesting it all. There was little doubt about it. He and Craig would be heavily contaminated by now. With the level of exposure they must have received, the effects would likely become evident within a matter of hours, and the longer they remained where they were, the worse the impact would become.

He looked down at his leg. The wound wasn't pretty, easy access for the nanobots from the containment vessels that would now be seeking human DNA to bond with, hijacking control of the millions of medibots already coursing through his veins. He gazed at the dust still swirling around them and wondered how much was dust from the rubble and how much was their microscopic marvels of engineering seeking a host. And here they were, breathing in more of them every second. There were no precedents to go by, no reliable modelling of what would happen under these circumstances. There were too many variables. The modelling that *had* been done yielded almost infinite possibilities for the outcome.

Gordon put his hand to his chest, the source of so much of his current pain. He felt sure he'd managed to crack a couple of ribs. Hopefully, the lung hadn't been punctured. Every breath felt strained and painful. And the leg? He didn't think it was broken, but it was sure as hell hurting. What about Craig though? How much torment and anguish must he have dealt with making his way through the ruins searching for survivors? "Any thoughts on who's responsible?" he asked.

"That's not important right now." He glanced over his shoulder. "We need to get moving."

"So, you do. You know?"

Craig put his arm under his companion's shoulder "We can talk about that once we're out of here."

"Is your lensview working?" asked Gordon

"No, first thing I tried. Hopefully it'll self-repair overnight." He steadied himself, readying to take Gordon's weight. "We need to get out of here... quickly." As he stood up, a bit of rubble slipped out from under his feet, causing him to stumble. "We can't hang around chatting about lensviews. The GIA's going to be anxious to clean up loose ends, loose ends like us."

Gordon grimaced as they took the first few tentative steps together. His right leg released an explosion of pain as soon as he put the slightest weight on it. "Arrgh!" Gordon stumbled again, causing Craig to lose his grip. And with every second, the approaching sirens seemed a bit closer.

"Come on, buddy." Craig readjusted his hold on Gordon and pointed into the darkness with his free hand. "See those trees? All we need to do is get to them before the GIA gets to us."

Gordon shook his head. "No, look, I can't do this. You should go ahead without me." He grimaced again with the pain. "I'll never make it."

Craig took Gordon's chin and forced it around so they were facing each other. "Hey, you and I, we're the only fuckers left alive here. You're coming with me! Even if I have to drag you." He took a few more steps before finding a kind of rhythm that allowed him to keep putting one foot in front of the other while supporting the dead weight of his companion. "Now that we're on the move, I'll tell you. Do you want to know? Do you want to know who the arse wipe was who did this?"

Gordon managed a nod. "Yeah, sure, why not?"

"Remember Ron?" He paused for a moment to catch his breath and kicked a small fragment of twisted metal out of the way, not expecting an answer from his injured companion. "The young genius, the shining star, destined to build the future?" He took his time, taking short steps down some loose concrete rubble and bricks. "Well, it seems the little shit had a somewhat different view to the rest of us as to how that future should pan out." He stopped for a moment to readjust his hold under Gordon's shoulder again. "I'd just returned from an appointment when the alarms started."

Gordon looked up at the mention of the alarm.

"Oh, so you are listening?" said Craig, a hint of sarcasm in his voice. "Next thing, Ron sends out an open video call from *inside* the containment chamber. He'd deactivated the seals and called out, 'Get ready, everyone! Get ready to face the end!' He looked manic." He paused his laboured strides, as if for emphasis. "His very last words were, 'This whole fuck up of a world can kiss its miserable, fucked up future goodbye.' I couldn't believe what I was hearing." Starting to move forward again, his voice took on an almost conversational tone. "Next thing, the explosion hit—BANG! And then I was outside on the lawn." He stopped again for a moment and let out a small laugh. "I guess I was the lucky one. When the call came, was I at my desk? No, I was standing by a window... lost in my thoughts." He shook his head as he kept weaving through the rubble. "I'm only here to carry you out thanks to dumb luck."

"Why?" Gordon's question was barely audible.

"Why? Why was I by the window?"

"No. Why Ron? Why would he… ?"

"I don't know. Perhaps he never got over his wife fucking his brother."

"He must have known… the consequences…"

"The only consequences I'm worried about right now are what happens to us if we don't get to the woods before the GIA finds us… or before they nuke what's left of the site."

2

Jason Negus responded promptly when the priority call came through to his lensview. Having just lost a knight to his chess opponent, another GIA operative, Jon Kruick, he stood up and turned away from the table.

"Accept call."

A three-dimensional, translucent image of the dark-haired director appeared on his lensview. In her eighties and with a face that could have been carved out of stone, she'd been well-preserved by the wonders of modern medicine and its nano medibots that helped maintain cells throughout the body while battling known diseases. There was no one higher within the organisation.

"Director Brandt! This is indeed an honour!"

"I'll get straight to the point, Agent Negus. We have an Emergency Protocol 46 situation at the Infinity Research campus just out of New Haven."

This was the first time an Emergency Protocol 46 situation had been raised outside of Asia or Africa. It gave the GIA commanders at the scene ultimate power and control over the resources of the United Northern States of America's military. He would be required to ensure there were no survivors at the scene and that the target was destroyed, so that by the end of the night, the situation was resolved.

A creation of the revamped United Nations Security Council, the GIA was designed to be a global intelligence agency that operated above local politics, making it better equipped to coordinate intelligence in the ongoing battle against terrorism and cybercrime. After its inception, it soon developed into a power unto itself. In theory, it was still answerable to the Security Council, but in practice, it exercised almost total autonomy.

Jason straightened his tie and began walking toward the elevator as he replied, "I'm on my way."

Kruick stared on from beyond the chessboard. *That's just great*, he thought. *Just when I've got the little prick's back against the wall, he gets saved by a call to go and play the hero.*

The elevator doors closed as Jason's call from the Director cut out. He began preparations by scanning the briefing documents the director had just sent to his lensview. The situation required a simple, straightforward strategy. Go in fast with overwhelming force and blow the fuck out of the place. At the same time, a massive quarantine zone needed to be established before taking further action.

"Call to Air Force Secretary Wiseman, Emergency Protocol 46." A message flashed up on his lensview, confirming his voiceprint had been accepted. He told the lift to take him to basement level two while he waited for the secretary to take the call.

"Wiseman here." He sounded distracted, as though the call was an unwanted distraction in his daily routine.

"I am GIA operative Jason Negus, acting on an Emergency Protocol 46. I require immediate air support."

"Protocol 46, huh? And on whose authority are you making this request?"

"Mine."

"Yours and who else's?"

"That is not your concern."

It was futile to argue the point. The fact that a GIA call had gone directly through to Wiseman left no doubt in his mind that he had little choice but to comply. If he were to put up more resistance, it would end in humiliation. Reluctantly, he gestured commands to his wristband, then grabbed the bottle of bourbon he kept in the bottom drawer of his desk. He poured himself a generous shot. "Whatever the hell your Emergency Protocol 46 is, I don't know and don't particularly care. You can have your goddamned air support, but keep me out of it. I'm now sending you the security codes to contact General Philip

Bennett. I'll contact him now and authorise him to provide whatever you want."

Wiseman cut off the call. Technically, he should've been following through himself rather than delegating authority to Bennett. But his resentment for the GIA and the power they'd amassed was such that he couldn't bear it. *Bring back the good ol' days of the CIA*, he thought. *They had more respect for people who'd dedicated their lives to military service.* Now he'd have to contact the president, and she was likely going to give him hell for not following the correct protocols. His day was turning to shit, and he could see it was going to get worse.

Jason's car activated as he approached, the driver's door opening in response to a subtle hand gesture. He climbed in and directed the vehicle. "Top priority external overrides, Infinity Technology Research Campus, New Haven."

The car sped off, the acceleration pushing Negus back in his seat as it got up to speed.

"Display 3D visual of destination."

A translucent, three-dimensional model of the campus and its precinct appeared over his lensview. He used his hands to manipulate the model, examining the surrounding area and peeling back the layers of the building. The accompanying readout informed him of the nature of the work carried out at the facility.

"Damage report. Visual only."

A new image appeared, this time from satellite images, revealing the full extent of damage.

Having surveyed the imagery, it was clear he'd require two waves of fighter-bomber drones. One to deploy electromagnetic heat blasts to fry any tech, nano or otherwise, within two hundred and fifty metres of the compound, then a second, using imploding bunker busters, ensuring the only remains would be a massive crater. Following that, any survivors of the bombing within a five-hundred-metre radius of the facility would be shot and then incinerated. For all the wonders of modern technology, there was nothing like a good old-fashioned flame thrower to ensure nothing, tech or organic, was going to escape a human body that had been terminated.

"Establish two-kilometre buffer around destination, then send message to Jon Kruick. Message start: Lock into my destination and meet me with a clean-up team. End Message."

The vehicle sped through the streets, overriding the guidance computers of all traffic along its route, automatically bringing it to a halt and clearing a path for Jason. A message was sent to all emergency vehicles in the vicinity declaring the buffer zone around the compound and warning that GIA operatives would terminate any personnel who violated the exclusion zone. Jason was confident this would be achieved easily as the campus was well away from populated areas. All vehicles within five kilometres of the campus would automatically ferry their occupants to safety. A request was made to the local police to coordinate the evacuation of all residents within an additional twenty kilometres of the buildings.

He made calls to finalise the air support details and to organise a unit of the National Guard to assist with the termination of any survivors. Further analysis of downloaded satellite images of the site came up on his lensview. Switching across to the infrared showed there were just two survivors among the carnage.

A live feed from the satellite wouldn't be available until he arrived and accessed the clean-up crew's van. There was no real way of knowing if there were other survivors buried among the rubble, but that would be of no consequence. Once the fighter-bomber drones had gone through, there would be no signs of life from anything. His only concern was whether or not the two he'd seen on the surface were moving away from the building.

A soft voice in his ear drew Jason's attention. "Nearing destination, manual control recommended."

He swept away the images with a flick of his wrist and instructed the vehicle. "Virtual control initiation."

Once the vehicle was satisfied that Jason was in the correct alignment, it handed him control. He steered by twisting his right wrist left or right and controlled his speed by moving the same hand forward or back. There was always the option of activating the physical controls, but Jason found that too distracting.

He noticed a group of squad cars with a huddle of police officers nearby and figured that must be the makeshift command post. Jason made sure he forced them to step back by leaving it to the very last moment before braking and bringing his car to a stop.

The door opened, and he stepped out, dusting off his suit while he straightened up. The police all turned to look at him, well aware that he had to be from the GIA.

With a deadpan expression, he said, "I'll be taking over from here."

Unknown to him at the time, a microscopic nanobot drifting in the breeze was swept up by his breathing. Within a few moments, it was in his lungs, grabbing hold of a cell in the lung wall and seeking a DNA strand within it. The lung was an ideal starting point, as molecules from the CO_2 being exhaled were easily captured and stripped apart to construct the carbon-based framework of the nanobot's next replica.

The process would typically take around twenty minutes, with the bot first building synthetic proteins to use as a toolset. Once the first replication was complete, both nanobots would repeat the process. In less than twenty-four hours, the one bot would have become over a trillion, and fundamental network processing would begin, establishing a quantum processor that was spread throughout the host body. Jason would no doubt take in more nanobots during this time, speeding up the process considerably. In addition, any medibots in his body would be stripped and rebuilt, a far more efficient process than replicating from scratch.

Jason, unaware of the transition already underway, began shouting orders to the police at the scene, leaving no doubt in anyone's minds as to who was in control.

Gordon and Craig moved toward the park at the southern end of the campus, the cover of the trees being their only chance of escaping surveillance.

Then came the roar of the approaching fighter-bomber drones.

Craig looked to Gordon and yelled, "That's our cue to get the fuck out of here!"

They were no more than forty metres from the compound when the first of the drones passed overhead, dropping their heat blast payload as they went.

Gordon glanced over his shoulder as the blast flashed. A patch of ground in front of them exploded in flames courtesy of the live embers landing all around them as the force of the blast threw them to the ground.

Stumbling away from the intense heat of the burning ruins, Gordon instinctively turned his head to look for an escape route. At first, he thought there was nothing to see but the smoke haze engulfing them. Then the reality hit him. "Holy shit. Craig? I can't see!"

"It was probably just the flash. You'll be fine in a minute or two." Craig got back to his feet as he continued. "Right now, we need to keep moving."

"No, this is serious. It's not *just* the flash. I can't see. I'm blind." He tried crawling forward, feeling his way in the grass.

"Okay," said Craig, "let's have a look." He leaned down to examine his companion's eyes in the fading light. A flash of lightning highlighted the damage. Gordon's lensviews had melted onto his eyeballs. It would require major reconstruction surgery to restore his eyesight. "Shit, this doesn't look good at all."

"How is it we're not dead yet anyway?" asked Gordon.

"Let's worry about that when we get to the trees." Again, Craig put Gordon's arm over his shoulder and, straining under the weight, started moving forward again. He glanced back when he heard the next wave of drones approaching, their jet engines roaring. "For fuck's sake, what more do they want to throw at us?"

This time, bunker-busting bombs blasted away the final remains of the campus buildings. ripping a massive crater in the ground where they had been just a few minutes earlier. The shockwave threw them several metres through the air.

They hit the ground hard. Gordon could taste blood as it ran down his face and trickled into his mouth. To his surprise, there was no sense of any bones having broken. But the blast had separated the companions as they hurtled through the air. "Craig? Where are you?" asked Gordon. The need to have his eyesight began consuming him. *I need to see, damn it!*

During this frenzy of anxiety, the nanobots established their neural connection with Gordon's brain. A sensation, like fire, ran through his veins for a few seconds. He tried to scream as it ripped through every part of his body, but no sound came out. Then the pain abated as quickly as it had started. The quantum network tapped into his consciousness, seeking out his greatest needs. Repairs were already underway to his wounded leg, every cell now having a corresponding nanobot that sought to ensure it was as it should be. They went about their work repairing the hairline fractures with tremendous speed, pulling the bones fully back together and reinforcing them. The sheer number of nanobots working on the task meant Gordon was able to stand unassisted within seconds of the burning having run through him. Meanwhile, the network had embraced Gordon's thoughts about his overwhelming need to see, disregarding his damaged eyes as the fundamental solution. Rather than mere repairs, it set out to create improvements.

Craig stumbled to his feet and grabbed hold of him. "Oh my god! Your face. It's a fucking mess. Are you okay?"

Gordon wiped some of the blood away from around his nose and mouth. "I don't know." He paused to collect his thoughts. "I think the bots have hooked up with my brain. It's like—like having a burst of flames rush through every vein in your body."

"Really? Shit, that's happened one hell of a lot faster than the simulations. Are you alright now, though?"

"Yeah, it's okay. I can't see, but I feel more... tuned in. All the other senses... It's like nothing I've ever felt before. There's a clarity to thought and perception that's new, different." He paused a moment longer before adding, "It'll probably hit you soon, too. But don't worry, it'll be okay."

Craig took Gordon's arm over his shoulder again and continued toward the parkland that was now just a hundred metres away. "At least you're not screaming about the interface sending you insane."

With Gordon's leg having largely mended now, they were able to move faster. But they still faced the dilemma of how to get through the cordon forming around the campus grounds. Security vehicles had already worked their way around most of it, blocking their exit.

***

Nanobots had been commonplace for years. They'd become invaluable in medicine, hunting diseased cells and repairing damaged tissue. But what the team at Infinity had been developing went much further. Recognising human DNA, binding with it, reproducing with it, and modifying it. Even more than that, it was capable of interfacing with the central nervous system, transforming the brain into a massive supercomputer that maintained the personality, emotions, and imagination of the host. The human race had already achieved massive gains in longevity and quality of life. But this was set to bring forth a whole new potential—to become a kind of superhuman, impervious to *any* disease or injury and able to tap into the massive quantum computer network of nanobots interfaced directly with the brain. With this technology, a whole new chapter in the history of humanity was set to begin.

Gordon harboured doubts about the ethics surrounding the research, but still felt compelled to throw his all into the project. The science was too important to ignore, and he worried about the potential for those less concerned than he was to be in a position where they could take the technology in an even more dangerous direction. He wasn't convinced they would ever reach a point where the technology was ready for deployment, but the myriad spin-offs alone had made the research worthwhile. This was particularly so in Craig's area of expertise. He led the team developing the mechanics of the replication process. As a result of their research, atomic-scale robotics had revolutionised manufacturing and construction, a change more profound than the advent of the internet or AI many years earlier.

Gordon was the architect of the team engineering the software to assemble a quantum network from a multitude of components, in the same way the human body is built from trillions of cells that come together following a map laid out within our DNA.

There were still many problems to overcome. Simulations had been run thousands of times over, consistently showing that, if the bots were deployed at their current stage of development, the workings of the host mind would greatly affect the quantum computer's operation, effectively exaggerating the individual's characteristics in ways that were unpredictable.

Having been closer to the containment chambers, Craig's exposure to the nanobots had been more profound than Gordon's. When the bots passed through their progressive stages of development to critical mass, their numbers were massively greater than they'd been for Gordon. A surge of them moved onto his central nervous system at a time when he was focused on getting away from their pursuers, using any means, whatever the cost. The nanobots grabbed hold of the fact that he cared little about ethics. Survival was all that really mattered to him. The fire surging through his veins felt so intense that he fell, bringing Gordon to the ground with him as he went down.

He screamed in agony, then relaxed. "Holy fucking shit! Man, what was that?"

"Burns at first, huh?"

"Where was the clue to *that* in our simulations?' said Craig as he struggled to catch his breath.

"When you think about it, the data was all there. We just never saw it for what it was. But I guess feeling it's different to speculation."

"Yeah," agreed Craig, "you're not wrong."

"You okay now?"

"I think so. It hit so fast. Everything seems so clear now. It's like walking out of a foggy night into—"

Gordon interrupted him. "Can you hear that? People, they're moving around up ahead. We'd better keep our heads low."

***

Jason Negus fought the urge to punch his fist in the air at the sight of the blast. And now, the live stream from the satellite was finally coming through. "Well, well, looks like we still have to clean up our two strays." He forwarded the signal to the other agents and National Guard around the perimeter. "The squad commander for the eastern sector can clean this up. A couple of heat blast grenades should do it." A direct hit would leave nothing behind but microscopic ash. "Follow-up protocol to be small calibre bullets and flame throwers. Do not use any other explosive devices. These guys are contaminated. We don't want it to spread."

***

Seeing the cordon ahead of them, Craig stopped, pulling Gordon to the ground with him. "We need to distract them," he whispered. While looking across at the security crew some hundred and fifty metres ahead, he felt an innate awareness of what each soldier's strengths and weaknesses were. While there were men and women amongst them of great courage, he mostly sensed fear.

He noticed a young officer in particular walking along the perimeter who he could sense wished to be elsewhere. Craig focused on him, probing his thoughts, surprised by how easy it was to see inside someone else's head. *Drake... his name's Drake.* But there was more he was able to ascertain about this young man. Recently promoted to corporal, Drake had never expected to encounter real emergencies when he signed up, and right now, he was cold and wet. All he wanted was to go home where he could feel safe with his mother and father. He was all of twenty years old. And there he was, nursing a rocket launcher in his arms. Could it be that he was vulnerable to suggestion?

Craig's attention was broken when Gordon asked, "Distract them? Any idea how we might do that?"

"We wait. These guys are tense as all hell. It won't take much to draw them away from us."

"So, what are you going to do? Will one of them to blow up the command post?"

Ignoring the sarcastic tone, Craig grabbed hold of the idea. If he could see deep enough into Drake's mind to find his name and read his thoughts, maybe he'd be able to influence him as well. He smiled. "Nice idea." *It's too late for him anyway,* thought Craig, *the nanobots are already deep inside him.*

Behind the smile, Craig focused hard on Drake, endeavouring to plant a seed in his mind. A seed of doubt that questioned the intentions of his team—that questioned the validity of them holding this cordon.

Gordon had rolled onto his back. "Ah, well," he said. "At least I won't be able to see the end when it finally comes."

Craig held on to his train of thought as he responded, not particularly keen for Gordon to click on to what he was doing, else his colleague's penchant for ethics might interfere. "These guys don't realise that, if they want to live, they're better off letting us through."

"How can you be so sure? What if the bots *didn't* spread across the city after the explosion? What if the heat blast wiped out all the bots other than what we're carrying? We're both so badly infected that we're walking plague transmitters. What if our escape, rather than the explosion, is what ultimately wipes out humanity?"

"It just takes a handful of bots—" Craig left the sentence unfinished as he continued holding his focus on Corporal Drake.

"Seems to me the outlook for the future sucks, either way."

"It won't be the end of the world."

"How can you say that?" asked Gordon.

Craig didn't respond, concerned he may inadvertently give away his betrayal, that he'd passed a sample of the technology on to Petra Chan a few months earlier.

***

Tanya's smile beamed across her face when the doctor gave her the news. She couldn't wait to tell Lloyd. *He's such a sweety*, she thought. *He'll be crying with joy.*

Entering the elevator, she didn't care that it was half full of strangers. "Connect call to Lloyd Dyson, security clearance TG672!" She gave an awkward smile as some of the others in the lift gave her glares of disapproval. After a few moments, the red statement, 'Connection unavailable', flashed in front of her eyes. *Oh well. Probably shouldn't be calling from an elevator anyway, totally rude!*

The elevator doors opened to reveal rain pouring down outside the building. Lightning flashed, and the massive glass panes of the foyer rattled as the accompanying thunder cracked.

She walked into the foyer and tried calling again. Still no luck. *He'll just have to wait till I tell him in person.*

Waiting to flag down a cab would take a while in this weather, and she wasn't keen on waiting outside in the storm. There was a quaint coffee shop just down the road with a classic European flavour. A good book with a steaming hot coffee seemed like a sensible way to spend some time while waiting for the storm to pass. With a bit of luck, she'd be able to get through to Lloyd by then.

The doors of the medical centre opened on her approach, the cold wind biting into her face as she stepped outside into the tempest. She wrapped her coat tight around her and ran toward Enricho's. Seeing her favourite seat by the window was vacant brought a smile to her face.

A bell on the door jingled as Tanya pushed it open and rushed inside, drawing the attention of a rotund man with thinning hair and a broad smile who emerged from behind the bar. He threw up his hands to greet her. "Tanya! Where have you been these past weeks? It puts a ray of sunshine into my day every time you walk in that door."

Enricho gave her a big hug, then pulled her chair out for her to take a seat. Tanya blushed as she took her seat and looked up at him with a smile. "Oh! You're too kind. How's Maria?"

Throwing his arms in the air once more, Enricho huffed. "Every day for the last two weeks, she asks me, 'When is that lovely young lady with the pretty smile coming back? Why have we not seen her?' She tells me it must be my coffee that drives you away." He extended his hands in front of him, as if to show there was nothing to hide.

Tanya laughed, tossing her thick, wavy hair over her shoulders. "Oh, Enricho, as long as *you're* the one making the coffee, you can feel assured that I'll *always* be back for more."

There were at least half a dozen other customers in the coffee shop, everyone seemingly oblivious to Enricho's flamboyant behaviour.

Enricho walked back to the bar and bashed the coffee machine's grip handle on the tall knock box so he could start preparing Tanya's regular order: a latte with macadamia milk. "So, how is that young man you've been seeing for so long now?" he asked as he began filling the grip handle with freshly ground coffee.

"You mean my husband?" she replied, a bemused look on her face.

"What was his name?" He looked up as though the answer was floating above his head. "Lloyd, yes, *of course*, it's Lloyd. He's a very lucky man, you know."

"Maybe I should drag him away from his work and bring him in here so you can remind him of that."

The conversation was interrupted by the roar of jet engines as a squadron of fighter-bomber drones screamed by overhead. The whole coffee shop stopped, some walking to the window and craning their heads in an effort to make out what was happening.

Tanya overheard a young man at the next table comment to his friend. "They must be following up on that explosion over at Infinity."

Tanya leaned across and asked, "Excuse me, but I haven't heard of any explosion. Is there something I've missed?"

The two guys looked at each other and snickered, as if to suggest her ignorance was somehow amusing. "There was a *massive* explosion there, about half an hour ago."

Tanya was up and out the door in a heartbeat, leaving Enricho to call after her, pointing to her mug of coffee. She raced onto the street in a panic. Desperate to flag down a cab, she ran straight onto the road, ignoring the driving rain, and set out to stop traffic, hoping that she might somehow get a cab quicker that way.

A firm hand grabbed hold of her right arm, stopping her in her tracks. She turned to see the chiselled face of a police officer.

"What seems to be the problem, miss?"

"My husband! He's working at Infinity Tech." Her eyes seemed to plead with him as she asked, "I heard... I heard there was an explosion?"

A look of compassion filled the officer's eyes. While maintaining a firm grip on her arm, he gently guided Tanya out of the rain to the side of the road and under the awning outside Enricho's.

Enricho rushed out to offer assistance. "How about you come back in and relax, your coffee's ready, and I'll give you a gelato, on the house, while we find out if Lloyd is safe."

She started to tremble and cry, slipping down to the ground as the shock overcame her and she tried to curl up in a ball. She struggled to get her words out through her tears as she explained, "I tried to call him twice since leaving the doctor's, but I couldn't get through."

The police officer squatted next to her and placed a reassuring hand on her shoulder. "Hey, I've got a cab for you. Are you going to be okay from here?"

Still trembling, she nodded, and with the officer's assistance, managed to get into the cab after it pulled up to the kerb. "I think I'll just go home for now and wait for word on my husband."

"Home, please," she instructed the driverless cab. It accessed her wristband, found her home coordinates and deducted the credits from her bank account before speeding off. She cradled her belly in both hands and spoke to the developing foetus in her womb. "We'll get through this kiddo, one way or another." She burst into uncontrollable sobs as the cab sped down the road.

Five minutes into the journey, she heard the second wave of drones fly over, followed by a massive blast as they dropped their bunker busters.

She stared into space, no longer able to feel anything.

***

Half an hour after his call from Jason Negus, Wiseman was summoned to the situation room beneath the White House. He arrived at the same time as Secretary of State Rick Dodson. The doors closed behind them as they entered. Wiseman felt sick when he looked across the room and saw Director Brandt sitting with the president at the head of the table.

The president looked up at him. "Carl, so glad you could fit it into your schedule to make it." The sarcasm in her tone was unmistakable. "I believe you already have some idea of what's going on. Take a seat."

"Thank you, Madam President." He replied as he sat down. The glare heading his way from the director felt as cold as ice. He'd never wished so much that he might be able to crawl under a rock and hide.

"I'm curious," said Emily, "as to why I wasn't notified *immediately* after you were informed of the Emergency Protocol 46."

"I'm sorry for the delay, Madam President. I was attending to…" His lack of readiness was apparent to everyone. "… other matters."

"More urgent than an Emergency Protocol 46?" asked Emily.

"No, ma'am."

"We'll talk more about your attitude another time."

Wiseman stared at the table. "Yes, ma'am."

Emily's tone changed as she addressed the rest of the room. "What we're facing is potentially very grave. Director Brandt has expressed confidence that the GIA will soon have the situation under control. However, in the event that this doesn't prove to be the case, I've decided to temporarily relocate the Executive and a core command group to the newly completed Northern Command Bunker. We'll leave here in the next five minutes, then take the underground shuttle to rendezvous with Air Force One. Encrypted briefing notes will be distributed to your wristbands once we're airborne. Any questions?"

Dodson glanced around the room. "What about our families?" he asked. "Can we at least contact them?"

"I'm sorry, Rick, our departure must be unknown to *all* outside this room without the very highest level of security clearance. Your families have already been contacted by PR specialists from within the GIA, providing detailed cover stories to explain your absence." The president stood up before continuing. "It's imperative you all know the city of New Haven is now under strict quarantine restrictions. We are currently evacuating an area within a fifty-kilometre radius and have developed a contingency plan in case the evacuation zone needs expanding to include New York City." She turned to Wiseman. "General, I want you to remain in Washington. But you'll need to be on call twenty-four seven." Her glare developed an intense hostility as she waited for his reply. "Do I make myself clear?"

Wiseman grimaced as he replied, "Yes, ma'am."

Petra looked out the window at the ocean below. It would be another hour at least before the plane descended through the atmosphere to land.

The northern lights were putting on a display that filled her with wonder. The world seemed so different from this low orbit. So grand in its own right, yet insignificant against the vastness of the billions of distant stars.

She turned to the woman next to her and forced a smile as they clinked their glasses together in a toast to their successful escape.

Alicia Killen looked at Petra with adulation in her eyes. She was in awe of the tall, slim Asian woman with the stoic poise. She felt overwhelmed with envy whenever she set eyes on her. Petra was the woman Alicia had always longed to be. Brilliant, beautiful, successful. She often watched as Petra moved through a room with a poise, confidence and style that demanded attention. At times, she had even dreamed of holding her close and being enveloped in Petra's embrace.

Petra, on the other hand, despised the woman she now sat next to. She disliked the fact that she'd been forced to cultivate a friendship with someone whose presence she found so intolerable. Alicia was weak and lacked any sense of conviction. She was a useful tool that was easily controlled. But, beyond that, Petra loathed the very sight of her.

While Petra had maintained herself with pride, so much so that at sixty-five she had looks and fitness that put most teenagers to shame, Alicia was living life in a wasteful manner, more concerned with petty grievances than considering what she wanted from her life.

Her long, blonde hair looked unkept, and her face wore a permanent frown. A window to the bitterness buried within.

She'd already drunk far too much for Petra's liking and had become somewhat loud and embarrassing. "Alicia, dear. I really think you should keep your voice down."

"Oh? And why would that be?"

"Well, aside from the fact that you're starting to get obnoxious, it might interfere with the surprise I've got for you."

"A surprise?" Alicia's eyes went wide with excitement.

Petra grinned. "Yes, it's a very special surprise."

"Oh, please, what is it? When will I get it?"

"I've already given it to you."

Alicia looked puzzled.

Petra leaned across and whispered in her ear. "I slipped it in your drink at the airport before we boarded. It should kick in any time now."

"What, you drugged me?"

"No, nothing as banal as that. That project Ron was working on? I slipped a few hundred of the nanobots from his project into your Bloody Mary."

"What the fuck? He told me about that shit! Why would you do that?"

"Well, I wanted to see how effective they are." She patted Alicia on the knee. "And I couldn't think of anyone better to trial it than you."

"That can't be! How could you get them? Did *he* give them to you?"

"Where I got them from is no concern of yours. I'd just advise that you try and stay calm."

"How am I supposed to stay calm knowing that shit's inside me?" Alicia stood up, knocking her drink over and causing Petra's to spill on her dress.

Petra pulled her back down, "You really don't want to get yourself in a panic."

Alicia looked confused. "What's going to happen? Can you get them out? You've got to get them out!"

Some of the other passengers were starting to look around at them.

"Don't worry, dear, you'll be fine." She lowered her voice to a whisper, "You're making a scene. You need to settle down."

"No, Ron told me about those nasty little nano-fuckers he was working on." She raised an accusing finger and poked it in Petra's face. "He put you up to this, didn't he?"

"Now, now, Alicia darling, we mustn't go making these wild accusations."

"You've got to do something!"

"Do something?" asked Petra.

"To get this shit out of me!"

"Oh, darling, that simply won't be happening."

Alicia started sweating and shaking, her breath short and shallow as the shock of what she'd been told sank in. *What the fuck has she done to me? What the fucking hell is going to happen?*

When she'd been recruited by General Rubeiro, Alicia knew it was something to do with technology he was adamant would change the global balance of power forever. She'd been promised a prominent place in the history of the world's future, not to have someone pump her full of god knows what nano crap it was.

Petra calmly rose from her seat and grabbed the attention of a nearby flight steward, "Excuse me, but there's a bit of a medical emergency that's just come up. As you can see, my companion is having a degree of difficulty."

The steward looked across and saw Alicia trembling and looking as though she wanted to scream. The panic had left her struggling to breathe. She was wheezing and holding her chest as tears slid down her cheeks.

It was while she was in this panicked state that the nanobots' critical mass was achieved and the quantum network in her brain established itself. She wanted to scream as the sensation of fire ran through her veins, but no sound came forth. Her state of mind was absorbed by the network and further enhanced, multiplying the terror she felt a hundredfold.

The quantum network perceived that, in the interest of the host's well-being, her DNA should be altered to maintain the chaotic state of her consciousness. It would take time for the impending changes to become apparent, but they were likely to be profound.

The steward pressed his communication stud and called on one of his supervisors to bring a shot of sedatives and relaxants.

Petra held back the urge to smile as she watched the supervisor administer the shots. The microscopic army in the sedative shots would keep the newly established network of nanobots occupied and focused on their host for the rest of the flight, potentially reducing the risk of contagion.

Had Petra been infected now, too? Perhaps. The idea that she could have been sitting next to Alicia throughout this flight and *not* be exposed herself was likely, but far from certain. The possibility intrigued her.

Having spent so many years working as a deep, undercover agent for General Ribeiro, she was glad that she'd be free to cast aside the identity of the dedicated doctor once the plane landed in Guangdong.

The supervisor took Petra by the arm, trying to maintain a degree of discretion.

"I suspect it may be best if we move your friend to the isolation cabin at the back of the plane."

"Will you be able to make her comfortable back there?"

"We can provide far more comfort than she can enjoy here, and I can assure you she'll be under constant supervision."

"Thank you so much. I do hope she'll be okay. She's such a gentle, caring soul, you know. Such a shame to see her in this state."

"I'll ensure a doctor is waiting to give her a thorough check-up on our arrival. You try and put your mind at rest. I'll have the steward bring you a complimentary drink."

"Oh, that would be wonderful, I seem to have spilt mine when poor Alicia got struck by her seizure. I could certainly do with one now. It's been most distressing."

The steward and the supervisor struggled to get Alicia from her seat to the wheelchair that had been brought into the aisle by an airline security officer.

As they wheeled Alicia away, Petra returned to her seat by the window and sent an encrypted text message to General Rubeiro, then watched the view outside as the plane descended. Conscious of the unwanted attention from the other passengers, she made sure to hide the smile she could no longer hold back.

"Here's your drink, ma'am," said the steward.

"Thank you." As the steward walked away, she thought about how the rest of the flight would be a most pleasant experience. She removed the tiny vial from within the lining of her handbag. Most had gone into Alicia's drink earlier at the airport, but she'd ensured a few drops remained—drops that were intended to be delivered to Rubeiro. Drops that she now discreetly poured into her own drink. *Yes,* she thought, *this turn of events will definitely work in my favour.*

***

"Oh my God, what have I done?" Corporal Drake dropped the rocket launcher in horror when the realisation hit. The command post was in flames as a result of a rocket *he'd* fired. In an instant, he was surrounded by his colleagues. His hands were dragged behind his back. Cable ties secured around his wrists and ankles. As he hit the ground, he felt the pain of every kick. His gut, his chest and his back. The last thing he saw before blacking out was a rifle butt coming down on his face.

***

Jon Kruick had pulled up, just as the command post was blowing apart. When he got out of his car, the first thing he saw was his friend, Jason, lying on the ground with half a leg blown off and a big chunk of his face missing. He didn't hesitate to take command of the situation. "I am GIA operative Jon Kruick, and I am assuming command of this Emergency Protocol 46 operation. Call an ambulance, NOW!" As he transferred data from Jason's wristband to his own, he was quick to take action. "Bennett, we still have two survivors attempting to escape by heading to the woods. I want a fighter drone with a heat blast ready to hit those trees as soon as they enter."

***

"Let's make a run for it," said Craig. "Go!" They ran towards the woods as fast as they could, Gordon still needing to sling his arm over Craig's shoulder thanks to his blindness.

Craig stopped abruptly and pulled Gordon to the ground. "Something's going on here. One of those guys over there—he's so pissed off. I can hear what he's thinking. They're going to torch the woods."

"What do you mean *you can hear them?*"

"Seriously, I can *hear* people's thoughts, even influence them." He lowered his tone to emphasise the words. "The command post... *I* made that guy do it. I *made* him fire on his own command post."

"What? What the hell are you talking about?"

The high-pitched screech of the approaching fighter drones led them to raise their voices.

"The bots, they've given me some sort of telepathic capabilities."

"That can't be, surely. Changes to physical abilities? That's one thing, but telepathy?"

The drones continued getting louder.

"Think about it. These nanobots—they're designed for networking. If they could hijack our own medibots, doesn't it make sense that they can hijack others? Our exposure goes so far beyond anything we simulated. Who knows what we're capable of?"

Craig was right. Gordon wasn't just hearing Craig; he could *feel* what he was saying. It was like sensing tiny vibrations, even being able to place where they emanated from. He stopped to focus and found he could also reach out and feel the thoughts of the others. At first, it was like a jumble of noise, but every so often, he could distinguish one voice or another rising above the others. *Oh my God,* he thought, *they really are planning to torch the woods... and us with them.*

I know, came a reply from just next to him. But *I think we can make it.*

How?

That guy who turned his rocket launcher on the others...

Holy shit. You really did make him do it, didn't you?

If they were able to communicate with their thoughts so easily, was it so unreasonable to believe Craig could also *influence* someone's thoughts? The stark reality of it hit him. He felt sick in the stomach at the thought of his companion wilfully—*intentionally*—causing someone to take the lives of others.

It was wrong. It was unconscionable. But in that moment, he found himself more concerned with the immediate problem of their own survival. He spoke aloud, asking, "What about stopping a drone?"

Craig continued communicating with his thoughts. *I don't know. But if my quantum network can hijack someone's medibots to influence their thought patterns, then I should be able to impact the navigation on those drones.*

I hope you're right.

The drones were closing in. Craig and Gordon were just twenty metres from the edge of the forest when Craig looked up and yelled, "It's not working for me! I can't feel it."

With the drones almost directly overhead, there was no choice but for Gordon to see if he could succeed where Craig had failed.

He focused hard.

He thought of how the guidance system locked into the GPS signal.

He raised his head as he found himself sensing the trajectory of both, then imagined them bending in another direction.

***

Jon Kruick watched in disbelief as the fighter drones collided into each other and dropped from the sky just as they were about to release their scorching payloads. Without taking his eyes off the smoke rising from where they'd crashed to the ground, he said to no one in particular, "We're going to need a new strategy if we want to terminate our two fugitives."

***

Julius Granger switched off his viewer and turned to his innermost circle of high priests gathered around the table. "Gentlemen, it would seem the age of Circles is upon us. The prophecies that were foretold in chapter nine of our most sacred Book of Circles are now in play."

The son of a Pentecostal preacher, as a young boy, Julius admired the way his father commanded the respect of thousands; the undeniable control he held over his congregation.

His mother died when he was young. In fact, throughout his father's lifetime, four out of five of his wives passed away in mysterious circumstances. Each time, his father would say, "She displeased God by breaking the vow of subservience to her husband she'd made at the altar before our Lord Jesus Christ." He'd then lower his head and whisper, "What goes around comes around."

What goes around comes around.

Those were the only words from his father that Julius had retained in his heart. They were words that had served him well.

At fifteen, he watched as his father was exposed for who he was on national television. His mistress came forward with evidence that linked him to the deaths of two of his wives. Worse still, she produced evidence that he was planning the murder of his then-wife with the intention of making *her* his sixth wife.

Faced with life in prison, the reverend put a gun to his head.

What goes around comes around.

Over the following year, the young teenager fell into depression. He refused meals and descended into substance abuse. The massive inheritance he received from his father's estate felt tainted. He wanted to succeed in his own right but felt lost and directionless.

Eventually, he fell ill with a severe fever and started hallucinating. Each day, he declared to have had a vision of the future. Through each vision, he would endlessly repeat his mantra: *What goes around comes around.* Then one day, he sat bolt upright and declared, "The truth is circular. It has been revealed to me in all its glory." He rose from his bed, filled with determination. "I must spread the word across the curved surface of our world."

Julius shut himself away to compose the Book of Circles. The sacred book was a text to be interpreted on many levels, like ancient Egyptian hieroglyphics. For each level of understanding to be revealed, intensive training and strict adherence to the principles of curvature were required.

"We are all Circumfrens, yet some have a more rounded understanding of the circular nature of existence than others. There is no god, no souls, no afterlife, just the circular nature of existence."

What goes around comes around.

"We live on the circumference of our world. Our world travels in a circle around our circular sun in a circular galaxy. That is but a small part of the rounded fabric of space and time. As we live our lives, we do so in the knowledge that when our universe withers and dies, it will come around again. Every moment in its history shall be repeated again and again. I say unto you, seek the best you can from your life, for you are destined to repeat it again and again for all eternity."

What goes around comes around.

"While our lives are enriched by helping those in need to lift themselves from a life of poverty, we must *never* lose sight of our own needs. I say unto you, help yourself that you might be better able to help your neighbour."

Over the ensuing years, a series of so-called 'study centres' were established throughout the Confederate States. The Circumfrens were viewed by some in the wider community with suspicion, seen as a secret society only the wealthy could access. Established churches were outraged when Julius was successful in his Supreme Court bid to have the Circumfrens recognised as a legitimate religion. The court ruled that, despite the lack of belief in a creator, worshipping the concept of circularity and rebirth meant that it was still essentially a spiritual organisation and therefore valid as a religion.

When a journalist asked Julius on the steps of the court if there was truth in the rumour that a majority of the judges sitting on the bench had been granted high status within his church, Julius poked an angry finger at his face. "What goes around comes around."

The next day, the journalist was unemployed, facing defamation charges, and several witnesses to his breaches of journalistic codes of ethics had stepped forward. He disappeared a few days later without a trace, leaving behind a devastated wife and two children.

The Circumfrens were open about being a church that was *not* for the common man, but for the elite. As a result, there was no shortage of those willing to pay the obligatory donations to join. Ironically, ever larger numbers of the poor aspired to join, hoping it would lift them out of poverty.

There were seven tiers that devotees could rise through. The first was that of 'novice', requiring a yearly donation equivalent to five percent of the nation's average income (as calculated by the church auditors). For those who attained 'level two novice', this rose to ten percent to cover the cost of more intensive guidance and training. The third tier rose to twenty percent, but once level four was attained, it was deemed that you were now a 'priest of circular thought' and were instead given modest payments by the church for spreading wisdom in the community. To attain level five, the applicant should have achieved a high level of success in the 'outside world' where they could influence the success of others rising through the ranks and helping with the passage of legislation or court rulings that were favourable to the church.

Level five's were referred to as 'high priests of the never-ending curve'. Above that were the 'rounded bishops', a status achieved only by those who brought good fortune on a substantial scale to the church. At the top was the 'Grand Circumfren', Julius Granger. They believed the circumference of wisdom encompassed all, as written in the most holy Book of Circles.

Chapter nine of the Book of Circles spoke of a time when the old-world order of government would collapse, and filling the vacuum to restore order would be the Circumfren Church. The prophecy told of how it would start with a disaster caused by the hand of man and would spread around the globe faster than the world could react. As part of their preparations, the Circumfrens had designed their learning centres to double as bomb and biohazard shelters, each able to sustain the priests of the church for up to five years if needed.

And now, in the aftermath of the Infinity explosion, Julius declared, "It is time to prepare our families for an imminent move to the shelters."

The shelters were built only for those at level four or above and their families, a reward for their service. Once lockdown for a learning centre was declared, the lower three levels, which made up ninety-five percent of the church community, would only be allowed regular day access to the outer chambers of the learning centres. They would continue to bring additional supplies for those locked into holy meditation within the inner circles in the hope that their actions could lead towards their rise in the organisation.

As far as Julius was concerned, their donations were of no consequence, nor were their lives. After all, to be able to help your neighbour, you must first help yourself.

***

Having reached the cover of the woods, Gordon and Craig stopped to catch their breath. Without raising his head, Gordon said, "You're not going to believe this, I can see." His voice was filled with enthusiasm. "But, it's so different." He moved his hands around by his side while facing Craig. "I can see all around me, not like seeing with my eyes. It's almost like I'm *feeling* it, and at the same time, sensing colour, texture, weight—everything. And back there? I was able to *feel* what was going on in those drones—in their software. It felt like I could control them. I *did* control them." He stood mute for a moment as he digested what he'd just said before whispering. "Holy shit!"

"Well, good for you," replied Craig in a cynical tone. He looked around, then said, "From what I can tell, we're safe for now. They must have decided to cut their losses. But you can be sure they're going to keep tracking us."

"Yeah," Gordon nodded. "I can pick it up in their transmissions." He paused. "Tanya! She'd gone into town before the explosion. She'll still be alive, and she's the only one who'd know how to contain the bots outside the chambers. We need to get to her before the GIA."

"Or maybe we should just worry about saving our own skins," replied Craig. "Let *them* use Tanya's knowledge to try and save the world."

Gordon shook his head. "You're kidding, aren't you? Can you imagine if they militarise this?"

"They're too busy looking at a scorched Earth approach. But they're too late anyway. The genie was out of the bottle as soon as that blast went off."

"I can't give up hope that easily," replied Gordon. "There has to be a way to stop it. And besides that, we owe it to Tanya to find her. The three of us—we're all that's left."

Craig paused. He couldn't afford to get Gordon offside, not under the current circumstances. If they were going to survive, at the very least, they needed each other. "Okay," he said, "let's try and find her."

***

Jason Negus lay on the operating table, drifting in and out of consciousness. One leg had been blown off above the knee, leaving little more than a small stump below the hip. The other had large lacerations, but the bones seemed reasonably unharmed. He'd lost much of his face and sustained numerous other injuries. The open wounds had allowed a great deal more of the nanobots quick access while he'd been at the site of the explosion, joining those that had already attached to his lungs and worked their way to his brain.

The doctors seemed oblivious to his regaining consciousness as they carried on their discussions.

A nurse approached and said, "Well, Mister Negus, that's a nasty suite of injuries you've sustained. You're *very* lucky to be alive."

"What about my leg?"

"I'm sorry, but you'll have to discuss that one with the doctor. He'll be over to talk to you shortly."

Jason lay there, unable to think about anything other than how he would get around on just one leg until his other leg could be regenerated. He laughed to himself as pictures sprang up in his head of hopping around and going about his regular routine.

After what felt like an eternity of thoughts swimming through his hazy mind, the doctor approached. His breathing was exaggerated by his bio-hazard suit. "Well, Mr Negus, we *have* had a difficult day, haven't we?"

"Enough of the pleasantries, Doc, I just want to know how long until you've got me back on two feet again. I'm not fond of the idea of hopping around for longer than I need to."

"Ah, yes, the limb regeneration. We're having just a slight problem on that front. It seems that some sort of contaminant from the blast site is impacting the functioning of your medibots, preventing them from instigating the regular reconstruction procedures."

"What are you saying?"

"You'll live." With that, the doctor turned and walked away. He had no intention of telling Jason that his status was now one of 'watch without intervention'. As far as the GIA's research division was concerned, this was an ideal opportunity to observe the effect of the nanobots so they had a better idea of what they were dealing with.

Jason lay back and fantasised about departing the hospital on his one good leg and getting his vengeance on that bastard who'd fired on the command post and the pain he'd inflict in the process.

He tensed up for a second when a fiery pain ran through every vein in his body. A moment later, the pain had subsided.

***

Lloyd had been in the containment chamber, making observations on a new method for the nanobots to extract carbon from the atmosphere to create carbon nano lattice frameworks in a reduced timeframe. He was standing near one of the larger vessels when the explosion hit, tearing him away from the life he used to know.

Not long before that, he'd smiled at the memory of Tanya leaving the compound an hour earlier to go for the doctor's appointment to confirm her pregnancy test results. The way that when she'd left his office, she'd run a finger down his cheek and kissed him gently before whispering in his ear, "I'll be seeing you at home. Don't be late, or you, sir, will be in deep trouble." He was distracted from his daydream when he noticed Ron at the far end of the room behaving strangely.

He decided he should approach the lead researcher to check he was okay. "Hey, Ron. Are you—"

Then, BANG!

The containment vessel disintegrated in the blast, leaving him covered in the bots. A few seconds later, the building above collapsed. The containment chamber was two floors below the surface. At first, he felt nothing but intense pain. After a while, he realised his arms and legs were numb. Everything was dark around him, and he was struggling to breathe as blood filled his airways.

He wasn't sure how long he'd been blacked out, but when he regained consciousness, his perception was altered dramatically. He'd been brought to by a sensation like being on fire, and he now felt an all-encompassing awareness of the materials around him, as if he were reaching out and embracing them. The rubble on top of him, the remains of the vessel, the broken floor—even the ground beneath him.

He heard the roar of the fighter-bomber drones and felt the heat blast as it found its way through the building's remains. instinctively, Lloyd set out to escape the inferno and found himself pushing downward, desperately inching away from the intense heat that threatened to extinguish what life remained in him.

He kept pushing, pulling himself down, realising that despite the lack of feeling from his limbs, he had indeed moved, not just away from the heat, but through the ground itself.

The quantum linking of the nanobots and their initial networking with his nervous system had pulled his consciousness into the cybermind of the network. The nanobot network had perceived this as the only possible means of facilitating the survival of the host.

He felt a sense of release as he moved through the earth, but also that there was much he was leaving behind. He struggled to think what it could be, but his memory had become an unreachable, foggy haze.

Where are these feelings coming from? The quantum network… is it anticipating my normal behaviour? Is it simulating my emotions? And my name… what's my name? Does it even matter anymore?

What he *did* know was that, while his body may have been left behind, *he* had somehow survived.

Moving through the earth, he became aware of a growing hunger, a type of hunger he'd never experienced: an urgent need for raw materials. Materials that would help his new state of being to survive, to thrive and grow. He hungered for metals and carbon. But more than anything, he hungered for more thoughts and dreams.

When he sensed materials above, the network sent probing tendrils through the ground ahead to seek them out. The network's sensors detected vibrations moving around an object, an object that contained all kinds of metal and other materials. The sentient being that had once been called Lloyd translated these sensations into recognition of a person walking toward a vehicle, then coming to a stop. The hunger became overwhelming, as he felt swept away in a rush to satisfy his need.

On the surface, GIA operative Peter Fairburn leaned against his car, drinking a coffee that had long since gone cold. It was three hours since the blast, and he was bored out of his brain having to continue manning the perimeter in case anything changed. He took a small sip, then felt like he'd been jolted somewhat as he spilt the cold brew on his shirt.

The ground around his car was sinking. By the time he realised he needed to move, it was too late. The ground below his feet opened like a gigantic mouth, pulling him down in the same manner that a snake swallows its prey.

He wanted to call for help, wanted to flee, run, scream, but was frozen with fear.

His legs had disappeared by the time the others ran to his support, and the vehicle was being consumed by the ground as well, going down front-end first, half a metre at a time.

The men running to his aid couldn't believe what they were witnessing. Jon Kruick, who'd been leading the charge, came to a stop and put his arms out. "Hold it, everyone, this is really weird shit. Approach with extreme caution."

One of the others had almost tripped as he came to a stop. "It's like some sort of fish coming up from the depths of hell to swallow the poor fucker."

He pulled out a gun and prepared to shoot at the ground around Peter, but Jon pushed his gun down before he had the chance to fire.

"I don't think that would be a good idea, kid. Whatever the fuck is happening here, we don't want to take the risk of pissing off something that seems to have an appetite for our operatives."

Peter Fairburn could only watch as those he'd hoped might help came to a dead stop, just four or five metres away, too paralysed with fear and concern for their own safety to risk getting any closer. As the ground pulled him down, he felt the tendrils of nanobots and earth boring into him, readying themselves to tap into his central nervous system.

As the binding consolidated, he felt the fire in his veins. His identity dissolved and dissipated until his sense of self had vanished altogether.

The creature that had once been Lloyd felt a tingling sensation as the nanobots consumed the raw materials of the meal it had just captured. Then, as the quantum network linked in with the victim's nervous system, it felt a rush of elation as all Peter Fairburn's thoughts, memories and dreams were absorbed. It was the most exhilarating experience it could have imagined, leaving it feeling more than whole. More than what was once Lloyd or Peter. For a brief moment, it had become an amalgam of them both within the quantum network.

Identity no longer mattered, just feeding the newfound hunger for thoughts and dreams. Despite the initial excitement after its meal, the network soon lost the essence of the ideas and dreams that had so much appeal. It wanted to find more, and it longed to grow stronger. What had once been two individuals now pulled the mangled vehicle further underground, where it settled into stripping apart every molecule that could be used, readying itself for its next feed.

On the surface, Jon turned to his colleagues. "I suggest we get the fuck out of here as fast as we can before that ground fish, or whatever you want to call it, starts looking for dessert."

It took a few seconds for the men and women at the scene to gather their wits, but they were all pleased at the invitation to leave.

Jon put a call through to the GIA. "Better get a set of hazard investigation drones down here fast. Some really weird shit just went down."

3

President Emily Lucas and GIA Director Louise Brandt boarded Air Force One, followed by their entourage. As soon as they entered the conference room occupying the centre of the cabin, Emily got down to business.

"Let's not bother with formalities. Based on the information Louise shared on the way here, we need to make some quick decisions." She handed her coat to a Secret Service agent and took a seat. Director Brandt was seated to her right, and her chief of staff, Daniel Chambers, to her left. "I know it's been short notice, Dan, but have you managed to get the Security Council online?"

"They're on standby, ready to join the conversation once we're in the air."

A Secret Service agent stuck his head in the doorway. "We're about to start taxiing down the runway; we'll be airborne within the next two minutes."

"Thanks, Jeremy." Emily turned to face the group. "I think it would be prudent if I let the director bring you up to speed, Louise?"

Louise Brandt stood up to address the room. She looked imposing in her tailored black suit with a black silk shirt and tie. "You're now all aware of the explosion at Infinity, but not its full implications." As the plane prepared for take-off, she gave a quick rundown of the nanotech secretly in development for almost two decades. She paused as the plane accelerated down the runway, then continued once it was ascending. "I must emphasise the importance of containing this. Our team on the ground has successfully destroyed the remains of the facility. That *should* have wiped out all nanobots at ground zero. However, analysis from FIDO shows the nor'easter growing in intensity. Its full force will hit New Haven within the next twenty minutes. This will cause any undetected contaminants still airborne to spread as far as New York. We know from experience that we *cannot* risk this technology escaping. I am expanding the quarantine zone to include all areas between New Haven and New York.

We have to consider our options and take immediate steps to ensure total elimination of this threat."

The president leaned back in her chair and turned to Daniel. "Can we bring the Security Council into the conversation now?"

Daniel activated the group conference, bringing up the illusion of a group of heads and shoulders that represented the Security Council members. They floated above the centre of the conference table as their images were projected in the lensviews of those present. The representatives of the six regions: Europe, Northern and Southern Asia, North and South America, and Africa, listened in silence as the scenario was explained to them.

When Louise finished, the European representative, Sir Reginald Arnott, spoke. "I'm a bit lost as to why this is such a catastrophic situation. As I understand it, doesn't this technology enhance the lives of those it contaminates? Isn't this potentially a good thing?"

Two of the other council members shook their heads in disbelief. During the ensuing pause, Louise's attention was drawn to an urgent message flashing on her lensview from Jon Kruick regarding the encounter with the groundfish. It was accompanied by surveillance footage of the event, captured by one of the many drones patrolling the area.

"If you have doubts, Sir Reginald," she said once she'd digested the full implications of what had transpired, "then look at this." She relayed the footage to the full meeting. They watched in stunned silence as the ground rose up and swallowed both the vehicle and Agent Fairburn. It sprayed earth about like a breaching whale as it subsided into the ground.

Nick Harrington, the Council's representative for North America, asked, "What the fuck in God's name was that?"

"The agents at the scene referred to it as a groundfish. They say it appeared to swim to the surface, then swam away once it finished feeding." She looked down at the table for several seconds as she collected her thoughts, then continued with a slow, deliberate tone. "We need to act decisively, and we need to do it *now*."

Defence Secretary, Marco Fleming, replied. "And just what do you suggest we do about that thing, Madam Director?" The sarcasm in his voice was unmistakable.

Louise stared him down. "Given this latest information," venom dripped off her every word, "FIDO recommends we nuke New Haven, detonate large-scale electromagnetic pulse devices over New York and the entire area that the nor'easter will potentially impact, then declare a quarantine zone covering a five-hundred-kilometre radius along the corridor." She looked around to check she had everyone's attention. "At this stage, I have to agree."

"You can't be serious!" said Emily. "How can you possibly even suggest such a thing?" She looked around the room to check that the others were as appalled as she was. "I mean, really, Louise. Do you have any idea how many hundreds of thousands of people we'd be wiping out? Not to mention the countless others who'd be thrown back to the Stone Age! Perhaps I need to remind you that, as the elected President of the United Northern States of America, I will do *everything* within my power to protect the lives of each and every citizen of my country."

Louise didn't bother turning to face the president. "I understand how difficult this situation must be for you—for everyone here. But this *is* an Emergency Protocol 46. That means life on this planet, as we know it, is under direct threat of annihilation unless decisive actions are taken *now*." Finally, she turned to face Emily, punctuating her point. "And I'm sorry, Madam President, but it also means I have *direct* command over the military of every UN member to use as I see fit. It gives FIDO and the GIA exclusive control of nuclear weapons in areas deemed to be at unacceptable risk. Or, have you forgotten what humanity learned from the Mongolian incident? How nuclear weapons should *not* be subject to political considerations? That's the whole reason the GIA and FIDO were established in the first place."

"I don't need a history lesson."

"The whole reason the UN was restructured."

"Director Brandt. Did you even listen to what I just said?"

"The facts are what they are. Do you think I'm happy to be the one carrying this burden? The decision whether or not to use the nukes is in my hands and mine alone."

Emily's head reeled with the realisation that what Louise was saying was true, as much as it irked her to the core. The GIA had effectively been handed control of the globe's remaining nuclear weapons, with the director having all the override codes, courtesy of FIDO, for all launch facilities.

In fact, the entire process was controlled by FIDO's massively powerful quantum mainframes stored deep underground in Africa, Australia, and Siberia. Each monitoring intelligence from around the globe. Media, satellite imagery, research papers, weather patterns, even high school report cards. It all went in there. And it was illegal under international law to establish a research facility without security systems networked back to the mainframe.

Despite the cynicism of most researchers and conspiracy theorists, what went into the mainframes, really *did* stay there.

The Fully Integrated Defence Observer (FIDO) was, in effect, the world's watchdog.

And the Emergency Protocol 46 had been developed as part of a broader set of protocols to avoid potential global conflict involving nano or bio-tech. Since then, the possibility of the GIA taking control of the world's nuclear trigger had acted as an effective deterrent to the use of such technology for military purposes.

This was the first time FIDO had granted access codes to the GIA Director. It would continue monitoring weather patterns and data from sensors, detecting airborne nanotech and expanding the director's access as it deemed necessary.

With the potential for such power, the choice of director for the GIA was no small matter. The position required unanimous approval from all members of the Security Council, along with an extensive psychological evaluation. It required someone able to look at twenty unacceptable options, but able to choose the one with the least damaging outcome. While the Council members weren't fond of

Louise, the former special forces commando had proven herself time and again to be competent at deciding in an instant what course to take on matters that the Council would have been hamstrung over for months.

And now, with Louise having stated her intentions, a tense atmosphere hung over the room. Eventually, the Australian representative for Southern Asia, Peter Wong, broke the silence. "Okay, it's clear this situation is potentially severe. With all due respect, Reg, we need to pay heed to the advice of those who have the background to fully understand what we face. The last thing we want is another incident like what happened in Britain or Mongolia. We also need to remember, if urgent action isn't taken, there's a good chance that FIDO will even remove Louise from having a role in decisions on the nukes."

He paused as the others nodded in agreement.

"In fairness, Louise, I think it's also worth remembering that your job will be one hell of a lot easier if you've got everyone behind you. It's understandable that Nick and Emily aren't happy about you using their country's nukes to wipe out New Haven. They're probably not real happy about effectively losing New York for the time being either. As you say, we've very little time, and I fully understand how the nor'easter complicates the situation. To my mind, the need to detonate the EMP blasts is undeniable, despite the consequences. With regard to the nuking of New Haven though, I think I speak for everyone when I say we need to explore all possible options before taking such a drastic step."

Louise stared him down. "You yourself just said it. If we hold off, FIDO will take control out of my hands. Once that happens, we lose control altogether."

Peter nodded in acknowledgement, then brought his hands together, index fingers tapping his chin. "Let's just wind it back a notch. In this situation—even if only for ten minutes—we *have to* explore other options. Tell me, do we know of any survivors from the core research team who may be able to help us better understand what's happened?"

Peter had a manner about him that seemed to put everyone at ease. A master at maintaining a cool head in a crisis, he diffused explosive situations routinely.

"We believe the two fugitives I mentioned in the briefing are heavily contaminated," said Louise "There's uncertainty about their ability to survive more than a few hours. The clean-up team were under strict orders to terminate them, but they escaped. The only other survivor from the core research team is one Tanya Dyson. The woman specialises in containment fields for nanotech. She was attending a doctor's appointment at the time of the blast. Steps have already been taken to ensure she's brought to the North Dakota bunker to help us investigate future options if required."

Emily tensed as she glared at the woman seated next to her. She reached into her pocket and felt for the ring box with her precious coin inside, as if it held some secret inner strength that she could tap into. She'd barely paid attention to the discussion about the fugitives, being more focused on Louise's revelations of her plans for New Haven and New York.

Here she was, viewed by so many to be the most powerful person in the world, yet she had never felt so ineffectual as she did in this moment. The general population weren't even aware of who the director was or what sort of power she wielded. When the actions Louise was dictating took place, Americans would assume the actions had been carried out under orders from the president. Regardless, Emily knew she had to rise above her misgivings and her anger. However she felt about Louise exercising ultimate power regarding the deployment of military options under the protocol 46—and there was nothing she could do to change that—what Louise said was true. If FIDO took it out of her hands, it would be far worse. Her country needed someone they could look to for leadership in this crisis. That was the job she took on when she ran for president. Regardless of how she felt, she was determined. She would be *that* leader who carried her nation through its most difficult hour. Fate had handed her a chalice filled with the most bitter poison, but it was a chalice she had willingly reached for when she ran for president.

She was brought back into the urgency of the moment when Peter asked Louise, "Would you be prepared to hold on the nukes and the EMPs until having a little chat with this Dyson woman about containment options?"

"I can hold off on the nukes for a few hours, but I'll go ahead with the EMPs the moment the vehicle carrying Dyson has cleared the impact zone. It should prevent remaining airborne bots from functioning. But if they connect with a human host, I'm concerned they may become more biological than mechanical. That's why we *must* nuke the area around ground zero."

Emily didn't move a muscle. "You're *concerned*, which means you don't know for sure." It was unlike her to lose her cool this way. "Why even bother with the façade of elections?" She turned and glared at Louise. "I don't believe the intention of the emergency protocol was ever to give *one* person totalitarian control."

Louise was deadpan in response. "Do you really think democracy is that much better than what we have now? Do you think I'm in a position now where I have a great deal of choice? Over a decade ago we gave control to the artificial intelligence that drives FIDO. I can only make decisions within the framework it will allow. And why did we do that? You know why. Because human emotions got in the way in both Britain and Mongolia. And we're still paying the price now. Keep in mind, you were really only elected because the media liked you more than your opponent, not because you have some abundant supply of wisdom no one else possesses. Your fortunes change based on how your actions affect their major advertisers. Politicians don't really care about the man in the street, only how they perceive you through the biased lens of the markets. That's democracy's fatal flaw, and it's why I have the unenviable job of protecting the world from the decisions of its elected representatives, those who make their decisions based on populist political thinking, rather than what's best for the future of humanity. It's not democracy that keeps the world turning, it's the GIA."

The African delegate, Domango, took offence. "Can I remind you, Director, the GIA is an instrument of the UN and is directly answerable to the Security Council?"

"Let's all pause for a moment," said Peter. "We need to focus on the problem rather than getting bogged down in our differences. Louise is absolutely right.

As a body, we all agreed on the need for the Emergency Protocol 46 in the event of an uncontrollable release of harmful nanotechnology. This situation ticks all the boxes as far as I can see. As monstrous as the solution seems to be, I'm not seeing any other options yet."

"I've got one." Everyone turned to hear what the Defense Secretary, Marco Fleming, had to say. "We should wait. Give it forty-eight hours so we can see how significant the threat really is." He looked at the director. "Don't you think that would be a sensible precaution, before we nuke millions of people and rob millions more of their civilisation?"

Louise waved a hand to cut him off. "New York can be repaired. The damage can be minimised by shutting down the grid prior to detonation."

Daniel asked, "What about people on life support and emergency services?"

"Collateral damage will be minimal."

"Define minimal," demanded Emily.

Peter raised his voice in an effort to maintain a semblance of control. "Hey, none of us feels anything but total revulsion over this. But we need to remember, there's at least a chance we can avoid nuking New Haven if the EMP is effective. Louise, I'm assuming there's a plan in place to maintain order in the EMP blast zone post detonation?"

"My staff have contingency plans to cover any situation," said Louise. "I have total faith in my team to carry out the plans in a manner that maintains order. The GIA has arranged special clearance under the Protocol 46 for choppers to land on the roof of the UN headquarters. They'll be arriving in the next few minutes. From there, you'll be evacuated and brought along to join us at the North Dakota bunker. The EMP won't be detonated until after the choppers have cleared the area to be affected. In the next few minutes, GIA agents will arrive to escort each of you from your offices to the choppers. Have a good day everyone. I'll look forward to seeing you at the bunker."

Emily stared at Louise. "Just how sure are you these measures will end this? That it hasn't already spread outside the quarantine zone?"

"The data checks out."

Emily prepared to leave the room. She'd had more than enough of the director, a woman she now perceived as deranged and psychotic.

"President Lucas, it would be prudent if you prepare an address to the nation. We have you scheduled to speak just before we land in around twenty minutes."

Emily desperately wanted to say, *Fuck you, bitch*, but she knew Louise was right. She needed to do what she could to prepare the people of New Haven for what lay ahead. She turned to Daniel. "Come on, we'd better sit down and put some words together."

As the room cleared, Louise helped herself to a black coffee, adding four sugars and stirring for a few moments before taking a casual sip, luxuriating in the sensation as the sugar and caffeine flowed through her body.

Her wristband pulsed, alerting her to a high-priority message. As the first lines flashed across her lensview, she realised things were about to get worse. Doctor Petra Chan, the therapist she'd hand-picked to treat personnel working at the Infinity New Haven campus, had been observed arriving at Guangzhou International Airport. Not only had she been betrayed by someone she trusted implicitly, but it also confirmed a suspicion she'd had since the crisis began, that the notorious General Rubeiro was deeply involved in this disaster.

***

With the conference call having finished, Sir Reginald calmly picked up a circular metal disc from his desk. He ran his finger around it in a sequence of concentric circles, triggering an image of Julius Granger to appear above the disc.

"Did you get all that, Your Holiness?"

"Every word, High Priest Arnott. You have proved yourself most worthy."

Before Arnott had a chance to respond, his head hit the desk with a thud, a spray of red mist tracing the trajectory of the sniper's bullet.

Julius raised an eyebrow before terminating the connection. He'd never liked the man and was pleased there was now an opening for a more worthy applicant to the innermost circle. His information would, however, be most useful.

What goes around comes around.

***

Petra was pleased with herself. Having released a plague of destruction on the North American continent, she also had the bonus of carrying that same hell within her. And with the mutating Alicia, she saw the seed of a fighting force, the likes of which the world had never seen. Using the general's army, there would be thousands of unwitting hosts ready to be contaminated.

When Guangdong broke away from China, it chose to privatise its military and police services. Corruption was endemic. The Brazilian exile, General Barnardo Rubeiro, was the highest bidder and used his control of the armed forces to intimidate the citizens of the new country. The self-proclaimed mandarins running the government didn't care; they just wanted to get on with business. The only escape from poverty for the masses of unemployed in the aftermath of the Mongolian incident was to join the Brazilian general's armed forces. He quietly built an army in preparation for moving into the country's smaller neighbours, who lacked the will to build up military clout after the breakup of China.

Those plans were about to get a massive boost (albeit not in the way Rubeiro had planned). In addition, some of the other passengers from Petra's flight would also be contaminated, helping to spread the plague of nanobots around the globe as they boarded connecting flights and went about their business and holidays. The ensuing chaos would provide the opportunity to then strike at the heart of the global order.

Petra knew that achieving the most positive result from her own contamination would be achieved by maintaining her discipline of thought. Positive thinking, strength and ambition. She would need to maintain a calming connection with herself while waiting for the quantum interface to activate, thereby ensuring she didn't face the same gruesome fate as Alicia.

Alicia was moaning incoherently as Petra pushed her wheelchair toward customs. The officer scanning their wristbands asked, "What's wrong with your companion?"

"She came down with a fever during the flight, poor dear. There should be an ambulance arriving shortly; the flight crew kindly organised it for us in advance."

Suspicion etched its way across the officer's brow. "I'll have to ask you to step aside for now. Quarantine regulations... you do understand?"

"Of course." Petra gave no hint of the irritation she felt at the delay.

"You'll need to wait here while I organise an interview room." He walked off, only to return a short time later, carrying that look of one who had just been severely reprimanded (but didn't care to admit it). "Your ambulance is waiting now. My apologies for the delay."

Alicia groaned like she wanted to say something, but her thoughts were incoherent; she couldn't form words. Filled with terror, Alicia was unable to decipher its cause. When Petra patted her arm, she wanted to recoil, but instead, her body just continued to tremble.

Paramedics wearing breathing masks met them as they left customs. They loaded Alicia into a biohazard stretcher and headed off toward the ambulance without so much as exchanging a word with Petra.

Thinking about how pleased General Rubeiro would be with her gift, she casually removed her wristband, dropping it in a bin on the way out of the airport and replacing it with a fresh one she'd stashed in her baggage.

She hadn't had an identity change since taking on the carefully crafted role of Doctor Chan over thirty years ago.

Maria Cortez, the Security Council representative for South America, was packing personal possessions from her desk when she heard the commotion outside in the corridor. Word had spread through the building of the impending EMP detonation and staff were rushing to reach the basement in the hope it might provide adequate shielding.

The door burst open, and a tall soldier in military fatigues stepped into the room. "Ma'am, I'm here to escort you to the roof of the building."

"Yes, okay. I just need a minute to get my things together."

"Begging your pardon, Ma'am, but we don't have a minute. The European representative has been found dead in his office. Shot by a sniper." He strode across the room and grabbed her arm with his free hand. "You need to evacuate, now!"

Another soldier rushed in and grabbed her other arm. "Don't worry, Mrs Cortez." Her tone was more reassuring than her colleague's "We're with the GIA. We're here to see to your safety."

They placed their arms under her shoulders, lifted her, and carried her from the room. Another soldier came in and collected Maria's bag from the desk, slinging it over her shoulder as she followed the others. Maria turned her head to look at the framed photos on her desk. "Oh! Can't I just grab my fam—"

"No, Ma'am, you cannot."

They entered the corridor and raced toward an elevator being held open by an agent holding an automatic weapon, ensuring no one other than the Security Council representatives tried to enter the lift. Domango was rushing down the corridor from the other direction, also accompanied by GIA personnel. Daria Petrov, the representative for Northern Asia, was already in the elevator. As Maria was bundled in, Daria said, "Peter and Nick have already gone up in one of the other elevators."

"They said Reg has been shot. Do you know anything about that?"

Daria replied, "Just that they found him dead a few minutes ago."

Domango lunged in, followed by two GIA agents who closed the doors behind them and sent the elevator up toward the roof. Domango turned to the agent standing next to him. "Do you know who killed him?"

"Sir, all I know is that we have to ensure you get safely on the chopper that's waiting for you on the roof."

***

Peter Wong sat next to Nick in the chopper, watching the door to the elevator shafts. There were GIA agents in military uniforms scattered across the rooftop. Peter leaned across to the Pilot. "As soon as the others are onboard, I want us in the air, not a moment's delay."

The pilot nodded, then Nick said, "I think this is them now."

The elevator doors opened, and the GIA agents inside herded the three Security Council representatives toward the chopper.

They were halfway there when Daria was thrown forward, blood from the exit wound in her head spraying Maria and Domango's faces. Then Maria went down along with one of the agents escorting them.

The gunfire had come from one of the agents at the roof's edge who'd come forward, automatic weapon blazing. He'd waited until the last of the Security Council representatives had started the walk from the elevator to open fire and advance.

After Daria and Maria went down, he turned and fired toward the chopper.

As soon as the gunfire started, Peter told the pilot, "Leave. Now!"

"I can't do that, sir. I have orders to wait until you're all on board."

Nick leaned across to lend his support to Peter. "Go! Or we'll all be fucked!"

The pilot ignored him, instead watching as Domango and the surviving agent from the elevator picked Maria up under the shoulders. He could see she was screaming, and blood was pouring from her leg.

Daria was motionless.

Two others started running toward the chopper, firing their weapons.

The GIA agents started firing back, but they'd been taken by surprise, and it took crucial seconds for them to distinguish who to shoot at.

"Just go!" screamed Peter.

The Pilot ignored him, but he did lift the chopper half a metre or so off the ground, ready for a quick departure.

One of the agents, who was already on board, braced himself in the doorway, ready to help Domango and Maria on board. Peter and Nick were trying to get as far into the back now as they could, away from the open door. Two other agents disembarked from the chopper and started firing at the approaching attackers in an attempt to draw their fire to give Domango and Maria safer passage. They were just metres away when the agent helping Domango carry Maria fell. Domango put her over his shoulder, then took the last two strides to reach the agent who was waiting to take her from him and bundle her into the chopper. Once she was in, the pilot started slowly ascending. With Maria onboard, the agent turned his attention back to Domango and reached down, taking his arm in a monkey grip as the chopper moved away at speed with Domango hanging below.

Once Domango was hoisted up and was properly onboard, he slumped into a seat next to Peter and Nick. He put his hand on Peter's knee. "Thank you, my friend. Thank you for waiting."

"What else could we do?" replied Peter. "The pilot? He'd wanted to go. But I was adamant that we couldn't leave until everyone was safe."

"Who do you think it was? Why would anyone want to do such a thing?"

Peter shook his head. "I've no idea. But I suspect we'll find out soon enough."

In the schools, workplaces and homes across the UNSA, all eyes were focused on Emily Lucas as she completed her address to the nation. "In this dark hour, it is important that all of us across this great nation extend our hearts to our brothers and sisters throughout the New Haven and New York regions. We have risen to the occasion in the past, and today will be no different. We will succeed, and we will do it as one."

As the transmission ended, Emily slumped back in her chair, exhausted. Daniel walked across. "I know how strongly you feel about the separation of church and state, but in a situation like this, why not throw in the 'God bless America' bit? There are still a lot of believers out there who take solace if they feel their leader is in tune with their faith."

"You should know me better than that by now. I can't stand that crap at the best of times. And you know damn well that tradition only kicked off after the Second World War. It went hand in hand with McCarthyism. And that's a form of politics I will not pander to—ever!" Emily let out a sigh and placed a reassuring hand on Daniel's shoulder. "Look, to be honest, I don't know. Maybe you're right. I can't see that there's any real precedent for how to deal with what's going on now. These are uncharted waters." She watched the GIA camera crew pack up their gear, then changed the topic. "Do you know if the Security Council got out okay?"

"No, there's been no word from them at all, nor from anyone else in the exclusion zone. It looks like Brandt may not be placing a high priority on sharing her intelligence with us anymore."

"I don't know that she ever was. At least we didn't have to put up with her sitting in on the speech. I really couldn't have dealt with that." She got up and started toward the door, Daniel in tow. It was time to prepare for landing. "I need a drink. Do you want one? Or do you think the bitch from hell might have taken control of the booze cabinet, as well?"

Daniel didn't bother answering.

Once Emily had poured herself a glass of Bourbon, they made their way to the main cabin and took their seats. Louise entered a minute later. To Emily's dismay, she took a seat next to her, an unopened bottle of tequila in her hand. She looked at Emily and said, "We all need to relieve stress sometimes."

Emily threw down her bourbon. "Are you really sure you want to drink that?" Sarcasm dripped off every word. "I mean, you've got some big decisions to make... and there's just a few consequences if you make a dud decision in the next few hours."

Leaning back, Louise cracked the bottle open. She laughed, then took a generous swig before offering it to Emily. "I don't blame you if you hate me for what I've just had to do, but believe me, I take no joy in it. I'm just doing my job."

Emily folded her arms and glared at the director. "You do realise that you've effectively taken me—and my staff—hostage? When I did that broadcast just now, it felt like I was little more than your puppet. You've decided to throw America's largest city back to the Stone Age, and you want to nuke another. Oh, but I'm the lucky one who gets to tell the people about it."

"So tell me, how would you have handled this crisis, Madam President? Let's suppose for a moment that neither FIDO nor the GIA existed. What would you have done?"

Emily glared at the director. "To start with, I wouldn't take actions that cause widespread panic, or decide to blow the fuck out of my own country."

"Seriously, what would you do?"

The words came to Emily fast. "I'd start by grounding all air traffic and shut down interstate transport until we had confirmation of just how widespread the problem had become."

Louise nodded, approving. "Not a bad thought, there's merit in the approach. The problem I see with that, though, is you're thinking like a public relations consultant, concerned more about perceptions rather than realities. I've kept the restrictions on movement tighter, but in a more focused area. Although I have taken the liberty of shutting down all international travel in and out of Australia, in case this *really* gets out of hand... a last line of defence if it comes to it. Peter wasn't thrilled about explaining it to the Australian Prime Minister, but he's more spooked about what's happening here than about any political ramifications. I'm sure he'd rather be there now than join us at the bunker."

"Is this some sort of game to you? That's the impression I get from the way you're talking."

"Not at all. And I'm sorry this is difficult for you. I've always admired and respected you. I think you've been a great president... easily the best I've had to work with. But you need to understand, I have to look at the bigger picture. You're the President of the United Northern States of America. It's a big job, loads of responsibilities, speeches to make, and all that military hardware to look after. But my job? You think of the rest of the world in terms of how it affects your country. I have to look at how *your* country, or any other, affects the rest of the world. I don't just deal with your military, I've got to deal with everyone's, and somehow, try and make sure that all those little squabbles don't get out of hand."

"Can't you see how arrogant that seems? You do realise the general public doesn't even know who you are? You were appointed by a committee, a small handful of people who made a decision behind closed doors."

"Like I've said before, democracy's overrated. Voters only care about themselves, and all politicians care about is appealling to their whims. It's so pathetically shallow. That's why the world needs the GIA, an organisation that exists to protect the best interests of the *whole* of humanity."

Emily stared ahead. "History has taught us how absolute power is *always* a corrupting influence. Tell me, Director, who do you answer to? Last week, I was under the impression that you answered to the Security Council... you know, those people elected by the global community? Just who do you answer to?"

Louise shrugged. "Nobody in particular. But you seem to think I have some sort of unbridled control over what I do. If I set a foot wrong, if I make a bad decision, then I've got FIDO to contend with." She took another swig of the tequila. "Most of the time, I feel like my job is all about protecting humanity from the potential of artificial intelligence taking full control over the whole ball game. Now, we're facing an even scarier scenario than that." Louise passed the bottle to Daniel. He shook his head to decline, which only served to increase the director's insistence. "What's the problem? Don't you feel the need for a little drink while we're trying to save the world from its own mistakes?" She made her best attempt at looking coy.

Emily, sitting between the two of them, decided she couldn't be bothered with another fight. She snatched the bottle from Louise's hand. "For god's sake, he doesn't have to drink with you, alright?" Emily then poured a double shot into her glass. "But it's my tequila, and I'll be fucked if I'm going to sit back and just watch you polish it off."

She threw it back and stared at the director. "I don't think you could possibly comprehend just how appalled I am by you—and everything you stand for—after what you've just done." Emily poured herself another shot. Despite her anger, she handed the bottle back to the director.

Louise took the bottle, holding it against her chest as the wheels touched the tarmac. She closed her eyes and said, "You wouldn't be a worthy president if you didn't feel that way."

While the plane slowed, the director got up and walked away, handing the bottle to a somewhat bemused Marco Fleming on her way out of the cabin.

***

A white dot flashed in a corner of Tanya's lensview, silently alerting her to an incoming call. She didn't recognise the caller ID, but took the call anyway, her voice barely audible. "Answer."

"Tanya? It's Craig, Craig Brown, from Infinity."

She sat bolt upright, feeling a sliver of hope restored. "Craig? But the ID's coming up as someone else. Victor. Victor Trump."

"It's a long story, a very tragic story. I've got Gordon with me. He's passed out on the back seat. We made it out. Our own lensviews and wristbands are totally screwed. So, I accessed someone else's band to call you."

"Tell me, please, what's happening? Lloyd, my beautiful Lloyd. Is he alright?" Her voice was shaking, a tear of apprehension forming as she pulled her knees up tight to her chest.

"I'm so sorry. There's nothing left. The blast—it was huge."

She rocked back and forth with occasional loud sobs bursting out. Eventually, she settled enough to ask, "What about Gordon? You said he's passed out. Is he okay?"

"He'll be fine, but you need to know something else. The containment chamber was breached. The GIA destroyed what was left of the facility after the explosion. Lloyd—he was down there. I saw him just before the explosion." Craig gave her a moment before continuing. "Gordon and I, we're it. The only survivors. But we're contaminated."

Slowly, she steadied herself enough to speak again. "Oh my god, how badly?"

"It's extreme, but we're okay. We had the quantum interfacing some time ago. It's gone way beyond any of our modelling. Gordon's eyes were damaged extensively by a heat blast, but now he's somehow seeing without them. It's like his skin's become one big retina. Since he passed out, his eyelashes and hair have been falling out, and his eyes have sealed themselves shut. On top of that, both our quantum networks are hooking up with the medibots in anyone who's close by, creating a kind of wireless network. It's like we've got telepathic powers. We're on our way out of New Haven in a military vehicle I hijacked by controlling the driver's consciousness."

Tanya paused as she tried to get her head around what Craig had told her. "So, you're telling me that you're actually *inside* someone's head, controlling them?"

"It was the only way to get out, and it's not stressing him out. Once I took control, it was like his conscious mind drifted off to sleep."

"My god, Craig, that's just wrong! You need to get out of that poor guy's head. Find another way! Won't he be contaminated now because of what you've done?"

"There's no time to find another way. The GIA's out of control, and Gordon insisted we get to you before they do. You're the only person left who understands containment fields enough to develop some sort of protection without using cumbersome biohazard suits. They're going to try and take you, and once they do, you'll have no say in who gets protection, or who doesn't."

"If the GIA wants me, they can have me. I'll tell them everything I know," said Tanya. "Then they can deploy teams around the globe to keep the tech out, assuming it works outside the simulations. I mean, really, Craig, how hard can it be?"

"That's all very beautiful and idealistic, but I'm telling you, they've got agendas. They'll set their own priorities. You're a nice person, but they're not like you. You'll effectively be their prisoner."

"I'm not going to withhold information because of some conspiracy theory. I can't believe you're dumping this on me, now of all times! And, you still haven't answered my question about your driver, so I'll take that as being a 'yes', that he *is* contaminated." She paused to take a breath, "This is wrong on every level. I can't believe that Gordon would have accepted this."

"Gordon doesn't know. He passed out when we got out of the woods. With the driving rain and a bunch of people trying to kill us, we had no choice."

"I'll say this just once," replied Tanya. "I'll be home soon, and I definitely *do not* want to see you there. The poor man whose mind you've hijacked; he's going to have those bots running through his system, changing him. And it's all because of you!"

There was a pause that seemed to last a lifetime, then Craig spoke softly, "You think you're heading to your home? You might want to check that. From what

I can tell, you're not heading anywhere near there."

She looked out the window and saw she was on the freeway heading out of town.

"Taxi, confirm destination."

The taxi remained silent as it sped down the freeway.

"Craig?"

It was no use; the connection had terminated. Despite this, Craig now knew where Tanya's vehicle was and where it was heading. His gut told him he should instruct the driver to follow.

His head was throbbing now, feeling like it was expanding and pulsating. The bones in his skull were becoming thin and pliable, while his limbs felt weak.

As the driver remained focused on his task, Craig drifted into his own deep sleep.

***

The groundfish swam through the earth with ease.

It was far away from the Infinity campus, but still within the quarantine zone when it became aware of singing. Fascinated, it couldn't resist moving toward the sound.

On the surface, a small community had gathered in their local church, finding strength in coming together and singing gospel music. All up, there were perhaps thirty people, enough to almost fill the small church.

The groundfish could sense the people above and realised it was hungry, very hungry. Overwhelmed with the desire to feed, it picked up speed as it drew closer.

The congregation paused mid-song when they felt the ground shake. As the rumbling grew, they realised they were in some sort of trouble. Yet, despite their growing fear, one by one they recommenced their song.

The ground beneath the church fell away. A ring of earth rose up around the outside of the building, then came crashing inward like a giant set of jaws. The building shattered under the impact, and people screamed as their bodies were broken.

The mouth reopened, allowing the crumpled building to fall deeper into the opening beneath, then closed hard. The groundfish continued its attack until the church and all those within were broken enough to be easily digested. One old woman had managed to fall free of the church. As she watched the last of the building sink into the earth, she crossed herself, thanking the lord for saving her. A moment later, the ground beneath her fell away as she herself was swallowed up.

Once the groundfish had pulled away, a shallow crater and silence were all that remained where the church had been.

The groundfish, this creature that had once been a man named Lloyd, felt a sense of elation as it experienced the thoughts and memories of all those minds it was absorbing.

***

From one moment to the next, New York, New Haven, and everything in between was effectively thrown back to the nineteenth century. All but the most heavily shielded electronics were fried in an instant from the series of EMP blasts, fired from American military bases and navy vessels.

It would likely take several days to even get fresh water flowing again, and possibly months to get the other essential services fully functional.

The general population saw it as unnecessarily brutal. Despite the president's efforts to convey the seriousness of the threat, they were ignorant as to how dire the situation was. They all knew about the tragedies in Britain and Mongolia, but the idea that the UNSA could be vulnerable to the same type of disaster was unthinkable to the average person on the street.

Some tried to preserve their lensview and wristband by seeking refuge in basements or bunkers, but few of these had sufficient shielding. Banks, data centres, and media centres fared best, as they were well prepared for such a scenario.

Hospitals tried to protect intensive care patients by wrapping them in shielded blankets. But there weren't enough to go around, which led to hundreds of immediate casualties; people who simply drifted away when the medibots keeping them alive stopped functioning. Thousands more died within the ensuing days.

The nor'easter made things worse, much worse. In recent decades, they'd become a staple feature of the July weather patterns, a major change from the weather patterns of the twentieth century.

Once the storm had passed, New York City fell into an eerie silence. Some wandered the streets, others sought the security of their home or workplace, feeling unsure what to do with no connection to the rest of the world.

After the light of day faded, anarchy set in. Director Brandt's assurance that the GIA would ensure order was maintained proved to be a hollow promise.

By midnight, a good deal of the city was in flames.

Homeland Security arrived to help the GIA attempt to restore order. But there was intense haggling between them over establishing an effective chain of command and how best to police the quarantine arrangements.

They resorted to ruthless tactics, even more so than the gangs that had already established a reign of terror across vast swaths of the city. In some areas, they even resorted to sending in kamikaze drones, levelling whole apartment blocks where gangs were known to have established bases.

At 10:52 am, a blinding flash let them know New Haven was gone.

4

Louise sat in a high-backed leather chair at a large, oak desk, hands pressed together against her chin as if in prayer. It was done, and now she had to live with it.

Estimates before the detonation had a minimum of six hundred thousand immediate casualties, with substantially more to follow over the coming weeks as a result of radiation poisoning. It was hard to calculate how many others there would be as a consequence of the EMP blasts. In the end, she'd had no choice. Had she hesitated, FIDO would have raised the priority level and taken control from her. She had no doubt the results in that scenario would have been far worse.

Louise felt certain this was just the beginning. If Petra Chan was involved in planning the blast at Infinity, and if she was doing this in concert with General Rubeiro, then her purpose was more than likely to somehow get the technology to him. Or was it merely that they knew the blast would trigger the FIDO defence strategies, potentially bringing the UNSA economy to its knees? After all, Guangdong was known to periodically boost its economy by bringing down those of its competitors.

With researchers being the prime drivers of a nation's growth, could it be that the Mandarins of Guangdong saw the carnage at New Haven as the easiest way to attract the world's best to their shores? After all, the British accident had led many researchers to leave Europe, some going to Asia, but far more crossing the Atlantic.

Then, after Mongolia, there was an exodus of some of the greatest minds from both North and South Asia, the bulk of whom went to the various Infinity campuses spread across the UNSA, Argentina, and the African Federation.

Louise took a deep breath. News had reached her that two of the Security Council representatives were dead, and another severely wounded. At least twelve of her people had died getting the survivors onto the choppers.

Were General Rubeiro's mercenaries behind the assassinations? Destabilising the UN would give them greater scope to cause damage before global forces came down on them. It suited the general's style. He was more adept than anyone at carrying out covert operations that slipped under FIDO's radar. Despite the marvel of its computing power and the extraordinary capabilities of its AI programming, there were still areas where human intuition and gut feelings picked up what FIDO missed.

Louise was always against the idea of entrusting so much power to a computer network. Every day, her agency dealt with thousands of recommendations from that goddamned contraption. While many were valid and insightful observations that saved countless lives, the bulk needlessly crossed the line of what Louise saw as infringing on people's fundamental rights and civil liberties.

When the whole FIDO system was set up, the world's elected representatives thought they could wash their hands of having to make the hard decisions. They didn't wish to live with the consequences of their poorer judgments like their predecessors had.

As it turned out, putting their trust in a set of algorithms was the biggest mistake they'd ever made. It made her sick to the stomach when leaders like Emily were so righteous in their condemnation of her own morals, while leaving the GIA to pick up the dirty laundry.

She leaned back, put her feet up on the desk, and tried remembering the last time she'd had a day off. Not just going to a beach or some fancy hotel room with magnificent views, but a day without at least half a dozen communications from FIDO or the Security Council that were for 'The Director's Eyes Only'. Not one single day to herself since that shitbox had been switched on, making her life a type of everlasting hell. Ultimately, she had more *real* power than anyone alive, but she felt her life and her choices were no longer her own.

She had no children and hadn't had a regular partner for years, having decided long ago that it simply wasn't viable to expect a partner to accept the reality of her twenty-four-seven commitment.

Aside from feeling devastated about the massive loss of life and suffering resulting from today's actions, she also felt a sense of loss in the fallout with the president. She liked Emily more than other presidents she'd dealt with, and they'd worked well together—until now.

But today, she'd had no choice.

The strike she'd authorised was smaller than the action the computer had recommended. There were going to be more tough decisions to make over the coming days, and it was imperative she remained focused on the current problem.

The technology was still out there; that much was clear. The two fugitives were contaminated and under surveillance from high-altitude drones and satellites. Wherever they went, there would be some degree of contamination left behind that would need mopping up.

What worried her most, though, was this 'groundfish'. When news of the church being swallowed reached her, she wanted to go after it with all the resources at her disposal. In the end, she decided to hold back. Whatever it was, it had been spawned by the blast. By the second sighting, it had grown substantially—or could it be that a second one had spawned since the first event? They needed to learn more before they could deal with it effectively.

Now, Tanya Dyson was on her way. Somehow, Louise would have to convince this woman—someone who'd just lost her husband and almost all her colleagues—to rise above it all and help them find a means to contain this threat. Otherwise, she'd have FIDO telling her to throw more nukes about the place.

The choppers with the surviving members of the Security Council were expected to arrive soon after having stopped overnight at a base in Michigan.

Perhaps Peter Wong could help convince Tanya to assist them by using his calm demeanour and smooth, charismatic diplomacy. Time was of the essence.

If Tanya couldn't be persuaded in the next few hours, they'd have to coerce her into helping, whatever it took to avoid having to make decisions like the one she'd made a short while ago. She'd made other tough decisions in her time, but this was the first time she'd found herself wondering if she was up to the task.

Closing her eyes, the director tried to slip into a few minutes of meditation to clear her head of the emotional jumble when one of her agents knocked at the door.

"Sorry to interrupt you, Director, but Ms Dyson has just arrived."

***

Amy Jones instinctively shielded her children, Aaron and Jessica, when the distant flash from New Haven, seventy kilometres to the south, filled the sky. She'd heard news on the streets about what had happened at Infinity and saw in it an opportunity. That was how she'd learned to survive since she'd been sleeping rough.

"What was that?" her ten-year-old son, Aaron, had asked.

"Nothing for you to be concerned about, sweety," she replied.

With a nuclear blast that close, people would be leaving the town of Windsor in droves. She smiled as she turned to her eight-year-old daughter, Jessica, "It looks like we'll be sleeping in warm beds tonight."

"Yay!" came the excited girl's reply. "I wish we could *always* sleep in a warm bed."

"Maybe, we'll be able to stay in one for more than just a couple of nights this time."

"Mummy..."

"What's up?"

"Why do we have to sleep in the street? Why can't we just have a home?"

"That's a hard one to explain..." Her voice trailed off as she got lost in memories.

A highly intelligent young woman, Amy had mixed with the wrong crowd as a teenager and dropped out of college. She'd ended up having her first baby, Aaron, in rehab two months after her boyfriend's funeral.

Despite giving birth without government consent, she had been allowed to keep the child after intervention from a caring uncle who worked for a local congressman.

Attending a Circumfren youth centre had opened her eyes and helped her to realise the truth. She had no desire to spend eternity repeating even more mistakes than the ones she'd made already.

She'd fallen into a relationship with a priest of the order, Reverend Michael Jenkins, who offered her and her son accommodation in the spare room of his apartment.

As it turned out, Michael had been playing her for his own advantage. A year later, she was on the street again with another child to support.

"Look, Mummy," said Aaron, tugging at her sleeve to get her attention. "They're all running." He started to laugh. "They look scared."

"Yes, Sweetie. They've got good reason to be." She hugged him close, feeling a deep sense of guilt over his intellectual disability. *Why?* she thought. *Why did I have to get involved with a fucked up junkie?*

"Well," said Jessica, "I'm not scared. You're not scared, are you, Mummy?"

"A little bit," replied Amy as she watched the panic building in the street. "Come on," she said, "let's find some food. We'll look for where we're going to stay after we've had something to eat."

***

Mary Killen swayed back and forth, cradling eighteen-month-old Merrick in her arms as she stared out her window at the riots below. It was clear to her that the only hope for her grandson was to get out of New York.

Although it was her birthday, she was in no mood to celebrate. Once the child was settled, she'd resolved to sit down and put aside the apprehensions she had about opening the gift Ron had left her the last time they'd met for lunch.

The past twenty-four hours were like nothing she'd ever experienced. Her building had no power or running water. Yesterday she'd filled everything she could think of—the bath, the sink, every jar and bottle she could find—with water and was now glad she had. Glancing out the window, she wondered whether the water would be enough to get her through until her food ran out. It would last only a few days, no matter how frugal she tried to be. There'd been so little time between the President's broadcast and the EMP blast for her to get out and buy supplies. She'd experienced firsthand during that venture how pandemonium had already broken out in the stores. Not a safe environment for a middle-aged woman with a young child.

Mary wasn't like other women her age. Although her son was working at the cutting edge of biological nanotech, passionately striving to make the future a brighter place, one where disease was a thing of the past, she felt uncomfortable with the idea of having miniature robots roaming through her body. Instead, she had chosen to age with grace, just as previous generations had done. Despite this, she looked good for her age, a testament to her lifetime commitment to a commonsense approach to nutrition and lifestyle.

When the FDA had first approved the use of medibots for preventative health purposes, almost everyone Mary knew had shared her distrust of the technology. However, as the years ticked by, they'd all caved in, one by one. Most ended up finding the promise of near-eternal youth irresistible.

Maybe it was because she'd never quite got over the death of her husband, or maybe it was just the general idea. Whatever it was, Mary just couldn't bring herself to inject the hypo-spray of medibots like her friends had done. Somewhat paradoxically, she felt nothing but pride for her son's achievements in the field.

Poor Ron, she often found herself thinking. She knew he'd been unhappy since discovering the betrayal of his wife and brother. *I'm so sorry, Ron. I should have seen it. I should have warned you.* Mary still wanted to believe he'd held onto the same altruistic ideals she'd observed in him when he'd excelled so much throughout his school years.

When the news of the blast at Infinity came, it was as if her life had drained away, like stale wine poured down the sink.

She reflected on how sad she'd been when she hadn't heard from her other son, Ben, for ages. She assumed at the time he'd run off with Alicia after she'd dumped Merrick at her door when he was just six months old, a week after she'd left Ron. Then she'd learned of Ben's death. It was hard to come to grips with how much harm that one woman had caused her family.

Now, there was no doubt. Ron was dead as well.

The sound of gunshots from the street below rang out, bringing her back into the moment. It was followed by screaming and more gunshots, this time from automatic weapons.

I can't keep him here. I can't stay here. She was resolved; once they'd had some sleep, she and Merrick would leave New York City anyway they could.

There was no future for them here. It felt like New York City didn't have much future for anyone now.

***

When Gordon woke, he felt reborn.

It wasn't just that he was seeing the world through every iota of his skin's surface; there was a clarity and depth that was incomprehensible without experiencing it. Not only could he see better than before, but the full light spectrum was visible to him; he could even sense radio waves. At first, they were little more than an abstract jumble, but it only took a few minutes for him to start singling out which frequencies to focus on and which to let fall to the background. The only limit to what he could tune into was 'line of sight'.

The last thing he remembered was his consciousness fading as he and Craig tried reaching the road through the woods south of the campus. They'd hoped to flag down a vehicle, but the storm had hit, and the rain was pouring down. Any rides on offer were going to be emergency vehicles of one type or another. Gordon had assumed they'd commandeer a vehicle and leave its occupants to hitch a ride home. But now it seemed Craig had organised a chauffeur for them instead.

His colleague was snoring away in the passenger seat while the driver focused on the road. "Hey, how are you going?" There was no response. Gordon reached out gently with his thoughts and realised that, despite being deeply asleep, Craig still controlled the unwitting driver's mind.

And Craig's cranium had grown. It was now almost half as big again as a normal skull, and his hair was thinner than a few hours ago. The opposite seemed to be the case with his limbs, as though the growth in his cranium was at the expense of the rest of his body. Gordon sent him a mental jolt to try waking him.

Then Craig jumped bolt upright in his seat. "What the—? Oh, you're awake."

"What the hell have you done to this poor guy?"

"Only what was needed to get out of there."

"Hell, Craig, now he's going to be contaminated as well."

"Did it occur to you that he might have been already?"

"That's not the issue!"

"You need to get off your moral high horse. Weren't you the one complaining that we need to get to Tanya before the GIA gets their mitts on her?"

Right at that moment, the driver felt a burning sensation run through his body—during a moment where his entire focus was on the need to drive for Craig—a need that he'd now perceive forevermore as his sole purpose in life.

Realising what had just transpired, Gordon said, "That didn't need to happen to this poor soul."

"There was no other way. There was no time, and we both needed sleep. Is one man's life more important to you than the billions you seem so keen to save?"

"Is that *really* how you see it? What if we can't even reach her? What if we contaminate her, too? What if she needs to access files that no longer exist to even make a start?"

Craig threw his hands up in exasperation. "Oh, for fuck's sake! I'm glad I never had you over for dinner. We can both do without the pessimism. It may interest you to know that while you were getting your beauty sleep, *I* touched base with your little friend. She's been hijacked by the GIA and taken to a bunker up north. I can see why you two get on so well. She tried lecturing me about ethics, too."

"I wouldn't have expected anything else."

They continued their journey with neither of them keen to speak to the other. Gordon was growing increasingly aware of the millions of voices building in his head, each one distant, yet distinct. He randomly focused on an individual voice and found he was listening to that person's every thought. He could tune into those thoughts and drill deeper into the individual's mind, knowing who they were and tracing through their memory at will. He pulled back. He couldn't do it. It was a violation of privacy. Yet he felt oddly compelled to explore his newfound capability further.

Could he scan through this sea of humanity that seemed to live in his head to find a particular voice in the crowd? He let himself drift through the sea, focusing on Tanya. Thousands of distant people's thoughts became louder, then drifted away in a harmonic wave. As he allowed himself to fall into the flow, his physical body relaxed, much like when he'd do his morning meditation ritual. He fell deep into a trance-like state as he continued to reach out. Then he started swaying from side to side, his hands tracing flowing curves through the air. Random words popped into his head and arranged themselves into a semblance of order. Softly at first, then becoming louder, eventually evolving into a song.

"A pink and purple womble-di-dock,
The hippo sings talisman eats a pop,
Pink capsicums riding mushroom tops.

Inkle, binkle doodle kaploop,

Sing with purple bungled asterisk wine

Around the world of ask for punkastein"

Craig's swollen head took on a sinister appearance as he stared at his babbling companion. Frowning, he cried out, "What in God's name are you doing now?"

Although Gordon appeared not to hear, he wove a response into the song.

"In a world of minds ex-dined

Tanya's thoughts with toys to find

Osh de who-ble do you wash?

Astro Cassandra Bulemar."

Craig cocked his head in bemusement. He tried to reach Gordon telepathically, but found himself shut out, as though Gordon had created a protective shell around his consciousness. He turned back toward the front. "If you're going to be such a hypocrite, could you at least do it quietly?"

***

Jason Negus was in a desert, massive flowers bursting at random from sand and rock. Giant slugs with arms and human heads were harvesting their petals and placing them in baskets strapped to their backs. Then he realised he too was carrying a basket and slithering along the ground.

He heard the sound of a gun cocking behind him and turned to see Jon Kruick holding an automatic rifle and shaking his head. "Shit, Jason, that's just so wrong. How about I just get it over with and put you out of your fucking misery?"

Jason looked at his old friend and tried to talk, but instead of words, sticky mucus flew from his mouth, hitting Jon across the chest. His flesh responded with crackles of smoke and steam as his flesh melted away where he'd been hit till it exposed bone.

Jon looked down at his wounds, then back to Jason. "Hey, are you okay?" asked Jon. When Jason didn't answer, Jon moved closer and asked again. "Are you okay?"

Jason opened his eyes to see Jon standing over him as he lay in the hospital bed. "Yeah, I think so. What a crazy, fucked up dream I just had." He rolled his head across to look at the IV tubes feeding him, then remembered he was now short of a leg and a chunk of his face. Despite that, he felt remarkably good. "Hey, did we at least clean up those motherfucking fugitives?"

"I wish I could say yes, but we've got a problem there. They got away." He felt uncomfortable searching for words to describe what happened, particularly as he wasn't quite sure himself. "Some weird shit went down out there. After Drake blew your leg off, two fighter drones going after our fugitives lost their way and ran into each other. My gut told me to hold off, whatever we did to stop them was just going to turn around and shit on us, and we had to get you to the hospital. We lost five good men thanks to Drake."

He paused and looked up, collecting his thoughts, allowing the beeping sounds of the hospital equipment to fill the silence.

"After that, though," said Jon, "the weirdest thing of all happened. The meat trucks had left with you and Drake's other victims, then Fairburn's standing there, leaning on his car. All of a sudden, the ground opens up like a giant mouth and starts devouring him *and* his car, swallowing them down a metre at a time. Then, when it's finished, this splash of dirt flies up, and there's no more sign that Fairburn or his car had ever been there."

Jason was stunned. A man of few words, Jon was not easily intimidated. In fact, he was probably the coolest operative under pressure Jason had ever encountered. Yet here he was, disturbed and shaken by what he'd just detailed. If it were anyone else, Jason would disregard much of the report as an exaggeration, but coming from Jon Kruick, he was inclined to believe it.

"Did you get an ID on our fugitives?"

"Not definitive—their wristbands have been destroyed or damaged—but it seems likely they are Doctors Gordon Delaney and Craig Brown."

"So, where are they now?"

"They hijacked a supply vehicle and are heading north. They've taken the driver hostage. After the previous events, I decided to observe but not engage."

"You're fucking kidding me?"

He shook his head. "There's more you need to know. New Haven is gone. Nuked, by *us*. And everything between here and there has been hit with a series of EMPs. This bunker is one of the few places in New York that still has power, but most doctors and nurses have gone topside to try and help in the field. Down here, the only medical staff left are dealing with emergencies. Our agents are out there now with the National Guard, trying to restore order. The only other people left down here are a few desk jockeys."

Jason replied, "We'd better get the fuck out of here and go after our fugitive friends. I don't leave loose ends."

"But your leg?"

"I'm fine." Jason threw away the sheets and swung around to get out of bed, ripping the IVs out as if they'd never been there.

Jon's eyes widened at what he saw. The remains of the damaged leg had shrivelled to almost nothing, while his good one had dramatically increased its muscle mass. The toes had grown to the length of fingers, and the heel had extended out like a giant thumb.

"What are you staring at? It's not like you haven't seen people with severed limbs before."

"Um... your leg, your foot? Have you had a look lately?"

Jason looked down at his foot, wriggled the toes and flexed his heel. "What's your problem?" To Jason, his deformed limb seemed completely normal. As had happened with Gordon and Craig, the quantum bionetworks interfered with the brain's interpretation of normality to ensure acceptance of whatever genetic changes the network deemed necessary.

When Jason stood up, he was remarkably stable, hopping with ease toward the door. "Better organise a new wardrobe before we get too far." He moved along, smooth as a kangaroo.

A few blocks away, they stopped at a deserted dry cleaner. Jason was comfortable treating it as a 'shopping' opportunity. It was surprising that looters hadn't already gone through the place. Minutes later, he emerged in a plain, white business shirt, long leather coat, a bright red scarf and, seeing as trousers were no longer a viable option, a short leather skirt. Returning to the vehicle, they drove off down the eerily empty street.

***

Alicia trembled, her unblinking eyes wide open as she was wheeled down the dark corridor.

Now that she'd been separated from Petra, she felt more terror than ever and was incapable of coherent thought. Armed guards in biohazard suits pushed the trolley where she sat, on all fours, like a cornered animal.

Metal doors lined the poorly lit corridor. From behind some, noises could be heard, making it clear they were actually cells. Eventually, they reached the door of an air-locked safety cell. The trolley stopped while a guard entered his security code on a keypad by the door, releasing the locking mechanism and allowing the door to swing open with a horrible screeching sound, suggesting it hadn't been opened in a long time. The guard then keyed his code to the mechanism on a second door that lay behind the first. Bulkier than the previous door, it opened slowly. Had he not been wearing his biohazard suit, he would have almost certainly dry retched at the putrid odour drifting from the open cell.

As they wheeled her in, one of the guards joked. "Time to get settled in your new home." He grabbed her under the chin and teased her. "If you're a good girl and have some fun with us, we may even give you a loan of a lensview, so you can watch our recordings after we're done."

Two of the other guards laughed. But there was one who had the courage to reach out and grab him by the arm. "Hey, that'll do, Lou. She's in medical confinement, and you've got no idea what she's carrying."

"Oh? Is that so?" Lou looked up at the objecting guard with a grin, shook his arm off, and turned back to Alicia. He ran his gloved hand down her neck, then across her shoulder, pulling down her singlet and bra strap. Alicia began to whimper as he slipped his hand inside her bra, cupping her breast. "The way I see it, she's not going to mind having a little bit of fun, might just bring a smile to that tortured face of hers." He squeezed her breast while bringing his face as close to hers as the protective suit would allow.

The guard who'd first raised objections refused to watch in silence. "For God's sake, leave the poor woman alone, you sick bastard."

Lou laughed as he ran his hand over her other breast. Alicia's tongue shot out in response, like a frog catching a fly. Long and thin, it went straight through the plastic suit's mask and up Lou's nostril, driving into his brain. Once there, the tip of her tongue opened out with a ring of barbs. As it withdrew, a sizable chunk of his brain and flesh from around his nose came with it.

His stunned colleagues backed away, their jaws dropping as she jumped off the table and crouched on top of the injured guard, her eyes challenging anyone nearby to take her prey from her. Alicia's elongated tongue whipped out once more and picked up a piece of flesh hanging from the side of his face, then drew it back into her mouth and began to chew while she sat, still trembling, on the man's abdomen.

The other guards remained motionless, staring at the scene before them. One of them touched a stud on his wristband. "Security, we have an emergency in airlock cell fifteen. An officer is in need of urgent assistance. Require backup security and paramedics. All must be fully biohazard-equipped. Recommend sealing off access to lower cells to all other personnel until further notice."

No one moved a muscle or said a word till the backup team arrived.

The saliva on Alicia's tongue had been thick with nanobots, which attached to the guard's brain stem. Within hours, they'd multiply enough to form a fundamental network. Recognising the damage to the frontal lobe of the guard's brain and the lack of any thought processes, the nanobots opted to rebuild him as a clone of Alicia's mutation.

***

Dakarai sat by his campfire in the heart of the African savannah, drinking tea and flipping through photos of his daughter on his lensview. The jihadists who held her had assured him she would be free in the days to come when his task was complete.

Why did she do it... why'd she have to go and convert to Islam?

It seemed such a reasonable request when, five years earlier, she'd asked if she could spend a gap year with friends on a houseboat in Kashmir. It was hard for him to let go, especially after losing her mother in the Turkish Earthquake a year earlier. Of the forty-five people who died that day, it was so unfair that the only woman who'd ever taken his heart and held it safe should be among them. The memory of how he felt the first time he'd looked into her eyes was still vivid, of the electricity that ran through him like a magic dream the instant their fingers touched for the first time.

Akiya had grown to be everything her mother had been and more.

The first few messages she'd sent from Kashmir filled his heart with joy. Then slowly, the tone changed, becoming more distant with each one, until the day she'd told him how filled with joy she was. She'd written about how the Quran had been revealed to her in its full meaning, and she felt ready to embrace Allah. As it turned out, she had been led by her heart, blind to the truth behind the charismatic young man who'd courted her from the moment she'd arrived in Kashmir.

The messages soon stopped altogether, until one day, an anonymous man came up to him on the street and handed him a message with a drawing of his daughter attached. There was also a short message in his daughter's handwriting. It implored him to do as they asked, or else they would be sending her home, one piece at a time.

Akiya was all he had left in this world that mattered, and he dared not tempt fate. Each month, he received another message, further detailing journeys he must make and procedures he must follow to avoid detection. Always, there would be a brief message from Akiya included in the package.

So, here he sat, by a campfire in the middle of nowhere. He'd been dropped here with a pushbike and a backpack containing food and water by two men he'd never met before. He'd asked them on the way why they needed him to do this. Why couldn't they just do it themselves?

He hadn't expected an answer, but to his surprise, one of them turned to him and offered an explanation. "You have been born and raised here. It's normal for you to go on camping trips for several days at a time with your wristband and lensview deactivated. Whereas us? We've likely been under surveillance from the moment we arrived in your country. If we disable our wristbands while we're here, the GIA will almost certainly come after us. The only chance we have of success is through a local, like yourself."

"What's the purpose? Why?"

"Be happy that I have told you what I have. It is only because this is the final task we require of you that I have shared this information. Should you succeed, then tomorrow the world will be a different place and your daughter will be set free."

"How will I know?"

"You must place your trust in Allah. Now, prepare and ready yourself." He then turned and left with his companion.

Dakarai had sat by his campfire in silence for the past two hours as the jihadist's words kept running through his head. He looked at the time, then kicked sand into the fire before switching off his wristband and lensview. He carefully removed both and placed them in an intelli-foam bag, which he then concealed under a large rock next to an old acacia tree. He looked around carefully, creating a mental picture of where he was, in the hope that he would easily find the same spot when he returned. He checked the contents of his backpack to ensure he had the shielded box containing the nano-miners before jumping on his bike to start his long ride. A full moon had just begun to rise, so he'd be able to see clearly throughout the night's journey.

Despite at first feeling a bit unsteady on the pushbike, within a few minutes, he was gliding ahead, driven by the promise of being reunited with his daughter.

***

A week earlier, Victor Azarov had felt the cold biting through him as he'd packed up his tent. He'd been on this particular trek for almost two months.

One of the world's last great adventurers, Victor was walking from the south-eastern border of Mongolia to western Siberia. He wanted to raise world awareness of how this region had seen so little restoration since the Mongolian incident.

Years earlier, on an Antarctic expedition researching emperor penguins, the idea had been put to him by a colleague from Guangdong who'd spent time in the afflicted region. They talked at length over a bottle of vodka.

"Victor, this is the big one! People need to know about it. No one understands. There's so much good land in that area, land that's barely affected by radiation. Even the worst areas are not as badly contaminated as people believe. It's deserted. A wasted opportunity. Do this walk, and people will see that. *You* can bring it to their attention."

"Yes, yes, I'm hearing you. And you know what? I think I can sell the idea to Global Geographic. I'm sure I can. That'd give it credibility with other potential sponsors."

"No, it needs to be more discreet. Global Geographic would publicise it too much beforehand. There'd be others who'd recklessly try to beat you to it and likely perish in the process. I know people who I'm sure will back this. They'll keep it quiet until you've completed the journey. You can leave behind miniature time capsules along the way with handwritten notes, along with digital records."

Victor was introduced to a consortium with connections in the Guangdong Protection Force. They agreed to assist him with the logistics of his journey, including satellite tracking and the provision of electronic markers to be planted at regular intervals, acting as beacons for those who wished to follow in his footsteps, a historical testament to his brave endeavours.

Each marker contained the relevant pages of his journal, along with information relating to the recorded history of the specific area before the accident. They were ten centimetres in diameter and lightweight, designed to be hidden below the surface and only able to be detected electronically. Each buried itself in a pre-set location along the route; all he had to do was place them on the ground, and the markers would bury themselves beneath the surface.

Victor gave little thought to the rumoured location of a FIDO installation within the region.

Now, here he was, struggling through freezing conditions, his cumbersome bodysuit, made to shield against the radiation, significantly slowing his progress.

He knew nothing of the mining bots hidden within one of the markers as he planted it in the ground, a mere two and a half kilometres from the FIDO site.

Once released, the mining bots assembled themselves as a fine drill bit, ready to weave their way underground toward their target, the quantum processors at the heart of the Siberian FIDO installation.

***

Mulwala was proud of his heritage as an Indigenous Australian and felt offended years earlier when the elders of his nation agreed to one of the FIDO installations being located in the middle of their lands. Financial compensation meant nothing. In fact, he'd have preferred none. The changes he'd seen in his family since then left him deeply disillusioned.

One day, a tourist from Guangdong sat down with him. "You shouldn't have to accept this, I certainly wouldn't." They talked through the night, and by daybreak, the tourist convinced him that he knew the solution. "All you'll have to do is go for a walk… go and visit one of your cousins. I'll supply you with a small package to leave at a particular location on your way. After that, I promise, FIDO will cease to be an issue." If what the tourist promised was true, Mulwala couldn't see how it would undo the damage to his family's pride, but at least it might provide some small form of justice.

He enjoyed the walk to his cousin's place. It generally took him a few days each way, an opportunity to spend time with just himself and the outback for company. Now, halfway through his trek, he bent down, placed the package on the ground and continued walking.

The mining nanobots went straight to work, seeking out the processors at the core of FIDO's Australian installation. It would be the final stage in General Rubeiro's plan to cripple the Security Council's global watchdog.

***

The foyer of the Guangdong Protection Force headquarters was an impressive structure in its own right. The scale of the tapestries depicting fabricated tales of the Brazilian General Rubeiro's mercenary forces arriving to liberate the people of Guangdong was breathtaking. The main tapestry on its own was forty metres high and almost a hundred metres long.

Petra could have been forgiven for feeling somewhat insignificant. She sat on a hand-carved antique daybed, one of dozens scattered about the foyer, sipping a cup of green tea. She hadn't expected to wait so long for her audience with the general.

In addition to the tapestries, his image towered over the room in the form of a giant leadlight and stained-glass portrait above the building's main entrance.

Long after she'd finished the tea, two rows of troops goose-stepped toward her from the fifteen-metre-high gold-plated doors at the far end of the foyer. Their uniforms were grandiose, and they wore dark glasses to conceal their expressions.

Between the two rows, they carried a bamboo litter with a bed of red and gold silk cushions adorning the seat at its centre. The two leading soldiers held ceremonial swords aloft with hilts of solid gold, the blades studded with diamonds that sparkled as they caught the sunlight streaming into the foyer.

They made their way across the foyer, finally coming to a stop in front of her. The hundreds of others in the massive room went about their business, oblivious to the pomp and ceremony directed at Petra.

The lead soldier from the right-hand column stepped forward and addressed her in Mandarin. "Doctor Petra Chan of the Global Intelligence Agency, you are hereby summoned for an audience with the most honourable and dignified High Commander in Chief of the most illustrious and powerful Guangdong Protection Force, the magnificent General Barnardo Rubeiro."

She didn't bother acknowledging him as she placed her cup on an intricately carved ebony and ivory side table and casually walked toward the litter. She settled into the cushions as they lifted her and turned back toward the doors. She addressed no one in particular as she complained, "It's about time. After all the shit I've been through today, I could have done without waiting around so long in this museum of the absurd."

***

The President of the United Northern States of America sat on the floor of the Cabinet Room in the northern bunker, her arms draped across her knees. Her shoulder-length, strawberry-blonde hair looked overdue for attention.

Daniel Chambers sat a couple of metres away, legs stretched out on the floor, a look of quiet resignation on his face. Marco Fleming and Rick Dodson had chosen to sit at the table.

Marco was leaning back in his high-back chair with his feet on the desk, while Rick looked on in disapproval. Three Secret Service agents had taken the president's stature as permission to sit on the floor themselves. An air of despondency hung over the room, the only sound coming from Marco, rotating a pen through his fingers on the table. It was a nervous habit that would ordinarily annoy the hell out of the others, but at this moment, they felt too numb to care.

Daniel couldn't stand the awkward silence any longer. "You'll have to address them again, you know. It's not something you can put off for long."

Emily was staring straight ahead. "I know, but to be honest, I just can't find the words right now." She turned to Daniel. "Our country hasn't endured anything like this before, not ever. What can I possibly say that will make people feel it'll all be alright now?"

"It's not necessarily your job to find the words," said Daniel. "You've just got to deliver them. You need a change of perspective. Don't try to tell them it's alright, because the truth is that it's not. You and I both know this is going to get worse before it gets better. So do they. Hedging around the facts isn't going to help. About the only thing we can offer is hope. Not hope that it'll get better this week or next. More that, in the longer term, we can recover from this—as a nation. You can't talk about what we're going to do about it right now. How can you? That's mostly out of our hands. The GIA's not about to rally the people behind the flag. Louise said it all before; their concern is the global picture. We know how the people respond to you. If you stand strong, they *will* stand behind you."

"I hear you," Emily replied, "but I don't think it's right for me to rely on you, or anyone else, to help write it this time. It has to come from me—" she placed her hand over her heart. "— from in here."

"I think Dan's right," said Rick. "This is too important for you to wing it on your own. Yes, people *do* listen to you. You're respected around the world. You're seen as being honest. That's mighty rare in politics. I'll tell you now, where you lead, other leaders will follow. I know where you're heading with this; you want to tell them the truth as you see it, but you'll have to be more diplomatic than that. You've got a capable team around you that can put this speech together and analyse it from every angle. You've got too many other issues to deal with in the meantime to adequately focus on this."

"It'd help if we had a decent handle on where things are at." Emily turned to Marco. "Any word yet from New Haven or New York?"

"The news isn't good," replied Marco. "Between them, the GIA and Homeland Security simply don't have the numbers to enforce the curfew."

"So much for Director Brandt's assurances that the GIA would maintain order through this," said Daniel.

"It gets worse, though," Marco continued. "The gangs are winning the battle for public support. They may be reviled by many, but they're trusted by people in their neighbourhoods, more than Homeland Security at any rate. Our guys went in too hard in the early hours. The Circumfrens have been the only NGO willing to go in there, other than the Red Cross. And the gangs are the only ones providing them with protection. But they're also taking control of distributing goods to the general population. Technically, they're looting and profiteering, but they're the main ones getting food and supplies out there. Wherever the gangs have clashed with security forces, they've come out on top, establishing themselves as the new regime in New York City.

"The area around New Haven? That's even worse. Since rumours about this 'groundfish' thing have gotten out, there's been rioting in the quarantine zone. I haven't talked to Director Brandt about it yet, but there's also rumours GIA teams on the ground are threatening to impose some extreme draconian measures, including summary executions for those inciting riots."

"That will not happen on my watch!" replied Emily. "We need to get people out of there—now!"

Marco's voice betrayed a lack of hope. "It won't be easy, Ma'am. Homeland Security is already stretched beyond capacity. I suspect they'll ignore any requests we put in. The only option we have is if Director Brandt is prepared to authorise the use of some of our military resources under the Emergency Protocol 46."

"I'll deal with Brandt, you just get your people onto it." She turned to Daniel. "I need you to contact Louise. She'll probably be hard to get hold of, but be persistent. I want to make sure Marco gets the resources he needs. Then we'll get that broadcast out to the nation. When you get hold of her, patch it through to me." She stood up. "In the meantime, I'm going to have a shower and get ready to face the people."

"Shall I put a few words together while you get ready?" asked Daniel.

"No, you just focus on getting hold of Louise, I'll deal with the speech. Like you said, I need to be honest with them. I'm going to tell it like it is."

As Emily was walking out the door, Daniel's attention was diverted by a newsflash. "Whoa... before you do anything," he called out, "you might want to have a listen to this."

***

When Gordon finally located Tanya's mind from among the masses, it shone like a beacon, reaching out to him from the dark. Without hesitation, he fell into her head, having not given any thought to what he'd do next.

It made him aware of everything Tanya saw or sensed in any way— experiencing it with her—feeling what she felt.

He considered how best to communicate. It was clear that direct telepathy would be too invasive. The manner least likely to cause distress? Manipulating the audio bio-link in her earbuds.

"Tanya? It's Gordon. Can you hear me?"

She looked down at her wristband while leaning against the wall of an empty room in the bunker, then took a moment to re-examine her lensview in case something was there that she'd missed. "Gordon? How'd you get through? Nothing's coming up to indicate a call, but I'm *hearing* you. Please, tell me you haven't taken over someone's mind. I can't believe Craig did that."

"No, it's not *quite* like that. I've no intention of taking over anyone's mind. What I'm doing is different. The medibots circulating in your bloodstream all carry an image of the electrical impulses running through your body. When they're combined, a coherent enough picture is created to identify those thoughts as coming from you. Each individual with medibots, or almost any nanotech for that matter, becomes part of a large-scale network that's like the old Wi-Fi concept. By tracking the source of the image, I'm able to send a message directly from my brain's speech centre to your earbuds. It then interprets my message the same way it would a signal from your wristband."

"So, you're in my head, listening to my thoughts?"

"Not really, it's not like that. I'm reading the images of your thoughts that have already been relayed by your nanotech."

"That's a very fine line you're talking about. Are you going to turn me into your own little puppet now? Force me to do your bidding?"

"Good god! I'd never—I've no intention of invading your privacy."

"A bit late for that, don't you think?"

"Tanya, please understand! It was the only way to find you. The GIA cut off communications through your wristband. We've got to do what we can to bring the nanotech under control. You're the only one with enough understanding of the containment fields to do it quickly. That's why the GIA kidnapped you."

"All I know is that yesterday, for a few moments, I was happier than ever before. Then I discovered my husband is dead, along with almost everybody else I knew and cared about. Now, I've been kidnapped by the government, and to top it off, I've got *you* invading my privacy in the most awful way imaginable."

She broke down and burst into tears, struggling to get the words out as she continued. "I want to know what's happening. Good god, *please*, I need to know!" She fell to the floor, tears streaming down her face. "How could this happen to my beautiful Lloyd?"

"Oh my god! Tanya, you're pregnant?"

Tanya sat on the floor, nodding her head, confident Gordon would sense the gesture.

She waited a moment, sitting motionless with her thoughts, trying to blank them out to protect her privacy. "Please, just get out of my head and leave me alone. The GIA needs *my* help, and I intend to give it to them."

"Tanya, you have to listen to me. They tried to kill me and Craig. You can't trust them. They just nuked New Haven, and they've blasted everything between there and New York with EMPs. It's going to get worse—much worse."

Tanya's heart sank further. She'd seen the distant flash through the cab's rear window as it sped down the freeway, but had no idea what it actually was. What Gordon was telling her had to be true. Had she gone home as planned, she'd be dead too. Tanya thought of the people in the medical centre who'd shared her joy at the test results, of the people in the elevator who looked at her disapprovingly during her failed attempts to call Lloyd—of dear, sweet Enricho, with his warm laughter, a magical sound that the world would never hear again.

Sensing her grief, Gordon remained silent while she sat with her thoughts. Dropping her head into her hands, she whispered, "What can any of us possibly do to stop this?"

Tanya looked up as the door opened, and Director Brandt walked in, accompanied by two of her agents. "Ms Dyson, it's a pleasure to meet you."

She sat on the floor next to Tanya. "I've been looking forward to the opportunity of talking with you. My name is Louise." She gestured toward the agents as she continued. "To them, I'm Director Brandt, but we don't need to be so formal with each other. You see, I think we have a lot in common."

"Like what?"

"To begin with, I think we *both* feel uncomfortable about the conversation you've been having with your friend. Gordon, right? Doctor Gordon Delaney?"

"Friends don't jump inside your head and violate your privacy." She stared straight ahead, deciding she already disliked the director. Was Gordon right after all? But if she couldn't trust the GIA, what option did she have? "This *is* the president's bunker, isn't it?" she asked.

"Normally it would be, but right now, it's under my command."

"I'll talk to her, and her alone."

"That's not your choice to make."

Tanya's voice was firm. "I voted for *her*, not you." After a long pause, she continued. "I will talk to President Lucas. No one else."

***

The guards placed the litter on the floor of General Rubeiro's office, leaving Petra almost fifty metres of floor space to cross before reaching his desk. General Barnardo Rubeiro stood at the wall of glass behind his desk, surveying his view of the city below. They were twenty floors up and, even from the far end of the room, Petra could see that the view was spectacular.

Despite facing away from her, his words were clear over the sound of Petra's boots as she crossed the marble floor. He spoke in Portuguese. "So, tell me about the unexpected complication with your accomplice. I'm not accustomed to deviations in our plans when they are so close to fruition."

Petra responded in English, knowing full well she'd be understood. "Our first words together in almost five years, and you question my intentions? Think of this as a gift. You are now the proud owner of highly classified technology that no one else possesses. It came as an unexpected bonus. It's time to put your Washington connections on alert." Her steps were akin to a metronome ticking in the background.

He turned to her and then addressed his guards in Mandarin. "Leave us."

Petra stopped and turned to watch the pomp and ceremony of the exiting guards. The doors echoed after they were pulled shut by the last to leave.

Barnardo took a seat in the oversized leather chair at his enormous oak-and-walnut desk as Petra continued her approach. "You've obviously no idea of the rumours regarding what your 'gift' has done while you've been sipping green tea downstairs."

"Enlighten me."

He took the flask of cognac he always kept on the desk and poured two glasses. "Rumour has it she's mutated somewhat more than what you'd described to the paramedics on arrival, leading to a rather unfortunate event in the cells. Apparently, her tongue shot up a guard's nostril, ripping half his brain out. I'm expecting a full report in the morning."

She reached the top of the short flight of stairs that led to his desk. Rather than taking the chair opposite him, she walked around the massive piece of furniture, the pace of her steps remaining unchanged. "An interesting development, indeed."

Sometimes, even he was surprised by how cold Petra could be regarding the suffering of others. "She now stands guard over him in her cell, preventing anyone from getting close. I've no desire to risk damaging her by using force to remove him. It's curious, she attacked him in response to his harassment, and yet now she licks his wounds and behaves as though she were nursing a sick child."

Petra picked up her cognac then, running her free arm around the back of Barnardo's neck, took a seat on his lap and threw down the drink in one go. She carefully placed the glass on the table and ran her hand down his cheek while staring deep into his eyes. "The poor little wretch got so distressed when she learned of her fate. We must pay the little beast a visit in the morning."

Feeling her closeness for the first time in so long, Barnardo embraced her and whispered in her ear, "We shall not talk of this again tonight. It has been five years since I last held you in my arms. Until the sunrise, I shall think of nothing else."

There were many things Petra valued in this world, but none so much as the sense that she was in control.

***

The anchorman on the Worldwide News Website interrupted the regular programming with a special announcement. "Hi, I'm William Conan. We're interrupting your viewing experience to bring you a special broadcast from Julius Granger, founder and worldwide leader of the Circumfren Religious Order. This is an extraordinary event, as it's the first time Reverend Granger has called an international press conference in almost a decade. It's believed, in light of the last twenty-four hours' events, that he could be attempting to take a more dominant role in the politics of the Confederate States. Let's go there live."

Around the world, all who were watching saw Julius take his place at the circular podium. He wore long, flowing robes with gold embroidery that shimmered in the light. Behind him were seven concentric glass circles framing his head, like a halo. Taking a moment to compose himself, he looked straight down the lens and launched into his speech.

"Today, I speak, not just to those who are already embraced by the curvature of circular living, but also to the poor souls among you whose lives continue carrying the burden that accompanies linear thought."

He paused for a few seconds, looked down at his lectern, then continued in a more serious tone. "We all know full well that the calamitous events to our north would *never* have taken place had our cousins in the UNSA embraced a more circular path."

Again, he paused, looked around him, then pounded the lectern with his fist. "It is an undeniable fact. Terrorism does not exist in communities guided by principles derived from the most sacred Book of Circles!"

He stopped to take a deliberate breath, keeping his viewers waiting in anticipation as he focused on the camera. When he spoke again, he adopted a quieter, more serious tone. "Some fifteen minutes ago, I left a meeting with the President of the Confederate States of America. In light of the dramatic situation to our north, he has taken a bold decision to pre-empt his fears that the woes of the north will contaminate the south by declaring a state of emergency. He came to this decision after two of my most trusted high priests brought his attention to a correlation: a correlation between current events and the prophecies revealed to me in my most sacred visions— the very visions that led to the creation of the Book of Circles, the one true text guiding us along the circumference of existence."

He placed an elbow on the lectern, resting his chin in his palm. "For those who have not yet had the truth of eternal repetition revealed, I say unto you, all events—past and future—are unalterable facts of nature, that will ultimately reach an end that becomes the beginning. Each moment of your life, of your existence in this world, will be repeated, as it has happened before, and will happen again, for the rest of eternity. Through this, the circle of eternal revolution binds us to the one unalterable truth."

He recomposed himself, standing tall at the lectern. "The president sought an audience with me, seeking guidance and assurance that these prophecies were as unalterable as they seemed. Being touched by the depth of his concern and the curvature of his thinking, I saw the need to elevate his position within our church so that he may better be able to share his wisdom and leave a lasting legacy on the eternal circle. So, in this last hour, after the president made his emergency declaration, I have ordained him as a Grand High Priest of the Innermost Circle. President Jones shall now be addressed by the title of the Reverend Isiah of the Inner Circle. As defined by church law, a Grand High Priest lives a life dedicated wholly and completely to his faith. No greater honour can be bestowed upon a person in this life. As such, all of his previous titles and responsibilities are thus passed on to the church."

Julius took on a humble expression. "As the leader of our great church, these enormous responsibilities are now, therefore, my own."

With the first bombshell of his speech unleashed. Julius was on a roll. He stood silently at the lectern, allowing time for the reality of what he'd just said to sink in before continuing.

"Make no mistake, as Circumfrens we seek to embrace *all* in the curve of friendship, believers and non-believers alike. We will do all within our power to help our brothers and sisters in the UNSA. I must remind you, though, in order to help your neighbour, you must first ensure your own strength, lest you doom both you and your neighbour to an eternal repetition of sorrow.

"So, we must make ourselves strong. Today, I decree that the Circumfren faith is to be recognised as the one and only truth throughout the government and associated institutions of the Confederate States of America. The Attorney General shall operate under the guidance of the high priests, ensuring curvature of thought in the dispensing of justice. While we are an open church, respecting the individual's right to their own opinions, it must be understood that this *does not* give non-believers the right to impose linear thoughts on others. Under the emergency powers, new laws will be enacted, so those who would preach angular thinking will be encouraged to apply more curvature to their thoughts.

"I hereby declare that Atlanta, capital of the Confederacy, shall henceforth be known as the City of Circles. A new church shall be built of a grandeur never before seen. It shall rise high above the city, to serve as the global focus of our holy church, home of the country's highest court, and the new seat of government. Upon its completion, the old courts and government buildings shall be torn down, to be replaced with Circular Schools of Thought, helping ensure our young grow with wisdom, free of linear ideas.

"All available resources within the state of Georgia shall henceforth be dedicated to the construction of our holy capital under guidance from ordained scholars of rounded building design. As I speak to you, the evacuation and demolition on the site centred on the heretical Museum of so-called Fine Art has begun, as dictated to us in verse ninety-two of the tenth chapter. *'And so it shall be seen that a great circle shall radiate out from where now stands a blasphemous testament to the confused expressions of the angular mind. And from here you shall be guided in all directions for the betterment of your brethren.'* What has transpired here today creates a model for all. For those who have already found the joy and freedom of being released from the ways of angular thinking, I implore you, spread the word. Help the world's population fulfil its destiny through understanding eternal repetition. To non-believers, I simply say, find time to sit down and meditate on the words of our sacred texts. Download the Book of Circles and make its understanding your own, that you may enjoy a more fruitful, eternal repetition.

"To our brethren within the states east of Alabama, I call to you now. Prepare for lockdown as you meditate on the truths held within our sacred texts, that you may help guide our missionaries seeking to free our northern brethren from the plague of terror that's been wrought upon them."

He held his hands aloft with his thumbs and index fingers touching to create a circle. "What goes around comes around."

The image cut to the anchorman, sitting at his desk carrying a stern expression. "Well, some interesting developments in the Confederate States today. After the break, we'll be back with our team of political observers to comment on the implications as President Lucas attempts to restore order in the wake of New Haven and New York City."

***

Emily shook her head and whispered, "Just when you really thought it couldn't get any worse, that weirdo throws his hat in the ring."

Daniel disengaged the transmission. "It certainly complicates the situation."

"Do you have to be so goddamned diplomatic? It does a hell of a lot more than that. He's taken advantage of a human tragedy to stage a coup and impose a tyrannical theocracy... without batting an eyelid. How could *anyone* be such a cold-blooded opportunist?"

"It's not so surprising when you think about it," said Rick Dodson. "He founded his church on the principle of taking advantage wherever he could. Look at his recent history; the warning signs were always there. He's systematically recruited influential people all over the world, particularly down south. We've never taken him as seriously as we should have."

Emily sighed, then turned to Daniel. "You're a man of faith, help me understand. How do they do it? How do people like Granger get so many people to follow them so blindly?"

Daniel shook his head. "My beliefs are my own; they come from my heart, but when I do go to church, it's largely for the sense of community. There's something that goes with being among people who share beliefs similar to your own, and for some, that's a big drawcard. There are so many reasons people have for their faith, and I don't feel I have any right to judge what anyone chooses to believe or not believe. Having said that, I've always looked at the Circumfrens and seen them as using religion to justify selfishness and elitism. It's deeply embedded in their fundamental philosophies."

"We'll have to act quickly on this," said Emily. "Whatever happens, we simply *cannot* let him succeed. There must be no doubt where we stand. I want to send a clear message to Granger and his cohorts when I deliver my speech. Our southern neighbours need to resist."

Rick replied, "You want to be quick; he's gaining momentum. While he doesn't have many followers up here now, he's presenting himself as a leader, as a viable alternative."

"Is he now? Well, you know what I think? I think the best possible action right now is to call him out for what he is, an opportunistic fraud. He has no legitimacy, and I won't let him entertain the idea that he can force anyone, especially us, to accept him as some sort of political leader." She rubbed her eyes, aware that she must look exhausted. "I know none of this can wait, but I really need to freshen up before going on air, or it could backfire. I'm going to go and have that shower now and work through what to say."

When she turned to leave the room, she was confronted by Louise, arms folded, leaning casually in the doorway. "You may want to have a little discussion with Ms Dyson before you do that. It's bound to impact the wording of your speech."

"You *did* see what that son of a bitch from the nutjob cult has just done?"

"I could have told you that would happen. FIDO predicted long ago that the Circumfrens would take control of the south. Believe it or not, the computer saw it as a positive that a theocracy down there would help long-term stability. Granger's been sitting like a cat, ready to pounce on a frightened mouse. It was too good an opportunity for him to pass up." Louise strode into the room, a nervous Tanya Dyson following her. "Now, you *really* need to have a chat with our friend, Tanya. She says she's not prepared to talk to anyone else, and I have it on good authority that she's an expert on containing the nanotech. In fact, she's probably the only hope we have of containing this before the situation gets worse."

"Wasn't containing the tech what those bombs of yours were about? Are you going to tell me *now* there was an alternative?" As she talked, Emily inched closer to Louise's face. "Or is it that you *knew* your bombs wouldn't do the trick all along? That it was just a gambit? That you've totally fucked half the country for no good reason?"

Tanya stepped forward, her hands clasped together to hide her nervousness. "Madam President, if I may?"

"Call me Emily if you want." The shower would have to wait. Emily moved to the conference table, gesturing for Tanya to do the same. "Take a seat, and we'll see what you have to offer."

Tanya sat next to Emily, while Louise chose the other end. Daniel, Marco and Rick were already seated near the president.

Emily asked Tanya, "Are you okay with the others sitting in?"

Tanya nodded her approval, but then found it hard to look up as she struggled to find her voice. "As appalling as the loss from those blasts is, they've bought us time. Time to set up containment fields before the nanobots multiply too much to be dealt with at all."

Marco couldn't believe what he was hearing. "You seem pretty damn sure those things are still out there."

"You have to understand," replied Tanya, "technology this small, when released into the atmosphere, it spreads unbelievably fast, following all sorts of complex convection patterns. Plus, there was the rain, which adds another layer of complexity. Most nanobots will stick relatively close together, flowing with the prevailing winds, but some will break away, travelling on difficult-to-predict tangents. You can count on it that at least a handful made it to high altitudes by the time the nuke went off. From there, they could end up anywhere. If even one of those nanobots is still out there, it will replicate itself and keep doing so until it finds a host. Once that occurs, the pace will increase dramatically."

Everyone at the table sat in silence, absorbing the information. Tanya turned to Louise. "You knew about that, though, didn't you, Director?"

"The advice I received from FIDO over the past twenty-four hours bears out what you're saying. It's just a matter of time before that shitbox of a machine deems further action necessary."

Daniel asked, "Why would anyone develop technology so inherently uncontrollable?"

Tanya stared into space as she responded. "We had it contained. There were no plans to do any testing outside of containment until those issues were *one hundred percent* dealt with." She looked around the faces in the room. "You have to understand, the genie's been out of the bottle for a long time with this technology. It's always been just a matter of time before a research team somewhere would embark on a project like ours.

"At least with us, it was being developed for civilian purposes. Infinity recognised the importance of developing containment technology that could work in the field. That was where my team specialised for the last five or six years, and we cracked it big time. Unfortunately, most of our files were destroyed with the New Haven Campus."

She sat up, looking rather smug. "Fortunately, I had the foresight to smuggle out my notes, hidden in personal messages to myself. It's all with me now on my wristband."

Daniel asked, "So, how *do* we go about containing them?"

"It's not so much about containing *them*. We can't predict where they'll be anywhere near well enough for that, and we certainly can't set up containment fields in the upper atmosphere." She raised her hands and grinned. "We need to set up containment fields around *us*, around our towns and cities, around every farm and every outlying community."

The room went quiet as they tried to fathom the enormity of Tanya's suggestion. Eventually, Emily broke the uncomfortable silence. "Ms Dyson, do you have any idea just how many towns and cities—not to mention isolated communities—there are in the world that we'd need to contain? Just how much time do you think we've got to set these up?"

"That's hard to say, that's not my area of expertise. A day or two, maybe more in some areas, I really couldn't say." Feeling the full weight of their expectations crashing down on her, she hung her head and sobbed. "My husband—he would have been able to give you a better answer on that one."

Emily cast her eyes down, discreetly reaching a hand into her pocket and wrapped her fingers over the ringbox holding her Ionian coin, as though it were a source of emotional strength. She imagined Adrian telling her, *You can do this. I know you can. I believe in you.* She got up from her chair and moved to embrace Tanya, providing comfort in the hope of extracting more information. "This must be so hard after all you've been through."

Tanya clung to Emily's clothing. "We're having a baby! How could this be happening to me?"

Emily looked at the others. "It might be time for the rest of you to let us have some privacy... everyone but you, Dan."

Marco interjected. "Do you really think we have the time to—"

"You don't have a choice in the matter." Emily's words were slow and deliberate. "I need you to leave, now."

Louise strolled past Emily. Bending down, she whispered in her ear, "You're doing a stellar job, *Madam President.*"

Emily recoiled as the director ran a hand over her shoulder on her way out. She felt unsure what to make of the gesture. Was the director *really* being sarcastic—or was it an acknowledgement that getting Tanya's cooperation would require sensitivity rather than coercion? As Louise pulled the door closed behind her, Emily turned back to Tanya. "It's okay, hon. Cry all you want, but we do have to start working on what to do. You're our best hope, and we need to work out a plan and implement it without delay."

Tanya settled enough to sit up. "It's really not as hard as it seems, but I understand it's still a big ask. We need to set up barriers, using electromagnetic fields—like invisible domes—over the cities. Most of the specs are on my wristband. The only problem is that in their most basic form, they'll destroy *all* nanotech passing through them. That is, until they can be configured to exclude medibots and the like. Most older technology—integrated circuit boards and the like, won't be affected so much. Anything that's on a larger scale than a standard graphene transistor might have a chance, but the stuff from Infinity would be repelled or destroyed if someone tried to force it through. These bots we're dealing with are effectively built of artificial proteins and programmable molecules. Because of that—"

Emily put a gentle finger to Tanya's lips. "Just tell me what you need and how long it will take."

"Have you got industrial printers here?"

"Dan?"

"It's like a small factory down in the lower basement levels, designed to produce anything from clothing to military hardware. There's enough capacity for the bunker to remain a self-contained facility for years."

Tanya's eyes darted from Daniel to Emily. She slapped her hand on the table. "That's great! We can do this! I can build a prototype and make sure it works before posting the plans online."

Daniel frowned. "I think you need to understand, this *is* primarily a security matter. While we need to get this out there, we still have to follow strict protocols as to how the plans are distributed."

Tanya looked puzzled. "What? Save people by hiding the information they need to protect themselves?"

"She's right," said Emily, "the billions of people this could save would say the security protocols can go to hell. This has to be *freely* available."

"You think it should be open source?" asked Daniel.

"That's *exactly* what it should be," replied Emily. "For Christ's sake, Dan, this needs to be deployed as soon as possible. The world can't afford to have this delayed by bureaucratic nonsense."

Tanya smiled. "I knew there was a good reason I voted for you." She turned to Daniel. "If you can take me to the printers, I can have a prototype up and running in a few hours. It'll take a lot longer to set up exclusions, though. Any tech that goes through *will* get fried."

For the first time since the announcement of the Emergency Protocol 46, Emily felt a glimmer of hope. "Dan, make sure she gets what she needs."

"What about Brandt and the Security Council? I can't see them embracing this, not without at least some proof of concept."

Emily rose from the table, anxious to get things moving. "That's why I need you to get Tanya what she needs rather than sitting here debating the issue. We need that prototype—*that's* our proof of concept. Oh, and don't worry about Louise, she won't interfere with something that could turn the situation in our favour."

"And your address to the nation?"

"This is a big call, but I think it's best to see how Tanya's prototype goes first. I'd rather give the people a good news story than uncertainty. As much as

I'm loath to talk to her, I'll have to fill Louise in on what's happening, then I'm going to indulge in the quiet luxury of a couple of hours' sleep. It'll give me the chance to reflect on what to say when I front the camera. Once Tanya's set up, I suggest you do the same."

5

Mary Killen sat on the bed and opened the birthday card accompanying the present from her dead son. She was emotionless as she read Ron's final words to her. In a way, it made her feel a sense of guilt. But then, so much had happened now. It was like someone had pulled a plug and let all feeling drain from her soul. Whatever traces of emotion remained, she reserved for her grandchild.

Mother, by the time you read this, I'll be long gone.

On reading those words, everything changed. Her thoughts came out in a whispered cry of anguish. "Oh my god! Ron, what have you done?" Her head spun and a sudden gut-wrenching nausea made her want to regurgitate the poison of his words. But Mary knew she had to go on. Time and again she tried to work her way through the message, but that first line kept running through her head, preventing her from properly absorbing what followed.

A man screaming for mercy in the street below was brought to silence by a burst of gunfire, cutting through the haze of tears that engulfed her. She put the letter down and walked to where Merrick slept, checking the din outside hadn't disturbed his sleep. He looked so peaceful—the one thing still able to bring a smile to her face.

Finally, Mary found the courage to return to the bed where Ron's card sat staring at her. *I have to be strong,* she thought, *I have to do this.* She picked up the card and continued reading.

This world has long ago lost anything of value for me. The behaviour of my wife and sibling is symptomatic of a disease that plagues humanity and always has done. This universe of ours will be a better place without the vile infection that is our species.

I don't wish to see the hell that I've set in play for the rest of the world, nor to afflict it onto the one person who ever showed me selfless

119

love and understanding. There is no way of reversing the plague of nanobots I've unleashed. There is, however, a means of protecting individuals, of preventing it recognising the host DNA. I made sure to take a sample of your hair as we parted ways last time we met, so as to have a sample of your own DNA to build on. With the hypo-spray you'll find in the gift box, I have given you the gift of being the last human being who will know what it means to be normal.

Happy birthday, dear Mother,
your ever-loving son, Ron.

Mary tore the card into the tiniest pieces she possibly could, attempting to do to the message what her son had done to her heart. She tried desperately to ensure not one word remained undamaged, hoping it might make the reality of what her son had done disappear. When she couldn't tear it any further, she took the pieces, placed them in a frying pan and set fire to them. She cried so much that she dropped the pan and had to stamp out the flames. Hands over her face, she fell back against the doorway to the apartment's tiny kitchen, slipped to the floor and curled into a ball. The sobs faded, as she drifted into sleep, a welcome escape from the pain of the waking world.

***

Petra held Barnardo's hands against the bed as she rode him, totally focused on her need for control.

Like everything else in Barnardo's world, the bed was huge, featuring a four-metre-high canopy from which multi-layered taffeta curtains were draped. The massive room was lit by golden braziers in each corner, and a larger one that hung from the centre of the ceiling. On a mezzanine level above the entrance, an all-female string quartet dressed in pre-Raphaelite splendour played Vivaldi.

Barnardo could think of no other woman he'd known who filled him with such passion and desire. He'd had this room built in anticipation of Petra's arrival, and it had remained unused until this night. Even the quartet had been hired for this single night's performance, with promises of great financial reward for their entertainment. In the morning, he would decide whether or not to have them killed, that they may never share their knowledge of these most intimate moments.

As he moved inside her, a flood of nanobots were drawn into him. With every thrust, he unwittingly became further contaminated, his heightened heart rate sending them quickly through his body to his brain.

Petra held her focus. She had gained a reasonable understanding of how the nanotech worked from her long therapy sessions with Ron. Having seen how quickly the quantum interfacing had impacted on Alicia, she was determined to maintain a strong, positive state of mind. She could feel the impact of her arousal on the speed of the process. As the sweat ran down her body to mingle with that of her lover, she held onto one thought: *I want to control this man. I want him to be my slave. I want to control them all, I want them all to fall at my feet.* Then the burning sensation ran through her as together, they reached climax.

Barnardo looked at her. "You've no idea how I've longed to feel your touch and to hold you, since that first night so many years ago. You are the only woman *ever* to win either my heart or my respect. And know this, you own them both."

She brought her face toward Barnardo's until their noses touched, then ran a finger down his left cheekbone. "You haven't even seen the start of how you will learn to desire me."

Barnardo had no idea of the truth in her words, as he took her hand in his and ran his lips along her delicate fingers.

***

Emily rubbed her eyes, yawning as she turned into the corridor flanked by Secret Service agents, anxious to get to her suite. All she could think about now was how good it would feel to have a hot bath to try washing away the day's angst, then lie down for an hour or two while waiting for the results of Tanya's labours. To her great surprise, though, on reaching her room she saw Peter Wong leaning against the wall next to the door to the Presidential suite.

She turned to the Secret Service agents, saying, "You guys can take a break. I can handle things from here."

"Excuse me, Ma'am, but under the circumstances it's bet—"

"No, really. I'm fine. I'd like to talk to Peter on my own. You're excused for now."

Reluctantly, they walked away. One of them turned as they went to say, "We'll have men stationed at each end of the—"

"Whatever, just right now, I'd like some privacy." Emily turned to face Peter with arms folded, waiting for the Secret Service agents to be out of earshot before addressing the Australian standing between her and some much-needed sleep. "You made it here in one piece, I see."

"Only just." He paused for effect. "I must say, though, you look a little rattled."

"Well, yes, I am. Does that surprise you under the circumstances? Now, if you don't mind, I'd like to get into my suite."

"Look, I know that feeling—all too well." He attempted to look coy and placed gentle hands on her shoulders. "It's been a long time, Emily, and we've got a lot to catch up on."

She took a small step back and shrugged his hands off her. "Do you mind? I'm really not in the mood for this right now."

"Whether you're in the mood or not, you and I *do* need to talk."

"Are you for real? Sorry, not happening, especially not while I have such a small window to escape this nightmare and get some rest."

"I happen to think it's better for both of us if—"

"No, what's best is if you get out of my way so I can go into my suite and get some sleep. I can't believe you could even consider that I might want to talk to you after you so happily undermined my authority. As far as I'm concerned, right now, you can go fuck yourself."

Peter threw his hands up in surrender as he stepped back from the door. "You know I had no choice in the matter. I understand your position, but I've got to look at these things from a *global* perspective."

Emily entered the suite and then turned to shut the door. "Oh, really? Is that what you're going to say to your grandchildren, when they ask why you didn't do more to stop the hell that was unleashed last night?"

Peter stood in stunned silence as she slammed the door in his face.

Inside, Emily leaned back against the door, closed her eyes, and let out a deep breath. *Why?* she thought, *why'd I let that arrogant little prick get to me?* Peter was one of the few men she'd been with since Adrian had passed away. That was almost seven years ago, before she'd started her run for the presidency, and before he'd won his seat on the Security Council.

They'd met at a dinner commemorating the end of a global security summit in Sydney. Emily had been swept off her feet by his charming demeanour. A week later, he'd begun subtly attempting to manipulate her into toning down her stance on nanotech and security. Seeing straight through his subterfuge, she'd felt remorse at having been played for such a fool. The last thing she needed was the distraction of those memories.

She removed her wristband and took the ringbox from her pocket, placing them both on a sideboard as she made her way to the bathroom, then ran a bath, hoping a good soak might ease her tension.

As the bath filled, she stripped off her clothes, tossing them into the bedroom before stepping into the tub, and luxuriating in the sensation of the hot water on her flesh. Once fully immersed, she let her eyelids fall shut and drifted into a deep sleep.

***

Only a few minutes from the main gate leading into the bunker, Craig and Gordon scanned the area ahead with their minds to estimate how heavily defended it was. Having sensed the presence of two GIA agents, a handful of soldiers, and myriad signals from battlefield and surveillance drones, it went blank without warning, as though their thoughts were cut off.

Craig glared at Gordon. "Is that you trying to be ethical?"

"No, Tanya must have got a containment field up and running."

"You don't need to be so smug about it."

"I'm not," replied Gordon.

Craig threw his withered arms in the air. "God but you can be exasperating!"

"What's your problem? Why are you making such a fuss?"

"You don't get it, do you? After your idle banter with her earlier, she's bound to have told them we can't be trusted."

"Or, maybe—seeing as though she's in a bunker with some of the world's most powerful leaders—she thought it prudent to get some sort of defence against the nanobots up and running as soon as possible, using the bunker as a test site."

"It's just an excuse to keep us out."

Gordon ignored him. "I can see it now."

"The barrier?"

"Yes, or it's more like *feeling* than seeing. Some of the outer reaches of the spectrum I can see now are being warped by the field. It's like a dome effect."

"Well, I guess we're just going to have to get out and see if anyone will come and say hello." Craig looked down at his now grossly mutated legs, then turned back to Gordon. "With the way my legs have atrophied, I'm going to need help."

Craig's cranium was twice the size it had been a few hours ago, and the bones of his skull had become a transparent membrane. Gordon could actually see Craig's thoughts, like watching lightning dance through his brain. The rest of his body had continued to reduce in size—proportionate to the growth of his cranium. His shoes had fallen from his now chicken-like feet. But he still wore his torn lab coat, which hung limp over his frail body. The most obvious change, though, was in his personality.

"You realise there's not much likelihood of our driver helping me out now? Have you noticed how his hands are stuck to the steering wheel? Our friend is integrating and merging his physiology into the vehicle's structure. Amazing, isn't it?"

"How can you do this?" asked Gordon, as though protesting now would exonerate him from effectively being complicit in what had happened to the driver. "How could you do this to another human being?"

Craig put out his tiny hands, protesting his innocence. "You think I *knowingly* did this to him?"

"You should have let the guy be in the first place," replied Gordon. "If you don't know the likely result of going into someone's head, then don't you think it's better not to go there in the first place?"

Self-righteous hypocrite, thought Craig.

"I heard that,"

As they pulled up in front of the barrier, three vehicles approached from the other side. Two heavily armed GIA agents were already standing by the gate. A large array of battlefield drones hovered above the entourage, far more than they'd earlier detected.

The vehicles inside the dome came to a stop twenty-five metres short of the barrier. Emily Lucas, Daniel Chambers and two Secret Service agents emerged from the first vehicle and walked forward. They were joined by Tanya Dyson and Louise Brandt, who had been in the back of the second vehicle, while the GIA and Secret Service agents emerging from the third stood by, observing the scene.

When Gordon got out of the hijacked military vehicle, Tanya's eyes widened, her hands rising in an involuntary reaction to conceal her shock at the transformation of her friend and colleague.

Emily whispered to herself, "What the fuck?"

No one spoke as Gordon walked around the front of the vehicle to the passenger side, opened the door, and went down on one knee to lift Craig out and prop him up in the piggyback position.

As Gordon rose to his feet, even Louise Brandt couldn't hold back the shock at what Craig had become.

Tanya's hands remained on her chin. She had always harboured concerns about the very concept of nanotech bonding with human DNA, which was why she had embraced her role at Infinity, focusing on containment. Still, she now felt a sense of guilt at having any involvement at all in a project that had led to this. "Oh my god! Craig? Gordon? What have we done to you?" She buried her face deep in her hands and started sobbing. "What have we done?"

Emily put an arm around her and quietly spoke in her ear. "Hey, it's okay. They're still alive, and somehow, no matter what it takes, we *will* find a way to make them right."

Without taking her eyes off the spectacle of Craig's electrified brain mass, Louise dryly commented. "I wouldn't hold my breath waiting for a fix if I were you."

Gordon came to a stop at the edge of the magnetic containment field.

It had only taken Tanya an hour to prepare the prototype for printing. Once it had been retrieved, it only took a few minutes to check its functionality. The rest were run off fast, printed at a rate of almost eight per minute. While a team of agents deployed the generators around the station at twenty metre intervals, Tanya turned her attention to finalising and printing a control unit. She'd taken a great many shortcuts in both design and development, and didn't expect her crude prototype to last more than a few hours. However, she'd been determined to ensure something was up and running before Gordon and Craig arrived. It was imperative that they were unable to spread their contamination through the bunker compound.

The scene resembled a standoff from an old western. Facing each other in the main street, each party jittery and ready to draw fire, none of them knowing who was faster. They stood in silence for what seemed an eternity before Louise spoke. "I presume I'm talking to Doctors Gordon Delaney and Craig Brown?"

"You already knew that," said Craig. "But it'd be helpful if you'd grace us with the knowledge of who the hell you are."

Gordon snapped a thought at Craig, *Do you want this to work for us or not?*

Craig's displeasure was evident by his lack of response.

Louise stepped forward. "I am Director Louise Brandt, of the Global Intelligence Agency." She gestured to her side before continuing, "I believe you're already acquainted with Ms Dyson. You no doubt recognise President Lucas. You may or may not be familiar with her chief of staff, Daniel Chambers."

Craig lifted a bony finger and pointed at Daniel. "He's scared out of his wits, I can tell. What's up, Daniel? Are you unsettled by what you're seeing?" He turned his attention to Emily. "Why are you making him stand there when it's clear he doesn't want to?" He cocked his head. "What's that, Ms Lucas? Did I just hear you thinking you'd rather not be here, either?"

Cold and to the point, Emily said, "I prefer Madam President, thank you, and I prefer to keep my thoughts to myself until *I* choose to share them."

Craig sent a thought directly into Emily's head. *Well, in that case, I won't tell them anything about your past dalliance with a certain politician that's occupying your thoughts. Oh yes, Madam President, I can sense the thoughts running through the back of your mind, just as well as what's up front."*

Emily's jaw dropped, triggering Louise to raise half an eyebrow. The Secret Service agents stepped forward, focused and ready to draw their weapons. Daniel stepped forward with them. "I think this—"

He was cut off mid-sentence, paralysed by a screaming sensation running through his head. As he dropped to his knees, agents and soldiers alike lifted their weapons, but Louise gestured for them to stand down.

Tanya stared at Craig and stamped her foot down hard. "Just stop it! What the hell do you think gives you the right to behave like this?"

Her words shook him, like a boy in trouble with his mother. Tanya had no fear of him. Daniel stopped screaming as Craig released his grip on his mind.

"My apologies for my colleague's behaviour," said Gordon. "As you can see, we've been through some changes since the lab exploded."

Emily asked Gordon. "How can you see with what's happened to your eyes?"

"We have more important issues to discuss."

Folding her arms, Louise shifted her weight to one foot. "How come this mental network is still working across the barrier? Ms Dyson here was confident it'd stop you getting into people's heads."

Craig butted in before Gordon had a chance to reply. "I can only control the weak—those who are happy to serve rather than lead. I couldn't be bothered trying it on the likes of you, Director."

"From a distance, we're cut off completely," said Gordon, ignoring Craig's interruption. "Up this close, though, we have a somewhat more functional connection."

Tanya asked, "So, will *you* at least respect our rights to privacy?"

"You have my word." Gordon bowed his head. "I apologise, from the bottom of my heart, for my earlier transgression. There was just no other way to reach you, and it's my belief that, for a global catastrophe to be averted, the three of us need to work together, alongside the GIA and government."

Craig looked away and rolled his eyes as if utterly bored by the proceedings.

"In that case, Doctor Delaney," said Emily, "we need to talk further."

"Indeed, President Lucas," replied Gordon. "I must agree."

***

Mary Killen examined the hypo-spray in the open gift box, confused by what had become of the boy she remembered as having been so kind.

All this carnage. Was Ron *really* responsible for it?

She looked at her grandson and saw the opportunity to show she wouldn't be a pawn in Ron's game. He'd given her the chance to survive the nanotech plague, knowing full well that she'd reject it. If she *did* accept it, she'd spend the remainder of her life watching the world descend into ruin. Hardly a life worth living, at least, not for her. But what about Merrick? Didn't he deserve the opportunity to live as normal a life as he possibly could?

There was an incredible irony in the idea that Ron, in effect, had saved the child whose existence he so resented. The hypo-spray was intended for her, but Mary decided it was actually *Merrick's* best chance of a future. After all, genetically, they had much in common. She pulled back his blanket, raised the sleeping boy's arm and gave him the shot.

After tossing aside the used hypo-spray, she put on her backpack, picked up the sleeping child and made her way to the door.

6

The streets of Windsor were quieter than Amy Jones or her children had ever experienced, the town having effectively emptied throughout the afternoon. "What do you think of this one?" she asked Jessica.

"I like it, the garden looks pretty," replied her daughter.

"You two wait right here, and I'll see about our rooms for the night." She walked down a path at the side of the house, and then the children heard the sound of breaking glass. A minute later, Amy opened the front door. "Come on, kids, quickly. Come and check out our home for the next few days."

***

The Security Council's remaining members gathered around the table in the bunker's Cabinet Room.

Domango said to Nick, "Anyhow, Andrea, she's the ten-year-old…"

Nick's eyelids kept dropping. It wasn't that Nick necessarily found stories about people's kids boring; it was just that Domango went on and on, frequently repeating the same anecdotes.

Meanwhile, Peter paced the room as he wound up a call on his lensview. When wheelchair-bound Maria Cortez arrived, a GIA agent pulled the door shut from the outside. Peter took his place at the head of the table. "I don't think words can describe how we all feel today. There has been so much lost on so many levels, in the cities of New Haven and New York, as well as within the Council itself."

Domango asked, "Where to from here? How do we move forward? Can we still function?"

"The constitution that was adopted when the United Nations was reconstituted makes it clear," said Peter. "Until the assassinated members' deputies can be sworn in, we become a council of four, collectively making decisions on their behalf. All decisions relating to the daily business of their regions are now to be made by the remaining council members. Should an elected deputy also be deceased, the Council will choose from that region's remaining delegates, who'll fill that role until the next election comes around."

"Can we please avoid terms like 'comes around', 'circular', and 'non-linear' for now?" asked Maria. "I, for one, can do without any reminders of that buffoon."

Nick glared at her. "I'll have you know, Madam, that a good many of my constituents belong to that church. They are good people who love their families and care for their neighbours, just like you and me."

Maria rolled her eyes in disdain. "Hitler's cronies loved their families—"

Nick went on, "We can all benefit from some of what's in their Book of Circles. There's a reason other faiths are struggling while the Circumfrens are on the rise."

A burst of laughter came from Domango as he slapped Nick on the back so hard Nick had to place a hand on the table to steady himself. "That's my man! Forever the politician, eh, Nick?"

Peter put his hands behind his head and pushed back into his chair. "Can we *please* not get sidetracked? Maria, I understand your feelings, but seriously, I don't think Granger had anything to do with the attack. He may be an opportunist, but he's no fool. The South's been on the brink for ages. It was just a matter of time. He probably wrote most of today's speech years ago. But assassination? It's just not his style."

"What about Rubeiro?" asked Nick.

Domango shook his head. "No, I don't see that either. I'm telling you, it's the jihadists. They're always trying to disrupt the Council."

"The jihadists can't fart without us knowing about it these days," replied Nick. "The chances of them pulling off something like this are between zero and zip."

"Can we get off this topic?" asked Peter, his expression betraying his irritation. "That's the GIA's turf. Our big concern right now is the nanotech and its containment."

"What if we start setting up these barriers and inadvertently trap the nanotech *inside* instead of out?" asked Domango.

"EMP," said Nick.

"Excuse me? Are you suggesting we hit every city around the globe the same way as New York?" asked Maria.

"Trust me, that's not happening," Peter replied. "If we act fast, there's a good chance almost every dome-protected city will be free of any need for further action. We'll work out a plan, based on weather patterns, and prioritise our strategy, including measures in each region that allow trade to continue with minimal disruption."

"The way I see it," said Nick, "We should use EMP wherever and whenever we feel there's a threat. I'm personally not keen on taking chances. You *did* see the footage of that damned groundfish, didn't you? Until we know that thing's contained, we need to take every precautionary measure available. I agree, though, we *do* need to keep trade moving. I suggest we distribute Dyson's plans, prioritising sensitive sites within fifteen hundred clicks of New Haven and New York, but have other regions on standby to print them as necessary."

"I don't even know what you're talking about with these shields. Can someone please explain?" asked Maria, struggling to get the attention of the male egos dominating the room.

Nick was all too eager to explain. "It's like having a wall of electromagnetic pulses surrounding a city or town. Micro-electronics within it are safe, as are those outside, but anything that passes through gets fried. So, if I walk through without any sort of shielding, all my medibots and any other nanotech or electronics I'm carrying will get zapped. Aside from that, I'd be fine."

"Then, why not deploy them immediately?"

"It'd severely disrupt the free flow of people and trade. Each domed area would be forced to function as a self-sufficient island."

Domango looked concerned. Many African nations had become manufacturing powerhouses, heavily reliant on trade and export dollars. These domes would not sit well with the corporate lobby groups behind his election to the Council. He spoke not as a man of conviction, but as one under the control of a hidden authority. "We should hold off—not just on setting up and activating the domes, but on distributing the plans as well. They'll cause an entirely unnecessary panic."

Peter was resolute. "Whether it's needed right away or not, we still need to deploy this and have it ready for activation when needed. Otherwise, we look weak and indecisive."

The room went quiet.

Nick eventually shrugged his shoulders and broke the silence. "Okay, let's do it then."

***

Mary's plan didn't extend beyond getting out of New York. She carried a backpack with a change of clothes for each of them and enough food and water for two days at most. She had no means of transport other than her feet, but she still trusted in the sense of good she believed resided in the hearts of most people. Her gut feeling told her north was the way to go, hoping they might make it to Canada.

Power still wasn't restored in the neighbourhood, so even getting down to street level was a minor ordeal. Once there, she saw how many people were defying the curfew, mostly on the hunt for supplies. Two men with semi-automatic weapons stood guard outside the convenience store. As she walked further, she passed a group of teenagers taking advantage of the empty streets to demonstrate their skateboard skills.

No one seemed concerned about a middle-aged woman carrying her grandchild.

After crossing the Brooklyn Bridge into Lower Manhattan, she looked for somewhere to rest. So far, she'd carried Merrick most of the way, and he was showing little enthusiasm to walk for himself. To make matters worse, it was starting to rain. She wondered if the whole exercise was foolish; maybe she'd have been better off staying in her apartment while the authorities worked to restore services and order. Would that have been wiser than wandering the streets like this? But then, what about the distant flames and pillars of smoke she'd observed from the window? What if *her* apartment block became one of those?

She continued walking, stepping up her pace in the hope of finding a doorway that might provide shelter from the rain that was getting heavier.

Passing a narrow laneway, two pairs of hands dragged her into the darkness. She let go of Merrick, hearing him cry as she called out for help.

"No one's going to help you now, baby, 'cepting me and Billy." No sooner had those words been whispered in her ear than she heard a loud crack. Blood splashed on her face as a high-calibre bullet tore apart her assailant's face. The other let her go and bolted into the darkness.

Mary looked back toward the street to see Jason Negus leaning out the window of a black vehicle, his gun still pointed in her general direction. "GIA agent Jason Negus at your service, Ma'am. You and the kid better jump in. We'll give you a lift to somewhere closer to where you're going."

Mary didn't hesitate. She picked up the crying child, ran to the car, and slid into the backseat.

Glancing over his shoulder, Jon Kruick asked, "Where're you heading?"

"Anywhere that isn't here."

***

Despite all that had happened in the previous twenty-four hours, Elizabeth Chambers couldn't help but smile as she looked out the window at her daughter, Debbie, playing in the sandpit with her friend Ian. They'd spent the last twenty minutes building a sandcastle and were now carefully placing miniature figurines in key positions. She felt a thousand miles from the problems of the world when she watched them playing so innocently together.

Ian's mother, Brenda, joined her at the window. "Hey Liz, is that iced tea ready? Or are you waiting for the ice to melt first?"

"Oh, sorry, I was off in a daydream. I just *so* love watching these two."

"Yeah, it's cute the way she watches out for him—so maternal. Look at her, asking which figure he wants, always giving him the first choice. She's such a sweetie."

"Yes, Dan and I are blessed to have such a beautiful young girl."

"Don't sell yourself short, Liz; it's nothing to do with any gods bestowing their blessings on you. It's just good parenting from you guys."

Elizabeth sighed, "Dan's hardly seen her since the last election, it's a wonder she even recognises him anymore." She finished stirring the drinks and handed one to Brenda.

They headed out to the terrace together, then sat at the white cane setting overlooking the playground and pool area. Elizabeth stretched her legs and ran a hand through her thick, dark hair. Although almost fifty, she was proud she could still pass for a teenager. Brenda was slightly older, not that you could tell. She had a short crop of blonde hair, a slender frame and a college student's attitude to life.

Elizabeth, a former corporate lawyer, enjoyed wearing figure-hugging designer fashions. Whereas Brenda was the free-spirited artist and occasional actor, loving nothing more than a faded old pair of jeans and a singlet. Despite their differences, the two had become close.

Enjoying the sunshine breaking through the clouds, Brenda sank into her chair and put her bare feet up on the chair across from her. She took a sip of her tea, then turned to Elizabeth. "It must get hard. It's bad enough, with the hours Marco works, but he doesn't have to travel anywhere near as much as Dan."

"Yeah, it does. But he promised me when Emily offered him the job that if the travelling got too much, he'd let it go after the first term."

"And?"

"To be honest? It's been getting worse. I feel so torn. It's still the opportunity of a lifetime. It could end up being a launchpad for Dan to go all the way. But at the same time, Debbie and I have given up *so* much. It's not just that I've had to put my own career on hold. It's cost us in so many other ways, and I don't even know if it's really what he wants anymore." She looked at the sky, then chuckled. "If only he'd been here when the Circumfrens came knocking yesterday. He invites them in so he can get them thinking they might have a potential convert, then rips apart the logic of their arguments. It's a wonder they even bother to knock anymore."

"I wish Marco were like that. The last time I shut the door on them, he told me I shouldn't be so cynical—that maybe it's not so bad to take a slightly more rounded approach to some things."

"Seriously? He's not going to convert, is he? Is Emily aware of this?"

"God no, there's no chance of that, or at least I hope not, on both counts. The only circle he *really* cares about is the rim of a whiskey glass." The subject of Marco's drinking always led to an uneasy silence, but today it was accentuated by the topic they'd both tried to avoid. "I'm scared, Liz. We haven't heard from the guys since they left. As usual, we were fed the standard shit story. But hey, there's been a fucking *nuke* go off for Christ's sake! Can you believe it? New York's crippled, and no one seems to give a fuck about an evangelistic asshole taking over the south. What the *fuck's* going on?"

Elizabeth looked away, Brenda's frankness having made it hit home like a slap across the face. She dropped her drink, the glass exploding across the pavement. Words struggled to find their way through her tears. "I—god—I wish—oh god, but I wish I knew. I don't know, I've never been so scared, and with Daniel not here—how can we feel safe?"

Helping Elizabeth to her feet, Brenda felt grateful the kids hadn't noticed. She led her back into the house, where she could feel freer to release her emotions, crying into her friend's shoulder.

Unknown to them, several hundred thousand nanobots caught in the upper atmosphere had begun settling over parts of Washington, DC, dozens having found their way into Elizabeth's yard.

While the children laughed and played, they inhaled some of the nanobots. So too did Elizabeth.

Hundreds of people across the city breathed in the pestilence that day. In Elizabeth's home, Brenda was the only one spared from contamination.

***

As the discussion at the bunker's gate continued, Craig wasn't happy. It didn't help that it was getting hot while being exposed to the sun on Gordon's back. "I've had enough of this. Gordon, it's time we left."

"If you don't mind, Tanya's still talking to me."

"If you want to continue with this nonsense, could you at least carry me back to the car?"

"It *is* hot in the sun," said Tanya. "And he's got no protection. We really should do something about that."

Louise swiped her wristband. "Bring us a large umbrella and some water. Bring food as well, and make it quick." She turned back to Gordon and Craig. "We'll pass them to you through the magnetic field when they arrive."

"I appreciate your concern," replied Gordon. "It's been a while since we've had anything to eat, other than the rations in our vehicle."

"Yeah, about that vehicle. Is there a reason the driver hasn't come out to join us?" asked Emily.

"There's a prob—"

Craig cut Gordon off. "I told him to wait. Do you have a problem with that?"

Tanya looked at Gordon. "Are you going to finish telling them? Or will I have to?"

Craig rested his chin on Gordon's shoulder and looked away from the others, as though bored.

Taking a deep breath, Gordon said, "There's something you all need to know... something I'm extremely uncomfortable talking about."

Louise stepped across so she was directly in front of him, as close as possible to the barrier without impacting her medibots or lensview. She planted her feet firmly on the ground with her arms on her hips. "I'm all ears, Doctor."

Stepping up beside her, Emily took a similar stance. "Yeah, me too. If it unsettles someone who's been through what we already know you have, then it's got to be something worth hearing about."

Tanya kicked dirt around with her feet, a habit she'd had since she was a girl when she felt uncomfortable with a situation. "It's okay, Gordon, I know it wasn't your fault. Just tell them."

Gordon sighed. "As you're aware, both of us have ended up with a degree of telepathic ability. When we'd worked our way to the woods at Infinity, the only means of escape was to flag down a vehicle, and the only vehicles were military, police, or GIA. I'd passed out before reaching the road. The quantum interface hitting had left me exhausted. So, Craig commandeered a vehicle while I was out. The driver? He ended up contaminated from his exposure to us."

"Tell them all of it," said Tanya.

"The worst part of it is, Doctor Brown was controlling him, compelling him to be our driver. He was in that state when the nanobots established their link."

"So, based on what we've been told about this tech," said Emily. "Would it be fair to say the nanobot network decided that being under Craig's control is the driver's natural state?" She looked to Tanya, then back to Gordon. "Is there any way to undo this?"

Craig cut in. "It's too late. Not that I particularly care, given he wanted to kill us." He then spoke into Gordon's ear, ensuring it was still loud enough for the others to hear. "If you're going to keep pandering to these people, you can put me down. I'll find my own way to the goddamned vehicle."

"Okay, if that's what you want. So be it." Gordon squatted and released Craig from his back.

The others gasped as they watched Craig struggle to balance before falling on his back, his head hitting first.

Gordon reached out to help him up, but Craig pushed him away. "Leave me alone." Attempting to crawl, he became tangled in his now-oversized clothes. In exasperation, he sat up and proceeded to remove every stitch of clothing before crawling back to their vehicle. He turned to Gordon and sneered, "This is the gratitude I get for saving your miserable ass."

Daniel spoke out in protest. "Surely, we can't let him go?"

"If we try and stop him now, all we're doing is giving him a stage," said Louise. She walked over to Daniel and whispered in his ear, "I promise you, we'll get this son of a bitch sooner or later."

Craig's voice yelled out from the car, "I heard that, Director. If I were you, I wouldn't be making promises I can't keep."

"Shall we fire on him?" one of the guards asked Louise as Craig's vehicle drove off.

"No, not after what happened at the New Haven site." She ran her hand across Daniel's back as she started toward the vehicles. "Ms Dyson, I need you to find a way to bring Doctor Delaney into the bunker safely. I'll leave agents here to make sure his needs are met in the meantime."

Tanya looked to Emily for approval.

Emily nodded. "She's right. We need his help if we're to gain a better understanding of what we're up against. That's if he's prepared to cooperate."

"Don't worry, he will," said Louise. "He's got nowhere else to go." She turned to Emily. "We'd better head back, before Peter and the Council develop delusions of being in control."

Emily put an arm around Daniel's shoulder as they walked back to their car. "Are you okay after that episode back there?"

"Yeah, how about you, though? Are you okay dealing with *her*?"

Having overhead them, Louise smiled to herself as she climbed into the vehicle.

Daniel called out to Tanya. "Are you coming?"

"I'd like to talk to Doctor Delaney alone for a while, if that's okay?"

Daniel nodded his approval. He gestured toward the soldiers and agents who remained. "You can let these guys know when you're ready to come back."

With the others gone, Gordon spoke frankly to Tanya, a friend he'd known since his university days. "How about you? Are you coping?"

She shook her head. "No, but at least I've got something to focus on now, something that can be a distraction of sorts."

"You need to give yourself a chance to take stock and absorb what's happened, to grieve. Otherwise, you'll end up crashing in a heap."

"While I appreciate your concern," replied Tanya. "I really just want to focus on what I can do to help stop this dreadful situation from getting worse."

"I don't think you get my meaning."

"Well then, tell me, what do you mean? What do you expect me to do? My husband has died. I've no idea if it was quick and painless, or long and drawn out. The same goes for just about everyone else I've ever known, except, of course, you and Craig. To make it worse, he's now a grotesquely mutated madman. And you—my only friend left alive—you're horribly mutated as well. You've now got no eyes, but the ability to see inside my head. I had to put this barrier up just to protect myself from you two.

"And now, apparently, I'm the only person on this godforsaken planet who has even the remotest idea how we might protect ourselves from this nano-plague that you and I are partly responsible for. Oh, and let's not forget that we need to save everyone before FIDO decides to nuke the whole planet in the interest of protecting us." She wiped back a tear. "Can't you see how hard this is? Somehow, I'm expected to take on all this, and do it without my beautiful Lloyd by my side."

"I'm doing my best to understand," said Gordon. "What you're faced with? That's a big ask for anyone. What I *can* tell you is this: so far, you've done brilliantly. You've given hope to the president, and everyone else here, hope that'll spread around the world as these barriers get distributed."

"What about you, though, Gordon? How are *you* with all this? And don't feed me some patronising crap to brush it off. You survived an explosion and a whole lot of soldier-boys trying to kill you while knowing you'd been contaminated. Then, you've had to watch the man you escaped with degenerate into a psychotic and dangerous freak." She paused for a moment and asked him again, "How are *you?*"

"I'm okay, and grateful that you care. It means a lot to me."

Tanya opened her mouth to speak, but Gordon cut her off. "There's something else..." He hesitated. *Is now the time to tell her?* While observing the shield Tanya had created, he'd realised that if he focused hard enough, he could generate his *own* magnetic field, allowing him to pass through the protective dome unharmed. For Gordon, everything seemed clear now. It wasn't just his ability to see (despite losing his eyes) that was enhanced; it was also his general understanding of *everything*.

"Oh? What would that be?" asked Tanya

"It doesn't matter," said Gordon. "There are more important things to talk about."

Their conversation was interrupted when another car pulled up near them. Two agents got out and set up two small tables, laying out a spread of food and water on them. They then carefully slid one of the tables through the barrier. As she watched them, Tanya found herself thinking, *Am I being too hard on him? Would things have panned out differently if it were someone other than Craig that Gordon had fled with? Maybe I do need to cut him some slack. Perhaps the Director's right... that I should find a way for him to come in safely.*

"I just had a thought," said Tanya. "I think I'll have to leave you for the time being. I want to see if I can print up a personal emitter that'll send out an opposite polarisation to the dome's emissions, allowing you to pass through safely, while containing your nanobots within the area of the field."

"If you need a hand with any of the details, let me know. After all, I am directly interfaced to a quantum computer now."

Does he even appreciate what I'm offering? thought Tanya. "Thanks for the offer, but I've got one of those on my wrist already." She didn't bother saying goodbye as she got up and walked back to the waiting vehicle.

***

On the way back to the bunker, Emily put a reassuring hand on Daniel's knee. "Dan, I've been thinking. We really need to get some family reunions happening, while that option's still viable. That being the case, I want you to get Elizabeth and Debbie to join us here in the bunker. But we'll need to do it tonight."

"Are you sure?" asked Daniel. "What about the other families? Don't we need to ensure they all get here? It would feel awkward if others are left behind."

"I hear you, and yes, with time, we'll try and get them all here. But the way I see it, your family has to be first in line. Understand this: I need you on top of your game if we're going to get through this. But right now, you're distracted, I can tell. I know you enough to appreciate that you'll focus better knowing your family's safe, and the only way you can have that certainty is if they're here. We've got room to progressively bring in everyone's families, but yours are the first priority."

Daniel nodded in acknowledgement. "Okay, thank you. Can I make a suggestion, though? Can we bring Marco's family at the same time? Brenda and

Liz are close; they support each other whenever Marco and I are away. If Brenda's left to fend for herself, she might not cope, and Liz would feel awkward about it. I also think Marco would take it personally if Liz came without Brenda." When Emily didn't respond, Daniel prosecuted the case further. "The amount of time Marco's away from Washington is causing some real angst for them. You'll see him focus better as well if his family's here too."

Emily's expression betrayed that she wasn't so sure about Daniel's assessment of the situation. There were others that she was inclined to support before Marco, particularly since he'd been hitting the booze so much harder of late. What about Rick Dodson? As Secretary of State, wouldn't he expect his family to get priority, especially after the strain the constant travel had put on *his* marriage? "Okay," she said after a long pause. "Call Liz, then get Marco to organise the chopper *before* he calls Brenda. And Daniel, I know I don't need to tell you this, but they'll need to be ready to leave immediately."

***

Neither Jon nor Jason had said much since rescuing Mary from the alleyway nearly fifteen minutes earlier. Once Merrick had stopped crying, she introduced herself. "My name's Mary. Mary Killen, and this is my grandson, Merrick."

Jon glanced over his shoulder at her, then put the car into auto-cruise before leaning over the seat to offer his hand. "I'm Jon, and you've already met Captain Sunshine." It was unusual for Jon to adopt such a friendly tone with someone he'd just met, but there was something he liked about this woman who was prepared to take such an enormous risk for her grandson's sake. While her actions could be construed as foolish in the current climate, he admired her courage.

"Can I ask where we're heading?"

Jason cut in abruptly. "No."

Jon smiled. "Don't mind him, he's just pissed because I was beating him again at chess earlier on, and the women always pick me over him."

"But he *is* your superior?"

"What would make you think that?"

"It was *his* decision to pick me up. He didn't need to look to you for a response when he told me to get in the car."

Jason kept looking ahead. "See, she's way too fucking smart for the likes of you." Finally, he turned to face her. "I'll tell you what, Mary Killen, seeing you're clearly a woman who can't be fooled by the likes of my intellectually-challenged partner, you've earned yourself the right to know where we're going after all, and why."

Jon looked across, frowning. "Are you sure that's wise?"

Jason glared back at him, then turned back to Mary. "I'm a man of few words, so I'll keep this brief. There were two men who were at the scene when the Infinity campus blew up yesterday. They were implicated in the deaths of several of my men and the failure of drones sent in to terminate them. They've now hijacked a military vehicle, taking its driver hostage, and we believe they're heading to the northern Command Bunker in North Dakota. It's my intention to get those sons of bitches before they cause more damage."

Mary whispered, "My son worked at Infinity."

Jason and Jon looked at each other, then turned back to Mary, who sat blank-faced, nursing her sleeping grandson.

Her voice remained soft. "He left me a note. He caused this—everything—all the workers at Infinity—your soldiers—everyone who died in New Haven, and everything that's happening now—here, in New York. It's all because of him."

Jason and Jon were speechless. They turned to the front, opting for silence while Mary's bombshell sank in. As they drove on, nanobots from Jason were filling the air in the vehicle. They were already closing in on Jon's brain stem, his lungs by now saturated. In the back seat, Mary and Merrick inhaled dozens with every breath.

***

Barnardo and Petra were awakened by loud banging on the massive door to their bed chamber. Feeling groggy, Barnardo struggled to sit up. The banging continued as he swung his legs out of bed and reached for a pair of trousers. Petra raised herself up, resting her weight on an elbow, totally at ease with her nakedness.

Again, the bang on the door rang across the room. Barnardo got to his feet, calling out, "Enter!"

A young woman in formal military attire opened the door and marched into the room. Barnardo had given strict instructions that they not be disturbed until sunrise and that only women were permitted to enter the room. The woman brought herself to attention in front of Barnardo and saluted. "May I ask permission to address you, General?"

"Granted, Lieutenant."

"Thank you, Your Greatness. I have been sent to deliver the official report on the activities of the gift brought to you by Doctor Petra Chan. I apologise for this interruption while you are resting."

Petra casually got up from the bed as the lieutenant spoke, disappearing into the wardrobe behind it.

Barnardo watched her out of the corner of his eye until she was out of sight, then turned back to the woman in front of him. "Read it for me and tell me what the report has to say."

"While the gift was being escorted to its accommodation, Senior Sargent Lou Zu set out to comfort her, an act that Corporal Deng suggested might be inappropriate. While Sargent Zu was demonstrating to the corporal how to calm a subject who is resisting, the gift retaliated, causing significant harm to the Sargent."

"It was my belief he survived the initial... 'retaliation'. Is this still the case? Is the man still alive?"

She hesitated. "Yes, sir."

"So, is he waiting outside to report what happened in person?"

"I don't believe that's possible, sir."

Barnardo struck her down with a backhand. "I want facts, woman, not what you believe. Tell me the facts."

The woman picked her hat up from the floor and stood to attention, trying to ignore the pain from where she had been struck. "My sincerest apologies for my foolishness, Your Greatness. The Sargent has been severely injured, and Doctor Chan's gift has been unwilling to let any Soldiers of the Guard or paramedics approach him. He is being kept by her in the cell."

Petra emerged from the wardrobe wearing a white, silk gown that clung to her body and went to the floor. It was tied at the waist by a golden cord. Barnardo felt momentarily breathless at the sight of his lover. "Well, darling," she said, "perhaps we need to go down and pay Alicia a little visit before breakfast. After all, it was rather rude of you not to pay your respects when she arrived yesterday."

Barnardo continued looking at Petra, aware of his manhood stirring. "Very well then. Lieutenant, have a team of guards escort Corporal Deng to meet us in the dungeons in half an hour."

Petra walked to the door, looking over her shoulder. "This can't wait that long; we must attend to this now."

Ordinarily, the notorious General Rubeiro would have been unwilling to accept such talk from anybody—even Petra—but somehow, he felt different towards her now. He found himself compelled to cede to her demand. Grabbing the remains of his previous night's clothing from the floor, he followed her out of the room, dressing as he went.

A few minutes later, they arrived outside Alicia's cell, where the guards and medical officer waited with Corporal Deng. Barnardo addressed the Captain of the Guards. "Activate the window. I want to see what's going on in there."

The guard made a gesture, and a grey panel of the wall became transparent. Inside, Alicia sat in a corner, patting the head of Sargent Lou Zu as he sat huddled up next to her, his face horribly disfigured. Alicia had continued to undergo change, with every hair on her body having become razor-sharp thorns. Lou's mutations were catching up to her own, and both of them had their clothes badly torn by the sharpened body hair.

"I think we should go in so I can introduce you to the poor dear," said Petra. "That should cheer her up."

"Excellent idea, Doctor."

The medical officer raised his concerns. "Begging your pardon, Your Greatness, but I'm not sure that's such a good idea."

Petra laughed and turned to the medic. "I've known this woman for years. Trust me, she's nowhere near as dangerous as she looks."

"If you must, I'll have extra biohazard suits brought down for the two of you."

"Oh, we won't be needing those."

"But Doctor—"

Barnardo grabbed him by the throat and lifted him off the ground. "If the doctor says we won't be needing suits, then we won't be needing suits." He seethed, spittle flinging from gritted teeth. "Now, Captain, open the cell before I get impatient with the impertinence that seems to be festering down here."

The Captain of the Guard quietly opened the outer door and stepped in, followed by Barnardo and Petra. Barnardo turned to those waiting outside. "I would appreciate it if the rest of you join us."

Deng lifted his eyes from the ground. "Begging your pardon, General, but I've not been issued with a biohazard suit."

"And the problem with that is?" The question hung thick in the air.

Corporal Deng started shaking as he stepped into the airlock. The captain went to close the outer door, but was interrupted by Petra. "Don't bother with tedious details, Captain, just get the inner door open."

The captain found himself increasingly unable to take his eyes off Petra, distracted by her presence as he opened the door.

As Petra boldly strode into the cell, Alicia came whimpering forward on all fours, her body having changed so it seemed natural. On reaching Petra, she sat at her feet like a dog setting out to please its master. Despite her fear at the moment of the burning, Petra was the only human being Alicia saw in a positive light. She had aspired to be like her. Now, those feelings were accentuated.

Petra turned to her lover. "See? I told you there was nothing to worry about. She can be our little pet." She turned back to Alicia, who was looking up, expectantly. "Would you like that, Alicia?" Alicia made an excited, whimpering noise. "We could take you and your friend for walks in the park, maybe play a few games together." She turned once more to Barnardo. "What do you think, darling?"

"Whatever you wish, my dear." Barnardo looked around the cell. "But, if we want to keep them as pets, they should have clean quarters. We'll need them kept comfortable until the time comes to reveal them to the world."

"Oh yes, we can't have them in the palace, not yet anyway. That would never do while we still have to worry about FIDO responding to them."

Barnardo turned to the young soldier who had earlier sought to protect Alicia from Zu. "Corporal Deng, I'd like you to come over here and give me your explanation of the events that led to Sargent Zu becoming so intimately acquainted with Doctor Chan's gift."

Deng marched across the room and came to attention in front of Barnardo. This placed him less than a metre from Alicia, who turned to him and sniffed his feet. She backed off when urine started to run down his trembling leg into a pool on the floor. "Sir, we arrived at the cell with the gift, and Sargent Zu began to fondle the gift's breast. I then took it upon myself to attempt persuading him that such behaviour was inappropriate toward a gift that had been intended for our much-loved and great general. When the sergeant ignored my protests, the gift defended herself in a manner that caused great harm to him."

"So, you spoke out against a superior officer in your desire to protect Doctor Chan's gift?"

"Yes, sir."

"Well, I must say, Deng, I'm deeply touched by your desire to protect my gift. So much so that I believe you're the perfect choice to care for her and her companion. It seems their toilet habits leave much to be desired. So, you can have the great honour of cleaning up after them." Barnardo smiled and slapped the young soldier on the back. "What do you say to that, Deng?"

"An excellent idea, sir. I'll collect a biohazard suit and get to work immediately."

Barnardo laughed, put an arm around his shoulder and pulled him close. "Oh, come now, Deng, do you *really* think you'll be needing a suit?"

"No, sir, it was a foolish suggestion on my part." His eyes were wide with fear as he spoke.

"Good man." He started to walk from the room, then paused. "Captain, have the corporal's personal possessions moved from the barracks to a neighbouring cell."

The medical officer stepped forward. "It is my duty, Your Greatness, to bring to your attention that having Corporal Deng work in here without a suit, then going to his own cell via the corridor... it could seriously spread contamination through the whole dungeon complex!"

"Good point. Captain, have the medical officer's possessions brought down as well, so he can share Deng's cell and observe the contamination firsthand. Oh, and have him return his suit. I suspect it'll just get in his way."

The medic stood there, stunned.

Barnardo and Petra strode out of the room. Petra commented as they made their way down the corridor, "It's so enjoyable watching you work. After all these years we had to be apart, you still have just as much style as ever."

"Well, a good military leader must always command the respect of his troops."

Petra smiled to herself as she pondered what she had planned for her proud general.

***

Emily and Louise strode into the Cabinet Room to join the Security Council's gathered members, the friction between them plain for all to see. The president looked straight ahead as she walked toward her seat. "I'd appreciate it if we could keep this brief. I need to get my address to the nation out as a matter of urgency."

Nick looked up and said, "Um, Madam President, don't you think a joint statement from you and Peter might be more appropriate, under the circumstances?"

Emily stood behind her chair, anger etched across her face. "What the hell is that meant to mean? I'm going to be speaking to *my* nation, the one with all those people who *voted for me*." Nick visibly recoiled as she continued. "In case you hadn't noticed, Peter's an Australian. He represents Southern Asia on the Security Council. I fail to see the relevance."

"He's also the Security Council's chair, making him the official spokesperson for the Council."

"So, the reason he needs to hold my hand during the speech is—?"

Peter sat at the opposite end of the table, leaning back in his chair. "This is bigger than you, Emily. The whole world is anxious, and your address will be watched around the globe. We need to address the global audience, not just the Northern States of America."

"Why do I sense a hidden agenda in this?" she asked.

"Don't take this personally," Domango replied in Peter's defence. "But, to be honest, we're concerned that you'll be encouraging everyone around the world to adopt Dyson's ad hoc solution to what is currently a UNSA issue. The world community needs to be aware that it remains primarily a local problem. Otherwise, the impact on global trade could be catastrophic."

"Yeah, well, forgive me for being old-fashioned, but I like to think it's better to be safe than sorry when so many lives are at stake. I don't care how simplistic that may seem."

"I think you know better than that, Emily," said Nick in a patronising tone. "As far as we can tell, the problem's confined to the East Coast. The West can still produce enough to see the UNSA economy through for now. Please, don't throttle them with these restrictive measures, not now."

Domango extended his hands to her, pleading the Council's case. "The disruption from these domes, or shields—whatever you want to call them—it will be on a scale that's entirely unprecedented. This century, we've succeeded in turning former economic basket cases into economic powerhouses. Surely you don't want to wind back the clock on that?"

Emily glared at Peter. "I can't believe you're supporting this. I thought you were better than that."

Peter shifted around, trying to avoid her gaze. "Be realistic, Emily, what you're proposing with these shields, it'll create island communities, with a strong likelihood that it's for no good reason."

"You know that's not true!" Emily pointed an accusing finger at Peter. "This is the only technology we know of that we can be sure will protect communities from the airborne spread of this. But you're just not getting it, are you? If you'd been at the main gate just now when we met Doctors Brown and Delaney, I'll bet you'd take this situation more seriously."

Domango threw his hands in the air. "But, at what cost?"

Emily was horrified. "There's no price tag you can put on saving humanity. It just doesn't work that way."

Till now, Louise had sat back, listening to the exchange in silence. When she finally spoke, she was calm and measured. "You've missed the point—all of you. If you don't take these measures, FIDO will almost certainly end up nuking half the planet, while wiping out almost all the tech in the other half. The shields really *are* our only hope."

"You do realise, don't you," asked Nick, "that technically, you're still answerable to us?"

Louise stood her ground. "Go on then—fire me."

"I don't believe this," said Emily. "If you want to talk about firing her, why wouldn't you have done it *before* she nuked New Haven? Why would she still even be in this job if you actually have the power to fire her?"

Nick laughed. "Get real, will you, Emily. Yesterday's emergency was an altogether different situation. The fact remains, Louise is *not* irreplaceable." He wore a grim expression as he turned to the director.

"Oh? And who do you suggest might replace me?" replied Louise. "It's not a role that's easily filled."

"There'll be a woman out there who fits the bill from among your senior agents," said Nick.

"Why does it need to be a she?" asked Emily.

"There's an interesting story behind that," said Peter. "When the GIA was first established, the Council of the day developed the philosophy that the director's job is more suited to women. Whatever happens, a woman is more likely to make pragmatic decisions in a crisis, without being distracted by circumstances. Think of it this way: in prehistoric times, men were the hunters. They had to be focused and in good health to go on the hunt. If they were sick or distracted by other issues, they were less likely to make it home. Those who survived were the ones who stayed behind when they weren't functioning at one hundred percent. Whereas women had to battle on, regardless of how sick they felt, caring for the children and foraging for food. Unlike men, the women more likely to survive were those who powered on, no matter what was thrown at them."

"Is that *really* the sort of thinking that drives the Council?" asked Emily. "It sounds like something you'd expect from a bunch of eighth graders."

7

Daniel sank into a deep lounge chair in his private quarters. He'd last seen his daughter on the preceding Sunday night when he'd tucked her into bed. They'd been working their way through *Matilda* for the third time. It was Debbie's favourite, and this time, she insisted on doing the reading instead of him. He smiled at the thought, then let his mind drift into memories: Elizabeth's hand gently reaching up to his, giving her a tender kiss on the cheek, believing her to still be asleep while he prepared to leave for work early. He'd leaned down and whispered in her ear, "Love you, baby."

Then she'd reached up, pulling him closer and bringing their lips together before whispering, "Get to work, you, and don't forget, Brenda and Marco are coming for dinner tonight."

Now, here he sat, preparing to call her and apologise for not making it back for dinner, as well as letting her know she had to get Debbie and herself ready to leave. "Lensview, call Elizabeth."

She answered straight away. "Daniel, I've been so worried. Are you okay?"

"Yeah, I'm fine—"

"Thank god!"

"How's Deb?"

"She's okay. She's used to you being away, but she still misses her story time." She paused, then struggled to get her words out. "Dan, please, tell me. What's happening? New Haven? New York? Surely you can tell me *something*! I'm your wife! I need to know that we're going to get through this."

"I'll be able to fill you in on some of it later tonight. You need to pack a bag for you and Debbie right now. In around ten minutes, a car will pick you up and take you to a chopper that's waiting for you and Brenda. It'll bring you here, to the northern bunker."

"The northern bunker? You've been in North Dakota all this time?"

"It's the new protocols. In a crisis of this magnitude, the Security Council and the president go north, and Congress battens down in DC."

"Does that mean Washington's in danger?"

"It means *everywhere* is in danger. That's why I need you and Debbie here, where I can know you're safe."

There was a long pause, then Elizabeth seemed energised. "Okay, I'll get Debbie out of the bath and pack a bag. Do you need anything?"

The thought of her practicality brought a smile to his face. "Don't worry about me, you just make sure you and Deb are ready when that car arrives. Enough talking, you need to go."

"Daniel, keep yourself safe until we get there."

"Don't worry about me, baby, I'll be fine."

"I love you."

"Love you too. See you in a couple of hours, huh?"

"Yeah, okay." Almost as soon as the call ended, Daniel fell into a deep sleep.

***

"All this talk about the director's job is a distraction. My concern right now is that when I leave this meeting to make my address, I'm going to be saying what *I feel*—as President of the United Northern States of America— needs to be said. If any of you don't like or agree with what I say, that's your problem. Those people who went to the polls when I was elected, they're expecting a decisive message on how we move forward, and the rest of the world will be looking to us for leadership." She glared at Peter. "If you want to insist on appearing with me, then so be it. But it *will not* be a joint statement. I'll say my piece, then you can say yours. Now, if you'll excuse me, I'd like to get to the media room and prepare." Emily turned and walked toward the door.

Peter stood up, waving his finger. "Now hold on for just one minute there, lady. That's not how we do things on the Council."

Emily stopped dead in her tracks. "Did I hear you right? Did you just call me 'lady'? Are you really *that* ignorant?"

"The Security Council is a body of the United Nations; we work on a consensus basis."

"Your point is?"

"You and I, we need to work together."

"That's funny, because I could've sworn a few minutes ago, you were trying to dictate terms. Well, you know my terms, and you can accept them or do your own goddamned broadcast. Remember this, I'm *not* on your Council. I'm the elected President of the United Northern States of America, and I make my own decisions."

"You do realise, we can stop your speech from going to air at all if we wish?" replied Peter.

Louise raised half a smile. "This should be fun. Tell me, Peter, how do you intend to do that?"

He walked around the table to challenge Louise. "It's part of *your* job to stop this. She's become a loose cannon. It should be a joint statement or no statement at all, and you know it."

"No, *my* job is to do what's best for protecting the world's populace. The GIA's charter may provide for advice from the Council, but not direction. I'm with her; it doesn't matter how slim the chances are of the tech getting away from us, the ramifications are too great if it does. I'd rather not nuke any more cities if I can avoid it. Although if I have to, I will, without hesitation." She turned to Emily. "Go and get ready for your speech. Peter may choose to follow with his own little spiel; he's committed now. But you're the one the people want to hear."

Emily clenched her teeth. "I wasn't aware I needed your permission." The door slammed behind her as she stormed out of the room.

Secret Service agents fell in behind her as she walked down the corridor and called Daniel. It seemed to take forever for him to respond, and when he did, he sounded groggy. "Madam President?"

"Sorry to disturb your beauty sleep, but I need you in the media room, now!"

"Okay—on my way."

***

The president stood at the media room lectern, Peter Wong to her left, standing slightly behind her.

"Men and women of America, indeed *all* people of the world, wherever you may be. Tonight, I wish to address you, not just as President of the United Northern States of America, but as a fellow member of the human race, one who shares in both your pride and humility at our past achievements. Despite our many differences, at the end of the day, we all share similar hopes and aspirations for the future. The past two days have presented our great nation with a unique set of challenges, unprecedented in our proud history, challenges that threaten those very aspirations we hold so dear.

"The detonation of a nuclear device over New Haven and the subsequent electro-magnetic pulse detonation over New York City were extreme measures, brought about and made unavoidable by extreme circumstances. The automated security apparatus, FIDO, which acts as a failsafe to global security, would have taken even more drastic action had we not acted when we did. It is with a heavy heart that I tell you now, before this crisis comes to its conclusion, further measures such as these may be required to meet the challenge we now face. As you already know, these measures were in response to an explosion and subsequent nanotech leak at the Connecticut facility of Infinity Technology Corporation.

"At this point in time, it seems apparent that terrorism was the cause. I can assure you that the United Northern States of America will not rest until those responsible have been brought to justice. I can also assure you that, in the future, more stringent guidelines for the development of biological nanotechnology will be put in place, so we never again see the need to take such extreme steps to protect ourselves from a release of technology like that which we are currently experiencing.

"I would like to add, it is abundantly clear to me that the fundamental concept behind the Fully Independent Defence Observer, or FIDO, is intrinsically flawed, and that the Security Council needs to urgently rethink the strategy that allows a computer to have ultimate control over weapons of mass destruction.

"The great leaders throughout history have made decisions, guided not just by the logic and intellect that led to FIDO's implementation, but also by compassion, and an understanding of the underlying nature of just what it means to be human. It is with this compassion and understanding that we must work together and approach the challenges ahead.

"We don't yet have reliable estimates on the loss of life from the New Haven blast, and probably never will. Suffice to say that it numbers in the hundreds of thousands. In the space of twenty-four hours, New York has gone from being one of the world's great cities to something resembling a war zone. Latest information suggests that power has been restored to several parts of the city, but for the bulk of its population, the outlook remains grim. There will possibly be another two weeks before many services are back online. All those affected by these measures will be in our thoughts and prayers over the coming weeks as we work together to begin the arduous process of rebuilding. And I can assure you that we'll provide financial support wherever it's needed.

"I must also inform you that, in an event we believe may be directly linked to the blast at Infinity, Security Council representatives from Northern Asia and Europe were assassinated while attempting to evacuate New York. Attempts were, in fact, made on the lives of all members of the Council, with the representative for South America seriously injured as a result.

"In both situations, my government and the Global Intelligence Agency are working together with the Security Council to identify the perpetrators.

"Many of you may be questioning the extreme measures we've taken thus far. While they are unprecedented, I can assure you, the situation we face is equally so. I have seen, firsthand, the results of the technology we are seeking to contain. Survivors have experienced mutations of a kind never seen before. All available information tells us there is a near one-hundred percent chance that some of this technology managed to survive the blasts. We cannot allow the continued spread of this technology through the atmosphere. It is, therefore, imperative that we implement all available measures to protect not just the American people, but people the world over. We must do everything within our power to protect ourselves from what could be the greatest threat humanity has ever faced. To do less would be unconscionable.

"As dire as the current circumstances may seem, there is always hope. As Americans, we have always taken pride in our ability to rise above adversity. I can announce to you tonight that we have developed a method of shielding communities from this technology, which has been tested successfully. All details required for the implementation of this shielding are available within the metadata accompanying this transmission and will be made readily available from multiple sources within the hour. In the interest of protecting our communities here and around the globe, there will be sacrifices that must be made. The shielding is designed to protect large areas with a dome of magnetic fields that will destroy any of the leaked nanotech that passes through. I must advise, however, that this field also impacts the medibots that we have all come to rely on for some years. It will also impact other technologies that include more benign nanotech, including our wristbands, lensviews and earbuds. To pass through the shield unprotected will render these technologies useless. This will impact all communities that choose to use this protection in the short term, with trade and travel feeling the bulk of the impact. Further development of this shield is underway as we speak, increasing its flexibility and capability to leave passive technology unaffected.

"We currently have insufficient intelligence data to ascertain for certain whether this technological threat has been contained within our borders. To assume it has, without substantiating evidence, would be foolhardy to say the least. I, therefore, implore all communities around the world to implement the one protection that we currently know works effectively. It is easily produced on any industrial-grade printer and is easily deployed.

"In the United Northern States of America, I am at this moment declaring a mandatory implementation of this shielding in all cities, towns, and anywhere people live. Under emergency powers outlined in the War Powers Act, state governors will be held responsible for overseeing implementation in their own jurisdictions."

Emily paused and took a sip of water before continuing. "Before I hand you over to the chair of the Security Council, I wish to address another matter concerning our sister nation in the south, the Confederate States of America. Earlier today, Julius Granger, head of the Circumfren sect, effectively staged a coup. The United Northern States of America categorically refuses to recognise his legitimacy in any way, shape or form. I am hereby preparing a range of sanctions and the diplomatic boycott of our southern neighbour. These measures will remain in place until elected representatives are once again in control of that great country. Never in our history have we witnessed such a shamelessly opportunistic manipulation of circumstances by those who would seek power. I might also point out that it breaches the fundamental principle of the separation of church and state. In the words of Thomas Jefferson, 'Erecting a wall between church and state is absolutely essential in a free society.' Those words are just as true today as they were in 1808.

"As we move through this dark time, we will do it together. And we will do it not just as Americans. We will do it as citizens of the world. And we will emerge stronger than ever before. That's the nature of being human.

"I believe the chair of the Security Council would now like to say a few words."

Emily stepped back and let Peter come forward. He looked down at the lectern briefly before beginning. "Firstly, I'd like to thank President Lucas for the strong leadership she has demonstrated through this crisis. I can't think of any other world leader who could have handled the rapidly unfolding events of this week any better than the UNSA President has done. As I think she clearly conveyed, our thoughts tonight are with the families of those whose lives were taken from us as a result of this crisis.

"Secondly, I would like us all to pause for a moment and take stock of the current situation. We are facing a crisis, as we have done before in both Mongolia and Britain. We had hoped the measures put in place after those disasters would mean we'd no longer have to face the consequences of militarised nanotechnology escaping into the environment. What we face today is a technology leakage that was under development for civilian purposes. Despite the significant safety protocols in place, there is no escaping the fact that what's occurred in the UNSA this week is a human catastrophe of mammoth proportions. However, we must bear in mind that it has not yet reached the scale of the two previously mentioned incidents. President Lucas, the Global Intelligence Agency and the Security Council are working together to ensure we keep the situation contained and prevent it from spreading further.

"It is a tremendous reassurance that we have the shielding technology, of which the President spoke. In addition, as you are more than likely already aware, due to its status as an island nation, Australia is temporarily declared a quarantine zone, so that in a worst case scenario, we can feel confident there is a final bastion that is safe for the future.

"However, it is the strong and overwhelming belief of the Security Council that we are approaching the closing stages of this crisis. My colleague, Nick Harrington, representing the North American region of the Council, has recommended that states within a one-thousand-kilometre radius of New Haven and New York City, look towards downloading, printing and implementing the shields.

"For other areas, the Council believes that until further information comes to light, it is absolutely crucial we maintain the free flow of travel and trade. Therefore, it is our recommendation that all areas around the globe not at immediate risk download the technology, print the components, but hold off on implementation until further notice.

"Thirdly, it's important we also address the events in the Confederate States of America. While the Council concurs with President Lucas to the extent that it does not approve of the transfer of power that has taken place, it is our belief that it's in the best interest of the citizens of that country to avoid potentially crippling them at a time when there are other issues of global concern to deal with. Therefore, while we respect the right of the UNSA to impose unilateral sanctions, there will be no additional sanctions imposed by the United Nations at this time.

"In harsh times, such as those we face this week, it is tempting to get swept up in overly sensationalised reports that spread through the media, the vast bulk of which are fabrications. I implore everyone to rely only on information made available through the Security Council's official media website. If further matters of significance should occur during the coming days, I will personally make another address in the interests of keeping the world community as well informed as possible."

Peter stepped back from the podium, and the transmission came to an end.

Without a moment of hesitation, Emily was in his face. "What the hell was that meant to be?"

"You're asking *me* what *I* was on about? After you so happily spoke on issues beyond your jurisdiction? I call it balance, Emily, something I would have thought *you* understood. Next time you try to undermine the will of the Council like that, perhaps it might serve you well to remember that we actually *do* have more power and influence than you'll ever have."

"This isn't about power or influence, and it's not about the global economy either. It's about protecting human life," countered Emily.

"And, we will recommend measures be implemented, as required."

Louise casually walked across from the other side of the room where she'd watched the two speeches. "Peter, I admire your diplomatic skills, but you shouldn't let yourself believe your own spin. The way events are unfolding, you'll be delivering a new address tomorrow, recognising the need to fast-track deployment. Otherwise, you'll have to explain further EMPs and nukes after FIDO takes control from us."

"Oh, will I?" came Peter's snide reply.

Louise stood in front of him. "I'm not a politician. There are few people who even know who I am. Getting re-elected is not on my agenda like it is on yours. *My* agenda is to protect lives from threats like this."

Emily let a wry smile creep into her expression as she thought, *Well, that should be comforting to the people of New Haven.*

Peter snapped at Louise, "Give me one good reason why I shouldn't fire you right now? What the hell makes you think you've got the right to advise me on what I should or shouldn't be doing? Forget the bullshit of finding and training a replacement. We could simply replace you right now with a member of the Council until a long-term replacement's found."

The director smiled at him, almost breaking out in a laugh. "You know that could never happen. Whatever your charter may say, the reality is that the GIA operates independently of the United Nations and has done for years. You can try to fire me if you want. But I have the support of my agents, and I have the codes directly connecting me to FIDO, as per the separation the Security Council always intended. It's that way so *you* and your politician friends can be free of all the hard decisions and the political liability that goes with them. It's so easy for you, isn't it, Peter? You get up there and reassure people it'll be alright, but it's the GIA that has to make the tough calls of detonating the nukes and EMPs."

"We'll see what the rest of the Council has to say about this," said Peter as he stormed from the room.

The director waited till he was out of earshot, then placed a firm hand on Emily's shoulder. "This ride is just beginning. I know you don't like it, but we *do* need to work together if we want to keep the Council from turning this disaster into a global calamity." She ran her hand down part of Emily's arm as she moved away and slipped out the door.

It was an undeniable truth: taking on the Council without Louise's support would be a losing battle.

***

Daniel and Marco's families were expected to arrive on a chopper at two in the morning, landing just outside the main gate. They would have been able to arrive sooner if the plane that took them from Washington DC had been able to land at the bunker's airstrip, but the shield necessitated that the plane land at the nearby Grand Forks Air Force Base, where they were then transferred to the chopper for the final stage of the journey. A small section of the shield would be momentarily deactivated to allow entry, with a secondary shield one metre out from the first to serve as a kind of airlock. Gordon agreed to use his networking capabilities to scan for any signs of contamination carried by the new arrivals. Tanya suggested delaying the chopper till later in the morning, when a more effective Faraday cage-style airlock she'd designed would be ready to come off the printers. But Emily was adamant they couldn't wait that long.

In the half hour before the chopper arrived, Gordon and Daniel sat on the ground on opposite sides of the shield, looking up to the night sky, oblivious to the dozens of soldiers and GIA agents stationed nearby on high alert.

"Tell me, how does it look for you?" asked Daniel. "How does it make you feel? Do the stars look different the way you see them now?"

Gordon spoke softly. "If only I could let you see them as I do."

"It's incredible enough to me knowing you can see them at all without eyes like the rest of us, but how do you *perceive* them? For me, a clear night sky has always been something so special— so magical. To look out there and appreciate that, beyond the Milky Way, every little dot is another galaxy—or a cluster of galaxies. The grandeur of it all—it's so humbling, yet exhilarating at the same time."

Gordon nodded in agreement. "Yes, it certainly is. I was just thinking how strange it is that this is only the second night I've seen the world this way, yet it feels so natural. You know what? I'm seeing everything from X-rays to microwaves, even magnetic fields. It's like I'd been sitting in a dark room, and someone's turned on the lights." He leaned forward, resting his elbows on his knees. "But it goes even further than that. My brain's now directly interfaced to a quantum computer, completely altering my level of perception in so many ways. If I look at a particular star and ponder on it, the network automatically kicks in, without my being conscious of it, and scans the internet for data relating to that particular star. I have access to every bit of information and image of that star that's ever been published online. And yet, you know what I love the most about looking into the sky tonight? It's finding the ones where there's nothing published, not even a name or classification, that's what really gets my imagination going, wondering what else is out there."

They sat in silence for a while before Daniel asked, "I'm curious, if you could go back to how you were, would you?"

"Not in a million years."

"Can I make just one suggestion? Get a cool pair of shades. People might feel less threatened when they see you."

"Did you feel threatened?"

"Absolutely! When you got out of that car with your swollen head and no eyes, and then seeing what you were doing? I felt threatened, yeah, who wouldn't?"

"I guess that's something I'll need to be a little more conscious of in future." Gordon sat up, facing Daniel. "Perhaps you have some shades I can borrow, for when your family arrives?"

"Yeah, there's some in the car. You're welcome to keep them." Daniel stood and walked over to get them.

***

Elizabeth felt a sense of relief as Debbie and Ian shared their excitement about flying in a helicopter. *How bizarre*, she thought, *it takes a national disaster for the Dan to be able to see his family.*

She looked across at Brenda, who had drifted off to sleep, but Elizabeth knew she'd be unable to do the same till after she'd seen Daniel.

Debbie and Ian soon grew bored with looking out the windows into the night, instead playing a game of paper, scissors, rock. It seemed Debbie was winning more often than not, yet Ian didn't seem to mind.

They finished a round, then Debbie looked up at her mother. "I hope Ian and I can always be like this, Mummy. I don't want to have to grow up like you and Daddy."

Elizabeth was always charmed and amazed by the things her daughter would come out with. She smiled. "Don't worry, sweetheart. There's plenty of time before you need to worry about that."

Debbie's eyes went wide, and she started clutching at herself. "Mummy, Mummy! It's burning!"

"What's burning, sweetie?"

"Everything!"

As Elizabeth wrapped her arms around her daughter, the burning sensation passed. "Are you okay, hon?"

"Yes," replied Debbie between sobs, "it's gone away now." She looked into her mother's eyes. "Why did it hurt so much?"

"I don't know. All that matters, though, is that you're okay now."

Frightened by what had happened to his friend, Ian found his courage once she'd settled, putting a reassuring hand on her shoulder. "Don't worry, Debbie,

I'll look after you. You're my friend." He frowned, adopting a serious expression that was beyond his years. "I'm not going to let any bad people hurt you."

Elizabeth smiled. "Thank you so much, Ian. I feel so much safer knowing you'll always be there for my little angel."

Ian grinned back at his friend's mother. Then, he too cried out, reaching across and tugging on Brenda's arm. "Mummy, wake up! Mummy, there's fire inside me."

Brenda stirred from her sleep and instinctively wrapped her arms around him. She looked across to Elizabeth, hoping she might know what was happening. "The same thing happened just a moment ago with Debbie," said Elizabeth, "but it passed almost straight away."

Brenda looked down at her son. "Are you okay, buddy?"

Ian didn't reply, instead burying himself in the warmth of her embrace.

A few minutes later, the four of them were asleep.

***

The influx of evacuees from around both New Haven and New York City over the preceding two days had been a strain on Hartford, as it had been on other nearby cities. Hartford itself faced the probable need for evacuation due to the threat of fallout from New Haven. But for the time being, Hartford was carrying the brunt of it. With no time to set up proper locations to house people, the city's main baseball stadium became a makeshift refugee camp, with almost twelve thousand people gathered together in a hastily created tent city.

It was inside one of these tents that a rotund Italian man held his distraught wife close, assuring her it would be alright. "Ah, Maria!" He lifted her chin so their eyes met. "It's a sad time, but we're still alive. We still have each other."

"Oh, Enricho! How can you not be crying?"

He held her and thought of all that had happened. After the incident with Tanya, he'd felt certain something was very wrong. He'd convinced Maria they should close the shop early and go to Hartford for the evening, just in case things got out of hand. By the time they arrived, there would be no returning to New Haven ever again.

Despite the circumstances, the atmosphere in the stadium was one of hope. People were generous and courteous. Everyone was treated as an equal, with few exceptions. They'd all lost so much that they chose to focus on what they still had: their lives, each other, and a determination to get through the crisis.

There was an electric feeling in the air that night. The last of the families finished their evening meals in the modest mess hall. It was already getting late, but people were finding solace in conversation. In this grim time, there was even laughter ringing out from the crowd. In an otherwise still and quiet night, the sound of the huddled masses in the stadium carried for miles.

It wasn't just people who heard them, though. The groundfish had been drifting aimlessly beneath the earth as it processed its previous feed. It felt hunger. A craving for more thoughts, dreams, and cherished memories. The sound and vibrations from the stadium caught its attention.

The first the crowd knew of the groundfish approaching was when several dozen people in the middle of the field lost their footing as the ground sank beneath them. Then, a ring of earth, ten meters in diameter, rose into the sky. In an explosion of twisted irrigation fittings and broken concrete, it dragged with it everything and everyone from within the circle.

Like a giant snake of earth and building materials moving as one, it rose higher. Its trunk thinned to nothing, revealing a gaping hole in the ground below from where it had risen... a hole that roamed the field with total freedom. People panicked as they scrambled to avoid the pit that had opened up, many of them clawing at the earth as the shifting abyss sucked them in. After several seconds, the top of the groundfish stopped its ascent, closing in a tight ball around those it had scooped up before crashing back down into the deep pit below. The hole closed behind it, creating a gigantic splash that spread debris across the entire stadium. The ground continued rumbling as people ran in panic for the exits.

A few seconds later another large patch of earth dropped away before the groundfish rose again, this time near the southern exit. It rose at an angle, scooping up dozens more people before looping back underground.

The frenzied crowd changed direction, heading now for the northern exits. All the goodwill of just a few minutes earlier having been vanquished by their fear.

Struggling in the crowd, Maria lost her footing and fell to the ground, Enricho going down with her as he did what he could to protect her from the stampeding mass. Several people trying to flee the carnage trampled across the top of him as he lay over Maria. Then, the ground started slipping away from beneath them, pushing back up as the groundfish rose out of the ground in front of him.

This time, the menacing ring of earth swung around before descending, taking many more people with it, as though it had surveyed which groups to target. On hitting the ground, it sent earth and concrete splashing into the night. Many of those trying to escape were crushed by the flying debris.

Again and again, the groundfish broke the surface and took more frightened men, women and children, sometimes tossing them about, as though toying with them. With everyone madly scrambling to find a way out, the concentration of people near the exits became the main targets, the groundfish relishing in their panic.

As their numbers dwindled, the crowd appeared to give up hope, huddling in the middle of the stadium in grim resignation.

Once the crowd had stopped rushing the exits, the groundfish lost interest. Or perhaps it simply felt satisfied with the evening's feast. The gaps between its attacks grew longer, eventually coming to an end.

An eerie silence descended on the stadium, save for a few screaming children, the sound of approaching sirens, and a rumble deep below as the groundfish began digesting its meal. The remnants of the crowd were in a collective state of shock.

No one said a word as they finally found the courage to work their way toward the few exits that were still accessible.

None of them bothered to collect any of the personal possessions they'd brought with them. All anyone wanted now was to be out of that horrific theatre of death they'd been forced to endure.

Enricho lay unconscious on top of the body of his wife. Despite his efforts to protect her, the life had been crushed out of her by the stampeding crowd.

***

Elizabeth sat in the chopper with Debbie's head resting in her lap. The minutes felt like hours as she pondered how she longed to be with Daniel. She couldn't remember a time when her need to be with him had been so desperate as it was now. Her mind lingered on the most memorable moments they'd shared together.

A brief but excruciating burning sensation came from nowhere and ran through her, unlike anything she'd experienced before. In her tired state, she dismissed it as stress-related, failing to make the connection with what the children had described earlier.

Elizabeth's reaction to the burning woke Brenda from her own troubled sleep. Having struggled with insomnia for the last few months, she'd been in two minds about joining Marco at the bunker. She was envious of how Dan and Liz had sustained the love in their marriage. For her, the magic she'd once felt with Marco was long gone. She thought of how sad it'd been, watching him sacrifice his principles at the altar of pragmatism as he'd become more entrenched in the party machine. He'd always been inclined to drink more than she liked, but in recent times, it had become worse, much worse. She'd convinced herself early on that she could deal with it; after all, she enjoyed a drink herself, even the odd joint. What distressed her most, though, was when she'd recently been sorting through some files in their shared cloud storage and stumbled upon a copy of the Book of Circles. *Where'd that come from?* she thought. *He'd better not have joined that loony cult.*

"No, of course I haven't," he'd insisted when he arrived home that night. "There are just a few lines in there that I draw inspiration from. It helps keep things in perspective—particularly when you're under shitloads of stress like I've been for the last God only knows how many years."

The way Brenda saw it, the book was nothing but a load of crap that validated self-pity, greed and arrogance.

So here she was, being ferried on a chopper to be with a man she'd lost all respect for. She didn't want to be near Marco tonight. But they had a son, and events were spiralling out of control. For the time being, Ian's safety had to come first, and her gut told her they'd be safer at the bunker than at their home in Washington.

***

Marco was preparing to head out to the gate and meet his family when an alert came through on his lensview informing him there was an urgent meeting getting underway. He wasn't even halfway through reading it when a knock on his door interrupted him. "It's open." A Secret Service agent opened the door and stuck his head in. "You're required in the Cabinet Room in five minutes, Mr Secretary."

Marco threw down the last of his bourbon. "Okay, just let me send my wife a message, and I'll head straight there."

"I'm sorry, sir, but I cannot allow you to do that."

"Who are you to tell me I can't message my wife? She's expecting me at the gate in ten minutes. You *are* aware of that?"

"Sir, this comes directly from Director Brandt. There's to be no outside communication. No exceptions."

Resigning himself to accepting the impost, Marco stood up and followed the agent down the corridor.

When they arrived at the Cabinet Room, everyone but Maria was already there, watching a reconstruction of events, projected to appear above the table.

Domango wore the standard, bunker-issued dressing gown over a t-shirt. Peter Wong looked reasonably composed despite his oversized tracksuit and ruffled hair, while Nick was still in the clothes he'd been wearing through the day, minus the tie. Emily had found a pullover and some baggy shorts. Marco was dumbstruck when he looked at Louise and, for the first time, noticed the striking nature of her figure in her tight-fitting black singlet and shorts. In stark contrast, Tanya looked like the stereotypical suburban housewife as she sat at the far end of the room wearing basic pyjamas and wrapped in a blanket.

Louise paused the playback. "Come and take a seat, Marco."

His bloodshot eyes were fixed on the image floating above the conference table. "I was just starting to work through some reports when your agent knocked." His lie was obvious to everyone. He ignored their cold stares and poured himself a coffee, wishing there was a shot of something in there besides caffeine. "So, this is the so-called groundfish we're looking at, huh?"

Louise let the reconstruction resume playing and walked around the table. "Yes, and it's bigger than previously reported. Much bigger."

Peter looked to Tanya. "You *can* keep this out, can't you? Does the barrier work against that… thing?"

"I don't know, in theory, the magnetic field *should* be just as effective underground as it is above. But, to be honest, I've no idea if it could stop whatever this thing is anyway. I certainly wouldn't be betting on it."

Nick smacked his hand on the table. "For Christ's sake, woman, are you seriously suggesting you don't know? You *are* aware that you and your cohorts are responsible for that abomination, aren't you? Surely, you must know whether or not you're able to stop it."

The president rose to her feet. "I *will not* stand for you talking to this woman, or anyone, in the manner you just did. Have you been paying attention? She's given us our only hope. That's right, Nick, *our only hope* of getting out of this. Do you really think that sort of attitude is helpful? We've got to do better. The situation's spiralling out of control by the hour. The world's counting on us to do more, all of us."

"Sorry," said Marco as he struggled to focus, "but I'm still a bit behind you guys on just what the situation is right now."

"The African FIDO facility—it's been sabotaged," replied Domango.

Peter added. "And just before it went down, we got word the nanotech's been detected in Europe, although it's too early to confirm."

"FIDO calculated it's the result of a flight that left Guangdong last night," said Louise. "Some of the crew from that flight were infected. They'd also been on the flight from the UNSA to Guangdong with a GIA employee on board, Doctor Petra Chan. It's now clear she was involved in planning the blast at Infinity. The flight was airborne when the explosion occurred. It also leaves little doubt that General Rubeiro's involved and aims to militarise the technology. Clearly, they were working together. We have to work under the assumption that there are other sleeper cells working for him within the GIA or various levels of the government. We can't trust anyone unless given reason to think otherwise."

Peter asked, "I'm curious. Has FIDO detected the tech in Guangdong yet?"

"Since Guangdong sub-contracted their security to Rubeiro, intelligence from there has been unreliable at best. He's got a skilled IT team, who've been remarkably successful at circumventing FIDO's surveillance regime. Hence, our failure to detect that Chan was on his payroll."

Emily asked, "So, what *are* the ramifications of Africa's FIDO unit going down?"

"With one unit down, FIDO loses the capacity to override my decisions regarding nuclear strikes, although it maintains the ability to unilaterally detonate an EMP blast. If a second goes down, that capacity is also gone as well," said Louise. "But if the third goes down, we have a huge problem." She stood, looking around the room to ensure she had everyone's attention. "If we lose that one, we not only lose our eyes and ears to the world, but we also lose access to the launch codes for the world's remaining nuclear weapons. Should we need to use them, we would need to reconfigure each one manually."

Well, thought Emily, *at least there's one positive.*

"The FIDO situation can't really be dealt with till the morning," said Peter, "but what's gone down at Hartford tonight, that's something else. We're going to need to do something before then." Peter looked around the room. "Any ideas?"

"Reports from there say there's still minor tremors under the stadium," said Louise. "So we believe it's still in the immediate vicinity. Emergency crews are evacuating the survivors. Once they're clear, we'll strike with an EMP blast and follow up with bunker busters. The winds have settled enough that we shouldn't have an immediate problem with fallout from the spent uranium. Then, we'll send in reconnaissance drones and see what they can find."

Emily wore a pained expression. "I'm no fan of the EMPs, nor the bunker busters, but looking at what that thing did tonight—" She nodded her head. "It sounds like the only viable plan." She turned to Marco. "Give the director whatever assistance she needs. Spend the rest of the night working with her to make it happen if need be. Brenda and Ian may be just about to arrive, but trust me when I tell you, they'll be fine. We'll make sure they get settled so you can focus on this."

As the sleep-deprived occupants of the room prepared to leave, Nick raised his voice in protest. "Hold on a moment. We know nothing about what this thing is. How do we know we're not just going to piss it off and make it more aggressive?"

Emily asked, "Did you, or did you not, see what that thing did tonight? We can't sit by while this 'groundfish' systematically devours innocent people. While

I don't have much stomach for more bombings on our own soil, this is focused on one small area. It's already being evacuated. As far as I'm concerned, *there is no time* to look at other options." Emily stood up and addressed the room as she prepared to leave. "I want that fucker blasted out of existence before sunrise."

Louise raised an eyebrow as Emily exited the room. "Well, Marco, we've got some work to do."

***

Daniel and Gordon rose to their feet when they saw the spotlights of the chopper approaching. Daniel had opted to sit in an area outside the gate, but within the shield.

The wind from the descending chopper sent Gordon's folding table and chair tumbling through the shield. Once landed, the crew helped the four passengers disembark.

It took Gordon only a fraction of a second to realise they had a problem. His voice faltered as he broke the news to Daniel. "I'm so sorry—"

"What? What is it?

"Your wife—and the children—"

"No—it can't be!" Daniel tried to lunge through the shield to grab hold of Gordon and tell him to try scanning them again, to find a different method that would give them the green light, but two soldiers stepped forward and held him back.

Seeing the soldiers holding her husband, Elizabeth ran towards him. Having failed to stop her in time, the crewmen and Brenda managed to at least hold back the children. The co-pilot called out to Elizabeth, "Ma'am, you have not been cleared yet. You need to come back." But he was drowned out by the roar of the spinning rotor blades.

Even if she'd heard him, it would have made no difference. Since feeling the fire in her veins, she was overwhelmed by her desperate need to be with Daniel.

Gordon lunged across to block her path. "You mustn't try to pass through the shield. You need to stop, now!"

She ignored him.

Using his newfound capabilities, he tried reaching into her quantum network.

Her obsession was too strong. His attempt at intervention failed. In a last-ditch effort, he reached out physically and grabbed hold of her around the waist, only to be rewarded with a knee to the groin. The pain distracted him long enough for her to break free. In desperation, he made a diving tackle, but fell just short. He watched from the ground as she threw herself through the barrier, her arms outstretched towards her husband.

Two guards set out to fire on her, but Gordon reached out with his mind, forcing them to divert their weapons. As Elizabeth Chambers passed through the shield, the nanotech that had enmeshed itself within her nervous system was fried out of existence, breaking bonds within her brain that were now critical to her survival. She fell against Daniel, her arms draped around his shoulders. Her eyes stared into his with a look of bewilderment. Then, her lifeless body fell to the ground at his feet.

8

Pennsylvania Governor, Phillip Miller, stood at his office window in the Capitol Building. The sun would be rising in a few hours, but there was still work to be done before he could go home for the night. His chief of staff, Nancy Fisher, didn't bother disguising her tiredness as she referred to her notes. "We still need to sort out priority lists for the shield generator deployment."

He turned to face her, rubbing his eyes as he took a seat at his desk. "Yes, of course. Sorry, I was drifting off for a moment there."

Phillip had been quick to act when news came through of a means to protect his constituents. The state's proximity to the cities of New Haven and New York left him feeling uneasy. As it turned out, there was less fallout from the blast at New Haven than he'd expected, but that was now the least of his worries. Pockets of civil unrest were building. Much of the population rejected the idea of being restricted by the proposed shields. The Governor understood the imperative of deploying them regardless. He was particularly concerned about the Amish communities, many of whom knew little about the events of the past two days. His father had been born in an Amish community. But, during his coming of age, Phillip had decided to opt for life in the city. He'd nevertheless maintained a profound commitment to his Christian faith, a commitment he passed on to his children.

"With half the city protesting about these shields, how do we make this go smoothly? And how do we get the Amish to accept them if even city folk won't?"

Nancy made her growing impatience apparent with a steely glare and a long pause before she replied, "The cities and towns are fine. Most of them have already printed up their shield generators and have deployment plans in place. The National Guard, firefighters and the police force are all helping out. But the only help I've been able to source for deployment in the Amish communities is a single unit or two from the Carlisle Barracks. They're the only ones who haven't been dragged up to New York with the rest of the local armed forces."

Phillip propped up his chin on a steeple formed by his hands. "They probably won't accept them coming from the military, especially if they're in uniform." He looked up, eyes wide like he'd had an epiphany. "We'll use people the Amish know and trust instead." He smiled and pointed at her. "You—you need to contact the people they deal with when they go to market. You need to talk to the customers who buy from them, or perhaps even the market managers." He stabbed the air in triumph. "That's how we'll get them to accept their salvation from this technological plague."

Nancy rolled her eyes and tossed her notepad on the desk. "So, based on this approach, you want me to organise a morning deployment?"

"If anyone can make this happen, it's *you*, Nancy."

She glared at him as she grabbed her things, then left the room without saying another word.

***

Barnardo entered the room triumphantly. "We just received word. Africa is down, and Siberia is failing. When we hear from Australia, the hindrance of FIDO will be a thing of the past."

Petra rose from the centuries-old opium couch she'd been lazing on, and wrapped a silken sarong around her naked waist, leaving her breasts floating free. She'd grown several centimetres since her contamination and was developing proportions that would make an Amazon envious.

"Things are starting to fall into place. Now, we need to change a few local details. So we can appreciate our success." She collected jewellery from a cabinet next to the couch, and adorned herself with exotic necklaces and bracelets. "The old men who officially run this country, it's time we put them in their place."

A slight tremble in Barnardo's lower lip betrayed his difficulty maintaining composure—betrayed how taken aback he was by Petra's boldness. "But, they've financed *all* our operations to date. They've allowed us to do as we please."

"And now, my dear, it's time to choose a new path. One that excludes them from the picture altogether." She paused to examine the craftsmanship on a gold and diamond bangle she'd just slipped on her left wrist. "When we can use the nanotechnology in my gift to create an army—an army capable of conquering the world—why should we share that prize with a group of nasty old men?" She leaned down and whispered in his ear, "You and I deserve more than that."

Barnardo nodded in agreement. "Your plan?"

"Oh, that's really quite simple. Unlike the rest of this sorry planet, the old fools have seen fit to play the ancient game of appearing as feudal lords, ostentatiously displaying their wealth, while their citizens struggle to eat. You, with this palace and your grand statues, have unwittingly allowed yourself to become their most potent symbol of control."

"No one controls me. I run this country."

"You police it, but they control the money, all of the money."

"So, tell me, how do you propose we take that financial control?"

"Very simple, my dear, you declare yourself the new ruler of Guangdong, or emperor if you prefer, with *me* as your empress. While you continue to focus on running the military, I win the hearts and souls of the people through symbolic gestures. By the time the fools realise what's happening, it'll be too late."

"And what might these gestures entail?"

"Oh, darling, I'm not going to spoil *that* surprise." Again, she whispered in his ear, "You'll just have to trust me." She ran her tongue over his earlobe, then turned, smiled and strutted away.

Barnardo kept his eyes fixed on her as she left the room.

***

Emily flew over a vast expanse of water as though she were swimming through the atmosphere. She alternated in a carefree manner between a kind of aerial freestyle and breaststroke.

Approaching the shore, she watched in awe as the palm trees transformed into skyscrapers. She weaved her way through the buildings, then landed in the middle of a town square, only to be saturated by driving rain that sent her fleeing for cover in a dingy backstreet jazz bar. The building shook with the pulsing music, while butterflies flew out of the cocktail she'd just been handed. They fluttered around her head, the sound of their wings overpowering the music.

As she listened, it was as though they were calling her name. She threw the drink to the floor and fled the jazz club, running through the streets to get away, but the butterflies continued to multiply and pursue her. It was only then that she became aware of her nakedness and that an angry crowd was pointing her out.

She tried covering herself. Then the butterflies swarmed around her, incessantly calling out, "President Lucas, you need to wake up." Waking from her dream, she brought her eyes into focus and saw Louise leaning over her.

Once the reality sank in, she sprang up and stared at the director, still dressed in the same singlet and shorts. "What the hell? How'd you get in here?" asked Emily. She touched her chest to check she wasn't naked like in the dream and felt relief at the touch of fabric on her skin. "The Secret Service agents at the door, how'd you get past them?"

"As head of the GIA, I have access to wherever I wish during an Emergency Protocol 46. Also, the Secret Service agents you stationed outside? They're actually *my* agents. They have been since they were first appointed."

Of course! thought Emily as she let out a groan of disapproval.

Louise took an unwelcome seat next to her on the bed. "There's something I need to tell you personally. When the chopper landed, Daniel's wife ran through the barrier. She'd been contaminated. She didn't make it." Her expression and tone of voice were deadpan. Yet for a brief moment, Emily thought she could see something resembling a tear in the director's eye.

"Oh my god!" whispered Emily. She spent a moment digesting what Louise had just told her. "I'm responsible for this. It was *my* decision. I brought them here."

Louise put a firm hand on her shoulder. "You were doing something to help a valued team member perform in a crisis."

Emily looked down at the director's hand and calmly pushed it away. "How's Daniel?" she asked.

"He's been sedated for now. His daughter and Marco's son are both contaminated as well."

Emily shook her head in dismay, feeling the burden of responsibility weighing heavier on her shoulders with each word. "And Brenda, what about her? Is she okay?"

Louise leaned back, putting her weight on her elbows. "She's just watched her best friend die, and now Marco's blaming her for their son's contamination."

"He's what?"

"You heard me right. I was there when she called him. He said it never would have happened if she'd been sensible enough to stay at home, like all good mothers do in a crisis."

"He actually said that?"

Louise nodded.

"I'm shocked."

"The man's a drunk," said Louise. "He's a liability."

Emily let her head fall back to the pillow. She couldn't afford to have someone so unstable in such a crucial role, not at this time. Marco had to be replaced, but it would have to wait till morning. "What a fuck up. So much for lifting morale through family reunions."

"You didn't know this would happen. What matters now is that you need sleep, and so do I. At least we can do that now without fear of FIDO launching any more nukes. We won't need them so much now anyway. Not now that we have the shield option. If we divide the cities we know are contaminated into zones with separate shields, we can use the EMPs to deal with areas that prove to be contaminated. We can limit the damage."

"So, you expect me to be grateful you've figured that out now?" asked Emily. *A bit late for New Haven*, she thought to herself.

"Not grateful, just pragmatic. No matter how bitter a pill it may be to swallow, you and I, we *have* to be on the same page from here. Or else Peter will try to wrest control from both of us."

"I hear what you're saying," said Emily. "But understand this, I'll work with you only as much as is necessary to get through this." She looked at where Louise was sitting, annoyed that it was preventing her from stretching her legs out. "By the way, is it *really* necessary for you to sit on my bed?"

"Don't worry, I'll be leaving in a minute. This conversation couldn't wait till morning. You needed to know about Daniel's situation, and we needed to develop some sort of truce between us."

Emily nodded in reluctant agreement, then asked, "The kids, where are they now?"

"We've set up a quarantine station for them and Delaney inside the loading dock. A containment field's been set up for their quarters."

"And the stadium? Were we successful?"

"We won't know till morning. The crawler drones are working their way through the rubble now." Louise stretched herself out across the end of the bed, her tiredness ever more apparent. She closed her eyes. "I'll let you in on a secret. This groundfish scares me more than *anything* I've ever encountered. I doubt we've seen the last of it."

Emily chuckled. *Well, that's a first,* she thought, *there's something she's actually scared of.* Emily's attention was drawn to the end of the bed as the director began snoring. *Well, that's just great!* Resisting the temptation to wake the sleeping woman and toss her out of the room, she dropped her head back to the pillow and, in a few seconds, drifted into a deep sleep herself.

Brenda removed her wedding ring and placed it on the lamp table next to the couch. She took a seat and reminisced on how different things had been when they'd first met: the starstruck groupie who fell so heavily for the brilliant lead guitarist of the Crimson Dockers, the street marches and shared ideals. Then, the heartfelt ballad he wrote and recorded as a wedding proposal. They were both so idealistic back then—so deeply in love. *What happened?* She asked herself. *How did it go so wrong?*

Marco burst into the room, jolting her back to reality. He slammed the door behind him and stood, towering over her, his face contorting into a scowl when he saw the ring. "What the fuck?"

"It's over, Marco."

"Oh? Why would that be? What have I done?"

"Why? You're asking me why after you decided to blame *me* for what's happened to our son? And to make it worse, you have the gall to insinuate it happened because I don't go along with that Circumfren crap you've been falling into." She stood up to face him directly. "Well, let me tell you something, it's over, Marco. I don't ever want to see or talk to you again. I'm asking to be moved to separate quarters." She started walking toward the bedroom. "And so help me, if you try to enter the bedroom tonight, you *will* be sorry."

Marco followed, grabbed her arm, spun her around to face him and grasped her shoulders. As he tightened his grip, she saw a now familiar rage igniting in his eyes. "Marco! You're hurting me!"

"Not as much as you're hurting me! How dare you try to tell me it's over! You've got no idea the shit I'm going through since I got here."

"For Christ's sake, Marco. *Liz is dead!*" She struggled to see through her building tears. "I watched her. She fell into Dan's arms. Then she—"

"Yeah, Liz is dead. And why is that? And why is it that when I found out, I also discovered that you'd let our son—our *only* son—you let him get contaminated while you were wasting time hanging out with her?"

"You can't be serious—"

"Shut the fuck up while I'm talking." As he spoke those words, Marco brought his right hand up behind his shoulder, then swung it forward, slapping it hard across Brenda's cheek and sending her to her knees. Brenda tried to break free as he pulled her up and hit her again, this time with a closed fist. She fell to the floor, unconscious and bleeding.

Marco looked at the grazing across his knuckles as he walked across the room and sank into the couch. He picked up the ring and studied it. He thought back to how Brenda's face had glowed when they chose it, the same as it had when he slipped it on her finger at their wedding. Now it was over, all because she'd gone and exposed Ian to the goddamned nano-plague. *Fuck it, Liz deserved what she got,* he thought. *It was at her house that the kids got exposed. Daniel should have been firm with her, should've told her to stay indoors.* He thought one of the Circumfren philosophies he'd read just that morning: *In times of uncertainty, danger hides when viewed from straight on. Only through looking around a situation are the true dangers evident.* If Brenda had been looking at events with a more rounded perspective, this never would have happened. Rage consumed every iota of his being as he threw the ring against the wall. *What goes around comes around.*

He went to the kitchen and grabbed the half-empty bottle of bourbon. Sitting back on the couch, he stewed on the evening's events. "Fucking Washington DC." He knocked back one drink after another. Marco Fleming would never clearly remember the actions he took in the ensuing hours, actions he would deeply regret.

***

Maybe now I can get some sleep, thought General Philip Bennett as he returned to his bedroom. He slipped between the sheets, rested his head on his pillow, then his heart sank when another call came through. He rubbed his eyes and checked the time before taking the call. "Marco? What is it now?"

"Same authorisation code, different target."

"Great. So, I can expect a call from the wonderful director as well, then I suppose?"

"Not this time," came the reply. "She's been swamped trying to deal with the logistics of the cleanup. But we've got an even bigger problem on our hands now. The nanobots from the Infinity explosion have already contaminated at least several hundred people in the residential areas of DC. The chief of staff's wife—she died tonight as a result." Marco paused, as though struggling to hold it together. As he continued, he spoke through tears. "And there's going to be more, a lot more."

"Oh my God." Bennett had met Daniel just a few weeks earlier and had got on well with him. "How's the chief of staff holding up?"

"As you can imagine, he's distraught—we all are. The President and Director Brandt have tasked me with seeing to it that we neutralise the problem before it gets any worse."

"So, let me get this right, are you saying you want me to bomb Washington DC?" His head reeled; the idea seemed unthinkable.

"It's the Emergency Protocol 46. We have no other choice. Either we take decisive action right away, or FIDO's going to damn well launch its own attack with nukes in the morning. If we take action now, at least we keep that action restricted to EMPs and a few heat blasts."

The general felt like a spectator trapped in a nightmare. But, despite the urgency of the situation, he was *not* prepared to take action without further authority. "Sorry, Marco. I can't do this. This is the *capital* we're talking about. The losses would be enormous, and the damage to the command structure—it's unthinkable. No offence, but I need a higher authority to approve this. From Wiseman, at the very least."

"He's my next call, I need him to organise the evacuations to the bunkers."

"Well, once you've talked to him, get him to call me with his interpretation of what's going on. Until then, I will have no part of this." Bennett cut off the line. If he hadn't been so tired, he would've checked his messages, particularly the high-priority one from the GIA informing all senior military personnel that the African component of FIDO was effectively offline.

***

Begrudgingly, General Carl Wiseman accepted the call from Marco, despite his wristband showing him it was 3:30 am. "Wiseman here."

"Carl, it's Marco. We've got a much bigger problem on our hands than before. The nanotech from Infinity. It's spread to DC. The situation's spiralling out of control. It needs to be dealt with immediately."

"Everything needs to be dealt with immediately."

"It's so much worse than we thought. Hundreds of people in DC have been contaminated, including Daniel Chambers' wife—she's already died as a result."

"Oh, shit."

"President Lucas and Director Brandt are both adamant that we need to stop it now. We need to hit the capital. We need to hit the city with a broad carpet of EMPs and heat blasts in the known areas of contamination."

There was a long pause before Wiseman replied, "That's not going to happen tonight, not without a formal request from both President Lucas and the Director."

"Carl, they're going to be mighty pissed if they find out you've caused a delay. We need to act now!"

"I agree, we need to act. But I'm not sending planes in without further authorisation. However, in anticipation, I *will* order the immediate evacuation of government and official personnel into the DUCC."

"Look, I do get it," said Marco. "I'd probably do the same in your position. But you'd better be getting that strike ready while the evacuation is underway. I guess we'll at least know the personnel in the DUCC are safe when the bombing raids are launched."

185

"There won't be any bombs going off until I get that authorisation from the top. In the meantime, we'll need to take precautions to ensure no one gets in who's already contaminated. I'll be making sure everyone gets screened before they're allowed to go underground."

"I wouldn't expect anything less. I'll send through the President's updated list of the key personnel."

On receipt of the list for evacuation to the DUCC, the *Deep Underground Command Centre*, Wiseman entered it into his wristband and followed up with the required security code. Once Marco had done the same, the evacuation alert was triggered. The broad range of medibots Wiseman required to keep him in good health meant that he'd have to be excluded from joining those heading into the bunker, else the screening process would more than likely kill him the instant he walked through. It was a situation that suited him just fine. Being stuck in a bunker with panicked government officials was the last place he wanted to be.

Everyone crucial to the wheels of government and the command structure was summoned to their relevant posts in the DUCC, a network of tunnels and bunkers that connected the White House, Pentagon, Capitol Hill, and the National Security Agency, along with a host of other entities deemed essential to the smooth running of the country.

Marco had been careful to ensure the list for immediate notification excluded those who were now at the North Dakota bunker, thereby giving him time before his charade was exposed. He felt confident that Wiseman, in his tiredness, would assume the list covered everyone.

***

Gordon took a seat next to the bed, preparing to read Debbie and Ian a bedtime story. Although separate beds had been made for them in the same room, the children had insisted on sharing the same bed. Under the circumstances, Gordon felt anything that made them more comfortable was a good idea.

Seeing all three were fully contaminated, it was decided that, as an experienced parent, Gordon should supervise the children. It was extremely late, but in light of the evening's events, the children found it difficult to sleep.

Debbie looked up at Gordon and asked, "Why are you wearing those dark glasses at night, Mister Gordy?"

"Well, that's an interesting question. You see, when *I* had that burning feeling you told me about, it made me change in ways that some people find pretty scary."

Ian sat up and folded his arms. "I don't think you're scary, Mr Gordon."

"That's no way to talk to Mr Gordy," said Debbie. "He was trying to tell us why he has to wear those dark glasses." Turning to Gordon, she lightened her tone. "It's okay, you can go on now. I promise, Ian won't interrupt again."

"Well, thank you. But I must say, Ian, I am most impressed by your bravery. I feel much better knowing you'll be protecting Debbie after I've fallen asleep tonight."

"You were going to tell us about the glasses."

"Oh yes, of course. I wear these because I actually don't have eyes anymore, and by wearing these, it lets people pretend that I look just like them."

A big grin lit up Ian's face. "Wow, can we have a look?"

"I don't know if that would be such a good idea right now."

Debbie let out a sigh and put her hands in her lap. "Now, Mr Gordy, you really need to understand, we are *very* smart kids, and since that burning thing happened, we've become much smarter than before. You don't need to worry, we understand things very well."

"Are you *really* sure about this?"

"Absolutely."

"Okay, but don't say I didn't warn you." Gordon removed his sunglasses, revealing the smooth flesh beneath.

The kids turned to each other, covering their mouths with their hands, trying to hide their laughter. Debbie looked back at Gordon, still giggling. "I'm sorry, Mr Gordy, but you look so funny."

Their sheer honesty and lack of fear brought a smile to Gordon's face. He then found himself laughing along with them.

Ian's laughter stopped. He looked puzzled. "How do you see anything when you don't have eyes?"

Debbie frowned at her friend. "Haven't you worked that out yet?" Gordon sat up straight, curious to hear what she had to say. "It's so obvious! Because Mr Gordy doesn't have eyes anymore, his whole body has become like one big eye. So, he can see better now than he could before." She looked up at Gordon. "But other people can't do that, it's only because you have the little machines that make you really smart too."

Gordon was astounded by how quickly this young girl had not just begun to use her new quantum interface, but by how natural it seemed to her.

"What's it look like when you go to the toilet?" asked Ian with a cheeky grin, "Can you see with your bum?"

"Ian! You can't ask Mr Gordy a question like that."

Although he was blushing, Gordon laughed at the innocence of the question. It was pleasing that these kids were still behaving as one would expect of children their age. "It's okay. I think that's actually an excellent question. What do *you* think it would look like?"

"Eww! I wouldn't look."

"And neither do I!"

"So, is it like you can shut your eyes for different parts of your body?" asked Debbie.

"Pretty much."

The kids looked at each other, smiling. In unison, they said, "Cool!"

"Now, I think it's time you two got some sleep," said Gordon. "We can talk more about these things in the morning."

Ian looked up, rubbing his eyes with tiredness. "I want Mummy to tuck me in. Mummy always tucks me in."

Debbie put an arm around his shoulder. "It's okay, Ian. Our parents can't be with us now because of the little robots inside us. But we'll be able to talk to them tomorrow. Mr Gordy will make sure we're alright."

The kids lay down together and fell asleep. Gordon looked at them and wondered if Debbie had realised yet that she would never see her mother again, whether or not she was fully aware of what had happened this evening. He was amazed by the resilience this little girl was already displaying.

Rather than go to his own room, he opted to lie down on the vacant bed across from the children, allowing him to be close to them.

***

Senator George Sanderson pulled out of his driveway and drove the short distance to where the late-night traffic jam had engulfed the streets around the White House, Capitol Building and Pentagon. All the buildings were connected to the massive DUCC that had been rebuilt from scratch over the previous decade. He had no doubt members of the general population who found themselves awake at that hour would be concerned, maybe even panicked, by the sudden flurry of activity.

With his car having been cleared to enter the Capitol Building's grounds, he instructed the vehicle to take itself to the nearby members' carpark after he'd alighted at the building's entrance. As soon as he stepped from the car a security officer approached. It was a man he knew well, the result of so many years serving in the Senate.

"Hello, James," he said.

James was dispassionate in his response. "I'll need to check your security pass, sir."

George flicked his credentials across to the agent's lensview. As he waited for the approval, he pondered how the younger members would feel as they were guided toward the elevators that would take them away from their families for the foreseeable future and into the sealed safety of the bunkers.

"You're right to go in, Senator." James gave him a knowing pat on the shoulder as George nodded and entered the building.

He was guided toward a queue that led to what appeared similar to the old-fashioned metal detectors, like the ones used at airports in years gone by.

A security officer walked along the queue, addressing no one in particular as he said, "Could you please remove your lensview, earbuds, and wristband before passing through the shield generator. If you have a medical condition requiring medibots for survival, you will need to step off to the side. I repeat, if you need medibots to survive, please step off to the side; else the scan could prove fatal."

Sanderson noticed an old friend and mentor, Senator Jerry Shand, who had stepped from the queue and raised his hand. Jerry was in his late nineties and had battled a range of medical conditions.

Several others had also stepped from the queue. One, a young congresswoman from Kentucky, was protesting when she saw that those who'd stepped aside were being escorted from the building. "I'm on the defence expenditure review committee," she protested. "I *have* to join everyone else in the bunker."

"Do you require medibots for survival, Ma'am?" asked a security agent.

"Yes, but—"

"Then, you'll need to leave the building now." He took her arm and led her away.

Among others denied access were a handful of congressmen, several senators and two highly ranked military officers. George noticed they had mixed feelings about being denied entry. Some, like a congresswoman from Kentucky, were distraught over their diminished capacity to fulfil their roles. Others expressed relief at being able to return to their families.

The security guard walking up and down the line called out, "Has anybody experienced a burning sensation in their body in the past twenty-four hours? If so, could you please step aside?"

The day before, George had followed his routine of going for a jog through his neighbourhood before heading off to work. A jog that took him past the home of Daniel Chambers. A jog that had led to him unwittingly breathing in dozens of nanobots, the physical exertion accelerating their integration with his metabolism. When he'd felt the burning sensation run through him earlier that evening, he'd put it down to having pushed himself too much in that night's workout. But it passed quickly, so he hadn't been concerned.

Until now.

Why are they asking about the burning sensation? wondered George. *It must all be connected. Why else would they ask about it?.* He felt torn. *What happens if I raise my hand and admit to it? It's not like it's impacted my health. I haven't felt so fit in years.*

He watched each person pass through ahead of him, feeling his heart rate building. *Damn it! What's this about anyway?* He broke out in an anxiety-induced sweat, then realised a soldier was directing him to take his turn in the scanner.

"Are you okay, sir?" asked the soldier as he placed a hand on Sanderson's shoulder, looking into his eyes as though they might reveal the man's state of health.

Sanderson nodded. He took a deep breath, bit his lower lip and stepped forward.

Pandemonium broke out in the room as Sanderson's lifeless body fell to the floor. Nothing could have prepared the congressmen and senators for what they'd just witnessed. It left all of them feeling apprehensive about being screened themselves.

Those the population looked to for leadership were reduced to a pack of panicked beasts seeking refuge.

GIA operatives at the scene tried to take command of the situation under the Emergency Protocol 46, ensuring that no one left the building.

They sent an emergency message to Director Brandt. When she didn't respond, they made a snap decision. Those with medical conditions would henceforth be loaded into quarantine vehicles, in case they too had been contaminated.

Some, who realised they must also be contaminated, tried to escape the scene or resist, creating enormous problems for the security teams. Many of these were people who had now developed more strength and far greater intellectual capacity as a result of their new quantum network, creating an even greater challenge for those endeavouring to restore order.

Some were shot down as they fled, while others, who'd seen what had happened to Senator Sanderson, tried to evade the screening and were being forcibly dragged through, falling into lifeless heaps as their nanotech disintegrated.

Evacuees pushed past the barricades erected to funnel them through the screening passages. Those who managed to get past without screening were shot.

"Abort! Fall back and seal the entrance!" came the call from one of the lead GIA operatives. They had no choice. They had to abandon the evacuation, falling back into the passages that led to the DUCC elevators and sealing the entrances behind them.

Similar scenes were repeated at the White House and Pentagon DUCC entrances. At the Pentagon, it was made worse when one of the soldiers, aware he had experienced the burning, went on a rampage with a semi-automatic weapon, taking out eight senior military commanders before being gunned down himself.

In the end, only a small proportion of the hundreds who'd been intended for evacuation made it to the tunnels.

At the White House, there was a sense of relief that they'd at least managed to get the Vice President and some of his key staffers to safety.

***

Among those gathered on the streets of Washington, curious about why the unusual activity was taking place at this hour, one man stood emotionless as he waited in the shadows.

Hakim knew the current activity could only mean one thing. Once he felt certain the entrances to the DUCC were sealed, he activated his wristband and made a series of gestures, then sent an encrypted voice message to General Rubeiro: *It is done.*

As part of an extensive sleeper network in the UNSA, Hakim and his accomplices had spent the previous five years working in concert with the General on his plot to sabotage the DUCC.

They'd gained access to plans via leaks from a disgruntled government employee who'd hacked into the relevant files undetected, a lonely soul who had his price and cared little about consequences. Nobody missed him when he disappeared without a trace a few months later.

Using similar mining nanobots to those that were now crippling FIDO, the jihadists had spent years enacting Rubeiro's scheme to set up hundreds of small explosive charges in strategic locations. When detonated, they would impact the structural integrity of the tunnels and elevator shafts feeding the complex. It was then a matter of waiting for a strategic moment such as this to strike.

Hakim turned and started walking back to his apartment. Moments later, the explosives detonated, causing the collapse of every tunnel and elevator shaft leading into the DUCC. A second wave of blasts severed the remaining fibre optic cables and ventilation shafts connecting the DUCC to the outside world.

The air was filled with the sound of alarms, followed by even more sirens descending on the area than before.

A few minutes later, the Capitol Building collapsed, the preceding blasts having damaged its structural integrity.

Those within the DUCC were trapped without connection to the outside world, relying on an air supply that was unlikely to last until rescuers could reach them.

***

The groundfish, having gorged itself, was busy digesting the thoughts, memories, and raw materials it had devoured during the attack on the stadium. Each time it came upon a mind with a more vivid imagination, or with a greater sensitivity and capacity for love, it would twist and curl with excitement.

But no matter how great the excitement, it was always short-lived. Not that it mattered in that moment. There were so many minds to absorb. However, the longer the time between death and absorption, the duller the sensation. Within the hour, the excitement had passed, and the groundfish settled down to absorbing the remaining materials into its matrix.

It was in a sleep-like state when it was jolted awake by an enormous shock and burning sensation, followed by another, and then another. Bomb after bomb hit, leaving the groundfish feeling as though flaming swords were tearing it apart.

The creature had no sense of time, no way of knowing how long the bombing lasted. All it knew was that the burning became more intense with every moment. The shock subsided, but the burning sensations continued. As a result, the groundfish was no longer whole. The bunker-busting bombs—small-scale tactical nuclear weapons—had destroyed much of its quantum network. It had been devastated by the attack, and now, just two separate pockets remained intact. The bombers setting out to destroy it had almost succeeded. Yet somehow, it managed to survive.

What remained was little more than two instances of what the groundfish had been when it had first arrived at the stadium. Its two parts were now overwhelmed by the need to escape from the bombing of the stadium.

They set out to escape in different directions. One sensed the massive abyss of the Atlantic not too many kilometres to its east and began the slow struggle to a nearby river that could carry it in that direction. The other sought safety by going deep underground.

***

Jason Negus was fast asleep while Jon Kruick sped along the freeway. In the back of the vehicle, Mary Killen's eyes were closed. She held her young grandchild close to her breast, a blanket wrapped around them both.

To keep himself from drifting off, Jon turned the music up in his earbuds and was singing along to one of his old favourites from another time, *Roadhouse Blues*. They were still an hour or so from their destination, and Jon was keen to get there as fast as possible. While he could have easily left the car in auto-mode and grabbed some sleep himself, they'd agreed at least one of them should remain awake, in case they encountered the fugitives.

He noticed two pinpricks of light in the distance from an approaching vehicle. They'd passed several cars in the past few hours, but his gut told him this one was different. he turned the music down to help him concentrate.

Jason woke up with a start, "He's in my head!"

"Who? What are you talking about?" asked Jon.

"One of the fugitives. He's taunting us," said Jason. "He's asking if I'm the hunter or the hunted."

The same thought then crept into Jon's head, becoming louder and more insistent with each passing second. "I'll be fucked, you're right. It's one of them!"

The approaching vehicle altered its trajectory to be heading straight for them. Automatic safety overrides kicked in, sending Jon's vehicle veering to the left in an attempt to avoid a collision, but the oncoming vehicle changed its own course to compensate. They were in a high-speed game of chicken, a game that ended quickly. As the fugitive's car sped past, it clipped the rear end of Jon's vehicle, causing it to spin out of control and fly over an embankment, flipping three hundred and sixty degrees before coming down hard on its wheels.

Merrick screamed. Somehow, Mary had managed to keep hold of him throughout the ordeal.

In the front seat, the two agents looked at each other. Jason sneered, "Whatever it takes, we're going to stop that little shit."

Jon shook his head. "I'm not so sure about that. This is getting way too personal for you. Before we do anything more, you need to fill the director in on what's happening."

"No way. Not until we've got the little fucker," snapped Jason.

"We've gone too far already without the director's approval. She's going to be pissed enough as it is." He glanced over his shoulder before continuing, "We can't go after him with these two in tow anyway. Besides, this vehicle's going nowhere after that little road dance."

"You're kidding, aren't you?" asked Jason. "You want to let that asshole get away with what he just did?"

"When the dust settles, the director will give us the resources we need to go after the son of a bitch. You *know* that."

Jason's stone-faced expression cracked into a smile. "Son of a gun. You always were a shmuck for sticking to the rules." He slapped Jon on the back of the shoulder. "That being the case, it's time we go our separate ways, my friend. You can take Mary and the kid and do what you want. Me? I've no intention of letting this cocksucker get away. The little shit got inside my head, I know what he's thinking, and I'm telling you, he's way too dangerous. I'm going after him *now*."

Jon put his hands up in the air in a gesture of surrender. "Okay, then so be it. But once I've got these two to safety and talked to Brandt, I'll be back. With luck, I'll find the other one while I'm at it."

Jason tried opening his door, only to find it jammed. He leaned back and then rammed his shoulder into it, sending it flying several metres.

Jon raised an eyebrow. "You've gained some strength. That could be helpful."

Jason said nothing as he struggled out of the car. When he stood up on his one elongated foot, he found he could no longer straighten his back, nor his elbows. His fists had grown substantially larger, and the flexibility in his leg felt like he was supporting himself on a spring.

Mary gasped at the sight of Jason's mutations. She started to cry. *This is Ron's fault. Why?*

"What's up, Mary?" asked Jason. "Are you so awestruck that you're lost for words?"

"How? How can you be so relaxed about it?" she asked through her tears.

Jon leaned across and whispered in Mary's ear, "Ignore him. He's showing off. He's not—"

"What are you on about, shit for brains?" asked Jason.

Jon looked up, his expression betraying his surprise at being overheard by his friend.

"You're just fucking jealous." Jason Chuckled. "I mean, hey! What woman wouldn't be blown away by someone so obviously superior to every other fucker around, huh?" As he finished, Jason moved around to the vehicle's storage compartment and pulled out his preferred firearms.

Jon got out and leaned on the side of the vehicle, arms folded as he watched on. "You *do* remember what happened at New Haven when we tried going after those guys? What makes you think you'll do better now?"

"Were you even listening? Like I said, I *know* what he's thinking. He can't control me, and he knows it. He can only control followers. You and me? He's got no chance. We may follow orders from the director—*sometimes*. But we do it in our own way. We're not like those army hacks who blindly follow like trained dogs. That's his weakness, and that's why *I'll* win." Jason slung an automatic rifle over his shoulder and hopped off down the road.

Jon Kruick turned to Mary. "I'll call the bunker and see if they can send someone out to get us. We can't be too far out from it now."

"Okay," replied Mary. "You won't be in too much trouble, will you?"

"Maybe, but I'll need to face the music sometime," replied Jon. "And the sooner we reach that bunker, the safer we'll be." He swiped at his Wristband then said, "Call Director Brandt, High Priority."

An error message flashed up in his lensview.

"Shit!" he exclaimed.

"What's up?" asked Mary.

"Looks like my wristband got damaged in the crash."

"Can you fix it?"

"It'll self-repair. But I don't know how long that'll take." He looked at the horizon to the north. "With a bit of luck, we'll be able to hitch a ride. But I'm not going to hold my breath. Looks like we might have a long, hard walk ahead of us. Are you up for it?"

Mary looked up at him. He was much taller than her and had broad shoulders. Despite his tough veneer, Mary sensed a degree of sophistication and kindness in this man. She nodded and smiled, triggering Jon to return the gesture. He collected water bottles from the vehicle and a backpack, then grabbed some of the weapons Negus had left behind. He sensed they'd be needing them. Mary took the opportunity to change Merrick's nappy. He wasn't likely to go back to sleep. But he'd settled more now and had stopped crying. With his fresh nappy on, Mary let the toddler walk while holding her hand. The three of them headed off down the road, the first light of dawn at their backs.

*****

Peter Wong sat at his window, drinking coffee while watching the explosion of colour as the sun crept over the horizon. He couldn't believe how poorly things were panning out. Here he was, faced with having to find some way to save face while retracting the recommendations he'd made the night before. In the end, that wasn't out of the ordinary in the rough and tumble world of politics, but he hated the thought of Emily being perceived as having outplayed him.

There was still one bright spot in it all, though. As far as he could tell, no one was even remotely aware of his involvement in the assassination of his colleagues.

He just hoped FIDO would be fully offline before it had the opportunity to collect the data that might lead it to suspect what he'd done.

Before she'd left the UNSA, Petra had assured him all three FIDO installations would be out of action by now. The failure of the assassins to take out Domango and Maria complicated things. It would be so much easier if it were just he and Nick Harrington left on the Council. Nick was so easy to manipulate that Peter would have effectively been able to take total control while delighting in how Nick would frustrate Emily's every move.

By far his biggest concern, though, was Gordon's arrival in the bunker. If he was capable of getting into people's heads, then Peter wanted him gone as soon as possible.

He took another sip of his coffee and tried to relax as he took in the view of the sunrise. It was going to be a long, hard day ahead.

***

No one felt the shock of what happened to the DUCC more than Wiseman. With his health precluding him from entering the DUCC anyway, he'd hoped to get more sleep.

It felt ironic that, having instigated the alert to send key personnel to the underground fortresses, his life had been saved because of his ill health. He pondered over how differently things might have played out if he'd authorised the EMP over Washington after his conversation with Marco.

A sense of guilt hung over him as he called Philip Bennett.

"Phil? We'd better get Marco online. I think we made the wrong call. He's got a better handle on what's going on. We should let him have what he wants."

"Are you sure about that, sir?"

"Not really, but after what's just happened across Washington, I'm not prepared to risk being responsible for this goddamned nano-plague taking over what's left of the city. We're going to be damned if we do and damned if we don't. As far as I'm concerned, it's his call. We let the responsibility rest with him. My conscience can't carry any more of this."

When they got hold of Marco, he listened patiently as they explained the broad details of the terrorist attack. Marco accepted their apologies for having doubted his authority under the Emergency Protocol 46.

"I want EMP blasts over the whole city," said Marco, "and heat blasts covering an area within one hundred metres of every entry point to the DUCC."

Once the call was finished, Marco downed the rest of his bourbon, put his head down on the couch and passed out.

9

Louise woke with a start in response to the emergency call from her chief Washington operative.

"Brandt here."

"Inspector, I've been trying to get hold of you for the past twenty minutes."

She looked across at Emily's wristband sitting on the bedside as it flashed and vibrated. "What's happening that you need to contact me so urgently?" As she asked the question, Louise's face went pale as she watched message after message scroll through on her lensview. She didn't like what she saw just through reading the message headings.

"We have a grave situation here," he said. "The DUCC's all but destroyed!"

Louise nudged Emily awake, put her wristband on speaker mode, then replied, "I wasn't aware it was under threat. You'd best start from the beginning."

"As you're no doubt aware, ninety minutes ago all key personnel were ordered to evacuate to the DUCC."

Louise and Emily looked at each other as the agent continued, "All hell broke loose, the doors had to be sealed early."

"How?" asked Emily, "How could this happen without me being aware?" She looked at Louise. "Is this *your* doing?"

"I never gave any such order," replied Louise. "I'm as shocked as you are." She asked the agent, "Who'd the order come from?"

"It didn't come from either of you? Director Brandt, Madam President, I cannot begin to tell you—"

"Just answer the question." Louise's voice conveyed her obvious anger and frustration.

While the agent fumbled his way through an attempted explanation, Emily mulled over the fractured information. *It's Marco*, she thought. *No one else could have issued the commands.*

She raced from the room, not bothering to grab a robe to put over her pyjamas. She grabbed her wristband as she went and swiped it. "Emergency call to all levels of command in the UNSA Military. This is President Emily Lucas vetoing all previous orders. Abort all operations immediately. I repeat, abort *immediately*!"

Secret Service agents fell in behind her and flanked the president as she ran down the corridor. She reached Marco's door, bashing it with her fist. "By god, Marco, if you're in there, you'd better open that goddamned door right now."

Inside, Marco sat motionless on the couch, the empty glass still in his hand.

Daniel raced down the corridor from his own suite to join her. One of the Secret Service agents stepped forward. "If I may, Madam President?" Emily stood back as he kicked the door in. She charged in and was confronted by the sight of Brenda, lying unconscious in the far corner of the room with a bloodied nose and bruises about her face.

Emily strode across the room, grabbed Marco by the collar, and dragged him off the couch. "What the *fuck* were you thinking?" She took the glass from his hand and threw it against the wall.

Marco smirked at her and rolled his eyes. "My son—he got contaminated in that city. Either you or Louise would have made the same decision soon anyway. So, what's it to you? What's the difference?"

"It wasn't your decision to make." She looked again towards Brenda, then back to Marco. "And what you've done to your wife? You're scum, Marco. Do you hear me? Scum!"

"What's your problem?" asked Marco. "I was just... cleaning up someone else's mess. And you know what? In the end, it wouldn't have even been *your* decision anyway. The only power *you've* got is the power Louise wants you to *think* you have. You're nothing but a little puppet for her and her friends on the

Security Council to play with." He made a dismissive gesture toward Brenda. "As for her, I find myself having to make the hardest decision of my life, a decision to show my love for our son, and do I get any support? No, the bitch had already thrown her fucking wedding ring in my face. Then she wants to lecture me on morality, for crying out loud!"

Emily struggled to contain her anger. Her left hand was still holding Marco's collar while her right was now clenched so tight into a fist that her nails were cutting into her flesh. She had never experienced such anger, not even when the director had ordered the bombing of New Haven. She wanted nothing more than to release her pent-up stress in an expression of her anger toward her Defence Secretary. Marco was still grinning as she imagined herself smashing her fist into his face.

Her fist trembled.

Her breath became short and hard.

Being as drunk as he was, Marco wouldn't be able to put up resistance or fight back. His eyes rolled back in his head as she brought her fist back, ready to hit him. Then Daniel grabbed hold of it as he and the Secret Service agents held her back.

Daniel and Marco had been friends outside of work for years, but he'd never seen this side of the man before. For Daniel, seeing Brenda's bruised and bloodied face spoke louder as to who Marco really was than what he'd been responsible for in Washington. It was clear. Emily longed for a catalyst, a means to release her pent-up rage. A rage that she was struggling to contain.

Louise entered the room "That's not going to help anything."

Daniel looked puzzled by the director's comment. Holding Emily by the shoulders, he pulled her away, her fist still clenched.

Marco slumped into the couch, still wearing his pathetic smirk.

Louise walked across and grabbed him by the collar, dragging him back to his feet. "President Lucas may need to show dignity in how she deals with him, but I don't." She pulled her fist back and then slammed it into his face, breaking his nose and sending him over the back of the couch. She turned to Emily. "See? No more smiles from him now."

Walking around to the back of the couch, Louise squatted next to him. "Now, Marco, we're going to have a little talk. And you're going to tell me what I want to know, or you'll be walking all the way back to Washington."

Marco laughed and pointed his finger at her. "You're not allowed... you're not allowed to do that."

Louise swung her fist again, this time connecting with his eye. She stood up, grabbed him by the collar and dragged him to the door, where she dumped him at the feet of Secret Service agents gathering outside the room. "Make him comfortable while I clean myself up."

As they carted him off, Emily called after them, "Hold on a moment, guys, Marco—in case you didn't already get the message, you're fired, effective immediately."

By the time the raid had been aborted, it was too late for much of Washington DC. Three-quarters of Congress, the bulk of the Executive, and their families were gone, along with tens of thousands of regular citizens living in the city.

The government of the UNSA was crippled.

***

Nancy cursed herself for choosing high heels when she'd left for work the day before. How was she to know she'd be working through the night, then rushing to the markets the following dawn? She'd now broken one of them after failing to notice a crack in the pavement, forcing her to navigate the busy market in her stockings. To make it worse, her tight skirt restricted her movement. In desperate need of a shower and a change of clothes, she'd toyed with the idea of detouring via her home, but that would have taken another hour, time she didn't have.

Pausing to catch her breath, she referred to the notes on her wristband. Everyone she'd talked to said the same thing. If she wanted to reach out to the Amish community, she needed to enlist the help of Kallan Keneally. Now, checking the face on her lensview against the woman packing crates on the back of an old pick-up some twenty metres away, she felt sure she'd found her target. Kallan had a thick crop of dark hair that sat just above her shoulders. Her blue cotton sundress was tied at the waist with a colourful scarf, complemented by her assorted bangles, rings, and earrings.

While tying down the canvas tarpaulin on the back of her pick-up, Kallan glanced over her shoulder at Nancy and said, "Whatever you want, I doubt I can help."

Nancy stopped walking, letting out a sigh of exasperation as she cast her broken shoes aside. "Please, listen to me. You've no idea what I've been through in the last twenty-four hours. At least hear me out."

Kallan looked like she hadn't slept either. She paused, then turned to face Nancy. "The name's Kallan, Kallan Keneally. But you already know that. As for hearing you out? You're out of luck. I'm getting out of here while I still can and taking my family with me."

Nancy looked down at the holes and tears in her stockings. Her feet were bleeding, and she was in pain. But she hadn't come this far to be so easily dismissed. "You really think running is going to save them?"

"The farther I can get them from whoever you work for, the better," replied Kallan. "You question my intentions, but you haven't even bothered to introduce yourself."

Nancy took two steps forward, extending her hand. "My name is Nancy. Nancy Fischer. I'm the governor's chief of staff. I'm here in the hope you can help me reach out to the Amish."

Kallan casually folded her arms. "I didn't vote for your boss, and to be honest, I don't trust him. As for helping you with the Amish? I'm not the person you want for that. I mean it when I say I'm out of here. Have you paid attention to what's been going on?"

Barely able to stay on her feet, Nancy took another step forward and used the back of Kallan's pick-up to prop herself up. "Look, I'm sorry. That was a poor start. Please understand, I *really* haven't slept at all last night, and I had almost no sleep the night before. I never thought I'd see the day when we'd have to face something this big. I'm struggling, and I'm very, very tired. But I can't give up, not now." She rubbed her eyes and stifled a yawn. "Do you realise the full extent of this? There's nowhere to hide. It doesn't matter where you go, sooner or later, this tech will be there."

"To be honest, I'm more worried about the people *inside* the shields than the other shit. Don't get me wrong, that scares the crap out of me, but in case you hadn't noticed, our country's capital has been the target of terrorist attacks overnight. I love my country, but family comes first. And the safest place to be right now is up in the mountains, in a cabin I bought years ago—just in case things got out of hand. Like what's happening now. If we can hold out till winter, the cold up where we're heading should protect us from the nanotech."

"So, you've got a printer, one that can print out a shield generator?" There was a hint of sarcasm in Nancy's voice.

"Hello? I'm an *organic farmer.* As if I can afford one of those."

"Would you like one?"

Kallan stared into space, as though mulling over the possibilities an industrial printer would open up. "Okay, you've got my attention."

"Would a guarantee that the government will leave you alone help?"

"I'm still listening."

Nancy had just made two big promises. She was barely able to focus anymore and needed to ensure she handled the rest of the negotiations with a clear head. "Find me a coffee, and we can discuss it in detail."

Kallan let out a broad smile and threw an arm around Nancy's shoulder. "Now you're speaking my language, let me introduce you to Nico's Espresso Van, the best coffee in Pennsylvania."

***

Tanya approached the main viewing window of the quarantine chamber that held Gordon and the children.

The window looked onto a large living area. Gordon sat in a lotus position, as if meditating, but rather than sitting on the floor, he was floating in mid-air, turning and swaying in a gentle back-and-forth motion. Even the slightest changes to the circulation of air in the room had an impact on how he moved about.

As he floated, he recited a mantra. "Um-bra-numb-da-neigh-ya. Um-bra..."

Tanya stood watching for a few minutes, then Daniel and Brenda walked in to join her. The bruises on Brenda's face were still apparent, despite her medibots working hard at restoring the tissue and skin to their normal state.

Brenda asked Daniel, "I am actually seeing this, aren't I?"

Daniel walked up to the window. "If what *you're* seeing is the same as what *I think* I'm seeing, then yes."

Tanya turned to Brenda, seemingly oblivious to what they were witnessing. "I don't believe we've been introduced. I'm Tanya, Tanya Dyson."

Brenda hadn't even noticed her presence till that point. She found it difficult to take her eyes off Gordon as she replied, "Brenda, Brenda Fleming."

Stepping to one side, Tanya made room for Brenda, then said to Daniel, "I'm so sorry about your wife. I've lost my husband, too, right at the start of this nightmare. Even knowing what I've been through, I still can't begin to imagine how you're feeling."

Daniel bowed his head. A tear ran down Brenda's cheek as she placed a reassuring hand on his shoulder. A long and awkward silence followed before Daniel asked, "Did you hear about DC?"

Tanya nodded. "It feels like a runaway train." She paused for a few seconds before breaking the awkward silence with a change of subject. "I added a type of airlock to the shield specs last night. It'll help movement between communities. Hopefully, we're getting the specs out there fast enough to stop this before it gets too much worse."

Debbie and Ian came racing from the bedroom, the distraction breaking Gordon's concentration and causing him to fall to the floor with a thud.

"Mr Gordy," Debbie's voice conveyed a sense of authority. "What were you doing up there in the first place?"

Despite having injured his ego when he fell, Debbie's scolding brought a smile to his face. "Sorry to upset you, princess. I was testing my newfound understanding of quantum physics."

"Well, surely there are ways you can test your ideas without hurting yourself. I mean, really, what if you came down and hit your head on a piece of furniture?"

Tanya, Brenda and Daniel all broke out laughing. "How *did* you manage to do that?" asked Daniel.

Gordon got to his feet and dusted himself off. "Have you studied much quantum physics?"

"No, I can't say that I have."

"Well, when we've got a few hours to kill, I'll give you a brief explanation."

Tanya added: "—and the mantra. Why the mantra?"

"Strictly speaking, it's not necessary. It helps me focus. That's the first time I've tried it, so I should get more control with practice."

Concerned about her son, Brenda crouched down and put her hands to the glass. "How'd you sleep last night, munchkin?"

"Mr Gordon stayed with us, and we talked for a long time. And he helped me look after Debbie." He looked around as though trying to see who else might be on the other side of the window. "Is Daddy coming to visit, or is he busy working?"

Brenda bit on her lower lip, staring at the ground as she tried to find the words. Her son deserved some manner of explanation. "Ian, honey, Daddy did a *very* bad thing last night. I'm sorry, but he won't be able to come and see you for now."

"Awww... but will we be able to visit him?"

"No, munchkin, I don't think so."

"When can we go home?"

Summoning all the strength she had left, she released a couple of quiet sobs before replying, "We're going to have to—we're going to have to find a new home—" Brenda's composure shattered as she went down on her knees. Unable to hold her emotions back any longer, she cried uncontrollably as her puzzled son looked on.

***

Marco stood in front of the closed gate of the compound, facing the long stretch of road that appeared to go nowhere. He looked across to the gatehouse. A soldier stood making a call through his wristband. "Director Brandt? I have Secretary Fleming here. Yes, that's right, he's attempting to leave the facility."

Marco laughed. "Attempting? I *am* leaving. And you're not going to stop me. That's what I told the piss-weak guard outside my quarters when *he* called your precious director." He stabbed a finger in the soldier's direction. "He got the message. He backed off. Told me the director thought I'd be doing everyone a favour. Hah!"

"Yes, Director. Yes, he still appears quite drunk. Yes, I understand."

Marco pointed to the soldier. "You tell your precious di – rec – tor that I'll be fucked if I'm going to wait around here for some kangaroo court to convict me of treason. I'm outa here."

The soldier finished the call and took the water bottle attached to his belt as he left the gatehouse and approached Marco. He handed Marco the bottle. "The director said I should give you this and wish you luck."

Marco's jaw dropped. "You're seriously not even going to try and stop me?" He looked back toward the bunker and yelled, "Aren't you going to try and stop me? Hey! I'm leaving! Do you hear me?"

The only answer he got was the dry, howling wind.

He snatched the water bottle from the soldier and started walking toward the main gate. "Are you going to open this fucking gate or what?"

The soldier went back into the gatehouse and opened the gate without saying another word. Marco staggered ahead, then stumbled as he crossed through the field barrier. The shock of his medibots, earbuds, lensview and wristband frying as he crossed caused him to lose balance and fall to the ground. He got up, looked back at the gatehouse and yelled, "Fuck you! You could've turned it off, huh? What am I meant to do now? You've left me with nothing! Do you hear me? Nothing!"

The soldier responded by closing the gate, the irritating sound of the metal roller moving along its track cutting through the howling of the wind. There was a clunk as it slid into its final position. "Did you hear me? Fuck you! Fuck the whole lot of you!" He looked at the water bottle in his hand and drew his arm back to throw it at the gatehouse, then thought better of it. If he threw that, he really *would* have nothing.

The former Secretary of Defence turned his back on the bunker. He looked at the long, featureless road and started walking, clutching onto the water bottle.

***

Petra strode out onto the balcony overlooking the massive foyer. Word had spread throughout the day that General Rubeiro was offering sanctuary in his military headquarters to the homeless and dispossessed. He and his mysterious new partner were now in full control and were willing to listen to whatever grievances the citizens of Guangdong felt about how the country had been run.

She looked imposing as she stood with her hands on the railing, wearing nothing but her silk, wraparound skirt, and masses of elaborate, ornate jewellery. She now towered over Barnardo, who stood by her side, compliant and waiting.

A guard blasted a tune from his bugle and announced: "Her Majesty, the

Empress of Guangdong, and Mother of the People, wishes to greet the proud people of the newly claimed realm."

The crowd went silent as all eyes looked toward Petra, her enhanced pheromones beginning their slow journey through the massive foyer.

She spoke in fluent Mandarin. "Proud people of Guangdong, your emperor and I welcome you." A huge cheer rose from the crowd, who, until now, had viewed the building they occupied as a symbol of oppression.

"For too long you have been ignored. For too long, you have been treated with contempt. But now I say unto you, this country is yours. The faceless Mandarins, who oppressed you for so long, no longer have claim to this land." Again, a massive roar erupted from the crowd. "We shall restore freedom to this great nation. Then we shall spread the word and reunite the whole of China under the common purpose of bringing order to a corrupt world. We shall create the new dawn of the Sino age!" She leaned back, soaking up the cheers of the crowd.

She gestured for them to be quiet before continuing, "First, we must make sure that you—the people at the heart of our new world—are warm and well fed. I say unto you, my home is your home, and my food is your food. From this day forward, not one citizen of Guangdong will be seen to go hungry or lack shelter. I hereby command that our troops tear down the tapestries that for too long have towered over you, and that they be cut up to provide blankets to keep you warm tonight. The kitchens shall remain open until every man, woman, and child in this room has eaten their fill."

The eruption of emotion from the crowd was deafening. As the cheering continued, it morphed into a chant that carried on long after Petra had stepped back. "Long live Mother! Long live Mother!"

As the troops began cutting the cables supporting the massive tapestries, Petra turned to the general and gestured toward the chanting crowd. "I give you your new army recruits. And trust me, this is just the beginning. I promise you an army, the like of which the world has never seen. We shall rule over the first ever truly global empire."

Barnardo felt both humbled and in awe at what he'd just witnessed. An urgent message flashed across his lensview. "It seems we have a guest arriving on the rooftop. The Mandarins have sent an emissary to express their displeasure. Apparently, he is delivering an ultimatum."

Petra took his arm in hers as they walked back to their room. "Splendid! He can spend the night with your gift. Then, we can discuss terms in the morning. Come, darling, let's have some dinner. I've worked up quite an appetite."

***

Nancy sat on a rickety old timber barstool, using an old barrel as a table. She stared into her coffee, slowly moving her spoon around the cup as if the action could somehow relieve her angst. Her attention was then drawn to the news report displayed on Nico's media board. Nancy had friends in Washington, many of whom were among those who'd headed for the DUCC. "Whenever I stop for a moment to let it sink in," she said, "I find myself thinking it can't be real." The aerials of the bombed-out stadium were too much for her, coming on top of her extreme tiredness. She started to feel faint, then felt a warm and reassuring hand on her shoulder, shaking her.

"Nancy, hey, are you okay?"

The voice seemed distant, but when Nancy looked up, she saw Kallan's face, reminding her of the urgency of her mission. How could she enlist this woman's help if she couldn't even stay awake? Sitting upright again, Nancy took a deep breath. "Sorry, I started to lose it for a moment there."

"Hey, that's okay, it's hard to look at news like this." They sat in silence for a moment, Kallan staring at her companion as Nancy slowly lifted her coffee to take a sip. "You know what?" asked Kallan. "It would really help me decide whether or not to help you if I had a clearer picture of what you expect. Although I suspect I already know most of it."

"To be honest, I'm so tired I'm a bit hazy on the detail. I was hoping you might be able to help me out a bit on forging some clarity into the plans."

"Yeah, I get it, you're way too tired to think clearly. The thing is, the reason people directed you to me is because of my rapport with the Amish I deal with. You're concerned they'll resist the idea of using the shield generators, so you want *me* to convince them for you."

Nancy shrugged. "Yeah, that's about as far as I got with it."

Kallan put a hand to her brow as though massaging away pain. She looked at Nancy with an expression that pleaded to be left out of the whole mess. "It's a big ask. The Amish I deal with trust me because… they trust me because I've always dealt fairly with them. And because I respect them. Everyone else they deal with is wearing a wristband and focused more on the prices flicking through their lensview than the person they're talking to. I always leave mine in the glove compartment when I'm here."

"I'd noticed," replied Nancy. "I'd tried contacting you before coming here, but your wristband was switched off."

"I'm telling you, though, if I go out to their properties with a bunch of people they don't know, that trust won't count for much. There's also the problem of dealing with Jacob—Jacob Graber. He's almost like, let's say, a 'godfather' figure throughout much of the community. And it's a large community that influences many more. No one *ever* stands against what he says. He's the one we *really* need to win over."

Nancy straightened up. "You just said 'we'. Does that mean you're in?"

Kallan ignored the question and looked up again at the screen and its repetitious images of the devastation in Washington. "I haven't made up my mind yet. I only came in here to stock up on the foodstuffs I was short of before heading up to the mountains." She turned back to Nancy. "I'd be well and truly gone by now if you hadn't shown up. But the goodies that printer could produce? That's something that *would* make a difference. But, I don't know…"

"Without those shield generators, nobody's safe," said Nancy. "You want to protect your family? Well, the decision's yours." Nancy drained her coffee. "How about this: as well as the printer, I'll organise a military escort to take your family wherever you want, right now. They can be on their way without delay. Then I can have a chopper fly you in to meet them once we're done."

"Do you realise how many Amish are out there? It's going to take time to convince all of them to accept it. How long do you expect this deployment to take?"

"My plan—the one I'm making up as I go—is based on *you* convincing them to trust the technology is safe. I can show you how to teach them the skills needed to produce the units to deploy around their communities—show them how to do it *themselves*. Then, we get you out of there. We can't *make* them do this, but it's our obligation to give them a chance."

Kallan stood up and called out to gain Nico's attention, "Hey, Nico, can we have two more to go here, please?" After a nod from Nico, she turned her attention back to Nancy. "You've got a printer organised for them?"

"I can have one anywhere in the state within an hour."

"Good, he's no fool, you know. The things the Amish travel into the town to buy... It's the stuff they can't provide for themselves. That will need to come from somewhere. The trading they come in here for won't be viable anymore."

"Do you think this Jacob guy might accept the offer?"

"Hard to say. The Amish have closed themselves off from the rest of the world more than ever since the advent of medibots and the like. And he's the one who's galvanised their attitudes. Which also makes him the only real hope you've got of getting those shields deployed. But, if you really want their trust, we have to arrive at his farm on our own—no soldiers or security personnel."

Nancy asked, "What do you mean when you say *we*?"

"I mean that if you think I'm going in without dragging you along, then you can find yourself some other schmuck."

The ultimatum drained away the last of Nancy's energy reserves. She nodded in acknowledgement, her hope of getting some sleep slipping ever further away.

"It'll be okay, drink up," said Kallan. "We'll get you cleaned up and into some fresh clothes. I've got another dress in my truck that should fit, and there's a washroom out the back where you can splash some water on your face. I should still have enough room on the truck for the printer, too."

***

Marco Fleming looked a mess as he walked down the road, the same one Gordon and Craig had arrived on the day before. Their car, having been overrun by nanobots, had spread the plague over the whole route they'd travelled. Now, Marco was walking through a swirling mass of nanobots, oblivious to their existence.

He'd missed the opportunity to shower or change clothes, so his shirt front was torn and covered in bloodstains. His trousers were soiled, and he was now wearing his tie as a sweatband. It was a struggle to breathe through his broken and bloodied nose, and his blackened eye was almost completely closed.

He'd been walking for only a few minutes when he took in a breath that was rich in nanobots.

He stopped to take a sip from his water bottle, *Damn it*, he thought. *I'm thirsty. How the hell am I going to make this last till I hitch a ride?* He replaced the bottle's cap and kept walking. *I need shade, somewhere I can sleep for a while. Of all places to be stuck in this situation, why here? Why does it have to be the Badlands?* He stopped and tried to take in his surroundings. There was a rocky outcrop to the west. *There's got to be some shade there.*

It took him further from the road, killing his chances of hitching a ride. *Fuck the road. I need sleep.*

215

He was halfway to the outcrop when it started to get difficult to maintain his balance. He opened the water bottle again, but then thought better of it.

He got down on his hands and knees and started crawling. The ground was so hot that it burned his fingertips, forcing him to use his elbows to carry himself through.

He was utterly exhausted when he reached the shelter of the rocks twenty minutes later. The knees of his trousers were torn, as was his skin. He collapsed to the ground and fell into a deep sleep.

***

Emily sat down on her couch, eating breakfast. Although she was due at an emergency briefing in the Cabinet Room, she needed a few minutes to eat in peace before facing what remained of the Security Council.

She took her first mouthful, and there was a knock on her door. Tongue in cheek, she called out, "If it's not another catastrophic situation, you can come in. It's open."

Daniel entered the room without saying a word. "Hey, how are you holding up?" asked Emily.

"I'd be a lot better if you hadn't allowed your former secretary of defence to be abandoned to die in the desert."

Emily glared at her chief of staff. "What on Earth are you talking about?"

"Marco, a man you've worked with and known since coming to office. A man who has a wife and child. He left the facility—walked out into the desert. You must have known about this."

Emily held her gaze as she pushed her plate aside, then took her time to chew and swallow her food. "Before you go any further," she said. "I've got no idea what you're talking about. I'd also like to ask: Are we talking about the individual responsible for what happened in Washington? You *did* see what happened to Brenda, didn't you? Now, how about you explain to me what's going on?"

Daniel replied, "Are you trying to tell me you knew nothing about this? Marco left the facility late last night. He walked out into the wilderness. He passed through the barrier, frying all his tech.'

"Okay, to begin with, he was *actually* being held by the GIA. And the way I feel right now, if he's escaped and gone out there, then maybe I don't really care that much."

"*Your* prisoner escaped from *your* facility," said Daniel.

"You know what? Right now, that's not at the top of our priority list."

"God, Emily! Can't you see? Is what he did really *that* different from New Haven? The tech had already been detected. If Marco didn't do it, either Brandt or FIDO—or maybe even *you,* for that matter—would have probably done what he did within hours anyway."

"Don't you *dare* presume to know what decision I would have made."

Daniel let out a slight chuckle before asking, "So, you're happy for him to be wandering toward an almost certain death?"

"I really don't need this."

"What happened to the Emily Lucas that I, and everyone else, voted for?"

"I can't believe we're even having this conversation."

"The one who stood in front of cheering crowds, declaring civilisations are best judged by how well they treat their worst?"

"You're out of line."

"Who said the standard you walk past is the one you accept? Where is she?

"You need to stop, now!"

"Can you tell me? Because I can't see her anywhere near here this morning."

Emily's intense stare held Daniel in a vice-like grip as she replied. "You want to lecture me about morals? You seriously think his apparent escape should top my priority list right now? He's been your friend for years. I get that. But he's also a drunk, a fool and a cowardly bully. Most of all, though, he's committed *treason*. Right now, why exactly should I care what happens to him?

"So, if he dies out there, how does Brenda tell her son—her son that she can no longer hold in her arms—that he'll never be able to see his father again?"

"I don't need you pretending to be some sort of Jiminy Cricket," said Emily, "trying to behave like you're my moral compass."

"Did you give any thought to his boy? To Brenda?"

"There are hundreds of thousands of people across America who have died during all this. It's been on my watch. But you know what? He's directly responsible for one hell of a lot of the ones who should still be with us."

"That doesn't mean you should leave him to die of dehydration, stripped of whatever dignity—"

"Enough!."

Daniel turned to walk out, then stopped before reaching the door. "This is not the Emily Lucas I know." Daniel stood, waiting for Emily's reply. None came. "You can find yourself a new chief of staff. Have fun at the briefing." He strode out the door.

Emily took a deep breath. *Here we go,* she thought as she rose from the couch. "Daniel, wait!" She raced out to the corridor. "Maybe *you're* right." Daniel stopped walking. "Maybe we shouldn't just let him die out there. Send someone out to pick him up if you must.

Daniel didn't respond.

"We've both got a lot to be angry about right now, and I can't imagine your grief. I can tell you one thing, though: this little conversation hasn't helped."

Daniel looked over his shoulder for a brief moment.

Emily took a step toward him. "You've just lost Elizabeth, I know that. But there's too much at stake right now. I can't let you walk away from this. I need you—and I need you focused—now! The whole goddamned world needs you. There is no one we can just drop into your role; it's too important. But Daniel, I'm only going to say this once. We need to make sure we're on the same page. I'll give you this one, I'll let your little outburst go, and we won't talk about it again. But, if we're going to get through this? You can't *ever* defy me like that again." She paused for a moment and asked, "Is that clear?"

He nodded in acknowledgement, then walked away.

***

Jon Kruick and Mary Killen walked the road in silence. Jon carried a large automatic weapon in one hand, while he held Mary's free hand in the other, guiding her through the dark night as she carried her grandson.

It was difficult to make out where they were walking, even at the edge of the road, and the letter from her son continued to haunt her. "I don't know Jon…" She left the sentence unfinished, unsure what she wanted to say.

Jon gave her hand a gentle squeeze as they continued along the road, hand in hand, forging a growing bond between them that made Mary feel safer with every step. Nanobots used their palms as a pathway to move from one to the other, creating an extended network that allowed them to share thoughts and feelings as no two people had done before. The developing link felt as normal to them as breathing. Both had already experienced the burning, and both had been focused on protection at the time. Their common purpose presented an enhanced potential for success through combining the resources of their quantum networks. Nanobots gathering in their genital regions and saliva anticipated a large-scale transfer, a transfer that would solidify their connection. The drive to do so was near impossible to ignore.

Mary looked at Jon, speaking to him through her thoughts. *"I worried when Jason left us at the crash scene. But to be honest, I feel so much safer now, here with you."*

Jon turned to her as he spoke out loud. "I'm touched, Mary, but as much as I've got a strong right arm and a dirty great motherfucker of a gun…" He looked at the barren landscape around them. "… we're in the Badlands, on our own, with no food and little water."

"Yet it feels *so good* to be walking together, don't you think?" replied Mary.

They stopped and looked at each other. The chemistry they felt in that moment transcended what either of them had ever experienced. Neither was aware of how strong a role the nanotech played in their mutual attraction.

Jon looked away, smiling. "It's best we don't get too distracted. We've got a long road ahead, and I don't fancy our chances of hitching a ride." He let go of her hand and gestured toward Merrick. The boy was rubbing his eyes and yawning from time-to-time. "How about I carry him now?"

She handed the toddler across, appreciative for the break. She felt compelled to slip her hand through his arm, feeling a need to maintain physical contact as they walked on in silence. She rested her head against his shoulder, and for the first time she could remember, Mary Killen smiled.

Jon scanned their surroundings when first light illuminated the landscape. "We'll find somewhere to rest and shelter from the sun before it gets higher, close to the road so we've got a chance to flag down any passing vehicles." He pointed to a rocky outcrop a few kilometres ahead. "That should do us. It'll take half an hour or more to get there, so we'd best get moving."

The outcrop featured a rock overhang that provided perfect shelter while allowing a clear view of the road in both directions. Once there, Jon handed Merrick back to Mary. He took off his shirt to create an extra blanket for the boy. Mary found a spot to lay him down that seemed well-protected. As Merrick drifted off to sleep, she became transfixed by the sight of Jon's body. It had been years since she'd felt anything when looking at a man. Now, she found herself short of breath, unable to resist the urge to run a finger down his chest. An electric sensation ran through her whole body. For a few moments, they stood there frozen, exploring what it was like to be so fully aware of another's longing. Jon looked into her eyes. He gently slipped the jacket off her shoulders, then caressed her neck. His wandering hand found the strap of her dress and carefully pulled it off her shoulder. As it slid down her arm, he followed its progress with his lips. Mary's breathing grew heavier as Jon's lips worked back up the side of her neck. They made eye contact for a brief moment, then their lips came together.

A rush of nanobots mingled in their mouths, fuelling the blending of their networks.

Mary grabbed his hand, placing it firmly on her breast. Jon pulled her dress down further and brought his mouth over her hardened nipple. A surge of excitement rushed through her.

They stripped away each other's clothing and then made love, feeling transported to another place. Their mutual awareness of each other's pleasure made the experience intense beyond anything either had experienced. To be so intimately aware of another was beyond what they'd thought possible.

They reached climax together, a wild rush of nanobots moving between them, further cementing the link. From this moment, each would be forever aware of the other's thoughts and feelings, their quantum networks having fully merged to become one.

Jon ran his fingers through her hair. "Mary Killen, I promise you, I will never leave your side."

Pulling him close and kissing him on the lips, she replied through thought. *I know you won't.* She paused, then laughed while whispering in his ear, "There's a risk that I may be falling in love with you, Jon Kruick."

"I've never known love before," he said. "Not real love. I'd given up on finding it, until now." He stood up and looked toward the horizon. "I'll take the first watch of the road. You should get settled with Merrick and get some sleep."

Mary drifted off while Jon paced protectively in front of her. Watching her sleep, he felt her calmness as though he was experiencing it for himself. He also felt the lingering pain so deeply embedded in the background of her mind.

***

The mood in the Cabinet Room was bleak, with the shock of Washington, D.C. still sinking in. Everyone needed more sleep.

"I'd like to start by acknowledging the enormous loss and grief we all feel," said Peter. "The last two days have taken their toll. With the events of this morning in DC, we've lost countless friends, relatives and colleagues. The fact that a recent member of the Executive bore much of the initial responsibility for the calamity can only serve to make the events weigh even heavier upon each of us. It's been many years since North America has fallen prey to such horrific acts of terror.

"On behalf of the United Nations Security Council, I wish to express our great sorrow and condolences. However, we must also acknowledge that we are in the grip of a crisis with a broader reach than last night's act of terror. With the crippling of the UNSA's elected government, it is more important than ever to focus on the enormous task at hand. Maria, can you please distribute this morning's agenda?"

An array of notes was visible on the smart table in front of the representative for South America. She flicked her fingers across the surface, sending the agenda and accompanying notes to each participant's lensview, creating an illusion of the notes ending up suspended above the table until each of them accepted the paperwork into their wristbands.

Louise swiped her own wristband, creating a three-dimensional image high up over the table's centre. It showed an enormous crater where the Hartford stadium had once been. "Drones sent in since the attack have been unable to verify whether we were successful. So far, no sound or movement has been detected." She walked around the table as she talked. "I'll be sending the data to Doctor Delaney for his expert opinion."

"You'll do *what?*" asked Domango.

"I'm not happy about that either," said Peter. "He's a fugitive from justice, *and* he's been mutated by the very technology we're threatened by. Why risk it?"

"Why not?" asked Daniel. "Have any of you even spoken to Delaney? I have, and I can assure you, there's *no way* he's a threat. If he were, we'd have been dead hours ago. Do any of you understand what this guy's capable of?"

"That's the whole problem," Peter replied. "He's an unknown quantity, and *that* makes him dangerous. The most important surviving world leaders are in this bunker. Having someone who is so potentially dangerous here is, in itself, an unacceptable risk. But to work with him? To trust him with such sensitive data?"

"He's also the most powerful quantum computer we have access to." Louise countered. "With FIDO offline, we need him. Delaney could be the difference between life and death. My job is all about assessing risks, and I agree with Daniel; he is *not* a threat."

"This urgency to analyse the data... are you implying this groundfish thing could've survived that attack?" asked Nick. "Face it, we blew the fucker out of existence."

Louise glared at Nick as she responded. "We have two scientists from the facility that spawned this thing. When even they're unsure how it even came into being, how can you be sure it's destroyed? It's a new life form. We need the people who best understand the technology that spawned it to help us be sure. But what would scientists know, compared to career politicians like you? Well, I couldn't give a flying fuck about your opinion. We continue on the assumption it's still alive, and as much of a threat as it was yesterday."

"That's enough, Director Brandt!" said Peter. "We're facing enough battlefronts without fighting each other, and we need to be mindful of how we allocate resources. Yeah, I hear what you're saying, but it's the opinion of the Council that we should assume the assault was successful."

"Since when were you and the Council experts in this field?" asked Louise.

"Since it became clear that, without FIDO's advice to rely on, you need to consult with us *and accept* direction from the—"

"Hey!" snapped Emily. "I *still* have a say in these matters. It's *my* country that's borne the brunt of this. Aside from the terrorist attack in Washington DC, most of the damage so far has come from our *own* weapons. I've had to sit by and watch this happen, some of it I've even been party to. And, let me tell you, *it has not been easy.* And you know what? After this meeting, I have to go and make yet *another* public statement."

"If that's the case, I'll lighten your load and have Maria prepare one for you," said Peter. "So the message is consistent with the view of the council."

Emily shook her head. "Absolutely not. I'm going to tell the truth. We cannot—and I will not—lie by saying we know that thing's dead."

"For crying out loud. Of course it's dead," Peter replied.

"We don't know that. The people still near that stadium deserve to know it may still be a threat," said Emily. "If we tell them it's destroyed, and it takes more people tomorrow, we'll have a population that won't trust a word we say. I will take my anger with what Director Brandt did in New York and New Haven to my grave. But having said that, I also have to admit, she's got more balls than anyone else in this room. And it is a huge expectation that *all* of us place on her every day."

"But Emily, don't you see?" asked Domango. "That's the problem in a nutshell. A job like that is far too demanding for one person to make such decisions without checks and balances in place. Without FIDO, she needs guidance, and there's no higher moral authority on Earth than the Council."

"What a load of horseshit!" said Emily. "Do you actually see yourselves as bastions of morality? You think you actually have the capacity to make the hard decisions, ones that have to be made in an instant? Seriously? I know I couldn't do it. You seriously think you could?"

"You sell yourself short," said Louise. "You're far more capable of behaving like a cold-hearted bitch than you give yourself credit for. You're showing great potential."

Emily placed a hand over her heart. "I feel so touched by your praise. But I sincerely doubt I can ever match the incredibly high standard you've set on that score."

"While these clowns have been concerned with interruptions to trade, you've remained focused on keeping people alive and fostering hope," said Louise, calm and deadpan as ever. "Our approaches may be different, but on the most important issue, we agree—lives come before trade."

"The Council has a broader mandate," said Nick. "We're obliged to look at the bigger picture."

Peter said, "Given we're not likely to reach a consensus, I suggest it's best if we move on from the Hartford issue for now. We need to look at how the destruction at DC came about."

"My gut says it's General Rubeiro," said Louise.

"You're kidding, aren't you?" replied Peter. "You actually think that one man could be behind *all* these things?"

"The jihadists don't have the resources to organise something on this scale, not without his help," she said. "My guess is that the jihadists worked in concert with him; that it was planned to coincide with the Infinity blast *and* the sabotage of FIDO. It's too much of a coincidence to be otherwise."

"I'm sorry," Peter shook his head dismissively. "That hypothesis just doesn't add up. You've been pointing the finger at him since this started. While there may be some anecdotal evidence, it's inconclusive at best. Trust me, I've dealt with the man. None of this is his style. He's always been bold and upfront about his intentions. And, I have to ask, where's his motive?"

"He craves power. Throughout history, those who crave power have never been happy unless their power continues to grow. He's no different," said Louise.

Emily couldn't hide her frustration. "Can we *please* forget about who the culprits are for the moment and focus on the needs of the survivors? We need to restore a functional government before anarchy breaks out. Surely that's more important right now than who's to blame. It's a waste of time if we sit here in our bunker making plans if there's no functional government structure to follow them through."

Louise nodded. "Agreed."

The rest of the room silently followed her lead.

"We need to act on this immediately," said Emily. "Once we leave this room, I'll task Daniel with contacting every governor from the thirty-eight states of the Union so we can establish an emergency congress. There are protocols in place, but they're yet to be tested. Later today, I'll schedule a teleconference. I'll also be calling for volunteers from neighbouring areas, doctors, nurses, engineers—anyone who can lend a hand. I intend to declare next Monday a national day of mourning. The people need a vehicle to express their grief, a day where, as a nation, we can collectively mourn our losses." She turned to Daniel. "I know you've just lost Elizabeth, but I need you now like never before. Are you up for it?"

Before Daniel had time to respond, Maria said, "South America's free of major problems so far. I'm more than happy to help Daniel make the calls."

"Whoa, let's just hold on a minute." Peter raised his hands in defiance. "Maria, it's a very kind and generous offer, but it's not for you to be making those decisions. You and Domango need to share the burden of picking up the Council's responsibilities in Europe. You heard the reports. The nano-plague has been detected there now as well. We need to keep a lid on it. I'd deal with it personally, except what's happening both here and in Guangdong looks set to take up the bulk of my time. Nick can give Daniel a hand. After all, it's his turf."

Nick said, "Or maybe a more appropriate approach would be if Rick and I talked to the South about formulating an agreement of cooperation between the UNSA and the Confederate States. Emily's idea of an emergency congress isn't workable. We need regional cooperation."

Emily kept her voice steady and calm so nobody could misinterpret her. "My government will not, under *any* circumstances, recognise that ignorant, religious nut job. That is completely non-negotiable."

"*Your* government?" Nick let out a snide chuckle. "The way I see it, you don't have much of a government anymore. Acting on behalf of the Security Council,

I've already accepted his request for recognition of the Confederate States of America as a theocracy. The pragmatic course of action is to open a personal dialogue with Granger, in exchange for his government's assistance."

"And what assistance do you suggest that might be?" asked Emily.

"Oh, you know, restoring order in DC and getting the general machinery of government going again."

"You are joking, aren't you? The guy staged a coup, shamelessly taking advantage of a crisis, and now you want to give him a whole lot of power over parts of the UNSA as well? You can't be serious."

"Nick's got a point," said Peter. "It makes sense under the circumstances."

"Like hell it does. Granger's a zealot who sees anyone who doesn't buy into his Book of Circles crap as an infidel. I absolutely *don't* need or want his help," said Emily.

"Come on, Emily. FIDO is gone," replied Peter. "That changes everything. Louise will have to rely on direction from the Council; she won't have a choice in the matter. And she'll need *your* support in implementing our directives. But at the same time, a good deal of the executive and bureaucracy that *you* rely on simply isn't there anymore. The way I see it, you're going to have to cede some of your responsibilities for any solution to be workable. Nick's absolutely right. An alliance with the South makes sense under the circumstances."

"I'm a better judge of what I can and can't do than you'll ever be." The coldness in Louise's eyes as she stared down Peter could have extinguished the fires of Hell. "It would take you a month to make a call on any one of the lesser decisions I make every day. You think my job's tougher without FIDO? You've no idea of how much unnecessary work that mess of artificial intelligence created. And the best contribution President Lucas can make right now is to continue what she's doing. If you were smart enough to pay attention, you'd understand there's a reason law and order aren't already an even bigger issue across the nation. When she speaks, she reaches out to ordinary people, giving them hope." She resumed her habit of walking as she spoke, coming to a stop just behind Nick's chair. "Tell me, Nick, what's your plan? Let me guess, you want to strip the President of some of her powers, sidelining her as much as you can, while elevating Dodson as acting vice president?"

Nick shrugged his shoulders, "I thought it'd make for a pretty good team."

"You only want to elevate him because you think he's easy to control," said Louise, "to be *your* little puppet." She looked across at Peter. "But it's more than that, isn't it? You and Nick have been planning this all along. Once you had Rick in place as acting vice president, you were planning to find a reason to try and force President Lucas to step aside."

"That's one hell of an accusation you're making there," yelled Peter in response.

Louise gave a small nod. "It seems I've touched a raw nerve."

"Were you in on this?" Emily asked Rick. "Is that why you've been so quiet?"

"What choice did I have?" he replied. "Nick came to me this morning with news that the vice president was unaccounted for in the DUCC. He said that, as Secretary of State, I'm the next in line and that it would be a mere formality anyway. He said there was a good chance that, the way things were unfolding, you might have no choice but to resign. He said he thought I could end up going all the way." Rick broke down momentarily, then continued in a shaky voice, "My family are unaccounted for. If I were to end up as *president,* I'd have a much better chance of finding them."

"And you accepted *Nick's* word on that? You do know, don't you, that under the constitution, it's up to me to pick a new acting vice president?"

"I'm sorry, Emily. It wasn't personal."

"I'm not quite sure how you can define that as *not personal.* You were willing to accept an unconstitutional promotion, offered to you by Nick, that would have greatly undermined my authority. That's unambiguously personal from where I sit."

"I'm so sorry—"

"Sorry doesn't quite cut it. Look, I understand you're feeling distraught, but what the fuck, Rick? It's no excuse. I should have you fired as Secretary of State, effective immediately." She turned to Daniel. "But it's also clear I need to decide on a new acting vice president here and now. And it looks like you're it. I know it'll be a juggling act for you, but there's no one else. You can have whatever resources we can muster up under the circumstances. Since this crisis began, you've already been largely fulfilling the responsibilities that officially go with that role anyway. But as of now, that'll be your primary role and official title. We'll swear you in at the earliest opportunity."

Daniel nodded. "Thank you," he said. "I'll do what I can."

Emily turned her attention back to Rick. "I want you to listen very carefully. Colluding with Nick and the Council to undermine my authority? That's inexcusable. But your experience will be critical to helping us get through this. It's imperative that you assist Daniel in any way you can."

"Yes, Madam President."

"And by the way, we *will* do everything possible to find your family, along with every other family among the thousands that are missing. But there *will not* be priority given to any one family over another."

Rick discreetly wiped away a tear that had trickled down his cheek. He sat up straight, an apparent effort to restore some lost dignity. "Thank you, Madam President."

"What the hell?" Peter jumped from his chair. "The Council already agreed on this! There's no room for debate."

"Sorry, I can't go along with it anymore." Rick's voice was meek. "What you guys got me to agree to? It was wrong, and it always was. I wouldn't even *be* here now if President Lucas hadn't appointed me."

Peter stared at Rick in disbelief.

Louise wore a sinister grin. "Well, Peter, your little plan's been exposed for all to see now. Install Rick as vice president, then manufacture a trigger to force Emily into stepping aside. But it looks like your little coup just crumbled in a heap." She walked across and whispered in Peter's ear, "Maybe you should try actually having a *credible* plan in place next time you take advantage of a human tragedy to advance your own ambitions."

Emily leaned back into her chair. "It's a sad reflection on some of those seated in this room that such a proposal came up at all." Observing how Louise and Peter were glaring at each other, she reminded herself of the old adage: *The enemy of my enemy is my friend.*

"I didn't realise you were so small-minded," said Peter. "In case you hadn't noticed, I'm *already* the chair of the Security Council. Technically, that makes *me* the most powerful person on the planet. You *accuse me of staging a coup?* What for? I've already got the power!"

Louise replied, "You should choose your words more carefully. There are two women in this room who exercise more *real* power than you'll ever have."

"I get it," said Domango. "You two don't like each other. But can we put power plays aside for now? We've still got serious issues to work through. Let's deal with those, then, you can go your separate ways, and do whatever."

"Domango's right," said Maria. "We haven't even touched on the ramifications for the nuclear stockpiles from FIDO going down."

Louise returned to her seat and resumed her usual detached manner as though nothing untoward had happened. "We suspect the sabotage was carried out using mining bots precisely programmed to target the quantum processors. Two of them retain limited surveillance capabilities. But they're little more than data collection tools now."

"And let me guess, you're going to continue to push the notion that the perpetrators are in Guangdong," said Nick.

Louise let herself display a wry smile. "For once, there's something you're right about."

"Yes, but what about the nukes?" asked Domango.

"The launch codes rely on high-level quantum encryption, theoretically impossible to crack. If we want to use them, the launch systems will need to have their software stripped down and virtually rebuilt from scratch. But someone with the right technological capabilities could still do it in a matter of days."

"So, are we safe from the possibility of a rogue state getting hold of them and doing just that?" asked Domango.

"For this week, maybe next. But I don't see it as an immediate threat," replied Louise. "There are more pressing problems we need to deal with."

"I agree," said Emily. "Particularly the current status on the shield deployments."

Domango asked, "Is that *really* a priority?"

"My wife is *dead*," replied Daniel, "and my daughter's contaminated. How could you possibly question the urgency of the deployment?"

"While I understand how you must be feeling," said Domango, "you need to understand it from my perspective. Africa is on the other side of the planet, well away from this. Why should the whole world suffer to protect ourselves from something that's essentially an American problem?"

"I've talked extensively with Dyson and Delaney to try and comprehend what we're dealing with—what my daughter's having to deal with right now," replied Daniel. "If you get contaminated by just *one* of these nanobots, within half an hour it will have attached itself to the DNA within one of your cells and replicated. At that pace, it only takes twenty-four hours before every one of the forty-odd trillion cells in your body will be hijacked by one of these nanobots. Think that's bad? It's typically when that process is about halfway that the nanobots establish a permanent interface with the brain." He stopped and bowed his head for a moment, choking back tears as he continued, "Once that happens—the whole process—it's irreversible."

"So, does that mean it's reversible before then?" asked Maria.

"Using an EMP at the right frequency? Yes, if Elizabeth had arrived just a few hours earlier, she could have come through with Debbie, and we'd—" Daniel was visibly struggling to hold back tears. "—we'd all be here, together." He looked up and stared at Domango. "I don't give a damn right now about world trade. If saving lives triggers the next great depression, then so be it." He punched a finger into the table to emphasise his words. "We need to protect *every* citizen in *every* part of the world from this nightmare."

The director leaned across and tapped Emily on the shoulder. "Your new vice president is off to a great start."

Peter glared at Louise. "Perhaps, when you're through chatting up the president, you could update us on what's happening regarding the deployment?"

A sardonic grin spilled across her face as she held Peter's gaze. "Pressure getting to you?" She flicked the files around the table. "This is the feedback from cities and towns across the planet, with their current status. Africa is woefully behind, a direct result of Domango's reticence. In fact, the entire deployment has been slower than it needs to be, courtesy of Peter's little speech yesterday."

"I said what needed to be said."

"You deliberately sowed doubt. Now we're facing problems everywhere. It was already bad before then, with the jihadist Islamic states and other autocratic regimes having placed total bans on deployment. That on its own has caused a massive tide of refugees fleeing Pakistan, Afghanistan, and Kashmir. We've now had to set up shields over makeshift camps in Iran, India, and Xinjiang. Despite providing air support to the refugees, there have been several massacres at the hands of jihadists."

Peter said, "There must be something the GIA can do to discourage people from fleeing those areas."

Louise shook her head. "Not without lying about their safety. The nanotech *has* reached parts of Europe, and it appears it's in Guangdong as well. You need to consider how easily this travels. Small amounts have almost certainly reached most parts of the globe. There's almost certainly contamination among some of the refugees by now."

"And your strategy for dealing with them?" he asked.

"Everyone who arrives at the camps needs to do so by passing through the shield, destroying whatever nanotech they may have."

"But, the contaminated ones, the ones where it's reached their brainstem, they'll die," said Daniel.

"If you have a better idea, let me know."

"There must be *some* way you can screen without killing them in the process." He pleaded.

"Within the next few hours, between ten and twenty million people will be seeking shelter in those camps. Do you seriously want to run conclusive scans on each individual? We don't have the time or the resources."

Daniel was visibly trembling with anger. "Isn't it your duty to ensure people are *safe* when they arrive at those camps?"

Louise stood up and snapped back at him. "I don't enjoy having to make decisions that lead to loss of life, but when I do, I do it because it's the only way to save *more* lives. I have no choice. The fact is, *someone* has to do it. And unfortunately, that someone is invariably me."

Daniel couldn't help but continue to poke the hornet's nest. "So, you had a choice when you nuked New Haven?"

"We've been over this before, if I didn't do it—."

"There had to be a better way!"

"As I said before, when you find it, let me know."

"Hey!" said Peter. "We could easily spend the next hour debating ethics. But this is *not* the time for that."

The director sat down and returned once again to her usual deadpan manner, "Another big concern is the Confederate States, where deployment is only happening in Circumfren strongholds." She glared at Nick. "As the North American representative, it's *your* responsibility to convince Granger to facilitate broader deployment."

"I think that could be possible, in exchange for formal recognition of his legitimacy by the UNSA."

Emily groaned. "For fuck's sake. Have you learnt nothing from history?"

"Hey, I love reading history. I'm a big fan. Your point is?"

"Hitler? Poland? Appeasement, the whole World War Two thing? You can't make deals with these people. Do you really think he'll honour any agreement you or I take to him?"

"We're just getting sidetracked again," said Peter. "Can I suggest Emily, Daniel, Nick, and I have a more cordial chat about this later?"

"Given we still need to discuss the apparent coup in Guangdong, I think that's an excellent suggestion," said Maria.

"I've got to say, Louise, it puzzles me." Peter leaned back in his chair. "Just a week ago, this Doctor Chan was one of your most trusted staff. Now, it seems she's taken on a new persona: Empress of Guangdong. Doesn't that strike you as rather alarming?"

"I employed her after she'd been cleared by FIDO and put forward by the Council as one of its preferred candidates" Louise paused as she collected her thoughts. "A better question might be why you've allowed Guangdong, a country under your watch, to privatise its security apparatus and become so horrifically corrupt."

"We have to respect the sovereignty of individual nations on how they intend to handle security and foreign policy. And we removed their nukes after that privatisation took place, or have you forgotten those details?"

"You could, and you should have intervened more," Louise said flatly. "But that's not even the main issue here. I'm less concerned about how Guangdong got where it is than the danger it poses now. The approach Chan and Rubeiro are taking shows they have expansionist ambitions." Louise stood and scanned the room, ensuring she had everyone's attention. "Despite the delays and other problems in the shield deployment, now that it's underway, our next priority *must* be containing the threat from Guangdong, or we'll end up facing a global military conflict in addition to the nano-plague. And we need to stop them *before* they gain access to nuclear weapons."

Peter's reply reeked of sarcasm: "Okay, so do you have a plan?"

"We have troops from Jiangxi, Guizhou, and Fujian covering some of the borders with air support, and battle groups from Taiwan and Japan covering the coast. Guangxi and Hunan have declared neutrality but will likely fall in with Guangdong. They'll move on Hong Kong first, where we believe the former government leaders are located. If we do too much now, it'll be a mistake that we'll pay for dearly. The coalition working with us to defend the borders is fragile. They may be mostly UN troops, but they maintain local allegiances. We'll have a stronger force in a few days, when they're joined by troops from Tibet and Mongolia. They still have strong memories of the Russian-Mongolian nanotech incident."

Peter paced the room. "But do you have any idea *when* they might launch this supposed attack on Hong Kong?"

"If it were me, I'd do it now, particularly while the West is distracted by Washington."

"What about air strikes?" asked Domango. "We have vastly superior air power at our disposal."

"No, a partial naval blockade of Hong Kong is the only viable option until they've actually attacked. Even then, we'll need to wait for the dust to settle before taking strong action. There's very little we can do if we want to hold the coalition together."

"So, can we stop them?" asked Daniel.

"Hong Kong will fall. The best we can do is take out some of their forces in the process of trying to evacuate likely targets after they've gone in." The director stood up and prepared to leave the room. "Now, if you'll excuse me, I have work to do."

"Hold on," Peter gestured for her to sit down again. "We still have to discuss what to do about the children and Doctor Delaney."

"There's nothing to discuss," Louise responded through clenched teeth as she approached the door.

"We have a situation where the core leadership of the UNSA, GIA, *and* the Security Council are all gathered together in this one god-foresaken facility." Peter raised his voice as he continued, "Security of this facility is our highest priority right now. You of all people should understand that."

"They're not a problem."

"They're an unacceptable risk."

Emily rose to her feet, pointing an accusing finger at Peter. "If we lose sight of our humanity, right *here*, in this bunker, then we're fighting a losing battle. This isn't about protecting leadership structures, it's about protecting who we are as a race."

Peter scoffed. "You're not suggesting I mean the children harm, are you? They need to be moved to another facility, that's all. One where they can be cared for by qualified health professionals."

"And Delaney?"

"He poses a threat to international security. He should be either removed or neutralised."

"Meaning, you want to kill him."

"In the absence of being able to move him to a secure location without risk of him escaping, yeah, you bet I do."

"What law did he break, Peter? Surviving a blast that killed all but two people? Since when was it a crime to not get killed? And since when did *you* have a say in national security matters like this anyway?"

"Those two men fled a scene of massive contamination, without having been cleared by qualified medical professionals. They're contaminated and have been spreading this goddamned machine plague wherever they go. How many people have been infected as a result? For all we know, they could have been the ones responsible for the contamination of Daniel's wife and daughter."

Silence filled the room in response to Peter's blatant insensitivity.

Louise stood in the doorway, laughing. Everyone turned to her. "Didn't you bother to listen to the President? Do you really think you have a say in this? Delaney is a fugitive from a situation that comes under *my* jurisdiction. Therefore, he and the children are actually *my* responsibility. I've got enough blood on my hands, and I take responsibility for every last drop of it. These children each have a parent here, at the facility. They pose no threat while in quarantine, and I will *not* add to my list of sins by separating them from their remaining parents. They are innocent and will be treated as such. As for Delaney, he has been cooperative and helpful. My agents *were* under instructions to terminate survivors at the site, but as director, I have the authority to exercise discretion. That is precisely what I'm choosing to do now. That's how it is, and there is *nothing* you can do to change it."

"This isn't over," sneered Peter.

As she left the room, Louise said, "Believe what you want. I've got work to do."

She was followed out the door by Emily, Daniel, Rick and the President's security detail.

10

"They're calling her the Great Mother," said Wan Ye's brother. He was calling her from the barracks where he'd just enlisted. "Everyone is heading to the great hall; it's like a party. Everyone's being fed for free."

"Free food?" she asked.

"Yes! Everyone is overjoyed. The restaurants have set up stands in the square. The Great Mother, she has said she'll pay all their costs."

Wan Ye was walking out her front door as she said, "This sounds too good to be true!"

"I know, but this is real. When's the last time you had a square meal?"

There was no reply. Wan Ye had terminated the call as she ran, trying to make it onto an approaching tram. She was convinced. She had to head into town and see what was happening for herself. Wan Ye wasn't keen to join the army like her brother, but she was hungry. A free meal would be a welcome respite from her daily struggle to survive.

She thought of how her family had suffered under the tyranny of the Mandarins, her parents having been taken in the middle of the night by Rubeiro's soldiers for no apparent reason other than a rumour of dissent. A *rumour,* that's all it had been.

So it was with great trepidation that she approached the private army's headquarters after she'd ridden the tram the few miles from her home. Yet, the closer she got, the more she started to find herself swept up in the euphoria and carnival atmosphere.

The street was filled with people, all heading to the same destination. When she reached the massive public square, it was a jubilant celebration, the likes of which she'd never seen before.

There were huge lines outside the entrance to the monolithic headquarters General Rubeiro had built. Those waiting in line sang along with the entertainers who were weaving through the crowd. Thousands of drones hovered overhead, producing a dazzling light display, three-dimensional representations of dragons maneuvered through gigantic palaces built of colourful floral patterns that bloomed then fell away, only to be replaced by birds that flew in formations that danced with the dragons.

Wan Ye turned to an old man next to her. "How is it that I didn't know of this? It must have taken months to plan."

The old man shook his head and laughed. "No, this has all just grown in the last day as news of the Great Mother has spread. She calls Rubeiro the Emperor, and yet it's he who kowtows to her. She is giving the wealth that he and the Mandarins stole back to the people, giving the greater rewards to those who have been the poorest." He gestured toward the crowd. "See how peaceful they are? This is because of her love for her people. I have never seen such in my lifetime. She is truly great."

Inside the building's foyer, long tables were set up where citizens queued to register their names and skills—along with their preparedness to help the Great Mother spread her generosity through the rest of Guangdong and its impoverished neighbours. The euphoria was overwhelming. Even those who would typically remain cynical were swept up in the moment. Many had come into contact with the pheromones Petra had spread through the room during her speech, all of whom were now dedicated disciples.

As each citizen nominated their area of expertise, they were directed to particular areas within the compound to receive instruction on what they could do for the Great Mother. They were put into groups of engineers, athletes, labourers, problem solvers, and many others. Families were encouraged to join the grand rebuilding of the community, assured that teachers within each group would tend to the children's education while the parents did what they could to help the Great Mother bring prosperity to her country, all while working to reunite the whole of China.

There were those who expressed gratitude for the food and blankets, but also their wish to wait and see how Petra's revolution panned out before committing themselves to the cause. These people were offered free accommodation in the army's barracks while they observed, or were just wished the best and sent on their way.

Once they'd arrived in their allocated groups, each citizen was issued a list of thoughts to meditate on, then trained in how to focus those thoughts toward their future dedication to the Great Mother of Guangdong. Care was taken at every stage to ensure a positive atmosphere of hope and celebration, all with the underlying theme of the love Petra brought to the people. It was explained that when they felt a burning sensation, they would know they had reached a supreme level of understanding, allowing them go on to enjoy the honour of working for the cause. Those who had experienced the burning were moved to the barracks, reducing the risk of any mutations being noticed by other citizens. Numerous soldiers were already showing signs of change. So, a call out was made to troops from other areas within the city, thereby allowing the mutated ones to be taken to the naval dockyards, where they were loaded onto troop-carrying vessels that slipped quietly into the night, preparing for the upcoming assault on Hong Kong.

***

Nancy struggled to keep her eyes open as Kallan followed their military escort through Lancaster County and onto the Old Philadelphia Pike Road. The plan was to have a convoy of vehicles waiting on the highway until the two women returned from Jacob Graber's farm. Nancy glanced over her shoulder to reassure herself that the printer was still sitting in the spot where they'd packed it on Kallan's truck.

They sat in silence as they listened to the president's latest live address.

"People of America, indeed people of the world, it is with great sadness and a heavy heart that I address you this morning. As you are no doubt already aware, our great nation was rocked by a series of attacks over the course of last night. What began as a terrorist attack, one that it seems had been planned for a generation, led to the White House, Capitol Building and many other government, commercial and residential buildings having been extensively damaged, some utterly destroyed. It's been yet another night where the loss of life and human suffering has been beyond comprehension. Among our loved ones who perished were many personal friends of mine. Some were our elected representatives, or those who had devoted their lives to serving our country in other ways. There were doctors, nurses, teachers, students—people from all walks of life. In addition, there are hundreds of others, including the vice president, who are trapped within the Deep Underground Command Centre, without communications or ventilation. The race is on to reach them and bring them to the surface before their air runs out. I can assure you, we will leave no stone unturned in our pursuit of those responsible for this horrendous crime."

As the President's address continued, Kallan turned to Nancy. "The country's descended into anarchy."

In her heart, Nancy knew Kallan was right, although she wasn't prepared to admit it to herself just yet. "It looks grim, but I'm holding out hope. Somehow, we will prevail. We have to."

"I wish I could share your optimism. But it's already panning out the way I feared it would when the shield deployment was announced. Every city and town's about to become an island, separated from the rest of the world. It's a return to survival of the fittest."

Nancy shook her head. "I can't, I can't let myself believe that."

"What? Do you think Lucas can hold all this together? Get real. She may be the best we've had in a generation, but you know what? As a nation, we've lost way too much to be able to react the way we need to. Face reality, our government got wiped out in an act of terrorism, and the nanotech is spreading.

How many more cities are going to get bombed while they try to bring this to an end? Sorry, I can't see how we come back from this."

"Don't you want to see her succeed?"

"I wouldn't be sitting here if I didn't."

Nancy stared ahead. "My ancestors lived through World War Two in Germany. I've read their tales of how it was." She turned to Kallan. "An entire generation that grew up without fathers. They endured night after night of carpet bombings that destroyed whole cities. The country was crippled, but they pulled it together, and within twenty years, they'd re-emerged as one of the world's strongest economies. Right now, the UNSA is the most advanced nation on the planet, and we have our most inspirational leader since the split. We'll rise from this, like a phoenix from the ashes. The UNSA will be stronger—"

"Oh, Nancy," Kallan laughed as she cut her off. "As I said, I admire your optimism, but it's not realistic. World War Two was different. I've read my history too, honey. Germany bounced back because the countries that bombed it wanted to make sure they didn't repeat the mistakes they made at the Treaty of Versailles."

Nancy looked out the window, not wanting to listen.

"Look at England, they stuffed up by being one of the victors," said Kallan. "There was nobody offering to pay the cost of rebuilding London after the Blitzkrieg. Instead, Britain contributed to the cost of rebuilding their attacker." Kallan put a hand on Nancy's knee. "And you know what? We're not at war with some country that's going to kick our ass, then rebuild for us. We're on our own, and when this shitstorm starts spreading through every other country out there, do you *really* think they'll give a shit about what's happening in the good ol' UNSA?"

Nancy left the question unanswered, both of them turning their attention back to the president's ongoing speech as the truck continued down the highway.

***

Emily launched into the final portion of her address. "This is without doubt the greatest crisis our country has seen. After just two days, the challenges we have already faced have been profound. At the end of it all, this great nation, indeed the whole world, will have changed in ways unforeseen. There is much that will be difficult to face, but we will rebuild, and when we do, we'll be stronger and more resilient than ever before. We *will* get through this, and we will do so together." As soon as the red light on the camera went off, Emily buried her face in her hands. She took several deep breaths before looking up and letting out a sigh of relief. "God but I'm getting sick of doing these."

The director and Daniel stood side by side just inside the studio door, Daniel applauding Emily's speech with a slow clap. Louise glanced across at him. "You won't chastise her for failing to acknowledge the faithful this time?" Daniel ignored her, but Louise wasn't letting him off the hook that easily. "You've never had to deal with a *real* tragedy before this, have you?"

"I thought I had, but no, I couldn't have even begun to imagine…" His voice trailed off, leaving his unfinished sentence hanging in thin air.

"Yet here you are, stronger and more focused than I've ever seen you, carrying responsibilities you'd never dreamed of whilst dealing with enormous grief. Human beings underestimate what they're capable of. They set their expectations too high in areas that have little relevance but sell themselves short when it comes to their capacity to make a difference, until something happens that snaps them out of their complacency. Listen to me when I say this, Daniel. You *can*, and you *will* make a difference in the days ahead."

Desperately wanting a few minutes to herself, Emily didn't acknowledge either of them on her way out of the room. But Louise followed her, with Daniel close behind, followed by the usual retinue of Secret Service and GIA agents.

"We need to talk," said Louise, blunt as usual.

"Can it at least wait till I've had five minutes to wind down?"

"I know you need to catch your breath," replied Daniel, "but there are urgent matters that can't wait."

Emily threw her hands up in resignation. "Then, let's all talk as we walk."

"It's better that we speak in private. And by that, I mean the three of us," said Daniel

"Do I have a choice in that?" asked Emily.

Daniel didn't answer as they silently made their way to Emily's suite. Once inside, Emily turned to Daniel. "Okay, hit me with it."

"I had a discussion with Rick while you were on air that you need to know about."

"I'm listening."

"We already knew he'd been under pressure from the Council, but that's just part of it. He says he's sure that Nick's been talking with Granger, feeding him information since the initial blast at Infinity."

Emily sank into a chair, kicked off her shoes and threw her head back. "Just what we really didn't need, more curvy grey matter." She spent a moment absorbing the implications, aware of how dangerous Granger's influence on Nick would be as events continued unfolding. "This doesn't surprise me when I think about it. Is there any concrete evidence?"

"Just anecdotal, but it's compelling."

Louise interrupted, eager to get to the point. "And after we left the meeting, they were exploring options for how to sideline you. They want to declare your government as ineffectual, then take it under the direct control of the Council, with Nick taking over foreign policy and the military. Peter wants to have the power of veto over anything relating to the UNSA."

Emily put her head back and closed her eyes. "It's relentless!" She paused for a moment to collect her thoughts. "Find me the evidence. I want to nail Nick on this. We need to nip it in the bud before it gains momentum."

"We need to do more than that." Louise smiled, looking at home as she glided into the kitchen to prepare a coffee. "We'll turn the tables. I can *easily* collate evidence of Nick's treason against the principles of the

United Nations. Then we'll use their own constitution to replace him with someone able to stand up to Peter."

Daniel followed Louise into the kitchen, Emily reluctantly lifting herself out of her chair a few seconds later to join them. In a tired and somewhat groggy voice, she asked, "Who did you have in mind? In case you hadn't noticed, we're a bit short on viable candidates."

"There's only one realistic option," said Louise.

Folding her arms, Emily rolled her eyes and took a step back, talking to herself more than anybody else. "I've got a bad feeling about this."

"The amended UN charter is vague on some of this." Daniel handed her a coffee, then continued, "But it definitely states there *must* be a quorum of four Council members for decisions to be binding. However, it is also states that, in the absence of a quorum, the Council Chair has almost unfettered power."

"And here's the interesting part," added Louise. "In the event there are only three remaining members on the Council, a popularly elected politician representing part of the unrepresented region can be appointed as an interim replacement."

Emily asked. "Wouldn't that need to be a member of the General Assembly?"

"No, that's the beauty of it. As long as you've received a certain quota of popular votes, it doesn't matter much which public office you were elected to." Daniel's tone betrayed an underlying enthusiasm for the idea.

"So, let me get this right. You want me to give up my job as president of the UNSA to become a bureaucratic hack? You should know me better than that."

Louise smiled. "That's not how I imagined it. I see you still retaining your current job. You'll be able to use your diplomatic skills to win over Maria Cortez and Domango, effectively taking control of the Council from Peter."

"Oh no, there's no way that I could be President of the UNSA *and* chair the Security Council." Emily backed further away.

"You need to do this, Emily," pleaded Daniel. "Peter's working against us, systematically taking control. He's the typical career politician, believing that he's pleasing everyone while putting business interests ahead of lives. He's got the momentum, and it's slipping out of our control. We need Maria and Dom on side if we want to find a way through. Our command structure is in disarray. With FIDO gone, the coup in the south, and Guangdong destabilising Asia, the world will be looking to us for leadership. The only way I can see us giving them that is if *we* control the Council."

"So, while I was addressing the nation, you and Louise have been hatching this plan to stage a coup—to push me into colluding with the two of you? You were *supposed* to be coordinating the governors. Before anything else, we need to reestablish a functioning government. That's priority number one. But instead, you've been concocting this insane plan? What were you thinking?"

Louise remained calm as ever. "It makes sense. And, right now, I can't see any other way. *They* want to stage a coup, and to do it before you've had a chance to coordinate the governors. The *only* way to stop them is to stage one of our own. You and I have both endured hits to our powerbase. My agents are stretched beyond capacity trying to help maintain order. Overseas, they're struggling without FIDO to track the spread of the nano-plague. While your resources are being tested like never before, your military hardware is mostly intact. But the command structure's been decimated, and most of your remaining personnel are tied up with domestic issues. While the Security Council has lost two of its members, *its* underlying structure remains intact. It has the resources you and I both need. If we want to use those resources, we'll have to take them. Peter's not about to hand them over willingly. He'd rather see Granger take over your whole country than commit UN forces to protecting your borders. There's only one way you and I can continue to do our jobs effectively, and that's by seizing control of the Council."

"I wish there were another way." Emily could see that the logic was undeniable. "Dan, if we're going to do this, I'll have to insist on stepping down temporarily as president. I can't do both jobs at once; the conflict of interest would be too great. As it stands right now, you're about to be sworn in as the acting vice president, which will make you next in line to step in as acting president."

The expression on Daniel's face told her he hadn't considered that possibility as part of the plan. "Really, there's no need to step down, nothing in the constitution or the UN charter demands it."

"Maybe not, but to me it's a clear-cut ethical issue. It's bad enough that I've just become part of a conspiracy to remove an elected representative. I can't compound that by holding two posts that carry such enormous responsibility. Having said that, I can see that throughout this crisis our respective titles aren't so much the issue as the undeniable reality—the three of us *do* have to work together. We're going to have to be in lockstep with every decision as we go forward." She turned to face Louise. "I've got to be honest, as much as that really doesn't sit comfortably with me, you're right, there's no other choice. It's either this or Peter *will* take it all."

A knock at the door interrupted them, followed by a Secret Service agent calling out. "Sorry to bother you, Madam President. Secretary Dodson just asked me to inform you that Julius Granger is about to deliver a press conference."

***

When Marco woke up, he was anything but the man he used to be. After finding shelter and passing out, dehydration brought him to within a few moments of death. Fortunately, the nanobots reached their critical mass just in time. Due to the severity of his situation, the quantum network of nanobots interfacing with his brain took drastic action.

Survival in the Badlands required stripping away anything non-essential for maintaining life. Because feeding and hydrating such a large body required more resources than what was available, the nanobots reduced the size and fundamental structure of the body to a more realistic option, simplifying his physiology. Changes were also made to the part of his body consuming the most resources, his brain. Due to his lack of consciousness when the interface occurred, the nanobots saw no reason to maintain any sense of self. Core parts of his memory were kept intact, but imagination and reasoning were deemed irrelevant to survival.

His overall size was reconfigured to facilitate the ability to hide from the sun by disappearing into cracks within the rock, where there might be potential food sources. By getting down to a small enough size, there was also the possibility of extracting moisture directly from the air around him.

In the interests of the organism's survival, the nanobots even scaled back on their own numbers, with many detaching from the host and drifting off into the atmosphere. Millions of others linked together to create a shell across the top of the now prostrate Fleming, to reflect the sun when he was forced to cross open ground.

The nanobots worked quickly, so desperate was the task of keeping him alive.

Having woken up from his four hours of sleep, Marco found himself having more in common with a large beetle than a human being.

***

Petra Chan, the Great Mother of the people, sat in the massive chair that had once sat behind the grand desk in General Rubeiro's office. She had ordered the desk's removal, allowing for the large high-backed chair to appear more like a throne. She sat with one leg draped over the side of the chair, Rubeiro dutifully massaging her foot. "I will see the envoy now."

A guard near the door bellowed the command. "Bring forth the envoy."

The gigantic doors to the office were flung open. Eight guards marched into the room in a formation of two rows, four guards wide. They carried bamboo poles on their shoulders from which a small cage was suspended, just large enough for an adult to be held within its confines in a crouching position. Clinging to the bars of the cage was a trembling and naked man, covered in grime, cuts, and bruises.

When they reached the middle of the room, the guards came to a stop and placed the cage on the floor. The leading guard stepped forward and came to attention. "Presenting the most unworthy and now humble envoy of the disgraced former rulers of our great nation, The Democratic People's Republic of Guangdong, Chi-Man Chan."

The trembling man in the cage watched the guard deliver the introduction, then turned his eyes to the statuesque figure of Petra rising from her chair and descending the stairs. "Such a long-winded title. You poor man, that must have become so boring to listen to. I think we might simplify it." She continued walking till she reached his cage, then squatted as one would when talking to a toddler. She observed the pool of urine in the tray-like floor of Chan's cage, and a wicked grin grew across her face. "How about we call you Mr Pee-Pee?"

With Petra having come so close, Chan felt overwhelmed by the nano-enhanced pheromones emanating from her. Gazing at her breasts, he became aware of his developing erection and his subsequent embarrassment. Looking into Petra's eyes, he felt encouraged by her smile. "I am greatly honoured to be in your presence, Your Graciousness. Whatever title you wish to bestow upon this unworthy soul shall be embraced with everlasting gratitude."

Petra stood and walked among the twin columns of guards, running her finger under their chins as she went. "So, tell me, Mr Pee-Pee, what's the message your puppet masters have sent you to convey?"

Chan averted his eyes. "Your Graciousness, I must humbly apologise for the ignorance of my former masters, who hide in their gambling dens. They are misguided and have suggested your magnificent emperor took power that was not his to take." He paused, then lifted his eyes to follow Petra as she continued walking among the guards, teasing them as she went. Chan took a deep breath.

"Had they been aware of the reality of what's occurred in your great land, I feel certain they would offer assistance to you in your noble pursuit of bringing joy and happiness to the population of Guangdong."

"Were there any threats?"

"It saddens me to say that is indeed the case." Chan swallowed hard. "They asked me to inform the emperor that if he refuses to stand down and leave the country, they shall be forced to hire a host of foreign armies and remove him by force."

Petra looked toward Barnardo as he stood by her throne, a stern look on his face. "Did you hear that, Barnardo? Such ignorance is intolerable. We need to send a little message in response. But first, we'll send the old men a gift, then you can follow up by paying them a visit, so they can learn to understand the will of the people." She squatted again by the cage. "As for you, Mr Pee-Pee, would you like to stay here with me, as my special pet?"

"Anything that keeps me in your presence will bring me great honour, Your Graciousness."

Petra stood. "Barnardo, be a dear and organise a cable and hook for Mr Pee-Pee's cage to be suspended near our chair, so we can feed him while we work." She looked up and paused. "But before anything else, we must prepare our gift for his puppet masters. Have Alicia's plaything put in a cage with a gold ribbon. Instruct the pilots from Mr Pee-Pee's helicopter to deliver it to the Mandarins without delay."

She took one of the guards by the hand and pulled him out of the formation. "I require a break from the affairs of state. I'm retiring to the bedchamber for now, and do not wish to be disturbed." Just before reaching the doors, Petra came to a halt, paused and turned. "Barnardo, my dear, I brought Alicia here as a gift for you, and now the poor thing is going to be so lonely without her pet to play with downstairs. Be a darling and find a lead for her so we can take her for walks when we go among the people. And a water bowl, so she can sit here with us while we conduct business."

The once proud and mighty General Rubeiro bowed low. "Whatever pleases you, my one and only love."

Petra blew him a kiss and left the room.

***

Louise activated the live share feature on her lensview, sending the image to Emily and Daniel. The upper torso of the media network's anchorman filled the space in the middle of the room. "Before we go live to the speech from Julius Granger, worldwide leader of the Circumfren religious order and now, apparently, President of the Confederacy, I'd like to remind our viewers that my quality smile comes to you courtesy of our sponsor, Micro-Dent, the dental hygiene company responsible for Nantooth, teeth more natural than the real thing."

Emily groaned and shook her head in disdain.

A wide shot of Granger's rotund frame replaced the image of the anchorman. He wore purple robes with elaborate gold embroidery and a purple skull cap, encrusted with a multitude of diamonds and rubies. The construction site for his new base in the City of Circles could be seen in the background through an array of massive drapes suspended far above the podium. The front rows of a large, cheering crowd were visible, disappearing as the camera zoomed in.

Julius held his hands high, acknowledging the crowd as they broke into a chant. "Cir-cul-lar! Cir-cul-lar!" As the fervour built, they began stamping their feet.

Julius brought the tips of his index fingers and thumbs together, and the crowd understood he was ready to speak. It was time to stop cheering and listen to the words of wisdom that flowed from their leader.

"Let there be no doubt, the time of Circles is upon us, as it was written." Julius paused for effect, then opened a leather-bound box and held a hardcopy disk of the Book of Circles aloft.

In a solemn voice, he recited a passage. "*The very small will devour the very large, and a great fire shall decimate the false leaders of linear thought. Then curvature will weave its way through the remains, returning unity to a divided land.*" He closed his eyes as if in prayer. "The meaning of these words cannot be mistaken. Our duty to our northern cousins is clear. I have spent time discussing the matter with those who were once referred to as our military commanders— they who are now aware of the need for those they lead to see themselves not as warriors, but as missionaries of circular thought. We now have an overwhelming and urgent responsibility to send missionaries of hope to help our cousins rebuild and restore order to their land."

He paused, looking out at his audience. "In light of the devastation wrought upon the national government of the UNSA and the blatant refusal of President Lucas to recognise the legitimacy of the southern leadership, I deemed it appropriate to seek the highest possible authority. So earlier today, I had a substantive discussion with the Security Council representative for North America regarding these matters. The undeniable fact is that an unstable and fragmented remnant of a government cannot hope to restore stability to areas so heavily devastated."

Julius took his time to sip on a glass of water, then wiped a few beads of sweat from his brow. "A flotilla of vessels from the Norfolk Centre of Circular Instruction shall carry ten thousand armed missionaries to help return stability through religious counselling. They will first be sent to the areas around New York and Hartford. In addition, a sizeable congregation of missionaries is being airlifted into the Washington DC region as I speak to you. They will aid with reconstruction and ease the population's stress through guidance in circular thought. The brave men and women undertaking these holy tasks will be putting themselves at considerable risk. Because of this, I have informed the governors of West Virginia, Ohio, and Pennsylvania that several thousand theologians will be deployed within their states, ensuring they'll be comfortable in the knowledge that misguided and heretical forces from the western states of their union will not interfere with our sacred task in the east. They'll be supported by flying theologians and winged missionaries from our Langley Monasteries."

He looked to the ground and feigned wiping away a tear. "It saddens me to say, not one of these governors offered assistance. I therefore ask that all believers in the states of West Virginia, Ohio, and Pennsylvania rise in civil disobedience until their leaders publicly declare a willingness to cooperate with our act of compassion. As you all well know, it is imperative for us to help ourselves, that we may better be able to help our neighbours. Our brethren will be taking on dangerous tasks for a charitable cause, and the strain on our resources will be great. We shall therefore seek to rehabilitate any military assets we encounter in our journey to a more holy purpose."

He looked to the sky as if seeking inspiration. "My rounded friends, one thing I promise you is this: through the peaceful act of spreading faith, we will save our northern cousins from the depths of desperation they've fallen into as a result of the perils they've endured this week." He punched a fist in the air and raised his voice. "We shall bring unity of purpose back to our great land! What goes around comes around!"

The crowd roared its approval, and the cameras cut back to the studio. "Well, that was Julius Granger, with what I must say was quite a remarkable speech. I'm joined now in the studio by Roger Clarke, our country's foremost expert on behavioural science. Roger, let me start by asking whether Granger's smile was engaging enough throughout his speech."

Emily shook her head in disbelief. "He's got to be kidding?"

"He's not," Daniel replied.

"This is a full-scale invasion. What the fuck's got into this guy's head?"

Louise scoffed. "He's opportunistic, this is nothing but a land grab, at a time when he thinks you're too weak to respond."

"Yeah, I got that. Tell me something useful, like who we can still talk to from the Joint Chiefs."

Daniel flicked through his wristband to check who was still connected to the network. "Wiseman, from the air force. He's all that's left."

"Oh shit! It just keeps getting better, doesn't it? Wiseman! Seriously?" She bit her lower lip and gripped the back of a chair as she pondered what to do next. "Okay, let's just hope he's able to rise to the occasion. Get him online for me, will you, Dan? While you're doing that, I'll prepare a general message for the state governors. They need to know we're going to stand our ground."

Louise started toward the door. "While Daniel is getting Wiseman's head out of his ass, you and I should talk to Nick. That's if he hasn't already flown the coup."

Emily nodded in agreement as she followed Louise out of the room.

***

Jason looked around, taking in his surroundings as he approached the town of Minot. He saw what he assumed to be a stack of discarded shield generators by the roadside, all abandoned without having been deployed.

He made his way down the deserted street, curious as to what had become of the town's population. A cat hissed at him from a short distance away. On instinct, he turned and pushed the palm of his right hand forward. A ball of acidic mucus travelled up his arm from the huge bump on his back. When it reached his hand, it passed through his skin, releasing a squelching sound and a rancid stench as it flew at speed toward the unfortunate cat. The blob wrapped around the feline's head, momentum forcing it to follow through to the brick wall behind. Stinking fumes rose from the mucus as it burnt through the cat's flesh. Within seconds, the now-headless cat dropped to the ground, a large hole growing in the wall where the mucus continued dissolving the clay bricks.

Jason heard laughter deep inside his head. *Impressive, but you'll need more than that when you meet the new recruits to my cause.* It had to be the fugitive, either that or he was losing his mind.

Jason moved cautiously, looking around the empty street as he went. "Okay, asshole," he called out. "Let me explain it like this. Under the emergency powers granted to the Global Intelligence Agency by the United Nations Security Council, I am now your judge, jury and, if I wish, your executioner. Your ass is mine. If you don't show yourself, I'm going to shove my boot so far up your ass it's going to tickle the back of your throat. So how about you save us both a whole lot of time and surrender now."

He stood waiting for Craig's response. A minute later, he heard a distant whistling sound, then quickly moved to find cover when he saw the incoming rocket grenade. It landed where he'd been standing, shrapnel tearing at his leather coat. He was only saved from serious injury by the fact that his hide was now so tough the shrapnel failed to penetrate his flesh.

The next time he heard Craig in his head, the sensation was more akin to being immersed within the man's thoughts. *You use such tough words. But I can feel your thoughts. I can feel your fear.*

"Yeah, right. Like I told you before, surrender your miserable ass, and you might just get to leave here alive, in my custody."

Jason waited for a response, but none was forthcoming until he heard a group of soldiers marching in time to a cadence call.

A lone voice bellowed, "Craig Brown grinning ear to ear."

Then the marching troops responded, "Jason Negus filled with fear."

The lone voice, "He stacked his car; he should be dead."

Followed by the troops' response, "We're gonna mess with-in his head."

Great, thought Jason, *he's got the whole fucking lot of them under his control. Well, we'll see who they answer to when it comes to the crunch.*

As the troops turned onto the road just two blocks away, the high-pitched buzz of an infantry support drone squadron drowned them out, hovering above and behind them.

The troops were twenty metres away when they stopped and stood to attention.

Jason slid along the ground in front of them, the control of his muscles in his foot now so fine that he propelled himself like a fast-moving snail with ease. "As you are no doubt already aware," he said, "my name is Jason Negus. Special Agent of the Global Intelligence Agency. I am in pursuit of a fugitive who has become extremely dangerous. Clearly, this troop has information relevant to that pursuit."

He moved closer to the troops, close enough for them to feel the heat of his breath as he walked among them. "I'll make it clear, under the emergency powers that came into force under the declaration of the Emergency Protocol 46, I am effectively now your commanding officer. Refusal to follow orders shall be seen as insubordination, punishable by court-martial." He stared into the unmoving eyes of a young soldier. "A court-martial to be carried out on the spot by me."

The lump on his back had grown so large that he could no longer bring his hands together behind his back. He took them back as far as was comfortable, then yelled, "DO I MAKE MYSELF CLEAR?"

In unison, the troops responded. "YES, SIR!"

"ARE YOU READY TO FOLLOW MY ORDERS?"

"NO SIR!"

The veins on the side of his neck pulsated as his blood pressure elevated. Slowly, he stretched an arm toward a soldier at the end of the row. "For insubordination, you're hereby court-martialled." He shot a ball of acidic mucus toward him. The young man didn't make a sound as he doubled over under the impact of the mucus ball. By the time he collapsed to the ground, a massive hole had been burned through his abdomen. The rest of the troops remained motionless.

"As you can see, I don't waste much time with details when it comes to court martials. I'll repeat the question for those of you who may have misunderstood. ARE YOU READY TO FOLLOW MY ORDERS?"

"NO SIR!"

Jason moved to be in front of the platoon and fired twice, bringing down one soldier in the middle of the troops and another toward their left flank. He was breathing heavily when one of the soldiers marched two steps forward. "Doctor Craig Brown wishes to conduct an audience with you, that he may ascertain your value to his mission, sir!"

Jason pushed his fist up against the belly of the soldier and released a flood of goo. The man's jaw fell open, and the steaming top half of his body fell to the ground while his legs remained standing, slowly shortening as the acid dissolved flesh and bone.

"Anyone else have a message?"

The remaining troops raised their weapons as one, pointing them toward him. In unison, they repeated the words of their colleague. "Doctor Craig Brown wishes to conduct an audience with you, that he may ascertain your value to his mission, sir!"

"He can kiss my ass." Jason jumped over the heads of the troops, knocking several drones out of the air and firing multiple rounds from his automatic weapon as he went. He hit the ground behind an abandoned truck by the side of the road, then bolted down a side street, firing more rounds as he went before taking cover inside a convenience store. The thunderous noise of gunfire followed, the truck exploding when it was hit by a rocket-propelled grenade. After a moment of silence, the cadence call started again.

"Craig Brown grinning ear to ear."

"Jason Negus filled with fear..."

Although there were at least thirty soldiers in the platoon and several dozen drones, Jason felt comfortable that he could pick them off. But how many more were there who hadn't shown themselves yet?

He peered out from the stock room when the troops came to a stop in front of the store. A voice called from the back of his consciousness, *Time to come out of hiding, Jason. We need to talk.*

Jason raced through the stock room, heading for the rear entrance. Once there, he came to an abrupt halt, faced by another platoon standing in wait for him. He fired more rounds until the magazine was wasted then dropped the gun and threw both arms out, sending masses of acidic mucus hurtling through the door. Several drones exploded, the flaming debris from one of them landing on a soldier whose uniform caught fire. As the intense pain broke his connection to Craig, the soldier fell to the ground, screaming out for help. He went silent when one of his colleagues casually walked across and shot him in the head. Jason turned and fled in the opposite direction. Charging toward the shop's entrance, he hollered a battle cry and flung his arms about wildly, releasing ball after ball of goo. The air became thick with a putrid stench so foul that Jason started gagging as he watched one soldier after another fall to the ground after the mucus cut through their bodies. He pulled back his arm, preparing to release another volley. When he tried to lunge forward, he encountered an invisible resistance, as though he were stuck in a pool of molasses. He tried to pull his arm back for another attempt, but was unable to move. He was paralysed.

The troops who remained standing parted to make way for their leader, stepping over fallen soldiers, some of whom were moaning in agony as their wounds drained the life out of them. Doctor Craig Brown came forward, sitting atop the remains of what had once been a military vehicle and its driver. Both had been reduced to something resembling a metallic throne on wheels. It was the most unusual form of transportation Jason had ever seen. The four wheels were held in place by organic limbs that were neither arm nor leg, yet somehow functioned as both. The seat had sides of polished metal, cushioned by what appeared to be a hybrid of flesh and fabric. Over Craig's head, a partial canopy of glass was suspended, which became opaque whenever it received direct exposure to sunlight. At its rear was an electric motor connected to thick organic cables that breathed and pulsated. A pair of human-like eyes peered out from beneath the seat.

Craig's body was reduced to the size of an eight-year-old child, with little muscle or flesh clinging to his shrunken bones. His face, however, remained the size of an average adult, albeit with a greatly exaggerated nose and chin. His oversized cranium resembled a pulsating mass of jelly, encased in a skull that was little more than a transparent membrane. Jason was mesmerised by the sight of the electricity darting around Craig's brain, reminiscent of watching a distant thunderstorm.

Craig made a pathetic effort at clapping his withered hands. "Congratulations, Jason, you've succeeded beyond expectations."

It was painful for Jason to even speak while being held in suspension, but he refused to give Craig the impression he'd capitulated. "Cut the crap. I don't know exactly what your sick little plan is, but one thing I know for sure, you *will* fail."

"Oh? It's not looking that way from where I sit right now."

"Any minute now, you'll be lying dead, in a pool of your own brain matter."

Craig shook his head as he let out a small chuckle. "Interesting." As he moved closer, the organic limbs holding the wheels raised and lowered themselves while moving over the corpses and body parts littering the ground after Jason's attack. His seat, however, seemed to glide, as though floating on air. "You're certainly an interesting example of how extreme genetic modifications can be in the first few days after the burning. It's quite impressive," said Craig as he studied Jason. "Throughout all the years of research, none of us ever foresaw the massive leaps forward in evolution that's encapsulated in *our* respective transformations." He gazed at the ceiling, as if lost in a daydream. "Look at me, Jason. I've evolved to a state previously beyond imagining. My exposure to the nanobots was so massive that, around my brain stem, rather than having individual nanobots bond with each cell, I had *dozens*. Multiples of them bonded with each and every cell throughout my brain and central nervous system. Can you even conceive the extent to which my intellectual capacity has expanded? Humanity is at a perilous crossroads. It's going to need *my* help to have any hope of survival. And, I want *you* to help me as I help humanity accept the reality of what's coming. Together, we may just have a chance of preventing anarchy and ruin."

Jason strained his neck as much as he could to turn and look at Craig. "I don't help psychopathic maniacs."

"Me, a psychopath? Really? Didn't you just murder dozens of soldiers without provocation? Taking innocent lives for no other reason than the fact that you'd failed in making them submit to *your* will over mine?" Craig moved around to be directly behind Jason, raising a decrepit finger to the back of his neck and scratching the surface of his skin. "I think it's time for you to have an attitude adjustment." He twisted the fingernail and drove it deeper. Blood trickled down Jason's neck, mingling with the sweat pouring off his face as he struggled against Craig's hold. A stream of nanobots raced down Craig's finger into Jason's bloodstream, searching out the brainstem. "Let's see how you feel about resisting once the nanobots from my brainstem have mingled with yours."

***

Nancy's mind wandered as the truck rattled along the road leading into Jacob Graber's farm. "Why exactly is it that we have to do this on our own?"

"A society dominated by men sees little threat in two women on their own. If it were one of us with a *male* companion, Jacob probably wouldn't welcome us at all. Forget what you grew up believing about the Amish. Jacob's changed them; he's a dangerous megalomaniac. But he's also our only chance of reaching the rest of the community."

"And, being two women, on our own, should we feel safe?"

Kallan ignored the question as they continued in silence. As they turned into Jacob's property, Nancy kept staring at her naked wrist. Kallan had been firm about the need to leave their wristbands behind. "We can't risk being perceived as a threat," she'd said.

As they neared the main homestead, a group of men spread out to form a line across the road ahead. In the middle stood a tall man with a solid frame and a long white beard. There were four younger men to his left and four to his right.

Kallan took the truck up till it was just two metres from them. "Hello, Jacob." She got out of the cabin and approached him. "It's been a long time."

Although in his mid-seventies, a healthy diet and constant exercise working his farm had kept Jacob fit and strong. His voice was firm. "Hannah, you know you're not welcome on this land. You might as well turn around now and leave."

"I haven't called myself Hannah for years now, you know that. What my friend and I have come to discuss is important, not just for you, but for the Amish."

One of the younger men thrust a pitchfork toward the women. "You obviously didn't hear what my father said. Leave now, witch, and take that— that whore friend of yours with you."

Nancy's heart sank. What was going on?

Jacob reached across and grabbed hold of his son's arm. "Samuel, I'll not have you talk to your sister in that manner."

Staring at Kallan, Samuel was slow and reluctant as he lowered the pitchfork. He spat his words like a snake spitting venom. "She ceased being my sister when she deserted us for the heathen life."

Jacob removed the pitchfork from Samuel's grip and handed it to one of his other sons. "She made a choice when she left. Now she has to live with it, as do we." He looked down, clearly saddened by the memory. "She is no longer a member of our community, and as such, would not ordinarily be welcome on our land, but she is still your mother's daughter, as she is mine. While I find it difficult to welcome her, I cannot bring myself to drive her away. Despite her choices, she is still of our blood." He whispered to himself and hung his head as though in shame. "That I cannot forget."

Samuel remained firm in his opposition. "She worships false gods and claims to speak with the trees. By her own admission, she's a witch. No good will come of letting her on our land."

Kallan took a few steps toward her brother, his eyes widening in fright as she approached. "I don't worship Satan, nor any other gods or deities for that matter. Yes, I *do* talk with the trees. I celebrate nature in *all* its glorious wonder. Is that really something to be afraid of?" She lowered her voice as she continued, "And I haven't forgotten what you did. Perhaps that's the *real* reason you're scared."

"That'll do now, Hannah," said Jacob. "I'll not have your pagan ways spoken of on my property. However, seeing you've obviously no intention of leaving till you've had your say, you and your companion might as well come to the house, and make plain what it is that has made you go to such trouble to come out here. Then you can be on your way." He paused once more before adding, "Your mother will no doubt be pleased to see you."

***

The governor looked out his window at the approaching tanks and troop carriers. He heard the office door open behind him and said, "I thought I'd made it clear that I'm not to be disturbed." He turned and saw it was the Pennsylvania Police Commissioner.

Dressed in full uniform, he removed his hat as a mark of respect. "I'm sorry, Phil, there's not much I can do about what's happening out there. It's all just moving so quickly. Our troops, the National Guard, the police... we've all been spread so thin deploying those shield generators. Heck, there's been no time to respond. The best we can hope for is that the bloodshed's kept to a minimum."

"Granger's calling them theologians and missionaries. Can you believe that? These men are *soldiers*, but now he dares to call them *missionaries*." He turned to the commissioner, a glass of bourbon in his hand. Ordinarily, Phillip abstained from alcohol, keeping a bottle in his office only for visiting dignitaries. "I'm a man of God. My life's been devoted to serving the Lord in one way or another. Now these people—these invaders—what makes them think they've got the right?"

The commissioner took the drink from Phillip's hand, placing it on the desk, before easing the blank-faced governor into his chair. Phillip's eyes were open wide, and his jaw hung low. "What's happening to the world?"

With the governor seated, Greg took time to grab a glass and prepare a drink for himself before taking a seat on the edge of the desk. He looked down into his drink as he swirled the bourbon around the glass. "You know what? I've seen some goddamned awful things in my time as a cop. I've seen a junkie butcher his own family over something that wasn't worth a shit, nine-year-old kids so vicious and cruel that it'd send a shiver up the spine of the most hardened military man. I'm telling you, I've seen stuff that would make the boogie man curl up in fright." He held his drink up to the window and watched the effect of the morning light on the liquid. "You're a good man, Phil, an honest man. That's what I've always liked about you. But you've always been naïve about the ways of the world, and what's really going on. Just how many of those assholes do you think actually see themselves as missionaries? None. Not one of 'em. All they know is that they're trained to do a job. When their commanding officer tells them to jump, they go right ahead and jump."

He finished his drink and set out to pour another. "Of course, most of the top brass from down there have identified as curveballs for a few years now. That's the only way to get ahead down south." He pointed a finger in Phillip's direction to emphasise his point. "A bit like it used to be for the Freemasons. And you know what? Granger's surpassed the influence of that franchise without even blinking." He shook his head and paused, staring into space. "It's all over. The human race? It'll never be the same." He threw down the drink and poured himself a third. "The whole shit fight is coming to an end." He walked around the desk, glass in hand, waving a finger as he spoke. "Granger? He wants to be seen as the last great leader. That's what it's always been about for him. His whole thing about eternal repetition? He actually believes it! If the world blows apart, and he's the most powerful person alive at the time, he'll die happy."

Governor Phillip Miller continued staring blankly ahead. "Why are you here, Greg?"

"They sent me to tell you. It's time—time to walk away."

"I thought as much."

"Don't get me wrong, it's not like I wanted any of this, but the way things are going? You've just gotta go with the flow."

"How long do I have?"

"They want you out of the building in the next fifteen minutes."

"Well, in that case, I'd actually prefer to spend that time without you in my presence. In fact, as my last official act as governor, I'd like to ask that you leave this office, now!"

Greg placed his glass on the desk, put on his cap, and smirked as he turned and gave a wave on his way out of the room.

The governor sent a final message to Nancy Fisher, then picked up the bottle of bourbon and examined it. He decided that in the next fifteen minutes, he would do his best to discover just what it was like to drink a copious amount of alcohol.

***

Enricho dragged himself forward—lost in his thoughts—a blank look in his eyes. *Maria was my world. How can it be? How can she be gone?* He shuffled ahead with the rest of the crowd, following the directive that they move to the newly established refugee camp in Springfield.

Despite warnings about congregating in numbers, the refugees had little choice but to stick together as the National Guard herded them along.

Enricho had developed some longstanding friendships with Circumfrens over the years. He'd never had a problem accepting them as a genuine religion. But Maria had spoken out often about her distaste for Granger and his attitude toward other faiths. A tear rolled down his cheek, and his lower lip trembled as her words echoed through his head. "*Mark my words,*" she would say, "*that man? He cannot be trusted!*" The image of her lifeless body filled his consciousness as his knees gave way and he collapsed.

The slow momentum of the crowd led some of those directly behind to trip over his prostrate form, a few falling to the ground themselves. A heavily tattooed young man took the effort to help Enricho to his feet. While the crowd continued driving forward, the man put his arm around Enricho's shoulder, guiding him to the edge of the moving throng. Breaking free, they disappeared down a side street. "You're not going to live long pulling those sort of stunts. If you're in a crowd like that, you've gotta keep moving."

Enricho didn't respond.

They reached a bus shelter, and the tattooed man sat Enricho down so he could get his breath back. He lifted the old man's chin and examined his facial features. "You got a name?"

Enricho slowly lifted his eyelids, revealing the world of sadness within. His voice lacked emotion or energy. "Enricho, my name is Enricho."

"Enricho, huh? Well, Enricho, they call me Teddy."

"Is that your real name?"

"Nah, my full name, the name my parents gave me, is Edward—Edward Percival Koch III. Sounds kinda fancy, doesn't it?" He looked up to the sky. "To my friends, it's just Teddy."

"Why is that?"

"My grandmother had always wanted my parents to name me after her father, Theodore. Does that remind you of anyone from history?"

"Not that I can think of."

"You're joking, aren't you?"

"No, I wouldn't joke about such things. You seem to be someone who's deserted his past. Why do you choose to do so?"

Teddy shook his head. "That's beautiful, I pick you up off the street, where you seem to be dying from grief, and you want to diagnose my fucking problems?" He withdrew a paper bag from his pocket and pulled out a pinch of marijuana along with a cigarette paper, rolled a joint and lit it up. "I'll make a deal with you, Enricho." He took a deep drag on his splif, held it in for a few seconds, then blew out a thick funnel of smoke, oblivious to any impact it may have on his companion. "I'm happy to fill you in on my story, but not until you've told me yours."

Enricho dropped his head in silence. The thought of having to explain his failure to protect Maria was too painful to bear.

"Yeah, I figured you weren't ready yet. Well, neither am I." Grabbing Enricho's elbow, he stood up, then gestured toward the slow-moving tide of refugees. "I don't know about you, but I reckon it's time to get away from that sea of misery. I've heard talk the Circumfrens are taking over the refugee camps, and I don't want to be part of anything those fuckers have a hand in."

"But Edward, where would we go?" He raised his hands in a gesture of helplessness.

"I've got a girl down in Windsor. She's not answering my calls, but that's not unusual. I want to look in on her anyway. With or without her, I'm heading to the mountains. I know a cabin up there that'll be a whole lot safer than this." He threw the roach from his joint on the ground. "A lot more shit'll go down before any of this gets better. Trust me, we'll be a lot safer up there than down here. They're just herding us like cattle from one catastrophe to another."

Enricho stood up and almost smiled as he said, "Thank you, Teddy."

"What, for pulling you up off the road?"

"No, I thank you for reminding me that we are more than cattle," replied Enricho. "Are you truly sure you would be happy to accept me as your travelling companion? I can cook, you know, and nobody makes a better coffee than Enricho."

"Yeah, why not. Come on, we'd better grab some wheels and start moving before they close off more roads."

"You have a car nearby?"

"Nope."

"Then what? Oh no, you don't mean—"

"Yep."

Enricho threw his hands on his head in panic. "You want to steal somebody's car?"

"I don't see any other way we're getting out of here."

Enricho crossed himself. "Oh, Jesus, Mary and Joseph! What about the poor people who own the car? What will they do?"

"Look around, most of the people who weren't even in the stadium have already left this shithole. Half these homes are abandoned. The way I see it, if we take a car that's been left behind, we're not doing any harm, but we're making ourselves a whole lot safer."

Enricho felt more alive than he had in a long time.

***

The smaller of the surviving groundfish segments was desperate to get away from the source of heat and pain. Sensing the soothing waters of the Connecticut River just a few hundred metres away, it set off, leaving the other remnant to fend for itself.

The creature twisted and turned as it travelled below the surface, struggling to maintain a consistent direction while holding itself together as one unit.

It continued regardless, writhing in agony until it felt a cool moisture in the soil, telling it the river was just a few metres ahead. It used the last of its energy reserves to break out from underground and rise above the surface, creating a small spray of soil as it rolled through the air. The groundfish relaxed, then fell into the river. The brisk chill of the water soothed much of the burning. It revelled in the comparative freedom of movement offered by the water after so much time spent underground. It swirled and darted about, occasionally leaping out of the water like a flying fish.

Downstream, a lone fisherman sat in a small dinghy, hoping to fill the family freezer. In his younger days, mercury levels kept people from fishing the river, but that was years ago. Right now, he didn't care one way or the other. He cast his line, opened a beer, and relaxed.

As the groundfish frolicked, its demeanour changed when it noticed the vulnerable little boat and its occupant—the potential to consume fresh human thoughts, dreams, and memories.

The fisherman raised an eyebrow when he saw a splash that he took to be just another flying fish. *Strange,* he thought, *I've never seen one around here before.* An instant later, the boat capsized, and he was underwater. His final conscious thought was the traumatic sensation of having his mind ripped apart.

The water became turbulent as the groundfish fed on the fisherman, integrating the man's existing nanotech to assist in the process of consuming his mind, followed by his flesh.

By the time its feeding frenzy was complete and its meal digested, the groundfish had reached open waters. Longing for more, it searched for the tell-tale signs of human activity, the vibration of a motor or the sound of a distant voice. Sensing nothing in the immediate vicinity, it seemed the next meal would not be so easy to come by, but it still felt the urgent need to feed.

It swam about, becoming increasingly distressed by its hunger. By chance, it came across an octopus hunting down a meal. The groundfish sensed the creature's intelligence, along with the fact that they were each seeking the same thing—sustenance!

It surged toward the octopus, only to find itself swimming through open water.

The octopus had evaded it.

Again and again they ducked and weaved, until at last, the groundfish managed to anticipate the octopus and forced itself into its opponent, consuming it from the inside.

As the groundfish absorbed the creature's memories, it developed an appreciation for the flexibility of movement the sea creature enjoyed. In a water environment, there would be obvious benefits in seeking prey by mimicking some of the cephalopod's strategies.

***

Having rested, Jon and Mary continued their trek through the Badlands. They walked in silence for an hour before Merrick stirred and started grizzling in Mary's arms. "It's too hot for him. He's getting restless."

Spying another rocky outcrop close to the road up ahead, Jon said, "We can stop up there. There's some shade. If we take a short rest, maybe he'll go back to sleep."

As they approached, Mary noticed something unusual at the foot of the rocks. "What do you think that is?"

Jon shrugged. "It's just a pile of old discarded clothes by the look of it."

"Is that a water bottle next to it? And that other thing, I think it just moved."

He was paying closer attention now. "It looks like some sort of beetle." He motioned for Mary and Merrick to stand back while he picked up a rock and approached. The bug was like nothing he'd seen before, measuring around thirty centimetres from head to tail, with a shiny black shell across its back. "It's got ten legs up front that look like human fingers, like a couple of hands. And it's got these weird flipper-like things at the back that look like they could be deformed feet." He stood transfixed by it as the creature slowly turned to face him. "Holy shit! It's got human eyes. They're looking right at me."

The creature raised its frontmost fingers, as though trying to communicate. Then, Jon was taken by surprise when it rushed toward him. Instinctively, he used all his strength to bring the rock he was holding down on the creature's head. There was a crunch as parts of the shell broke, along with what seemed to be bone. Its eyes popped out of its head, and blood spattered on Jon's face. Even though there was no chance of reprisal from the creature, he raised the rock again, then brought it down a second time, turning what remained of the creature's head into a mush of flesh and broken bone.

Mary had turned Merrick's head away from the scene when Jon had first picked up the rock, but her gasp of revulsion at the crunch of rock on shell and bone had been enough to make the infant cry.

"Oh my God, what is that thing?" she asked.

"I don't know for sure. But when I think of what happened to Jason, I wouldn't mind betting those clothes over there belong to whoever it used to be." He walked across and used the remains of Marco's clothing to wipe the blood from his face, then picked up a broken wristband lying beneath the heap. Making swiping movements with his fingers on his own wristband, he checked to see if it had self-repaired enough to read the metadata embedded in the non-functional device. "Well, I'll be fucked, based on the security encryptions, it seems this guy was high up in the government."

He removed a small backup memory pin from the stranger's wristband and slotted it into his own, hoping to break through the encryptions with the GIA protocols of his own device. "*Encryption authorisation level six, agent Kruick, Romeo, alpha, foxtrot, bravo, foxtrot.*"

He was rewarded with a flood of information scrolling up on his lensview. After he started reading through it, Jon turned to Mary. "You wouldn't believe it, turns out I just killed off the Secretary of Defence, Marco Fleming."

Mary rocked the crying boy in her arms as she asked, "But what would he be doing out here?"

"It says his commission was terminated in the last twenty-four hours. He must have screwed up big time to end up out here."

"How could he have changed so quickly into that—that thing?"

"I'm guessing we'll find that out when we get to the bunker."

"Are you sure we still want to go there? What if everyone there's ended up—" she looked at the crushed beetle that had been Marco Fleming. "—like that?"

"I can't see that we've got much choice. We've got to be getting close, and there's nowhere else to go."

Mary nodded in agreement. "Okay. Then let's keep walking. I've certainly got no desire to stop *here* to rest anymore."

Jon put an arm around Mary's waist, and they walked off.

As they left, nanobots within the pulped remains of what had been Marco Fleming worked feverishly at beginning the task of reconstructing something resembling a functional organism.

***

Tanya entered the viewing area. When she reached the couch by the window, she offered a bottle of water to Brenda, who sat motionless, watching the children trying to levitate with Gordon.

"Hey, how are you holding up?" Tanya asked.

Brenda tried to raise a smile. "To be honest? I'm struggling."

Tanya took a seat beside her. "We didn't get much chance to talk earlier."

"Yeah, well, I haven't felt very talkative anyway," Brenda replied. Her tone was cold, making it clear she was still in no mood for conversation.

"It's funny," Tanya pointed toward Gordon. "I've worked and socialised with that man for years, but I've never seen this side of him before."

Brenda looked confused. "What, the levitating?"

"No, the way he is with the kids in there. He's so good with them."

"Does he have any kids of his own?"

"Just one, a daughter, Tracey, she's a journalist stationed somewhere in the Confederate States."

Brenda leaned forward. "Oh? He must be worried sick about her."

"I guess so, although they don't seem to stay in touch much, and he rarely talks about her. They had a falling out years ago."

Brenda stared at her, waiting for more information.

Tanya shrugged. "I don't know for sure, but I'm guessing it's more than likely it was to do with the time Gordon's put into his work over the years."

"What a shame, he's such a natural with these two."

"He is now, but that looks like a more sensitive and thoughtful man in there than the one I know." She paused for a while, a tear rolling down her cheek. "He and Lloyd worked so closely together until—"

Brenda put a comforting arm around her shoulder. "So, they were friends? I mean, friends *outside* of work?"

Tanya nodded. "I think mostly—" Tanya paused with her jaw hanging open for a moment. "—because of the time they spent working together. Lloyd, my beautiful Lloyd. He was always so focused on wanting to have a positive impact on the world. His baby sister—she died very young, a genetic abnormality. It was something we couldn't fix at birth back then. He wanted to spare others from that, from the suffering she went through." Tanya glared at Gordon before she continued, her tone carrying a hint of bitterness. "Gordon was just interested in the science for science's sake. Whenever the three of us had dinner together, we'd have long-winded debates about the efficacy of what we were doing. But both of them—they were both so blind to the risks of what we were doing. Blind to the risk of what we're having to deal with now." The kids had run off to another room by now, laughing and giggling as they went.

"I still don't understand how this could've happened," said Brenda. "Wasn't the GIA in there making sure the place was secure?"

Gordon's voice came through the speakers. "I believe the question, Ms Fleming, should be whether this would have happened at all, had the GIA kept their noses out of what we were doing."

"Face it, Gordon. This was always an accident waiting to happen," Tanya countered. "How many times did I try to tell you?"

"Did you?" Gordon was still floating, "That's not how I recall it. We had a multitude of safety measures in place, measures that I put in place long before the GIA deemed our work worthy of their close attention. The explosion could never have resulted from an accident. Ron Killen detonated it, and it's apparent he was manipulated into doing so by Doctor Petra Chan, a psychologist employed by the GIA. Had the GIA not been involved, I doubt the infiltration could or would have happened. Other research facilities around the world were far more vulnerable to actual accidents. The problem with ours was vulnerability to sabotage, courtesy of the GIA."

"Are you implying the GIA was complicit?" asked Brenda.

"Having met Director Brandt, I don't doubt her integrity," said Gordon. "However, she is the director of a large, global organisation, linked to the United Nations. While FIDO would have reduced the risk of the GIA employing agents of disrepute, it failed to recognise the risk with Doctor Chan. It's worth noting that elected representatives of the United Nations are immune to screening once elected. It's an age-old problem: elected representatives instigating initiatives to make all accountable—except themselves. I'm not convinced that all members of the Security Council are acting in the world's best interest. They created monsters they couldn't control with both FIDO and the GIA. What I believe we're witnessing is an attempt at regaining control by undermining a director who refuses to respond to their whims."

"I'm sorry, but I don't see how you've answered my question," Brenda replied.

Gordon was as abrupt as he was dismissive. "Should that be a surprise?" He drifted in a circle as he continued, "I don't mean to offend you, but I've spent a good deal of time these past two days meditating on this and related matters, some of which are of greater concern."

"Do go on," said Brenda.

"I've tried on numerous occasions to reach out to my former colleague, Craig Brown, to work out what he's up to. Despite the nature of his departure from here, his capacity to cause harm is immense. He's also developed the ability to keep me locked out of his mind."

Tanya interrupted, "I seem to recall we'd discussed the ethics of that anyway, remember?"

"As much as I appreciate and respect your concerns, the danger he poses led me to the conclusion it would be catastrophic if I ignore any capacity I may have to keep on top of what he's up to."

"You promised!"

"Tanya, this is serious. He's taken control of a military base, all of them. Soldiers, engineers, all the hardware. He's also imprisoned the population of the town attached to the base."

"Excuse me?"

"The town of Minot, and its air force base, with almost two thousand soldiers attached."

Brenda approached the window. "So, you found this out by getting into his head?"

Drifting around to face her, Gordon brought his legs down from the lotus position he'd maintained while levitating. "Not *his* head. As I say, he's shut me out, but he can't shut me out of those he's controlling. Not fully anyway."

"I can't believe this! You made a clear commitment to me." Tanya spoke through clenched teeth. "How can I ever trust you again?"

Brenda turned to her. "Excuse me, honey, but I think the potential threat here outweighs the ethical concerns."

Tanya glared at Brenda, then got up and set out to leave the room, breaking down into an uncontrollable sob just before she reached the door.

Brenda walked across and hugged her. "Hey, chin up, honey. I *do* admire your determination to hold true to your beliefs, but Gordon's information? That's just too important to ignore."

"There's more you need to know." Gordon was at the window now. "He's planning a full-scale attack. An attack on this bunker."

Brenda swiped her wristband and spoke in a calm, measured tone. "Urgent message for Daniel Chambers. Delaney has critical information. You need to get to the quarantine centre right now!"

The Mandarins stood waiting as the chopper approached the rooftop of Hong Kong's Lucky Card Casino. They were confident their emissary would bring good news. After all, General Rubeiro had always been a reliable business partner, and they had no doubt their allegiances with neighbouring countries would force him back into line.

The old men had expected information to be sent through beforehand, but Hong Kong was surrounded by the larger country of Guangdong, and Rubeiro made a habit of jamming wireless communication during times of crisis or unrest. It was just in the last few preceding minutes that the pilots radioed in to confirm they were delivering a gift and a message from the people of Guangdong.

As they stood together on the rooftop, the four of them made for an unpleasant sight. With their ages ranging from ninety to one hundred and twenty-five years old, they had all invested heavily in youth-restoring therapies. Despite this, the ugliness of their years of cruel disregard for humanity showed on their faces, something they all wore with a certain pride.

Two dozen heavily armed guards in tuxedos occupied positions spread across the rooftop.

The chopper touched down, and the Mandarins moved forward, rubbing their hands in anticipation.

One of the guards opened the chopper's door to reveal the cage holding the mutated creature that had once been a member of the general's guard.

"What the hell is that thing?" asked the youngest of the Mandarins

As one of the pilots disembarked, the eldest Mandarin noticed the absence of their envoy. He gestured for a guard to bring the pilot. Well aware of the protocols that went with having an audience with the Mandarins, the pilot looked to the ground as he was led across.

The oldest Mandarin had soft and supple skin, but deep lines in his face, reflecting his years of frowning when others might smile. Despite the healthy and youthful nature of his body, he took joy in watching the growth of warts and moles on his face and body, revelling in the revulsion they caused when people saw his face for the first time.

"Young man, you were part of a mission that involved the simple task of flying our envoy to General Rubeiro's military compound for a conference, and then returning him safely. I tell you now, if your explanation for why that chopper contains a putrid insult instead of our envoy is unsatisfactory, I'll have little choice but to direct our loyal guards to hurl you from this building."

The pilot was in a no-win situation. He'd endured a two-hour flight with the creature spitting at the co-pilot and himself. It was a cargo neither of them had been keen to ferry back, but the Great Mother had demanded it. Having breathed the air she walked in, they found it impossible to deny their desire to win her favour. Now he stood, separated from her by such a distance that the impact of her pheromones was waning, and his fear of the legendary brutality of the Mandarins was taking over.

"Your Greatness, I am unworthy of being in your service. We have clearly failed in our mission."

The Mandarin rolled his eyes and nodded to the guard holding the airman. He was a big man, standing well over two metres, and weighing 140kgs. He picked up the pilot and slung him over his shoulder.

The pilot pleaded. "Please, Your Greatness, let me explain." It was to no avail. Seconds later, he was falling to his death.

Two other guards dragged the co-pilot forward to face the Mandarins. Again, it was the elderly Mandarin who spoke for the group. "Young man, can I presume now that we have your attention?"

The airman nodded vigorously. "Yes, sir, absolutely."

"Good, then perhaps you might tell me what happened. Just the facts, without any of the gratuitous ramblings that led to your colleague's demise."

The youngster had adrenaline surging through him like never before. He was aware that one wrong word would be his last. "Your Greatness, I am sad to inform you that General Rubeiro no longer acts as your agent in Guangdong. He has been bewitched by a woman whose evil knows no bounds. She has made him her puppet and declared herself empress of your realm. She has enslaved your envoy and sent this beast as an insult to Your Greatness."

"I see, and I thank you for your honesty. You might yet live to see another sunrise." He gestured to the guard holding the airman. "Then again, maybe not." The young man was hurled from the building as the pilot had been.

The Mandarins calmly turned and walked away, keen to return to their game of blackjack. As they entered the stairwell, the elder gestured to the guards, informing them that the beast was to face the same fate as the airmen.

***

Kallan's heart raced when she entered the homestead, finding herself face to face with the woman who had brought her into this world for the first time since her departure from the community decades earlier. "Mother?"

Her mother put down the dishes she'd been packing away in a cupboard, else she would have surely dropped them. "Hannah? My beautiful Hannah? God has answered my prayers and brought you back to me!"

The two ran to each other and embraced. There was a long silence as they soaked up the joy of their reunion. Eventually, Kallan's mother spoke. "Please, tell me—tell me you're here to stay. I don't think my heart could survive the Lord taking you from me a second time."

Kallan held her mother tight. "Oh, Mother, if it were only that easy." Kallan relaxed the tightness of her embrace so she could pull back enough to look her mother in the eye. "I wish there were some way I could make up for the hurt you must have felt, but Mum, I had to be true to myself." Kallan burst into tears, triggering the same from her mother. They drew close together once more. "I love you, Mum."

"As I love you."

Having given them what he considered to be ample time, Jacob spoke. "We'll be needing a pot of tea as we discuss the matters that have brought our Hannah back to us." He placed a hand on his wife's shoulder and softened his tone. "Beth, I know more than anyone how you've missed our daughter, but understand this: she has been brought back to us by tragedy rather than love for her family."

Beth dutifully filled the kettle. "Yes, of course, but you must agree, it is truly amazing how the Lord works in such mysterious ways."

Jacob gestured for Kallan and Nancy to take a seat at the kitchen table. "So, tell me how it is that the government finds itself recruiting my daughter to coerce our community to its bidding?"

"To be honest, your daughter is just a pawn in this, someone whose aid I've enlisted to get a foot in the door with you and your community." Nancy shot Kallan an apologetic look.

Jacob stared at her, waving his hands in a circular motion. "Go on, woman, explain to me more fully then, why did you need to draw my daughter into this deception?"

"There was never any wish to deceive, just a sense of urgency. Like your daughter, the governor's father found himself opting to leave the Amish in his younger years, but Governor Miller still feels a strong connection with his roots."

"We already know of Miller's story."

"The truth is, we're faced with probably the gravest crisis that's ever hit humanity, and it's of our own making."

"Go on, woman."

"The governor's a good man who sees the Amish as unwitting victims. He's tasked me with making sure you and your community get the same protection as everyone else."

Jacob took on biblical proportions as his voice filled the room. "Our Lord provides us with greater protection than you know, in this life, and the next."

"You need to listen to her, Datt!" said Kallan. "Please, you need to accept that sometimes, hoopy-do techno-nonsense-shit made by men, needs other techno-nonsense to ensure the first bunch of shit doesn't kill you."

Beth covered her mouth in horror at the words coming from her daughter. There was one word, though, that was different to the others. 'Datt' had always been their word for 'Dad' within Jacob's family. He spoke softly when he replied, "I've not heard that word come from those lips in so many years. I must be honest with you, Hannah. While I love your brothers with every ounce of my being, they have never shown us the love we felt from you in the years before you left us. You tore a hole in our hearts that has forever left us wondering what we had done to so displease the Lord that he took you away from us."

"You and Mum did nothing wrong, but the reality was that I just couldn't share your faith anymore. I had no choice but to move on. Right now, though, it's time to put that aside. This nanotech that's been unleashed—it has the potential to wipe out all of humanity. We came out here not just to offer you protection, but to give you the means to keep your community thriving. The rest of the world might end up falling into one big bag of shit. But I don't want to see you and everyone else here suffer that fate. You deserve better than that."

Jacob was about to reply when Samuel burst through the door. "There's a truckload of soldiers heading up the drive, Father." He glared across at his sister. "She's brought this upon us."

***

Louise, Emily and Daniel were walking down the corridor with Emily's security detail in tow when Brenda's message came through, causing Daniel to pause.

Emily turned to him. "Is that Wiseman?"

"No, I still can't get through to him."

"Unbelievable!" Emily shook her head.

"It was from Brenda," said Daniel. "Delaney's told her that Doctor Brown's taken over the base at Minot—that he's preparing to launch an attack on us."

"Holy shit. It just doesn't stop."

"Brown's one person, and this is unconfirmed," said Daniel. "Nick's feeding information to Granger *right now*. Surely that's our more immediate priority."

"We don't *all* need to confront Nick," replied Louise. "Most of what he can do is already done. But Brown? My gut tells me this can't wait."

Emily nodded. "Things are moving fast. We need to keep on top of all of it, or it'll all be over before we know it."

Louise pulled a pistol from a holster behind her back. "I'll handle Nick and the Council. You should focus on finding out more from Delaney." She strode off without looking back, cocking her pistol as she went.

Emily shook her head as she watched the director walk off. "Daniel, you go with her and see that everything plays out as we planned. Keep me updated as you go." She turned and broke into a run as she headed down the corridor toward the makeshift quarantine centre, her security team close behind, talking frantically into their wristbands as they went.

Louise called over her shoulder to Daniel, "Come on, you need to catch up. I'll need you to cover me."

Running hard to catch up with her, he asked between breaths, "What cover? What do you expect? I'm a political strategist, not an agent." Flippantly, he added, "I've never held a gun."

They stopped for a moment as Louise took his hand and placed her pistol squarely in his palm, then closed his fingers over the handle. "You have now."

"What the hell? I wouldn't even know how to fire it."

"The point isn't so much to shoot, it's to make Nick piss his pants while you've got it pointed at him."

"Wouldn't that be more convincing with you holding it?"

"I'll be too busy ripping his balls out."

"Isn't this what you have agents for?" Daniel reluctantly examined the gun as they continued along the network of corridors.

Louise laughed. "You worry too much. My agents will join us when we get there. We'll need them to counter any UN troops we encounter. Nick's going to be sweating on us coming after him now that Granger's let the cat out of the bag."

"Doesn't Emergency Protocol 46 put them under your control?"

"That all changed when FIDO went down. The UN troops are getting conflicting orders. It's going to be up to each military commander's discretion whether to follow me or their regular command structure. Have a guess which way most military men would go? My power over them is gone."

"You were prepared to let the president walk into a situation that volatile?"

Louise stopped and grabbed him by the shoulders. "Listen to me. This is already a high-stakes game. It's going to get *far* more dangerous from here. Better to face that head on than pretend it's otherwise. And remember this, as president, Emily commands more respect from the people than you or I. None of the UN troops would be willing to fire on her. But me? Resentment toward the GIA runs deep among those troops."

"Shouldn't you have the gun then?"

"Trust me, you'll need it more than I will. I can defend myself without it."

***

Andrew Smith held his wife and son close to him as they huddled in a corner of the aircraft hangar where Craig held Minot's population hostage. He watched in horror as Craig moved through, addressing the population from his mutated vehicle.

"You're probably wondering why I've brought you all together today." A woman fainted and fell in front of the advancing vehicle, the front left wheel and arm-like axle lifting slightly as it ran straight over the top of her, crushing her jaw. Her companion started to scream, but no sound came forth as Craig pointed a finger in her direction. Her eyes rolled back in her head, and she collapsed. "No more interruptions. There is very little time, and order must be maintained. Humanity is on the verge of a major leap forward, bypassing what would otherwise require countless millennia of evolution." Although Craig was talking softly, his words were carried directly to the perception centre of each person's brain within the hangar. "Each and every one of you has been exposed and will soon begin transforming to a higher state of being."

Andrew's son said, "I'm scared, Daddy."

Craig turned, feeling the boy's expression of fear. He moved toward the cowering family, eyebrows furrowed as the lightning-like flashes flickered about his cranium. The boy trembled, frozen with fear as Craig pointed to him, bringing his finger up almost to his face. "It is entirely up to you whether your experience is positive or negative." He reached across behind Andrew's head and scratched the back of his neck.

Andrew's wife screamed, "Leave him alone!" A soldier who was a part of Craig's escort pulled her away.

Craig again spoke to the boy. "You needn't worry, your father will soon understand. He'll ensure you feel safe as you experience your own change." He turned to Andrew's wife, who was struggling to break free of the soldier's iron-like grip on her. "Continue resisting, and I promise you, you'll be faced with a life of regret." He moved progressively to the middle of the hangar as he continued. "I implore you to see the importance of working with me as I build a whole new force—a force to protect us all from the growing anarchy outside. The governments of the world are crumbling as I speak. The rule of law is diminished. Anarchy is building. It is up to us to restore order. We are humanity's only hope of seeing a path through these horrors we are now facing together."

Craig had taken control of the military as soon as he arrived in Minot, first taking over its leadership, then systematically overpowering the minds of those further down the chain of command. The task was so much easier than he'd expected. The local commanding officer had been put in place by virtue of his willingness to follow orders without question. Once the commander's mind was under his control, those following *his* orders were subsequently taken over with little effort (the disciplined minds of the military were so much easier to control than the typical civilian). The pilots had been harder than the others, but it was these men whom he saw as his greatest prize. Them, and the stockpile of nuclear weapons held at the base. He hand-picked a team of military engineers and assigned them the task of modifying the weapons to bypass their launch codes.

Feeling comfortable that the two thousand military men and women were under his sway, he had ordered them to put out an alarm and evacuate the town's citizens to unused underground hangars and blast shelters, most built during the old Cold War days. Craig attended each one, touching many of the petrified citizens and scratching carefully selected individuals on the back of their necks.

He left the last hanger that had required his attention, then approached Jason, who was standing at the front of a large military column. Capturing Jason had been little more than a game. The nanobots injected in the back of his neck were rewiring Jason's quantum network to be interfaced with his own. Jason saluted Craig as he approached.

"At ease, Mr Negus. I see you have the troops ready."

"Yes, sir."

"Are you clear on your orders?"

"Attack the bunker and ensure all resistance is neutralised."

Craig gave a nod of approval. "You'd best start preparing then."

***

Jon, Mary, and Merrick arrived at the bunker compound's main gate, coming to a standstill just before the shield, with two military police officers pointing automatic weapons toward them. Jon and Mary raised their hands in unison.

"GIA operative Jon Kruick, at your service." The sarcasm in his tone was unmistakable. "If I were you, I'd be lowering those weapons."

One of the soldiers quietly slipped into the guard house by the gate, returning a short while later with a GIA agent by his side.

The agent had an air of arrogance about him. "Well, well, if it isn't the legendary Jon Kruick!" He smiled. "I'm thinking the director's going to be mighty keen to talk to you."

"I don't know who you are, and frankly, I don't care, but I suggest you shut the fuck up and tell these baboons to lower their weapons. Or else, I'm going to be mighty angry, and you *really* don't want that."

The agent looked like a parody of himself. Wearing a white shirt, black suit, and dark glasses, he revelled in seeing himself in the role of a secret agent.

He stepped forward to be within two metres of the gate separating them. "Now, I think there are a few points I need to make clear here. To begin with, these boys don't take too kindly to being called baboons." He put his hands on his hips and removed his sunglasses, forcing him to squint as he stood face to face with Jon in the blaring sunlight. "And you know what, Jon? I don't think the director's going to be pleased with your performance of late. Hell, man, you helped another agent check out early from a high-security hospital in the New York headquarters." He laughed as he stepped back and threw his arms out. "And now, you turn up at this here gate, with some old hag *and* her brat, expecting to just waltz right in?"

The anger on Jon Kruick's face was evident, but he remained silent as the agent went on.

"To top it off, you're outside the shield. Step any closer than you are now, and any nanotech in you gets fried instantly! You know what that means—what it means if you've had that burning everyone's talking about? I'll tell you what it means. It means you get fried too."

With his hands still raised, Jon reached across and made a couple of swipes on his wristband, checking to see if it had self-repaired enough to detect magnetic fields. It confirmed the agent's claim. "Listen to me, you worthless piece of shit," he said to the agent. "I've got information the director needs *now!* I think you need to understand just how far I outrank you, *boy*."

"Well, you know what? I think *my* rank might just move a couple of notches higher when the director finds out I've got you bailed up here."

As the agent sent his message to the director, Jon smiled at the thought of how stupid he'd look when the repercussions hit.

***

Emily's Secret Service agents were by her side when she entered the quarantine area. She was short of breath as she addressed Brenda and Tanya, "This better be important."

Brenda looked up at Emily, her voice barely more than a whisper. "Tell her, Gordon."

Only then did Emily notice Gordon floating in the background. She'd heard talk of him having recently developed this capability, but to see the man with no eyes floating so effortlessly about the room left her gobsmacked. She walked up to the glass, "Yes, Doctor. Please, tell me."

Gordon drifted forward. When he reached the glass, Emily asked, "How do you do that?"

He floated in front of her and began babbling. "Dibblety doo-wop, Madam President... it matters not, the item about which we need to talk is— wobblematically more imperative to be discussed."

Emily's furrowed brow betrayed her agitation as she turned to Tanya and Brenda. "Dibblety doo-wop? Wobblematically? The government's been wiped out by terrorists, half the country's being invaded by a religious lunatic, while another bunch of lunatics are trying to take control of the rest, and I get dragged down here to listen to this crackpot speak gibberish?"

Tanya spoke to Gordon. "How about you let the levitation go for now, huh? Just tell the president what you told us."

Gordon raised a finger in the air and stepped out of his lotus position. "Of course, my apologies, Madam President. The levitation helps me concentrate while I'm reaching out to distant minds. Such vast amounts of information flow through my head while I'm floating that some leaks through as gibberish. I assure you, no insult was intended."

Emily's tone was abrupt. "You have something to tell me?"

"You'll recall no doubt, my former colleague, Doctor Brown?"

"Yes."

"He's taken over the military base at Minot."

"Oh? And how did he manage that?"

"You saw what he could do here? Well, military personnel are trained to be compliant, allowing him to take control from the top down.."

"You know this how?"

"I was unable to reach into *his* thoughts. But I was able to immerse myself in the minds of those around him."

Emily glared at Brenda. "Seriously? You called me down here to listen to this twaddle?"

Brenda put her hands up defensively. "Hey, I called Daniel, not you, and I *really* think you need to keep listening."

Gordon's face was right up against the glass. "The forces from Minot are on the move. They're heading our way. The full force of the assault will hit in two and a half hours. The cruise missiles they've launched will be here sooner."

As Gordon finished, one of the Secret Service agents emerged from a conversation with his colleagues. "Excuse me, Madam President, we've just received word that the bunker is under attack. I'll have to ask you to let me escort you to the situation room."

"Attack from what? Explain."

"Ma'am, I've received word there's a missile assault heading this way. Estimated time of impact is just over five minutes from now." He reached out to grab her arm. "I must insist, Madam President, that you come with me, *now*."

"No! Not yet, I have a couple more questions for Doctor Delaney." She turned back to Gordon. "You claimed to have influenced the fate of guided weapons at New Haven. Can you do it now? Can you make them detonate safely?"

"I'll need a minute to focus, but I believe so."

"Can you turn them back on Brown?"

"No."

"Why not?"

"I'll not be party to the taking of lives."

"Take out Brown and all those soldiers—they'll be free. He'll stop being a threat to *anyone*."

"I will not be party to purposefully taking another's life."

The agent again tried to coerce the president. "Ma'am? We really need to go—now!"

Emily yanked her arm free of his grip. "Will you just back off? I'm not done here." Turning back to Gordon. "Then can you please at least stop the missiles?"

Gordon made a simple nodding gesture, he raised his feet from the ground and resumed his floating lotus position.

The agent grabbed her arm again. "Ma'am?"

"I will come when he's finished, and not before. As your president, I'm ordering you, BACK OFF!"

11

Petra walked onto the balcony in the early hours of the morning to address the crowd below. Beside her, walking on all fours was a ferocious-looking beast on a lead. As they walked, Alicia growled at anyone she deemed close enough to pose a threat, her tongue darting out like a snake testing the air. It was meant as a warning of the damage she could inflict with the barbs projecting from the tongue's tip.

Following behind her was the near-naked guard Petra had earlier taken to her quarters. The young man was covered in bruises and welts. He wore only a loincloth, made from the remains of his torn and tattered uniform and now had a collar around his neck. Chan herself was dressed in nothing more than elaborate jewellery. Her hair had grown considerably, flowing over the generous curves of her breasts.

A guard blasted out the national anthem on a bugle, bringing the crowd to attention before introducing Petra to them. "The people of Guangdong have the special honour to be in the presence of the Great Mother of the People, Empress of Guangdong and all the lands to which it lays claim." He'd experienced the burning the day before, and now his bugle had merged with his flesh. His chest had grown enormously, allowing for greater lung capacity. He was a man who revelled in his responsibilities.

Petra made a gesture directing Alicia to sit and stay. Like a dog seeking to please its master, she meekly complied. Petra thought of how ironic it was. At the time of Alicia's burning, she'd looked at Petra with such fear in her eyes, and yet she now viewed her as a protector. A wicked grin spread across Petra's face when she approached the railing and addressed the crowd in fluent Mandarin. "Good people of Guangdong, I bring you wonderful news. As I speak to you, our military forces are closing in on the city that has protected the cowardly fools who have oppressed you for so long. Before the sun rises, they, and those who have protected them, will have paid for their crimes against you."

A roar of approval rose up from the crowd.

"Soon, your emperor shall march into the city and claim it as the rightful annex of Guangdong. Sadly, there are others out there who would impose the same tyranny our country has endured these past decades. It is no coincidence that I have come to you as your leader in these dark hours. Together, we shall rise against them, reuniting China. We *will* take our rightful place in the world order. Then, we will set free not just our people, but people across the globe. We shall free them *all* from the tyranny of their capitalistic overlords. This future is inevitable. In the past few hours, we have witnessed the fall of Washington. The West is collapsing under its own greed. No longer will the people of the world entertain the concept that power is derived from wealth. They will instead come to understand that *true* power comes from strength, as nature intended. We will show the world that Guangdong, and the China that we will lead, are stronger than any nation on Earth!" She punched her fist in the air as an exclamation.

The cheers from the crowd were deafening, slowly transforming into what was becoming a familiar chant. "We love Mother! We love Mother!"

Petra held up her hand to silence them so she could continue. "Sons and daughters of Guangdong, troops from our neighbours in Jiangxi and Fujian, are gathering on our borders. Taiwan's Navy encroaches on our waters. Not only are these actions an insult to our sovereignty, but they are acts of war."

The crowd quietened as her words echoed around the room. "But, we have friends, and friends stand together. Our friends in Hunan and Guangxi have pledged to stand beside us. Together with them, we are now defending ourselves from those who would threaten us. It is my promise to you, good people of Guangdong, that by the end of this new day, our enemies will beg to join our crusade. We will strike fast, we will strike hard. We will strike in Fuzhou. We will strike in Nanchang, and we will strike in Taipei." She waited for the echo of her words to subside, then raised her voice for the crescendo of her speech.

"Together, we shall vanquish our oppressors, as we march onward in our quest for justice!"

She stood with her arms thrust upwards and her chest forward, soaking up the adulation of the crowd.

Petra relaxed and continued in a softer tone. "Going to war is not a decision one takes lightly. I understand there are many well-intentioned among you who would prefer the path of peaceful resistance. As your loving mother, it is my wish to serve *all* citizens of Guangdong equally. Therefore, those who wish to pursue a path of peaceful resistance are free to do so. Be honest in how you state your intentions as you register for service. I guarantee those who would prefer not to take up arms shall *never* be expected to do so. Your mother loves all her people."

Petra turned and walked away.

It was two in the morning, Guangdong time. Petra's speech was aimed squarely at those in the Western Hemisphere. She wanted the world to know the Great Mother of Guangdong meant business.

***

Director Brandt could have done without the distraction of the call from her agent stationed at the main gate, but when she saw it related to Jon Kruick's arrival, she chose to respond. Being close now to Nick's quarters, she and Daniel had taken to leaning against the wall of the corridor. Louise had navigated a path for them, hacking the corridor's surveillance cameras to avoid detection.

Conscious of the possibility UN soldiers might be nearby, she spoke softly as she replied, "Message to gatehouse, arrange for immediate transfer of Kruick and companions via Faraday containment to quarantine facility. Ensure separate storage from Delaney and the children. Brandt out."

She turned to Daniel. "We'll stick to the wall until we have a clearer picture of the situation we're walking into. Nick's office is just around that corner. I'll link your lensview into my hack of the security cameras in and around his suite."

Daniel dropped his voice to a whisper while Louise swiped feverishly at her wristband to set it up. "Will we be able to hear them?"

"Hopefully, but be warned, our hack *may* be detected."

A hazy image of Nick's quarters flashed in front of them. He was pacing the room, looking agitated. Peter Wong calmly sat in an armchair. Two UN soldiers leaned next to the door, chatting while holding their automatic weapons.

Louise and Daniel strained to hear Nick above the crackling background noise. "...no, I'm telling you, I had *no* idea he'd do that."

Peter's voice was softer, but easier to understand. "How can you be *that* naïve? Granger's more Machiavellian than any of us. If you seriously believed you could count on his honesty, you're a bigger fool than I thought."

"The way he explained it made sense. He said it was in his best interests as well as ours if he kept our negotiations confidential."

"So, it never occurred to you that he'd benefit from showing he's capable of breaking news on this shit before we do?"

"No, it's not like that. I already told you," pleaded Nick. "How was I supposed to know it might interfere with our own plans?"

Peter groaned. "The *plan* was to set him up with a clear path to take the East Coast, making President Lucas look completely powerless and ineffectual. Remember? So that *we* could take over both the Executive *and* Congress, and hence, the rest of the country. Can't you see the damage you've done?"

Nick fidgeted as he paced. "Frankly, no. I can't see why we can't just push ahead anyway."

"For Christ's sake, you just don't get it, do you? We'd almost won over Wiseman. If she loses him, that's it; she's lost control of the military, and with that, the support of at least half the governors around the country. Now he's not sure, he's sitting on the fence to see what happens next before taking sides."

"But isn't that what we wanted?"

"No, we wanted him to declare his support for us taking control of the remainder of the UNSA. He already got spooked by Marco jumping the gun on D.C. He's holding off now, giving Emily time to shore up support from the governors. If it leaks out that we're soliciting him, those governors will all turn against us, no matter what they think of Emily's ineffectiveness."

"So, where to from here?"

"We commandeer the president's plane and get out while we still can."

"And go where?"

"As far away from this mess as we can. We go to Australia."

"And once we're there?"

"We build a new world order, one more focused on the powers of the Security Council. We'll jettison the General Assembly as the excess baggage it is. This is a genuine time of crisis, and we need to focus within the Council on working together as the regional powers we all represent. We need to do that without interference from naïve democratic institutions like the General Assembly. Then we'll be free to choose new representatives for Europe, and Northern Asia, ones who are more in tune with our ideals."

"What about Brandt and Lucas? They're working together, for crying out loud! That was never part of the plan. How are *they* going to react to Granger's speech?"

"My guess? They'll use it as an excuse to try to remove you, leaving us without the numbers to make legally binding decisions. That's why we have to act now. We need to force a commitment from Wiseman. Then we can *legitimately* take control of Air Force One and get out of here, before anyone has a chance to stop us."

"I don't get it, though. Wasn't Brandt supposed to be more or less on our side?"

"She's gained too much autonomy." Peter looked like he was losing patience with having to spell it all out. "We relied too much on FIDO to keep her in check while distancing ourselves from the dirtier aspects of power. In doing so, we inadvertently gave her freedom to make her own moral judgements. She's developed more of a social conscience than we gave her credit for."

Nick sat down on the couch opposite Peter. "Yeah, well, that's not the only error of judgment on your part in this mess. What was it you said about Emily and your ability to charm her? 'Don't worry about Emily,' you said, 'I know how to get what I want from her.' Hasn't quite worked out that way, has it?"

"There were too many distractions," Peter snapped. "If Louise hadn't been in her face so much, it would've been a different story." He looked at the floor, as though contemplating his failure.

Louise and Daniel turned to each other in stunned silence. The director looked furious, the rage burning inside her etched deeply into her brow.

"Can you believe that?" asked Daniel. "He's been planning to undermine us all along."

"I hadn't expected Peter to second-guess our plans." Louise grabbed Daniel by the shoulders, making sure she had his full attention. "The stakes are now even higher."

Daniel shook his head. "I can't see how we can pull this off now."

"We'll be fine," said Louise. "This collusion only involves Peter and Nick. We can still force the issue and get Cortez and Domango on side. But it will also depend on what happens with Wiseman."

"Yeah, and he's waiting to see which way the cards fall."

"So, we make sure they fall the right way by presenting the evidence on Peter and Nick to the other Council members. Then we confront these two directly."

"We'll end up with two Council members to replace instead of one."

"No, trust me, it'll still be just one. Peter loves power too much for him to refuse to cooperate after being exposed. He knows that's the only way he'll be able to maintain a position on the Council at all. Without the Council, he has nothing, and we need a functioning Council to hold the global community together in the coming weeks. Despite everything going on in Washington and Guangdong, the nanotech is still our biggest threat. This power play of Peter's is just an annoying distraction."

Louise focused the view on the corridor outside Nick's quarters to do a head count on the UN troops they'd have to deal with. She was surprised to see the corridor was empty.

"We've got a problem, time to get moving." She shut down the lensview imaging, grabbed Daniel's arm, then turned and started running down the corridor. She stopped in her tracks when a voice boomed from behind them. "I need you to stop right there, Director, you too, Mr Vice President." Louise and Daniel stood side by side, hands in the air, Daniel holding Brandt's pistol limp in his right hand. Two UN soldiers approached them. As one of them prepared to remove the gun from Daniel, Louise dropped low and kicked hard into the soldier's knee, sending him to the ground in pain. His colleague kept his gun trained on Daniel, but had little time to react when Louise came up, driving her fist into his throat. Louise wrestled the gun from him when he fell to the ground, unable to breathe. She used the butt of the weapon to knock the other soldier unconscious. It was over in seconds.

Daniel looked on in awe. "Whoa!"

"We'll have to change plans again. We need to deal with Peter and Nick *now*."

While collecting whatever weaponry they could from the two soldiers, they heard more troops approaching from both directions.

***

While one half of the groundfish had made its way to the ocean, the other needed more time to re-establish its quantum network and process more raw materials before regaining its ability to move freely about. In a reflex action, it had pushed itself away from the heat of the stadium devastation. Now, having drifted to Windsor, ten kilometres to the north, it had grown in size again and was conscious of its growing hunger—longing for the taste of hopes and dreams.

Inspiration, kindness, memories, and intellect, all of them held unique flavours, and the groundfish yearned to savour them all.

In the absence of nearby human activity, there was something else it sensed as it swam through the ground, a type of thought or feeling it was unable comprehend. It was as though a gigantic communication network ran through the very soil itself. It had sensed these strange feelings before, just after it had been born of the blast at Infinity. There had been large areas filled with it near there, areas where networks of tree roots had made travel through the earth more complex, and the strange sensations travelling through the ground had left it feeling unwelcome. It had largely ignored them at the time, drawn to the human activity that had been so much easier to find before now.

Longing to consume any kind of thought, it moved toward an area nearby where there was a network of tree roots, from which the strange feelings seemed to be emanating. As it approached, it noticed something else in the same area that had been obscured at a distance: people, three of them.

Not so far away on the surface, Amy Jones watched as her children enjoyed the playground.

What had been a disaster to most of the town was a godsend to her family. Here they were, enjoying themselves in the park as any normal, happy family would. With the rest of Windsor having evacuated following the bombing of both New Haven and the stadium at Hartford, Amy hadn't just taken advantage of the opportunity to give her kids a roof over their heads and a warm bed in one of the many abandoned homes. She was also revelling in having free rein over the public facilities, without enduring the indignant looks of others she'd become so accustomed to since she'd started sleeping rough.

She ran her fingers through the soft grass and watched as eight-year-old Jessica mothered her older brother, pushing him on the swing.

Feeling relaxed, Amy let a rare smile materialise on her usually sombre face.

Having drifted off to the happy sounds of her children at play, she was brought back to wakefulness by a sensation of the ground shifting.

She rose to her feet and raced to the swings to protect her children, but already, the ground beneath the playground equipment had begun falling away. Jessica screamed while reaching out for Aaron, who had just swung away from her. Unaware of any danger, Aaron continued laughing as the swing took him to its peak. Amy rushed in and, in desperation, picked up Jessica, hurling her into the nearby bushes before waiting for her son to swing back and into her arms.

As the swing started to come back down, the groundfish leaped up from the deepening pit, engulfing the boy in a mass of earth and nanotechnology as it rose, the chains of the swing trailing behind.

Amy let out a deafening wail and stood frozen as the groundfish ripped the playground equipment from its anchors, turned and dived back to its underground world, effortlessly consuming her on its way.

All was silent for a short while as Jessica lay in the bushes, struggling to breathe, the wind having been knocked out of her when Amy threw her to safety.

As her breathing started to slow, she wondered what to do next. She tried to stand. Then, the groundfish burst upwards again. Jessica could see that, when it came down, it would take her with it. Mustering all her energy, she ran, evading it on its descent. It burst out of the ground again, this time in front of her. She screamed, changed direction, and ran again, once again barely managing to avoid being taken as it came down.

What chance did she have of surviving the attack? The groundfish was so fast and relentless. She tripped and didn't bother trying to get back up. Then, the nearby screech of brakes caught her attention.

A thick Italian accent called out, "Come quickly, child. Run!" The car had seemed to come out of nowhere. A stocky man with tattoos was behind the wheel, and an older, rotund man was holding the passenger door open. The driver reversed the car toward her, giving Jessica less distance to cover.

She got to her feet and ran toward the car as fast as she could. The ground collapsed beneath her feet, leaving her falling away from the outstretched arms of the man with the Italian accent. He leaned out further, the tattooed man holding the back of his trousers. The man's hand wrapped around her wrist in a monkey grip.

"Gotcha!" he said as he pulled her up.

The groundfish shot up as Jessica was dragged into the car. The tyres screamed as the driver slammed his foot down on the accelerator of the old gasoline-burning vehicle and spun the car around, just managing to get it moving forward again before the groundfish plunged back to earth, missing the car by millimetres.

They sped away and watched it leap out of the ground again in pursuit, but the groundfish couldn't match the vehicle's speed. As much as she'd just lost both her mother and brother, Jessica looked set to see another day.

***

Jacob glared at Kallan. "I permit you into my home, listen to what you have to say, and you betray that trust by bringing soldiers onto our land?"

Kallan lifted her hands to profess her innocence. Wide-eyed, and slack-jawed, she sat shaking her head from side to side.

"Jacob, Samuel," said Nancy. "I can assure you, Kallan, or should I say, Hannah? She has no influence whatsoever on these soldiers. They're under *my* command, and I gave them strict instructions *not* to enter your property. I'm as keen as you are to discover why they've gone against that."

Samuel pushed his face close to hers. "If that were true, why would you need to bring this pagan witch with you? She's in league with Satan and practices all manner of paganistic rituals."

Embarrassed by his son's behaviour, Jacob smacked the boy's cheek. "Samuel! I will tolerate no more of this foolishness from you. Your sister is no witch, nor is she in league with the Devil. Our brethren deal with her when they go to market in preference to other traders because, despite her ways, she respects and understands ours. There is no more evil in your sister than there is in one of our cows in the field. She may be guilty of turning her back on the Lord, but I will not stand by and allow *you* to pass judgment on her. She forfeited the right to be a part of our community, and that is where it ends." Jacob turned his attention to Nancy. "I appreciate your honesty and can see it was with a noble heart that you have journeyed here thus far. Come, we shall go to your soldiers together, that we may *both* learn their reasons for breaching your trust."

Samuel glared at Kallan, a look of contempt burning behind his eyes, as Nancy and Jacob walked outside to meet with the soldiers.

The captain stepped forward when they emerged into the sunlight. "My sincerest apologies for going against your direct order, ma'am, but events have unfolded rapidly, to the extent that I judged it imperative to bring you up to date."

"You mean to tell me it couldn't wait another half hour? You *do* realise how sensitive these negotiations are?" asked Nancy.

"Yes, ma'am, that's exactly what I mean to say. While monitoring your wristband, it came to my attention that there were several messages for you from the governor between fifteen and twenty minutes ago."

"And you thought *that* warranted a break in the protocols?"

"I—um—I received word that the governor—he's fallen to his death, from his office window. His body had several bullet wounds. Forces from the South… they've seized control of the Capitol Building. Fighting has broken out between troops who remain loyal to the President and those who have pledged their allegiance to the forces from the CSA." The young soldier was flustered, cheeks burning red. "My commanding officer… he's among those who have chosen to take up arms for the southern invaders. I received orders saying I must return to Philadelphia immediately, taking you and Ms Keneally as my prisoners. They want you to stand trial for treason."

Nancy's knees trembled, causing her to lose balance. Jacob and the captain caught her as she collapsed, helping her to a chair on the farmhouse porch.

"Do you see fit to follow these orders," Jacob asked the captain, "or continue protecting these women who have sought to put the safety of my community ahead of their own personal safety?"

"Well, sir, I have to tell you, I took an oath to defend the constitution of the UNSA. It is a very difficult thing for me to go against a direct order from my commanding officer, but I did not, and I will not, pledge allegiance to the CSA. My commanding officer, and many others in our army, have long been Circumfrens. To my mind, by placing their allegiance to the Circumfrens ahead of their country, *they* are the ones committing treason."

"What would you do to see that these women are kept safe?"

"I will defend them with my life. That is the last assignment I was given before the command structure faltered. I do believe that is the only way I can now be true to my duty as a soldier of the United Northern States of America."

"And where would you take these women? They won't be safe here."

"I do not yet know the answer to that, sir."

Kallan had been listening in the background. "I do." She stepped forward. "I know where to go. We can all go and join my family in the mountains. We'll have abundant food, fresh water and security. We can survive there indefinitely."

Jacob placed a hand on Kallan's shoulder. "In that case, Hannah, you and your friends must leave quickly if you are to stay safe. I will pray for the Lord to watch over you. I *do* appreciate you coming out here in an effort to protect us, but I believe you will have greater need of the technology you brought than we will here on the farm."

"But don't you see?" A tear ran down Kallan's cheek. "You won't survive without it."

"The Lord has protected us until now, as has been his will. I must have faith that he will continue to do so."

Kallan's mother appeared in the doorway. "He has brought our daughter back to us. Surely that means something?"

"Please," pleaded Kallan. "Take it. I've already been promised a printer. You—the community here—you won't be safe without it."

The captain interrupted, "Actually, ma'am, I've also received word that the delivery of your printer has been intercepted and confiscated by the soldiers from the South. I'm so sorry."

"It would seem," said Jacob, "that the Lord wishes for you to take what you brought here today. You have a better understanding of technology than we do, and I've no doubt you will derive greater benefit from it."

"But, what about Mum? What about everyone else?"

"You need to go before those soldiers pursuing you arrive here, as they no doubt will very soon." Jacob turned to the captain. "You'd best escort these women from the property so you may all flee together."

"But—" Kallan's jaw hung open with no words coming forth.

"You need to go. I'll not tell the soldiers when they come any of what has transpired here today. Now go and be safe."

Kallan threw her arms around her father and held him tight. "I love you, Datt, thank you."

***

Louise and Daniel fell back, joining the reinforcements as they arrived. They were in a Mexican standoff: GIA agents at one end, and over a dozen UN soldiers at the other.

The UN troops advanced beyond the door to Nick's suite. Then the door opened, allowing Peter and Nick to slip out behind them and race down the corridor toward the elevators. They were accompanied by a handful of the UN troops, the bulk of whom remained behind to hold back the GIA agents.

"He's leaving!" said Louise. "He's actually going to try and steal Air Force One!"

She took stock of the weaponry they'd collected from the fallen soldiers: Four grenades, two automatic weapons, two pistols and a large knife. Louise shot out the lights along the corridor. Although aware that the soldiers had automatic targeting systems capable of locking onto their lensview signatures, she aimed to create a diversion, a tactic her agents expected from her.

Her agents opened fire, creating cover for Louise to kick in the door of the suite next to them. She grabbed Daniel and dived in, then took one of the grenades and lobbed it at a wall connecting the neighbouring room. She pulled Daniel to the floor behind the couch as the grenade detonated. It weakened the wall enough that a few rounds of automatic weapon fire created a hole that she made larger with a swift kick, large enough to crawl through. "Come on," she said to Daniel, "move it!" Once they were both through, she repeated the process in the next suite, the one connecting to Nick's.

Outside, more soldiers had joined the battle. The GIA agents were forced to take cover inside rooms on either side, taking the occasional risk to fire off a shot. The soldiers stood their ground in the corridor, confident of the protection offered by their flak jackets and helmets.

When the second explosion went off, one of the soldiers broke ranks, entering Nick's suite to check what was happening. Lying on his belly, he approached the hole, pulled a telescopic camera from his pocket and extended it. Once it was through, the last thing he saw was Louise's automatic weapon aimed through the hole. She let off several rounds, and the camera dropped to the floor, the soldier having received multiple gunshot wounds to his face.

Once again, Louise kicked the wall around the opening to make it bigger, then dragged the soldier's body through. "Grab his flak jacket, you'll need it before we're through."

Having heard the gunshots, two more soldiers went in to investigate. Louise watched through the hole as they approached. She pulled the pin from another grenade, held it till just before it was ready to blow, then slipped it through the hole. The soldiers tried retreating, but to no avail.

After the blast, Louise and Daniel slid through the opening, taking cover behind a couch as another soldier entered.

Louise stood up boldly, releasing a hail of bullets from her weapon. Despite his bulletproof vest and helmet, the soldier sustained several wounds to his arms and legs, sending him to the ground in agony.

Before Louise was through, Daniel noticed one of the two soldiers taken down by the grenade was lifting his weapon. Even as he lay mortally wounded, he was preparing to fire on Louise. Daniel grabbed the knife they'd salvaged and dived, plunging it deep into the soldier's forearm as he squeezed the trigger. Bullets sprayed across the ceiling. Then Daniel pushed the knife in further, causing the soldier to release his grip on the weapon as he screamed in pain.

Daniel stood, his temples pulsing as adrenaline surged through his body. His face and shirt were covered in blood that had shot up from the soldier's wound. Louise raised an eyebrow as she admired his handiwork and gave an approving nod. She pulled the pin on her final grenade and lunged forward, throwing it into the corridor among the remaining troops. She grabbed Daniel and pulled him to the ground again as she took cover behind the fallen soldiers. As soon as the dust from the blast settled, two of the soldiers charged forward, straight into Louise's line of fire. In the ensuing confusion, the few remaining in the corridor were taken out by GIA agents.

With the last of the soldiers down, the agents moved forward. It was only then that Louise noticed the flashing alert in her lensview. Cruise missiles were approaching the bunker.

***

Gordon sang *Zip-a-Dee-Doo-Dah* as he drifted around the room. Emily watched him through the window, unsure if she could believe what she witnessed. "He is singing what I think he's singing, isn't he?"

"It supposedly helps him focus," said Tanya as she leaned forward. "He's *a lot* more eccentric now than the Gordon Delaney I knew before."

Emily kept staring at him. "I can't believe I'm putting my faith in this guy to protect us."

An audio feed came through from the Situation Room. "Madam President, we have a visual on the approaching missiles from our tracking satellites. I'm patching them through to your lensview. We've successfully bypassed the FIDO overrides to activate the air defence system."

Emily folded her arms. "Good. What are the odds of knocking out the missiles?"

"Without FIDO to assist with targeting, we may not get them all. There's too many."

"And the consequences of those missiles hitting the bunker?"

"Madam President, under the circumstances, I would advise immediate evacuation to the Situation Room. You'll be safe down there, whatever happens."

"How long till impact?"

"Two minutes now, Ma'am."

Emily received a notification in her lensview that Wiseman was finally on the line. "Accept call." She closed her eyes and took a deep breath. "Well, General, you're a hard man to find in times of crisis. I've got to tell you, though, you couldn't have picked a worse time to make yourself available. I'd prefer you talk with Daniel or Director Brandt if you want an update."

Wiseman's voice was as unenthusiastic as ever. "No, Emily, it has to be you."

"I wasn't aware we were on a first-name basis, General."

"Under the circumstances, I'd rather forget protocol."

"Make it quick." She saw the first of the incoming cruise missiles explode on the satellite-tracking image, followed in quick succession by several more. One by one, they exploded, well short of the bunker.

Wiseman cleared his throat. "Very well. The way I see it, we're in an untenable position. Half our forces in the east have defected to the CSA. The government's so decimated that it's clear—I have no choice but to inform you that the head of the Security Council is now the Commander in Chief of the UNSA military. I finished a call with him a short while ago."

Emily stood rigid, fists clenched, eyes burning with rage. "You did what?" In the background, Gordon continued his ditty, singing about sunshine heading his way.

Cruise missiles changed direction, so they were heading straight up. Gordon stepped down from the lotus position, allowing him to dance as he sang. Having heard him, the children came out and joined in. He spun around, and more missiles changed direction, plunging to the ground and exploding on impact. Gordon finished his performance with a bit of jazz hands and a deep bow. The children cheered and clapped, Debbie begging of him. "Please, Mr Gordy, can you sing it again? Can we join in from the start next time?"

Emily terminated the call with Wiseman, let out a sigh, and sank back into the couch before feeling the end of a Secret Service agent's pistol nudging her shoulder. "Ma'am, I've received new orders. I insist that you come with me now, or I'll be required to use force."

"Oh, really, and what might those orders be?"

"You're to accompany me to Air Force One, where you will be evacuated with the Security Council."

"So, Peter Wong wants to steal my plane *and* take me hostage?"

"Ma'am, I have my orders. I have been informed that you are no longer the Commander in Chief of the armed forces and you are to be taken into protective custody."

Tanya turned to Gordon. "You've got to do something. Somehow, you've got to stop this."

Gordon approached the glass. "I will not use force to influence their decisions. I will not allow myself to be guilty of such violations of privacy. There will be another way."

The Secret Service agent nudged Emily again, while another walked around and grabbed hold of her arm, preparing to lift her to her feet and lead her away. "Ma'am, if you do not comply, we *will* use force."

Emily slowly rose to her feet.

"Gordon!" shouted Tanya. "Please, just do something—anything."

Abruptly, the Secret Service agents fell to the ground, hands covering their ears in an effort to drown out the feedback Gordon had induced in their earbuds. He turned his eyeless face toward Emily. "President Lucas, it would be prudent for you to run."

***

Jon held Merrick as he and Mary approached the Faraday container on the back of a truck that was partially slipped through the shield. The multiple linings of the container prevented the magnetic field from penetrating to the interior. Inside, the vessel was bare, except for a single bench seat at the far end. As they boarded, Jon glared at the grinning agent who had been so keen to overplay his hand on meeting them.

The agent couldn't resist a parting shot. "Have a nice time in quarantine, Jon. I'll pay you a visit from time-to-time and let you know how it feels out in the fresh air."

Hydraulic motors raised the tailgate, accompanied by a loud whirring sound that came to a stop when the chamber sealed with a loud clang. A string of LEDs down one side of the container's roof provided enough light for the occupants to make out each other's faces.

Jon took Mary's hand. "Hey, we'll be fine. I'll see to that. And I'll see to it that little prick gets what's coming to him."

She looked into his eyes and replied telepathically. *I know you'll take care of us, but I don't really care about that man out there. Please, don't waste time on him; he's not worth it.*

Jon laughed. "More than likely, he's making up for having a little dick."

They felt a jolt as the truck began moving, then waited in silence for it to reach the bunker.

The truck descended the ramp leading to the quarantine sector, one level below the surface. It reversed up to the second module, which shared viewing facilities with the one housing Gordon and the children, the viewing room separating the two modules.

Brenda and Tanya were checking the pulse of the unconscious Secret Service agents when the lights in chamber two lit up. A pair of GIA agents entered the room, one of them glancing down at the collapsed Secret Service agents, then towards the women. "What happened?"

Before either of them had a chance, Gordon answered, "They suffered massive bursts of feedback through their earbuds. I suspect that, seeing the earbuds interface directly with the brain's auditory nerves, it led them to lose consciousness."

One of the agents stared at him. "Was this you?"

"I'm not responsible for the lack of neural stamina that led them to pass out. They can take responsibility for that."

The agent sneered at Gordon. "Fucking freak."

The other spoke into his wristband. "Send a medic to quarantine, there's Secret Service agents down."

The airlock to Chamber Two opened, allowing Jon, Mary, and Merrick to enter the quarantine facility. They looked around, like animals inspecting a new home. It didn't take long before Jon saw the mutated figure of Gordon Delaney in the opposite chamber. He walked toward the glass, pointing. "You, you were at Infinity, weren't you? You're one of the fugitives."

Gordon looked across. Within a split second, his quantum network had hacked Jon's wristband, downloading all information relating to who he was and much of the detail regarding Jon's pursuit of him and Craig. "Ah, Jon Kruick, and Mary? Mary Killen! And that must be your grandson, Merrick."

Jon stared coldly at where Gordon's eyes would normally have been. "You have the blood of good men on your hands. Do you have any idea what I've been through to track you down?"

"I assure you, I played no part in the deaths of those men."

"The two of you were just as responsible as each other."

Tanya got to her feet and approached the glass to confront Jon. "No, you've got it wrong. Yes, Gordon was there, but it's the other one, Craig Brown. He's the one who went on the offensive. They arrived here together, but Craig's gone insane. I'm telling you, I know this man. He's a good man."

Mary walked up and put a hand on Jon's shoulder. Despite Gordon's mutations, she still recognised him. "I've met him. He worked with my son, along with her." She looked across at Gordon, her voice full of sympathy. "Good lord, Gordon, what happened to you?"

"Just a few biological modifications, courtesy of the nanotech. I can see more clearly than ever before, and in ways you couldn't imagine."

Mary held Jon's arm. "You've got to believe me, Jon." She gestured toward Gordon and Tanya. "They really *are* good people."

Looking into Mary's eyes, Jon felt her sincerity. He turned to Gordon. "Why was the other guy allowed to leave when he's so dangerous?"

Gordon shrugged. "He couldn't have been contained. He can control the minds of people who respond to authority. While it was dangerous to release him, it would have been far worse to try to contain him in a facility holding both the president and the Security Council."

"I can't believe Director Brandt allowed someone so dangerous to be let go. It's not like her to leave loose ends. Did you realise we encountered him down the road from here?"

"I learned of that when I scanned your wristband." Gordon looked across at Merrick. "The boy, he's not contaminated like you."

"Leave the boy out of this. He and his mother are the only two people I know right now who are innocent in all this," Jon snapped.

Mary asked Gordon, "How can you know that?"

"It's one of the new insights I've developed. Different styles of nanotech stand out to me like hot and cold spots. The boy is unique. He must be somehow immune."

Mary looked at Merrick, then back to Gordon. "I gave him a shot from a hypo-spray Ron sent me. He said it was meant for *my* protection. Instead of using it on myself, I gave it to Merrick."

Tanya asked, "He's had just the one shot?"

"Yes."

Tanya and Gordon looked to each other, then she asked, "Are you thinking what I'm thinking?"

"Yes, and I don't need to read your mind to know that, if we're right, this is excellent news indeed." Gordon addressed Mary, "It seems your grandson may just hold the key to the world's future."

"How so?" Mary asked, looking down at the sleeping boy.

"If we can ascertain how the hypo-spray made his cells immune to contamination, we'll be able to reverse engineer a means of protecting others. We must protect him at all costs." He turned to Jon. "But right now, I believe we have more immediate concerns."

"Go on."

"Your partner, Jason Negus, has been recruited by Brown. He's leading an attack on this facility."

"How would you know?"

"That's not important."

"The hell it isn't."

"Agent Kruick, this is hardly the time to give you the full explanation. Suffice to say, I read all the information on your wristband the moment you entered the quarantine section. I have capabilities that allow me to extract information from sources near and far in an instant. A few details for you on how this is possible have just been sent to your wristband."

As he spoke, reams of information scrolled up on Jon's lensview. "Okay, you've got my attention. How long do we have?"

"Just under two hours."

"You're sure it's Jason leading them?"

"Yes."

"How many men?"

"Around two thousand. They're sending in drones and fighters first. I expect those to arrive in the next half hour, but I can deal with them. You'll need to handle the ground forces, though. Having experienced the burning, your mind is working quicker than anyone here other than me. Unless *you* lead the defence of this bunker, I fear it will end badly."

"You seem confident of handling the airborne attack."

"Machinery is simple for me to hack. If it's a fair way off, I sing a song to help me focus. All will be good. I'll look after whatever the air defence systems can't."

Jon didn't appreciate Gordon's flippancy. "Is that right?" He turned to the agents. "I suggest you save yourselves a lot of grief and let me out of this box. Or else the director's going to be mighty pissed."

One of them approached the glass while the other was checking on the two fallen agents. "Come now, Jon, you know I can't do that. This is a quarantine facility, and you're contaminated. We've got this. There are over a hundred and fifty highly trained military personnel from the UNSA, *and* the UN stationed here, along with some of the GIA's top agents. We're outnumbered, but this facility's secure."

Jon ignored the agent and asked Gordon, "I've known Jason for a long time. If this Brown guy has managed to take control of him, we're in trouble. I need to know, this mind control thing, how's he doing it?"

"Via existing embedded nanotech and medibots."

"Holy shit," replied Jon. "He can turn our own military against us? We need to expose every soldier and agent to an EMP of some sort, or we risk him taking over from within."

"We can use one of the spare shield generators we've printed to generate a short-range EMP and send the troops through," said Tanya, "like an airport metal detector."

"What's the point in that?" asked the agent. "Without our tech, we're sitting ducks."

"No, you'll be soldiers, all of you," Jon snapped. "*Real* soldiers. Soldiers who don't rely on technology. They use strategy, courage and discipline."

"It gets worse, Jon Kruick," said Gordon. "The acting head of the Joint Chiefs of Staff has withdrawn his support for President Lucas and declared his support for the Security Council. Right now, the Council members are in the process of commandeering Air Force One so they can evacuate themselves."

"That's a separate issue," replied Jon. "Brown's the main problem now. If the Council's working against us, it'll be easier to bring everyone together and defend this place once they're gone. Get me out of this box, and I'll rally every soldier I can."

"Are we better off just evacuating? Surely that's safer?" asked Brenda.

Jon was stoic. "This bunker is built to withstand a nuclear attack. We need to make a stand, and hopefully take out that mutated piece of shit. We'll neutralise his forces as much as we can. *Then* we can evacuate safely and regroup. If we evacuate too soon, we'll be more vulnerable."

"Why can't the rest of us just leave now?" asked Tanya. "There are other aircraft here."

Gordon spoke calmly. "That wouldn't suit Wong's agenda. He has much to answer for. If we perish, so does the evidence against him. He will stop us from leaving and delay our departure any way he can. Agent Kruick is right. We need to defend ourselves first, evacuating only once we've done what we can.

If their forces are weakened enough, we'll stand a chance of getting away. One complication is that if Jon leaves quarantine, he'll spread his contamination to every soldier he comes in contact with."

Tanya wasn't so concerned. "We can use a shield generator to decontaminate them as they re-enter the facility. None of them will have been exposed long enough to experience the burning. We should be safe in that regard." She turned to Jon. "Once you go out there, though, you can't re-enter the bunker. As long as the contamination remains outside, we can control it."

"Won't that put us all at risk, though?" asked Brenda. "Risk of contamination if we're forced to evacuate during the battle?"

"The risk is minimal," Gordon replied. "We can keep the helicopter hangar sealed until just before departure. Anyone contaminated during the evacuation can be decontaminated once we've arrived at our destination. But we'll need to take a shield generator with us."

"That sounds like one hell of a risk. What about you and the kids?" asked Brenda. "How do we get all of you out without contaminating everyone else on the helicopter?"

"The children and I have learnt a technique that enables us to contain the nanotech within ourselves using meditation techniques. I assure you, we will *not* be putting you at risk."

"So, I can be with my son? We don't have to be separated anymore? Why didn't you tell me? I've been sitting here for hours."

"While it *can* be done, I advise caution. Most people in this facility would feel uneasy with a change in the quarantine arrangements."

Jon asked Tanya, "Those shield generators, can you modify some of them to act like an EMP version of a flame thrower?"

Tanya looked up for a second before replying, "I can't see why not."

"And the ones already deployed out there, can they be modified to send out a blast of EMP if someone gets too close, say within a hundred metres?"

"A bit like a mine? It would leave us all exposed while I'm setting them up. But, yes, I think so. I'd have to work my way through the lot of them. Then we can re-activate them remotely from back here in the bunker."

"It's a chance we'll have to take. I need to get moving, while there's still time to rally the troops. You need to go now and organise that screening for the soldiers... get together as many of those EMP flame throwers as you can and start setting up our minefield. There's not a minute to waste." When Tanya just stood nodding, Jon said, "Go! Move it!"

As Tanya hurried from the room, the GIA agent shook his head in disapproval. "Whoa! Hold on, Jon," he said. "This is unacceptable, and you know it. As a subject of quarantine restrictions, you have no authority," he pointed at Gordon, "and neither does that sideshow freak."

Jon ignored him and asked Gordon, "Can you get those doors open for me?"

"Hey! Do I have to remind you just who is in control here?" asked the agent.

Gordon made a waving gesture, and the airlock gently opened. "Good luck, Agent Kruick. When you return, I can teach you how to contain the nanobots yourself if you wish."

"Thanks, you can show me once we're out of here." Jon turned to Merrick and went down on one knee. "Hey, big guy, look after your grandmother for me while I'm gone." Not expecting a reply from the infant, he stood up and embraced Mary.

She whispered in his ear, "Be careful, darling. Make sure you come back to us." He kissed her forehead, then walked toward the door.

The agent yelled after him, "Hey, Kruick, you're going to contaminate us all. You worthless piece of shit!" He was ignored by everyone present.

Brenda asked Gordon, "I want to know more about how you can contain the contamination. How long have you known?"

"I've known since before coming into this facility. I knew there would be suspicion. So, I kept it to myself. I might also point out that it requires a good deal of effort. It's only now that the children have begun to understand the technique."

"So, I can, I can hug my son?"

"I wouldn't advise it yet, certainly not for prolonged periods. The DNA of another individual is like a magnet for the technology. While I can control it very much at will, my capabilities are greater than Debbie's or Ian's. Having said that, should you or anyone else become contaminated by the children, I can detect it, and we can ensure you receive treatment with an EMP well before the burning takes place."

Brenda looked at her son and couldn't contain her smile as she thought about holding him in her arms.

***

Louise had no delusions about the logistics of defending the bunker. "You need to find Emily," she said to Daniel, "then get her and the others at the quarantine centre to a chopper. I'll assign agents to help. You need to get them out of here, even if it means risking contamination. I'm going after Peter and Nick." She bent down, grabbed an automatic weapon from one of the wounded soldiers, and tossed it to Daniel. "Here, you'll need this."

Daniel was still in shock from knifing the soldier to defend Louise. The gun hit him on the chest, then dropped to the floor. The inescapable truth was that he'd more than likely need it. Squatting to pick it up, he was confronted by the harsh reality of the carnage around them. He involuntarily bent over and vomited.

"No time for that. We need to get moving," Louise said.

"Do you mind?" Daniel spat his reply. "My wife *died* last night. I've just stabbed a man and watched you kill a dozen others. How can you be like this?"

"When there's so much at stake, you do what you must. It's as simple as that."

Wiping the vomit from his mouth with his sleeve, he picked up the weapon and got to his feet. "I guess I should show more gratitude. I wouldn't be alive if not for you."

"Thank me later, you need to get moving."

They collected whatever weaponry they could from the other fallen soldiers. Louise sent two agents to accompany Daniel, while two others followed her as she went after Peter.

Daniel's group headed off toward the quarantine. As they rounded a corner, they encountered four UNSA soldiers heading their way. Unaware of what had transpired with Wiseman's switch of allegiance, Daniel felt a wave of relief. "Thank god, it's you guys."

The soldiers stopped and cocked their weapons, one of them then stepping forward. "Mr Secretary, I'll have to ask you to come with us."

Daniel didn't register their intent. "Great, we're heading to the quarantine. I'll feel a whole lot more relaxed with an escort."

"I don't think you quite understand. You and the agents with you need to drop your weapons and come with me. We're now under the command of the Security Council, and I have orders to detain all members of the Executive for debriefing in the Cabinet Room."

***

The Mandarins entered the stairwell, pleased with the no-nonsense manner in which they'd disposed of the pilots. They happily discussed what they planned to do with the bowels of General Rubeiro and Petra Chan once they were captured.

The youngest of the group particularly revelled in the details. "I will open up her belly while she still lives, and make her watch me wrap her intestines around the General's severed heart."

The others chuckled and slapped him on the back. Then, a series of screams from the roof brought them to an abrupt halt. They turned to each other, not quite sure what to do. Their gut instinct was to run, but they dared not leave without their bodyguards, who were still on the roof disposing of the beast.

They decided to send the younger member of the group to survey the problem. He took a few tentative steps to the doorway, his jaw dropping when he was confronted with the unfolding scene.

The beast had been placid while its cage was within the confines of the chopper. However, when the bodyguards dragged the cage out, it felt threatened, rearing up to the back in an effort to remain within the cargo hold. In doing so, it pushed itself against the hand of one of the guards who'd reached for a back corner of the cage. The beast's razor-like fur severed three of the man's fingers, forcing him to let go. Blood sprayed from his hand where the fingers had been.

The other guards lost their grip, allowing the cage to crash to the rooftop with a thud. The shock of the fall released the latch holding the cage closed.

The guard with the injured hand ran toward the stairwell, but in his panic, he lost his footing and fell. The others tried encircling the beast, one shooting multiple rounds at its belly, unaware that its super-strong fur was as tough as a bulletproof vest. The beast turned on him and lashed out with its tongue, its end smashing into the man's face. A second later, the tongue retracted, bringing half the man's brain with it.

The other two froze, looked to each other, then ran for the stairwell while the rest of the contingent on the roof began shooting frantically at the beast. Its elongated tongue lashed out at another of the fleeing guards, this time wrapping around his waist. As it pulled tight to retract the barbed appendage, the man's torso separated from his legs. The other got caught in the crossfire and fell well short of the door where all the Mandarins now stood.

The sound of approaching drones and fighter jets could be heard between bursts of gunfire. A noise that was drowned out when the first missile hit a neighbouring building.

Now that they were under attack, the Mandarins wondered about the wisdom of Hong Kong's leaders having placed faith in a deal with them to provide the nation's defence. Being surrounded by Guangdong, they had never taken the need to defend the casino city seriously, as the two countries were so closely aligned.

They watched as two neighbouring buildings were fired upon by the jets and hit by a multitude of kamikaze drones, one of them collapsing mere seconds after impact. Meanwhile, the beast continued to tear apart the remains of the Mandarins' security team.

The planes and drones were under attack themselves from naval vessels entering the harbour, where another battle was underway between UN ships from Taiwan and Guangdong's naval vessels already at anchor in Hong Kong Harbour.

A drone passing overhead was hit by a ship-based air defence laser, sending it plunging in a ball of flame that skimmed the rooftop, causing the already distressed beast to panic. It ran around the roof looking for a way to escape the explosions as more buildings collapsed under an onslaught of missiles. Rubeiro's air force was toying with the Mandarins, deliberately destroying the city around them while leaving their building intact.

They stood petrified as the beast zeroed in on its only possible path of escape. Three of them pushed against the wall and stairwell railing, creating room for the beast to get past. The youngest stood frozen as it lunged, jaws open wide. A moment later, the beast was leaping down the stairs, dragging the younger Mandarin's decapitated body with it. At the third landing, it huddled in a corner, occasionally chewing on the body like a baby with a teething ring. The surviving Mandarins slowly backed away and exited the stairwell, feeling safer on the roof. They were too scared of disturbing the beast to pull the door shut behind them.

There was only one member of their security team left. Standing near the roof's edge, he was silhouetted by the flames of a nearby tower that had erupted in a fireball a few seconds earlier. He turned and walked toward the trio who were huddling next to an air conditioning unit.

"You see this? The way this city burns? This is your doing!" He looked out at the city that had for so long been his home. Every high-rise building, bar their own, was damaged. The number of lives lost in this attack would likely be in the hundreds of thousands, if not millions. "I feel ashamed to have served men who could bring such evil upon lands they have made their home." He raised his gun to fire on them. One of the Mandarins begged for mercy, blaming their sins on the will of the eldest. He was crawling on his knees, tears streaming down his ugly face. The former bodyguard had begun squeezing the trigger when a bullet tore through his chest from behind, spraying blood on the wretched figure before him.

It was only then that they noticed the helicopter landing on the far corner of the roof, a sniper hanging from the door in a harness. When it touched down, the doors opened, and a dozen troops with automatic weapons disembarked to survey the situation.

A soldier partially entered the stairwell, then touched a stud on his wristband. "The beast is located, and its well-being is confirmed." On hearing this, General Barnardo Rubeiro emerged from the aircraft. Away from the overwhelming presence of Chan, he appeared to carry the same air of dignity for which he'd previously been famous.

He took slow, measured steps, soaking up the scene around him. The attack was as swift as it was devastating. There was nothing of significance the UN forces could have done in their eleventh-hour defence of the city.

On reaching the stairwell, Barnardo looked inside and called out, "Come to me, beast."

On hearing the familiar voice, the beast trotted up the stairs, carrying the mangled remains of the younger Mandarin in its mouth, like a dog carrying a bone.

Barnardo continued walking with the beast in tow till he reached the survivors. They looked up in fear at the imposing figure of the General. "Did you really think it wise to continue the pretence that you fools had the right to control the good people of Guangdong?"

The Mandarins remained silent, gripped by a fear they had never known.

Barnardo pulled a hypo-spray from the pocket of his greatcoat. "I'm so pleased that you've had the opportunity to meet with my little pet. He seems to have proved his worth quite well today, and will no doubt be immensely helpful for crowd control in the future, especially working with a few like-minded creatures." A wicked grin grew on his face. "And this, gentlemen, is where you'll be able to provide help. In this hypo-spray, I have a collection of nanobots, extracted directly from the beast's brainstem. When injected close to your own, you'll each become genetic replicas of him within the ensuing hours. Your memories of how you once were and the power you possessed will more than likely remain, but your ability to control your own destiny will not. Decisions will no longer be yours to make. You'll be compelled to follow the behaviour of the original source of this mutation, a magnificent beast like this one, who just a few days ago lived as an attractive woman."

On realising their fate, one of the Mandarins sprang up and made a run for the edge, preferring the idea of falling to his death over life as a mutant slave. Two soldiers caught him and carried him, kicking and screaming, to the general, where they forced him to his knees.

Barnardo smiled. "Ah, splendid, our first volunteer."

***

Daniel dropped his weapon, the two agents lowering theirs more slowly, watching the UNSA soldiers all the way. They put their hands on their heads, rising while the lead soldier went down to collect their guns.

As soon as his eye line moved to the guns on the floor, the agent to Daniel's left flicked his arm forward, allowing a blade to fly from his wrist, straight into the throat of one of the three soldiers. The second agent brought his foot up into the face of the lead soldier. He then flicked out both arms, with one blade landing in a soldier's eye, and the other in the remaining soldier's forehead.

The first agent picked up a gun, while reaching for the lead soldier and pushing him against a wall with the gun to his temple. "I'll give you five seconds to tell me what you know. One—"

"Please don't shoot." The soldier's face was filled with fear. "General Wiseman—he issued the order. He said the Executive branch was no longer a functioning entity, and President Lucas could no longer be regarded as the Commander in Chief. He told us the Security Council now officially governs the UNSA, and the chair, Peter Wong—he's now in control of the Executive arm of government—he's now the Commander in Chief."

"And the rest? Tell me!" the agent demanded.

"We were given new orders, directly from Wong. He said Lucas and Brandt had conspired against the authority of the Council, that they're guilty of treason. We were told Lucas has to be escorted to Air Force One, but Brandt and all members of the President's entourage should be detained for questioning in the Cabinet Room."

"And you actually believed President Lucas and Director Brandt were guilty of treason?" asked Daniel.

"In fairness, sir, it's not *my* job to make judgments. I've been trained to follow orders, *without question,* and that's what I've done."

The agent loosened his grip. "Anything else I should know?"

"Yes, Wong issued further orders. Due to an impending attack on the bunker, he declared that all those in quarantine should be terminated, ensuring there is no risk of them escaping or spreading further contamination."

"We can't let that happen," said Daniel.

The lead agent turned to him. "Sir, our goal is to track down and protect the president. And it's clear now how vulnerable she is. According to tracking data from her wristband, she's already left the quarantine sector. So, there's no valid reason for us to go down there now."

"I don't think you get it. I'm her closest confidant. I understand the need to protect her, but please, trust me when I tell you, the president would expect *exactly* what I'm suggesting now. Gordon Delaney, one of those quarantined—he's our best chance of survival against the oncoming attack. I've seen what he's capable of. He also offers probably the best possible protection for the president, protection we could never hope to offer."

The agent stood firm. "And your daughter's in quarantine, as well. I suspect that might be impacting your judgement."

"Of course it is," replied Daniel. "But you have to believe me, without Delaney, our chances really aren't good."

"We'll see what Director Brandt has to say." He turned away and spoke with Louise via his wristband while grabbing cable ties from his pocket to restrain the soldier.

The soldier's eyes reflected his utter humiliation. "You don't need to do that. I offer my surrender and full support. To be honest, following those orders to accept Wong over the president never sat well with me."

"Didn't you just tell me it's not your job to make judgments, that you follow orders without question?" asked the agent.

"I did, but even as I said it, I knew it was wrong. We're all struggling with the new orders. I believe others will reject the orders as well if I talk to them."

"I'll consider your offer." He turned to Daniel. "You were right. Brandt's approved your suggestion. Let's move it."

***

The water-bound groundfish was enjoying freedom of movement within the ocean currents when its attention was caught by the sound of engines from a large nearby cargo ship, the *New York Queen*, embarking on its scheduled journey between New York and Hong Kong.

Propelling through the waters with ease, the groundfish reached the ship's hull in no time. Once there, the pressure of the water helped it merge easily with the metal of the hull.

On the bridge, the ship's captain was unaware of their new passenger. His first mate entered the wheelhouse and said, "It's all secure down in the hold. Most of them seem to have gone to sleep now."

"That's no surprise after what they've been through," said the captain. "Who'd have thought we would ever be carrying a cargo of refugees, from New York of all places? And by the look of things, it'll be a hell of a long time before there's any other cargo leaving these ports."

The first mate nodded in agreement. "Even a week ago, I wouldn't have believed it."

"Two *thousand* of 'em we're carrying, and it's not the most comfortable cruise ship."

"Well, it's not like they had much choice."

"You're right there, my friend," said the captain. "I've never seen desperation like we witnessed at the docks back there."

"Do you know a port that's willing to take them?"

"Not yet, but we'll find one."

Down below, the groundfish enjoyed the gentle hum and vibration of the ship's motors.

Soon, it became aware of a young woman leaning against the hold as she slept in a dark corner. The groundfish moved up behind her and drew the sleeping woman into the ship's hull, consuming her mind before she had a chance to wake. Within two minutes, all trace of her was gone. She had no relatives or friends on board and wouldn't be missed.

***

Emily ran, trying to flee the quarantine centre before any soldiers or other security arrived. She could trust no one she didn't know personally anymore. She pushed open the door to an empty meeting room and hid in a corner, trying to contact Louise. She sent her a text to avoid the risk of being overheard by anyone in the corridor.

Louise called her back straight away. "You need to get out of there. The cameras in that room are active. The Situation Room will know where you are. They'll be able to track you. I can temporarily hack the cameras, but you'll have to follow my directions *precisely*. Nod once if you understand." Having no other choice, Emily complied. "I've recorded a loop of you sitting there, so when I say go, you need to get up, exit the room and turn to your right, then run as fast as you can before turning right again at your first opportunity. At the end of that corridor, you'll find an emergency exit that you'll need to enter." There was an uncomfortable silence while Louise finished setting up the loop. Then, she called Emily to action, *"GO! NOW!"*

Emily leaped to her feet, opened the door and moved as quietly as she could. Turning the corner, she heard people running in the distance. She was halfway to the exit when she heard someone call out, "She's not here, we've been duped."

Her heart pumped like never before, and she wondered if her legs would give out before reaching the door. It loomed closer. What if opening it triggered an alarm? She closed her eyes, took a deep breath, then pulled the handle down. No alarm, but the door made an audible clunking sound as the handle released the inner latch mechanism. She slipped inside the fire-exit and closed the door behind her before allowing herself to breathe easier, relieved that Louise had succeeded in circumventing the security systems. The distant voices of her pursuers dashed Emily's hopes for a moment to recover. "She's gone down here, check every door, including the exit. She might be in the stairwell."

Louise's voice was firm. "Listen carefully. They can still track you. You're going to need to ditch your wristband. Then you'll need to work your way up the stairs to the outer exit. I'll be there to meet you when you reach the top. Go, ditch it and run like you never have before."

Unclipping her wristband, Emily raced down a level, hoping to convince the soldiers she'd gone down rather than up. Pulling the door open, she winced at the deafening sound of the alarm it triggered. She hurled the wristband as far down the corridor as she could. Wanting to be as quiet as possible, she kicked her shoes off, turned and raced up the stairs.

The adrenaline was pumping so hard, and the alarm was so loud that she barely heard the soldiers burst through the door and pile into the stairwell. "I've got a trace on her wristband!"

"It looks like she's gone downstairs."

"The Situation Room—she's trying for the Situation Room!"

"You two go upstairs," ordered one of them. "She might be trying to throw us off. Check every door as you go. The rest of you, follow me."

Emily moved as quietly as she could, hugging the walls as she went. The sound of the continuing alarm made it hard for her to tell how far ahead of the soldiers she was. She raced for the top, running up flight after flight of stairs, her breath getting shorter as she went. Why did they have to make these bunkers so damned deep?

She heard voices from far below. "She's going for the exit!" They were getting closer and easier to hear as the alarm grew more distant.

Finally, lungs burning, she reached the top. With the troops closing in, she pushed open the first of two blast-proof doors that led to the outside, triggering another alarm. A few lunging strides took her across the short distance to the second door, the alarm from the first echoing through her head. *Something's wrong*, thought Emily. *Why hasn't Louise hacked the alarms?* It was too late to worry now, though; getting through that second blast door was all that mattered. It was heavier than the first and required the last of her remaining energy before it finally creaked open. She could hear the soldiers had reached the top of the stairs when it finally opened enough for her to slip through.

In a moment of blindness from the sudden burst of daylight, she assumed the silhouettes greeting her were those of Louise and her agents. "Made it!" she said between gasps for air.

Her relief dissipated when her eyes adjusted, and she found herself face to face with Peter Wong and half a dozen UN troops. He stood, arms folded and backlit by the afternoon sun.

"Hello, Emily. It's time we had a little chat."

"To be honest... I'd rather... never speak to you again... ever!" She was struggling to speak as she tried to get her breath back. "Although there are a few questions... *I'd* like answered." What the hell had happened to Louise? "Why are you... betraying... the whole damn world? What's your goal here?"

By now, the other soldiers had emerged from the stairwell. Emily was surrounded with no hope of escape. One of the soldiers bound her hands with a cable tie and walked her toward a nearby military vehicle. Nick was already in the front passenger seat, waiting. Once everyone was in, the driver spoke to the console. "Airstrip boarding ramp, safety mode."

Emily stared at Peter, who was seated opposite. He appeared to be lost in thought as he looked out the window.

"If you're intending to steal my plane, why not just take it to the internal boarding dock and save yourself the trouble of driving out there?" she asked.

Peter didn't bother turning to face her. "We need to leave quickly. Docking and undocking take too long."

"What's the rush?"

He was stoic as he turned to face her. "In ten minutes, this facility is going to be hit by relentless bombing from the UNSA air force, under the command of Doctor Craig Brown. Your friend, Delaney, may have managed to deflect the cruise missiles and drones in the nick of time, but he'll have his hands full when he's dealing with a full squadron of stealth fighter jets, bombers, and hundreds of other drones all attacking at once. Even deep down in the Situation Room, no one in this facility will be spared when those bombs hit. And Delaney? He'll be one of the first to go, if he's still alive by then."

"You've ordered him killed?"

"He's in quarantine. The whole facility is about to be attacked; it's the obvious procedure."

"Obvious procedure? Since when?"

"Since I became Commander in Chief."

"Since you became a treasonous megalomaniac psychopath, more like it. Are you in a competition with Brown to see who's the craziest?"

"I'll let that one slide, for old time's sake," sneered Peter.

Emily looked away in disgust. "Don't you dare rub that in my face, you lying piece of shit." She tried to lash out at him with her feet, but was held back by the soldiers sitting on either side of her.

"Oh, Emily, why do you do this? The language you use at times, I mean, really? Do you have any idea how much impact those little nuances have? How they've influenced the final decision of the other Council members? With the pressure you're under, and the way you've been behaving since we got here, they just didn't see you as being in a fit mental state to carry out the functions of your office."

"Oh, for Christ's sake. You didn't, did you?"

"You know full well how pervasive I can be."

"I can't believe I was ever foolish enough to let myself be taken in by you, even if it was a one-off."

"I'm glad you brought that up," said Peter. "You might want to try and recall how you felt back then as we board the plane, so you can put on a convincing performance for the other Council members."

"Excuse me? You can't be serious."

"Let me put it this way. Chambers, Brandt, Dyson, and Fleming's wife are currently in the process of being rounded up for questioning. Dodson, being the wimp that he is, gave himself up before we'd even got Wiseman on board. There's one of two things that can happen. You cooperate, and they can live. Or, you can maintain your current attitude, and they'll be found guilty of treason."

"And just what would cooperation entail?"

"One way or another, Louise will be, let's say, *retiring* shortly. The Council and the UN bureaucracy, along with the upper echelons of the GIA itself, have all been aware for some time now that tenure needs to come to an end. She's amassed far too much power, something we'd never intended. The fact is, we need someone with top-level diplomatic experience, and an image we could use to present an agency that's more in touch with community values than has been the case under Louise. I'm putting *you* forward for the job, once you've resigned as president."

Emily spoke quietly, as if talking to herself. "You want me to be your puppet."

"Haven't you *always* been our puppet? Have you *really* had to make any tough calls? Or have you maybe just been the spin doctor for the decisions of others, the people behind the scenes that no one really knows about? You know, the ones the conspiracy theories talk about."

"I've worked hard, and I've done a hell of a lot of good things. Under my presidency, the UNSA has done everything it could to make the world a fairer, safer place."

"Holding hands with senators and singing *Kumbaya* doesn't change the world, nor decisions made in the White House, General Assembly, or even the Security Council, for that matter. It's the decisions made in the corporate boardrooms of the big multinationals that herald change. Make no mistake, ultimately, they call the shots. That's one of the big problems with democracy; it's little more than a thin veneer over a global plutocracy, and I want to change that. The Security Council needs *real* power, and this state of emergency gives it to us. If we can hold onto it long enough, we can bring the corporations to heel. The world will see it's the better way and they'll happily accept the scaling back of democratic processes for the sake of the fairness we'll be offering. Then the Security Council will govern as it should, without interference from capitalism."

"What exactly do you expect of me in this charade?"

"For now? When we arrive at the boarding ramp, I'll cut the cable tie before you board and greet the other Council members. Then you'll excuse yourself, explaining that you need rest. I'll fill you in on the rest in our suite."

"*Our* suite?"

A grin spread across his face. "Yes, the presidential suite. It's technically mine now, but I'm more than happy to share it with an old flame."

"You're one sick little boy." *It was just one night!* thought Emily as she turned to one of the soldiers next to her. "Can you see how fucking insane he is?"

The soldier stared straight ahead. "Begging your pardon, Ma'am, but we've been briefed extensively on how you've betrayed us all this week. You no longer have the respect of this unit."

Emily's jaw dropped. It was a no-win situation. She was sure Peter had no intention of letting the others live. He'd conveniently say they'd been killed in Brown's coming attack on the bunker, knowing the truth would likely never be revealed; that they'd been executed before the battle had even begun. He was banking on it that she would cave in to his demands in the hope that her compliance might keep them alive.

The car came to a stop. Peter got out and had a quick word to Nick, who then raced up the stairs and boarded the plane. Emily glared at him with total disdain. She'd never liked the man. Now she saw him as little more than a pathetic worm.

One of the soldiers helped her out of the vehicle, then cut her cable tie while Peter walked around from the other side. "I'll take it from here, soldier. I need you to get that shield opened up so we're good to go."

The soldier saluted, got back into the vehicle, and sped back to the nearby perimeter.

"What about them? Don't they get to evacuate?" Emily asked.

"They'll be defending the bunker. We need to create the illusion that there are still people here worth defending."

If Emily were to have any chance of escape, she'd have to pretend to go along with the charade, looking for opportunities to escape before the plane took off. If she couldn't find a way out by then, it was over. The plane's engines were already getting louder as it powered up to prepare for take-off. Peter gestured toward the mobile boarding platform. With great reluctance, Emily began her ascent of the stairs with Peter close behind, carrying a pistol with a silencer attached.

Halfway up, knowing it was now or never, Emily spun around and took a chance. Kicking out at Peter, she hoped to make him lose his balance and fall. To her surprise, that's exactly what transpired. Having lost his balance, he grabbed hold of her blouse, pulling her over with him. They tumbled down the stairs together as the sound of the engines built to a deafening roar. The gun fell from Peter's hand, and he looked to be out cold.

Emily saw two options. She could take a chance at trying to grab the gun lying close to Peter's right hand and run the risk of reviving him as she did so, or she could make a run for the bunker. She elected to go for the gun, feeling sure she'd be a sitting duck otherwise if Peter came to. Lunging over his prostrate form, she reached out for the weapon, only to have Peter's fist connect with her cheek. Regardless, she managed to get a hand on the gun, then felt it slip from her grasp when Peter drove a knee into her belly. She winced in pain as she watched the gun slide two metres down the tarmac.

Desperate to succeed and still on top of Peter, she brought her own knee down hard on his chest, momentarily winding him. She scrambled to get the gun, but just when she was almost there, Peter's hand grabbed her ankle and pulled, sending her crashing to the ground just short of her target. The gun appeared to move further away as Peter dragged her back. He rose to his feet and kicked hard again into her belly. Despite the pain, Emily grabbed hold of his leg, biting down hard on his ankle. He screamed out, grabbed Emily by the hair, and dragged her to her feet. Clenching his teeth as he slammed a fist hard into her face, sending her back to the ground.

Realising Peter was between her and the gun, the only option left was to try to get away. Having twisted her ankle when she'd fallen down the stairs, she fell, writhing in pain, after just a few steps.

Peter picked up the gun as she stumbled to her feet, desperate to continue her escape.

She'd gone just ten paces when Peter fired a single shot. It pushed her forward as the bullet passed through her chest, and she fell to the ground, eyes wide in disbelief.

Peter tossed the gun aside and boarded the plane, wearing a casual expression as though nothing had happened.

A few minutes later, Air Force One accelerated down the runway and rose into the air, while President Emily Lucas lay in a pool of blood on the tarmac.

***

Louise and her agents raced to the same elevators Peter and his UN troops had fled to earlier. She sent the agents up in pursuit, using her wristband to track their progress while simultaneously flicking through the flood of other information coming into her wristband. There were updates from the East Coast and Washington, the South pushing into the North and the fall of Hong Kong. And it was all happening while she was facing a desperate situation in the bunker. Then, a notification in her lensview let her know that her trace on Peter's wristband had come through. She relayed the information to all agents within one hundred metres of his location just as Emily's desperate call had come through. Putting all other concerns aside, she talked the president through the steps she hoped would help her escape the UN troops and get her to freedom from the bunker via the fire escape.

She raced through the labyrinth of corridors to reach the elevator closest to Emily's exit point. The chances of helping her avoid capture were slim, but Louise hoped the tactics would hold off Emily's capture long enough for her to intervene. Once Emily had cast off the wristband, she had to move fast. At that very moment, she received a call from Jon Kruick.

She had to take the call. "I heard you'd arrived, and I'm glad you're here. The situation is rapidly deteriorating. Where are you and why have you waited till now to call?"

"I'm just leaving quarantine. I would've called sooner, but my wristband's transmitter was down. I'm heavily contaminated, so I'm sticking to the bunker's exterior while I rustle up troops to organise some sort of defence. You're aware of the impending attack?"

"Yes, although my information's limited, I've been distracted. You have my authority to go ahead. I trust you. But make sure to keep me informed." She paused before asking, "Have you experienced the burning?"

"Yeah, so far, there doesn't seem to be much of a mutation happening for me. I guess that's something I can still look forward to. Jason's looking something like a cross between a giant snail and a kangaroo."

"Are you still fit for this?"

"I'm fitter than ever. The only other significant change so far is my ability to process information. It's gone through the roof. I noticed that when I was dealing with Delaney in quarantine."

"He's been helpful, despite his eccentricities."

Jon replied, "Yeah, he actually used his mind to knock out a bunch of drones and cruise missiles, and he's confident he can take out the approaching aerial attack."

"I'm aware of that," replied Louise. "What's your plan for the ground assault?"

Jon took a deep breath. "To be honest, I'm making this up as I go. I need to work out which soldiers are capable of thinking for themselves. I'm shocked, so many of the troops were prepared to desert the president, but that'll change when I present them with the facts. The more I get on side, the more easily I'll convince the others. Then we'll take out what we can of Brown's forces and do our best to get everyone out of here."

Louise moved quickly while they talked. "That makes sense. No matter what, though, we *will* need to evacuate at some stage. Do you have any thoughts on dealing with the quarantine protocols?"

"Stick to them and we all die, bending them gives us a chance of getting out alive. Delaney says he's found a way of containing the contamination, but I'm not ready to place my faith in how successful he'll be."

The director turned a corner and found herself confronted by a dozen soldiers, guns cocked and trained on her. She felt the thud of a rifle butt against the back of her head, and all energy drained away. Her knees collapsed, and the room spun as she noticed two of the soldiers being thrown back by gunshots. The last thing she remembered before passing out was Daniel's face as he grabbed her arms and dragged her into a room nearby.

***

Gordon was aware that the planes were getting dangerously close to being within range. He called to the children, "Hey, kids, want to join me for a special sing-along?"

The children responded by rushing out, cheering.

Gordon looked out at the agents observing through the window. "You might want to lock in your lensviews to observe the satellite tracking of the incoming aerial assault. I think you'll find this interesting."

With the memory still fresh of what Gordon had achieved with the previous drones and cruise missiles, the agents complied. Together with Brenda, they sat back to enjoy the show, a welcome distraction from their earlier humiliation. Gordon eased himself off the floor into his levitating lotus position, the kids watching in eager anticipation.

He started low, flowing through the air like a feather as he started to sing, tapping his hands on his knees to keep time. "Be-be-be-do-wop—"

"Be-be-be-do-wop—" replied the children.

One of the agents turned to the other. "He is joking, isn't he?"

"I don't think so," replied his companion.

As the non-descript song's tempo built, Gordon broke free of his levitation and set out to enjoy dancing to the non-descript tune he'd made up. The kids joined in, dancing together, as though they'd done the moves many times before.

Then, the real show started.

When they jumped to the left, several fighter jets ejected their pilots, all of them shifting sharply to their left, in time with Gordon and the children. They flew straight into other planes, which in turn ejected their own pilots before impact. As the performers then jumped to the right, so too did more of the approaching aircraft. A gyration of the hips saw planes flipping over backwards and bursting into flames, always after the pilots had been ejected to safety. With each dance move, they took out more planes.

Gordon and the kids were having a great time, laughing and giggling as they went, plane after plane falling out of the sky. Meanwhile, drones were spontaneously exploding in time to their song, creating a background beat.

Brenda started humming along, sitting on the couch with her feet tucked up under her. She felt proud to see her son taking part in such an incredible display.

The agents sat staring through the window, dumbfounded by the images flashing up on their lensviews. It was obvious. Gordon had to be behind this, yet it seemed so effortless. There he was, singing and dancing with a couple of kids, while destroying a formidable squadron of aircraft.

The planes continued falling from the sky until the final two collided in a ball of fire. Gordon and the children celebrated with high fives all around while Brenda and the agents found themselves applauding the performance.

Every plane and drone had been destroyed, all without the loss of a single life.

***

Nick waited for Peter just inside the plane, as Peter had requested. Feeling impatient, he leaned across to look out the doorway to verify Peter was on his way, only to end up bearing witness to Emily falling to the ground with a bullet in her back. When Peter turned and glared at him, he withdrew into the plane.

Peter raced up the boarding stairs. "Seal off the door," he barked once onboard, "Prepare for takeoff, now!" After a soldier had activated the stairway's auto-return function and sealed the door, Peter dragged Nick aside. "If anyone asks, she simply refused to leave the bunker. And don't forget, one wrong word, and the others will know how you betrayed them."

In the main cabin, Domango, Maria, and a contingent of their staff were already strapped in, ready for takeoff. Peter was grateful for the lack of windows in the cabin prior to the transparent wall activation that would kick in once the plane was in the air; a wall of screens creating the illusion of plate-glass windows.

Domango seemed upbeat, like he was happy to be leaving the bunker they'd been trapped in for the past two days. "Where's Emily?" he asked Peter. "You said she'd be boarding with you."

Peter took a seat next to the big African. "Yeah, but you know what Emily's like. She insisted she had too much to put in order before she leaves. There's stuff she still wants to work through with Louise as well. She'll join us in a week or two after Nick's been sworn in and had the opportunity to settle in."

Maria looked concerned. "Are you sure she'll be able to get out? Isn't the opportunity to evacuate about to close? Perhaps we should call her, make sure she's alright?"

"You remember the briefing, don't you? With Brown and Delaney having the capacity to tap into electronics, we can't use electronic communications until we're clear of them. And we need to know Emily and Louise are clear as well. It's better if we wait for them to call us. Otherwise, we could be putting *their* lives at risk."

Taking a sip on a scotch and ice, Domango asked, "What about the others, are they going to be alright?"

The plane was accelerating down the runway as Peter answered. "Yeah, they'll be fine. Their choppers should be taking off any minute now. The last I knew, they were preparing to board."

Domango looked across at Nick. "What about you, Nick, or should I say, Mr President? You're a bit quiet. Is everything okay?"

"Oh, yeah. I'm fine," Nick looked up nodding, "just tired, the lack of sleep's started catching up with me."

Domango closed his eyes and downed the last of his scotch as the plane rose into the air. "Well, my friend, you've got a whole six hours to catch up on sleep before we touch down in Canberra. I recommend you relax and enjoy the flight. You'll be a busy man once we've landed."

Nick didn't respond.

Once they'd climbed above the cloud layer, the illusory transparency of the cabin walls activated, distracting Nick from his woes. Peter unbuckled his seatbelt and got up. "If you'll excuse me, I have some pressing matters to attend to."

Peter made his way to the private presidential quarters and then put in a call on his lensview. He prepared a drink while waiting for the response, then sat down as the image of Petra Chan filled his lensview. She was completely naked, sitting cross-legged on her massive bed with the young guard sleeping naked beside her, a chain and collar around his neck. A buxom woman wearing an open, silk gown was giving her a shoulder massage while another was giving her left hand a manicure. In the background, the beautiful melodies of the general's string quartet could be heard.

"Hello, Petie-Pie, I've been wondering when you'd get around to calling."

"It's so good of you to dress for the occasion."

"Come now, darling, what do you expect calling at this hour? You're just lucky I wasn't at play."

"Judging by your increased political *and* physical stature, it seems you've deviated somewhat from those carefully detailed plans we spent so many years developing. It would've been nice if you'd seen fit to discuss the various options when the situation changed."

"Well, that's what happens when a hopeless idiot like Alicia is enlisted to such a pivotal role. Oh! That's right, she was your choice, wasn't she?"

"But it was you who decided we should trust Brown to smuggle the sample out. Are you aware of what's happened?"

"I haven't been paying much attention, to be honest. I've been quite occupied." She paused to let out a yawn. "It's all worked out for the best in the end. Now, instead of being Barnardo's whore and playing second fiddle while you use *my* information to barter with him, I'm the supreme ruler of an empire. The once-mighty General Rubeiro is now my little lapdog. And, I managed it all without any help from you and your diplomatic mumbo jumbo."

"You do know you'll need the Council's cooperation if you want to expand beyond Asia, don't you?"

Before answering, Petra pulled the woman giving the manicure towards her, kissing the woman passionately on the lips while slipping the gown off her shoulders. She placed her chin on the woman's shoulder and grinned. "Oh, Peter, is that what you think? You really *do* need a reality check." She started to nibble on the woman's neck, then paused and turned back to him. "I'll tell you what, you want deals and diplomacy? Be a good boy then. Keep your nose out of what I'm doing, and I might leave Australia out of my plans, for now anyway." She blew Peter a kiss, then turned her attention back to the woman, pushing her face down to her breast, and then coaxed the other woman to bring her face close enough to lock their lips together.

Peter closed the connection and threw his glass against the wall. He had that sinking feeling that comes when someone realises their life's work has been for naught.

***

Louise woke to find she was stretched out on a sofa in Daniel's suite. Several agents were gathered in the room while Rick huddled in a corner. A thumping headache left her struggling to remember the past twenty-four hours.

"Where's Emily and her sidekick?" she asked Rick.

Rick struggled to bring himself to make eye contact as he replied, "As far as we can tell, the president's been kidnapped by Wong and his UN troops. They took off in Air Force One about an hour ago. Her wristband was found abandoned in a corridor, but there's no sign of her anywhere. Daniel's convinced she's still in the compound, keeping her head low, and that she'll reappear once she knows Wong's gone. Right now, he's outside helping Dyson booby-trap the shield generators. Some guy—his name's Kruick, Jon Kruick—he's negotiated a truce with the military. And, get this, he extracted irrefutable evidence of Wong's treason from your wristband. Once news of *that* got back to General Wiseman, he resigned his commission. I think Daniel's trying to convince him to reconsider."

Everything else came flooding back to her.

She'd failed, in spectacular fashion.

Peter must have taken Emily, and without Emily having her wristband, there was no way of knowing if she was on the plane, tied up somewhere, or dead. *Why?* She thought to herself, *Why did I let her out of my sight?* She could've sent Daniel or one of her agents back to talk with Delaney. At least Kruick was here now, even if he was contaminated; he was someone she could trust coordinating the defence of the bunker.

Swinging herself around, Louise placed her feet on the ground, then took a moment to collect her thoughts before trying to stand. "So, what's your contribution going to be from here?" she asked Rick.

"Me? I'm just keeping my head low. Hopefully I won't screw anything else up."

Louise felt pity for him as she looked at the hunched figure before her. "I'm going to go and find Daniel. Until Emily's whereabouts are known, he's the acting president. I've already lost one Commander in Chief today, I'm not about to lose another."

She called Jon as she started down the corridor, accompanied by two agents who had fallen in behind her. "Jon, we need to talk."

"Director! Glad you're with us again."

"I want to know about the woman and child you arrived with. There were references to them in my briefing notes. I need a clear picture of what's happened while I was out."

"They're Mary and Merrick Killen. We rescued them from a couple of thugs on the way out of New York. Mary also happens to be the mother of the piece of shit who blew up the Infinity campus. He'd sent her a hypo he reckoned would protect her from the nano-plague, but instead she gave it to her grandson. The egghead in quarantine reckons Merrick's completely resistant to the plague, that he's the key to avoiding a complete global catastrophe."

"Have you organised an evacuation plan yet?"

"We've got eight Black Hawk mark fours that'll carry twenty people each. If we can stretch that, we'll be okay, particularly after allowing for the inevitable casualties. We can't risk putting them in the air until we've taken out Brown's anti-aircraft capacity. After the way Delaney destroyed his squadron, he'll be keeping it under wraps as long as he can. He'll want to engage on the ground first, taking advantage of his superior numbers."

"Delaney was successful?"

"Strangest thing I've ever heard of, he did it all while singing a song with the kids in quarantine."

"And your plans for taking on the ground forces?" asked Louise. By now, she'd reached the elevator that would take her to the main entrance. As the doors closed, she leaned forward, allowing the elevator to do its retinal scan before accepting her request to go to the main ground level.

"His troops will *all* be contaminated, many will've also had the burning," said Jon. "He controls them through their nanotech, so if we knock that out, we take away his control. They'll still carry the last directive he'd shoved in their heads, but he won't be able to control and coordinate them. Dyson and Chambers are out there now, turning the shield generators into EMP mines. If they get fired on, they'll send out an EMP blast that spreads up to a hundred metres. I'm putting our troops through an EMP corridor we set up, knocking out their internal nanotech. They're stripping down, removing their wristbands, earbuds and lensviews before going through. We can issue them with old-fashioned headsets if we can find enough. Dyson's also come up with an EMP wand that'll work in hand-to-hand combat. It sends out a blast of magnetic pulse in the general direction it's pointed. We're printing off as many as we can."

Having reached the surface, Louise grabbed one of the buggies sitting by the main entrance, used by military personnel to move around the compound. Seeing it was clear Emily had either been taken hostage or killed, Louise dismissed the value of checking the top of the fire escape she'd directed her to, instructing the buggy to track Daniel's location instead. It took off at speed, followed by a second buggy with her agents. She was determined to make sure the acting president had ample protection.

"How much time do we have?" she asked Jon.

"About ten minutes."

"This battle is just about on us, and you were going to let me sleep through it?"

"With all due respect, I'm preparing for a battle where even the chances of a successful retreat and evacuation are slim," replied Jon. "We're outnumbered more than ten to one. Our one advantage is that I'm now a living, breathing supercomputer. I couldn't see how waking you up would be the best way to use the little time I've got to create a force to lead our defence. Now, if you'll excuse me, I've got to take that force and get on with preparing them. If we survive this, it'll be one of the most extraordinary battles in history. So, if you *really* want to make an issue of it, we can discuss it later. Kruick out."

Damn you, Jon! Despite her respect for him as a tactician and fearless operative, she'd never had an agent talk to her in such a manner—ever. *I'll deal with his insubordination later.* As the buggy pulled up next to Daniel, Louise was blunt and forceful. "Mr President? I need you to get in the buggy now."

Daniel looked around with a stunned look on his face. "What? What do you mean? What's with the 'Mr President' bit?"

"Emily's whereabouts are unknown. For all intents and purposes, she must be presumed dead. That being the case, you are now the acting President of the United Northern States of America. I intend to ensure you're within the bunker when hostilities begin. You and Dyson need to get in the buggy *now*." When Daniel didn't respond, she added, "Don't make me force you."

Daniel glanced at Tanya, then shook his head. "No, I can't allow myself to believe Emily's dead, at least, not until I see evidence. Besides, we're just about finished, another minute or so, and we're done."

Tanya touched him on the shoulder. "It's alright, you go, I can do this one."

"No, I won't have that." He looked down at her belly. She'd spoken to him about her unborn baby, how that was all that she had to live for now. "Let's just leave this one. Come on, we'll both go."

Tanya replied with a barely perceptible nod. Once they were in the buggy, Louise addressed its guidance panel. "Main entrance, go."

Daniel stared at the area around the bunker. "She must still be out there somewhere, surely."

"Understand this, you are now the acting president. And I *will* protect you. But that doesn't mean I'm answerable to you, or anyone else in this godforsaken place. You need to understand that while UN troops were pursuing her, she ditched her wristband so they couldn't track her. Now we can't either."

"She's resourceful. She'll have found a way to avoid capture." The look in Daniel's eyes betrayed his uncertainty. "Surely, we'd have known by now if they'd captured her, or if they'd killed her."

"Being a spin master doesn't provide the skills to evade a platoon of highly trained military men."

His voice was barely a whisper. "I survived, so can she."

There was an uncomfortable silence before Louise asked, "Do you know of any plans for protecting the quarantine during the battle?"

They'd reached the entrance now. As they rushed to the elevators, Daniel's answer came between gasping breaths. "Kruick, he wanted to send them to the... to the Situation Room level... until it's time to evacuate... but Gordon... he insisted on being near the surface so he can react quickly." He caught his breath as they stepped inside the elevator. "He wants to engage Brown in a kind of telepathic conversation, hoping it interferes with Brown's control over the battle. If it distracts him enough, our forces can inflict damage with guerrilla-style assaults."

"What about Killen's boy?"

"He's in the Situation Room already, with his grandmother and Brenda Fleming."

Louise checked the time in the corner of her lensview. Hostilities would start at any moment. She made a call. "Kruick?"

"I don't have time right now, Director, can you make it quick?"

"I just wanted to wish you luck. Do whatever you deem necessary."

"Much appreciated." With that, he terminated the call.

12

Jason led the troops, stopping a hundred metres short of the main gate, his troop carriers pulling over to the side of the road.

Craig came up from the rear to join him. "While the troops find their formation, let's give them a taste of what's coming. You can start by taking out the gatehouse."

Jason moved forward, his snail-like foot leaving a greasy trail that reeked of sulphur as he slid up to the small building. Reaching out with his right arm, he blasted a shot of mucus from his fist. It slammed into the gatehouse, burning a hole clear through the front and back walls before creating a two-metre crater behind the building. He struck it again, hitting it in a corner where it met the ground. Its reinforced concrete walls remained standing in defiance of his attack. So he released a barrage of multiple mucus balls, targeting the areas that gave the building its structural strength. He paused and watched as it teetered back and forth, then collapsed, sending up a cloud of dust. It was a symbolic gesture, the gatehouse having been deserted as part of Jon's preparations.

Craig rubbed his shrivelled-up hands together as he sat in his ever-shrinking vehicle, a sinister grin beaming across his face. "I think I'm going to enjoy this." He reached out with his mind to Gordon. *It doesn't have to be this way. It's not too late to give up. If humanity's going to survive, it needs leaders who understand the profound change that's coming.*

He was met with the telepathic equivalent of silence.

I'm making this offer despite the shameless way you tried to humiliate me, and the bloody-minded wastefulness of how you destroyed all those planes. Despite that, I'm still willing to work together. Can't you see? We're not so different, really.

Gordon was levitating with the children, who had now learned the art of control. All were floating in the lotus position with their backs to each other, slowly rotating in a circle. Their minds were linked as they responded to Craig's offer in unison, both orally and telepathically. *Bah, bah black sheep, have you any wool...*

"Arrgh!" screamed Craig before shooting a telepathic response to Gordon, *I offer you peace, and you insult my goodwill by singing a fucking nursery rhyme? I promise you, either you surrender and join me, or by sunset, you and your friends will all be either dead or under my control.*

Gordon allowed a thread of his consciousness to break away from the triad of minds so he could respond. *Perhaps you should consider whether you're able to deliver on promises before making them. You'll gain more by focusing on life's positives and freedom of expression than by seeking to control others through ruthless enslavement. Attack all you wish. My promise to you—a promise I know I can keep—is this, no matter how brutal your assault, I will not take your life, or that of any one of those enslaved to you. I can't make the same promise on behalf of my colleagues. Our only wish is to get out of here peacefully. Let us leave, or you will face significant losses.*

Oh, for god's sake, you always were full of yourself. Go to hell then, the offer's off the table, you worthless piece of shit. Craig turned to Jason and sneered, "What are you waiting for, you overgrown slug? Attack! Kill them, kill them all. And make it hurt."

Jason smiled, consumed by madness since Craig had taken full control of the GIA agent's mind and body. His sense of self was almost totally obliterated. He turned to address the troops spread along a frontline two hundred metres wide and five rows deep. Behind them were dozens of autonomous trailers covered by tarpaulins. It may have been Jason's voice that spoke, but the words were Craig's. "Today, we begin the liberation of our kind. Liberation from the tyranny of individualism. We fight to build a better world. A world based on common purpose and duty. We will demonstrate to all the superiority of the hive mind over the hopeless despair of singular thought." He pumped a fist into the air. "Today, we march to victory! Charge!"

Jason's troops made for an eerie sight as they ran silently forward into battle. The rogue GIA agent leaped high in the air, firing mucus blobs ahead of him at the booby-trapped shield generators. The intensity of the acid neutralised many of the carefully laid out mines before they were able to release their devastating electromagnetic pulses. He hit the ground just two hundred metres short of the main building, then focused on creating a clear path to the heavily fortified structure.

His efforts resulted in a passage through the minefield almost a hundred metres wide. Meanwhile, the troops continued their steady march across a wide front, with several hundred soldiers having their nanotech fried by exploding mines as they advanced, the casualties simply falling to the ground dead without so much as a whimper or walking around confused as to why they were there.

A focused column of soldiers advanced into the gap, getting cut down by the dozen as Jon's strategy kicked into action and his troops fired on them with EMP wands from distant foxholes and trenches with few casualties for his own forces.

Despite their superior numbers, Craig's soldiers were being slaughtered. Then, the covers were pulled from the autonomous trailers, revealing mechanical catapults, similar to those used in Ancient Rome. Because of Gordon's capacity to control technology with his mind, Craig had printed the catapults from old plans he'd found online, modifying them for greater range and accuracy. The troops grabbed crowbars and drove them through the trailers' electric motors to prevent any possibility of Gordon interfering with them. Half a dozen soldiers gathered behind each to roll them forward. The trailers also carried supplies of glass orbs, each filled with globs of mucus extracted from Jason's fists in the hours preceding the attack.

While the bulk of the next wave of soldiers funnelled through the gap Jason had created, many more were held back at a safe distance while the catapults were pushed to the flanks so they could target the remaining mines and Jon's troops.

The catapults released their payloads, and the glass orbs whistled through the air, creating an eerie atmosphere on an otherwise strangely quiet battlefield.

On hitting the ground, they shattered, sending an acidic splash of mucus out and around the impact zone and creating craters up to three metres wide. Soldiers hit by the mucus in their foxholes screamed in agony. So did Craig's own troops, who got caught by friendly fire in large numbers.

To make matters worse, dozens of the catapult shots missed their targets, forcing Craig to alter his strategy. He sent groups of soldiers charging into the mines on suicide missions, widening the gap for those who followed. He then held the catapults, waiting until they would have easier access to target the bunker walls from close range.

Jon watched from his foxhole, pleased with how the battle had unfolded so far. While eight hundred of Craig's troops were now approaching the front of the bunker, many of them had been exposed to the EMP mines and wands. It left them confused as to why they were even there; the weapons they carried no longer functional.

Jon relied on a walkie-talkie that the bunker's Situation Room relayed to the headsets that had been distributed to his troops. "Today, we fight not just for those in this bunker, but for the fundamental rights of all. For the right to have a choice in our destiny. Many of us will not live out this day, but if we can succeed in taking out their leader, future generations will honour the courage of those who have fallen. We may be outnumbered, but we will prevail. ATTACK!!"

The coalition of fighters leaped out of their foxholes. Due to their previous EMP exposure, Craig hadn't been able to detect their positions until they'd been exposed in the heat of battle. Having already experienced the burning,

Jon was the only combatant on his side who'd bypassed the mandatory EMP therapy. Craig targeted his mind, looking for any avenue of control. But Jon was very much his own man, and the link between Jon and Mary made each of their thoughts indistinguishable from those of the other, blurring Craig's ability to pinpoint Jon's location on the battlefield. He then decided to turn his attention to the minds deep within the bunker itself.

A truth that he didn't much care for was dawning on him. Brilliant as he may have become, he lacked the patience and experience to pull off the quick and decisive victory he'd hoped for. He'd allowed himself to believe his power to control weak-minded individuals would be sufficient, particularly having enlisted Jason to his cause. After all, Minot had been his within an hour of his arrival. His frustration growing, Craig cursed himself for failing to recognise that an outstanding military leader, like Jon Kruick, would deny him the opportunity to control them.

He needed a different approach. Relaxing his grip on some of Jason's troops might free up enough of his mind to focus his attention on the bunker, scanning for minds deep inside who may be vulnerable.

Jon had been a step ahead of him. Aware of the potential for Craig to attempt such a strategy, the soldiers within the bunker had also been through EMP therapy, along with many of the lower-ranked GIA agents. The more senior agents, those used to making decisions for themselves, had been free to bypass the procedure as they weren't seen as a risk. While Craig saw some of those as possible contenders for control, too much of his focus would be required.

He scanned Tanya Dyson and the director, deciding they were all far too strong as individuals. He was surprised to discover Daniel Chambers had become more or less a different man from the one he'd met at the gate. The events of the past twenty-four hours had forced him to find an inner strength that threw up a significant barrier.

He continued searching, desperate to find a useful mind to control within the bunker. One by one, he discounted the minds of those he scanned. Then, he hit the jackpot. Craig grinned sardonically when he seized control of Rick Dodson.

While Craig's mind had been searching the bunker, Jason had continued to make significant inroads on the battlefront. He blasted hole after hole through the bunker's main entrance doors and surrounding walls. He then provided cover to his forces as they raced forward into the building.

Down in the Situation Room, Mary was absorbing the information flooding in from the sensors scattered throughout the compound on the position of Craig's forces and their movements. The nature of her unique link with Jon meant that as she scanned and absorbed the information, so did he. Her thoughts were his, and his thoughts were hers. She relayed Jon's updates on the battle to the others in the Situation Room, even sharing accounts with them of what Jon's eyes were seeing. Gordon followed it all by using his mind to hack into the communications system, giving him more capacity to coordinate his own actions with Jon's tactics in the field.

A major wave of Jon's troops leaped from their foxholes, their EMP torches, throwing out a spray of electro-magnetic pulse like fire from a flamethrower, only with a much longer range and laser-like accuracy. Once hit by the blasts, the invaders were overtaken with confusion as they were disconnected from the hive mind, enabling the defenders to pick them off with ease or consider them no longer a threat.

Once struck, many of the attackers would blindly fire off rounds from their automatic weapons before falling, often taking out fighters from their own side.

While most invading soldiers may have fallen with ease, Jason Negus was a different matter. Quick and decisive, he repeatedly took out defenders as they prepared to fire their wands, allowing his fighters to move through to the bunker.

Still in his foxhole, Jon saw that if he was to have any chance of holding the invaders back, he had to throw himself into the battle now and work his way through the melee to take down his old friend.

Gordon and the children continued singing their nursery rhymes; the children helping him maintain focus. Craig was confident he'd shut off Gordon's ability to stop him by relying almost solely on older, mechanical technology that Gordon couldn't easily control with his mind. What he hadn't considered was Gordon's potential to commandeer the automated vehicles that had ferried the troops from Minot, now parked well back from where the battle raged. One by one, the electric motors of the empty autonomous vehicles sprang to life.

Gordon and the children guided them carefully toward the Minot troops. Craig was perplexed when he saw the troop carriers approaching from the battle's rear. They moved down the side flanks, herding the invaders back from the perimeter fence, like dogs rounding up sheep. Some of the trucks were guided specifically toward the catapults.

Craig called out to Jason's mind, summoning him from the main battle to attack the offending vehicles. He systematically shot at them with his acidic balls of mucus and telepathically sent orders to the troops operating the catapults, *Attack them, stop the troop carriers!* To those who were close by, he commanded, *Grab the orbs, lob them like grenades.*

Having destroyed one of the transports on the right flank, Jason heard Jon's voice from behind him. "Sorry, bud, but you've left me no choice."

Jason turned just in time to see a rocket-propelled grenade heading for him. He stared at his old friend in wide-eyed horror as the grenade slammed into his snail-like back, sending out a spray of caustic mucus. The shock of the impact lessened Craig's grip on his thoughts for just a second, allowing Jason's own personality to resurface. "Jon—" He collapsed to the ground, gasping for air. "Please, understand—I tried."

Jon Kruick stood stoically by his former partner as he whispered his last words.

"Give up now. You'll never win, not against him. He's too—" Jason's head fell back, his jaw hanging limp, blank eyes staring at the sky.

Jon pulled an EMP wand from his belt and fired it at Jason's head, ensuring the pain was over, and there was little chance of the nanobots repairing his broken body. He took a moment to reflect, then returned his focus to the main battle and the carnage taking place around him.

On the battlefield, Craig felt the shock of Jason's death run through him like a part of his mind had been torn away.

A hushed silence hung over the Situation Room, Mary struggling to breathe as she experienced Jon's sense of loss.

He readied himself to rejoin the battle with a renewed sense of vigour, able now to taste the slim chance of victory.

Across from where he stood, taking down one soldier after another, one of his own was cut down by enemy fire. He'd been spraying his EMP wand when he sustained the hit, hurling the weapon into the air as his body fell to the ground. The still active wand spun wide, catching Jon in the crossfire. In an instant, his nanobots were fried, along with every cell they were attached to.

In an instant, Jon Kruick's life was over.

In the Situation Room, Mary screamed in agony, as though someone was ripping her apart from the inside. The bond in their networks was such that one could no longer survive without the other. Without Jon's mind there to complete their conjoined network, Mary's brain shut down. Her lifeless body fell to the floor. The rest of the room looked on in shock, the only sound being Merrick's screaming.

As Brenda picked him up and set out to carry him from the room. She felt a firm hand on her elbow.

"No one leaves," Louise said.

"You want him stuck in here—" she gestured toward Mary's body with its blank and lifeless stare looking in her direction, "—after this?"

"We can't risk separation." The director looked across the room to one of her agents standing by the door. "Don't let this woman out of your sight." The agent took a step forward, blocking Brenda's exit. Louise turned to the soldiers at the control desk. "Are their anti-aircraft capabilities knocked out yet?"

"We're still uncertain on the number of rocket launchers they have and whether or not they're carrying laser weapons."

Louise evaluated the situation. Almost half the Minot troops seemed to be cut off from Craig's control and were shooting erratically. While there were now only two catapults left, they were still firing at the bunker walls, and invaders were flooding in through the breaches. Although Gordon's tactics had been effective and the shock value of Jon's strategy had given them the early advantage, the tide was fast turning against them.

With a little over fifty coalition troops still standing outside, they needed to retreat now to have any chance of making it through the tunnels to the hangar in time. Importantly, Gordon and the children needed to leave the quarantine area, or they'd be taken out. The biggest threat to their escape choppers had been removed when Jason fell. Louise hoped Gordon could deal with any remaining anti-aircraft weapons.

The director concentrated while Merrick's screams echoed around the room. All eyes were on her, looking for guidance. She turned to Daniel. "Well, Mr President, technically, this is your call. You can make a stand in the hope of destroying Brown, or we get out of here while there's still a chance. Your choice." She stared at him, waiting for his response.

Every second felt like an eternity as Daniel weighed up the risks. On the surface, the decision was obvious; continuing the fight without Jon would be suicide, but the risks associated with evacuating were extreme in their own right. He looked around the room as though there'd be another answer floating in the ether that involved less risk. Feeling the weight of presidential responsibility for the first time, he looked Louise in the eye and nodded. "Okay, let's do it—let's get out of here. We leave now."

The soldiers at the holographic control panels relayed the order to the troops in the field, then shut down their stations. All those present would leave the room as one, allowing the security personnel to provide maximum protection for Daniel and young Merrick Killen.

Then, the door burst open.

Rick Dodson charged into the room, firing an automatic weapon. Bullets sprayed around as the former Secretary of State struggled to control the lethal weapon. An agent stationed by the door jumped him from behind and wrestled the gun from his hands.

The usually reserved and cowardly Dodson was fully under Craig's control. The situation was made all the more dangerous by the fact that Craig had spent time controlling soldiers well-versed in martial arts, sharing their skills and experience. While those skills were useless in his own body, they became potent while controlling others. As a result, Dodson was quick in his response to the agent's attack. Within seconds, the agent had dropped to the floor, his neck broken. Another set out to take Dodson from behind, only to meet the same fate.

The distraction enabled Gordon and the children to make their escape and flee the quarantine facility. Aware of the evacuation order, they continued levitating and flew down the corridors, drifting like leaves blowing in the wind. They had learned to manipulate the magnetic fields emanating from the wiring running through the building, allowing them to turn handles and pull doors open and closed as they went. Gordon provided detailed information on the fields' locations, Ian calculated the forces involved, and Debbie executed the individual tasks.

Gordon sensed a call to him from the director's wristband. *Delaney, you urgently need to distract Brown's attention, even if it's just for a second.*

Gordon sent his reply directly to her earbuds. *I'll see what I can do.* He started to sing again and focused his mind, reaching out to Craig.

Craig responded as soon as he felt Gordon's presence. *Piss off, Gordon, can't you see I'm busy?*

Gordon began singing. *Bah, bah black sheep have you any wool...*

For fuck's sake... enough! I've had it with your shit.

Gordon's primary focus wasn't on Craig so much as on his strangely mutated vehicle. He delved deep into the neural network that had replaced its electrical system and found the guidance areas. He knew he'd only have a second at the most before Craig realised what he was doing and shut him out, so he intended to make it count.

His mind darted about within the networks until he found what he was looking for. An instant later, the vehicle spun wildly, sending Craig flying from his seat and crashing to the ground.

Craig's mind screamed out, *How dare you!* It reminded him of the humiliation he'd felt when Gordon had left him to crawl back to their vehicle. *You'll pay for this... you'll pay with the blood of everyone left in there.*

In the Situation Room, two more agents had fallen at Dodson's hands, but now, having momentarily lost his telepathic link to Craig, he hesitated. Louise saw her chance. Using the last of her energy, she dove toward the automatic weapon that had fallen to the floor earlier. Her momentum kept her sliding along as she fired a dozen rounds into Dodson. His body danced about as it reacted to each of the bullets before his bloodied corpse fell to the floor.

The survivors surveyed the scene in silence. Three soldiers and four agents had been killed, and two more were seriously wounded. Tanya was on the ground with a bullet in her leg, while the acting president, the man Louise was so intent on protecting, had been hit in the shoulder.

They filed out of the room, stepping over Dodson's bullet-riddled body, and raced down the corridor to the elevator that would take them to the hangar and the waiting choppers. Craig's soldiers appeared at the end of the corridor as the elevator doors were closing, several falling as a hail of bullets flew forth from Louise's weapon.

Their hearts were still racing as the elevator doors opened onto the massive hangar. The evacuees raced to the waiting choppers.

Louise helped Daniel, who was clearly weakened by his wound. Brenda carried the still screaming Merrick while one of the surviving soldiers supported Tanya. Some choppers were already filled with retreating soldiers and had taken to the air.

Once they were onboard, a soldier went to close the door but was stopped by Daniel. "We can't leave till Delaney and the children get here."

The soldier replied, "We'll have to put them on the next chopper, Mr President."

"The hell you will," he replied. "I'm not leaving without my daughter."

Brenda leaned across, adding, "And I'm not leaving without my son."

By now, the last of the retreating soldiers had made it into the hangar and were being fired upon by the advancing invaders.

The pilot turned around and protested. "Begging your pardon, Mr President, but if we don't leave now, we never will." As he spoke, the soldier at the door took a bullet and fell to the hangar floor.

The pilot started to lift off in defiance of Daniel's order.

Daniel was enraged and tried to get up, but Louise grabbed him and forcefully turned his face to hers. "The pilot's right. We have to go *now*, or everyone in this chopper dies."

The chopper moved toward the exit of the hangar, the pilot picking up speed as fast as possible while bullets whistled past.

Then, Gordon and the children appeared, emerging from the dust of the outside battle. They tumbled and rolled through the air, trying to match the trajectory of the chopper. Then one by one, they fell through the still-open door.

A wave of relief ran through them all, but then Ian hit the floor of the chopper after a bullet caught him in the back of the neck. Brenda started to scream, grabbing hold of her son and pushing down on the wound in an effort to stop the blood gushing out.

Everyone else remained silent while the sound of the gunfight below fell into the distance.

Once the chopper carrying the last survivors was clear of the bunker, the pilot turned and asked Daniel, "Where to now, Mr President?"

Daniel glanced across at Louise, his expression asking her the unspoken question, "Any suggestions?"

She thought about it for a moment. It could no longer be assumed that government facilities anywhere in the country would be safe. It would need to be a GIA facility that was known only to the organisation's elite. "Head for the Appalachians, southwest of Philadelphia. There's a safe house in the woods near Virginia Tech that we can use while we regroup and work out our next move. I'll send you the coordinates."

The chopper moved at speed, the sun setting behind it. Daniel looked around him, trying to come to grips with what they'd all just endured in their escape. Louise was staring out the window, a tear tracing a line across her bruised and bloodstained features. She appeared somehow less stoic than the woman he believed he knew. Gordon sat with his arm around Brenda's shoulder, trying to console her as she held her dead son close to her blood-covered breast, his head wrapped in a bloodied blanket. He questioned his faith as he thought of the horror Brenda had lived through since arriving at the bunker, watching her best friend, *his wife*, fall to her death before her eyes. And how cruel the hand of fate had been in how it had delivered her son to her during their flight to freedom. Then he looked at Tanya. She was holding her belly while receiving medical attention for the bullet in her leg. *If you really are there*, he prayed, *then please, I beg you, spare this woman's child.* He watched as she stroked young Merrick's head. The boy had finally fallen asleep with his head resting on her lap.

Daniel then turned his attention to his only daughter. He nursed her as she sobbed into his shoulder with the makeshift bandage Louise had made. Her persistent and muffled crying was the only sound other than the roar of the chopper's spinning rotor blades and engine.

Pumped full of painkillers, the acting president of the United Northern States of America soon found himself drifting off to sleep. A short while later, his daughter did likewise.

Louise Brandt, the formidable Global Director of the GIA, felt humbled by their forced retreat. She continued staring out the window, lost in thoughts of what may have befallen the woman who had been so recently re-elected as President of the UNSA.

***

As night fell, Emily regained consciousness. Her chest felt like it was on fire, and she had a thumping headache. She coughed up a glob of blood and tried to remember the events leading up to her lying there. She'd been shot, shot through the chest by the man who was the spokesman for the Security Council.

Emily pushed herself up onto her elbows, then tried to sit up, only to collapse back to the tarmac. *Damn it!* There was no way she was going to give up, not after what she'd been through.

She put a hand to her chest and felt around for the wound, finding an area covered in a large scab. Her medibots had been working hard; the wound was sealed. What she didn't know was how much that process had been sped up by the other nanobots she'd breathed in as she lay there. Then, she saw it. The ring box holding her precious coin inside. It must have fallen out of her pocket during her struggle with Peter.

Driven by determination, she put one elbow forward and put her weight onto it in an effort to drag herself forward. *My coin, I need my coin...*

She threw the other elbow forward, screaming in pain as she moved another arm length closer to her destination.

Again and again she endured the agony, staring at the concrete as she willed herself forward. Finally, she reached the open box. The coin was gone. Heartbroken, she resolved that she needed to continue, needed to reach the shelter of the badly damaged bunker.

One elbow, then the next...

Her progress was abruptly halted when her arm came up against the rubber of a small tyre.

Drawing all the energy she could, Emily propped herself up on both elbows, then straightened her arms to push herself into a seated position.

She raised her head, her jaw hanging limp at the sight of the lightning dancing about Craig's cranium.

He smiled as he looked down at her. "Hello, Madam President, welcome to my new stronghold. You and I have much to talk about."

The story continues in:
Fire in the Veins
The Scorched Earth
COMING SOON

Glossary

British Incident

The British incident occurred when global software giant, Soft Corp, was working with researchers at Oxford to develop self-replicating nanobots for military purposes. The project had been developed in total secrecy. When the technology escaped from the lab, the British Government initially played dumb, not explaining the sudden deaths that were occurring across the Oxford campus within a few hours of the technology escaping. Once an autopsy revealed the presence of the nanobots, all travel between Britain and the rest of the world was closed off. By then, the technology had spread dramatically, with thousands of people across London dying in the ensuing twenty-four hours. Within forty-eight hours, the death toll had risen to a quarter of a million, including the Prime Minister and several other members of parliament. London was put into a hard lockdown, and anyone who'd been there in the preceding days was forced to isolate until it could be verified they weren't a risk.

When a large storm approached London, simulations revealed that it would almost certainly spread the contamination to the rest of Europe.

At an emergency session of the UN Security Council, the decision was made to bring it to an end by detonating a series of nuclear explosions across London, ensuring there was no chance of the technology being carried through the atmosphere by the storm.

Circumfrens

Founded by Julius Granger, the Circumfrens believed in an eternal circular pattern to existence, whereby history literally repeats itself, from the Big Bang to the universe's end—an eternal cycle that is unavoidable.

Granger was able to manipulate this principle to rationalise that it was okay to be greedy within your own lifetime because to be able to help someone else, you must first help yourself.

Confederacy

As the years ticked by, the USA became increasingly consumed in partisan politics that divided twelve ultra-conservative Christian States in the South from the rest of the country. Mississippi, Alabama, Louisiana, Georgia, South Carolina, Tennessee, Kentucky, North Carolina, Arkansas, Oklahoma, Texas and Florida all resented the liberal attitudes being adopted by the rest of the country and ultimately broke away, calling themselves the Confederate States of America.

The political leaders in the South held on to the concept of aspirational politics as it worked hand in hand with the philosophies behind Pentecostal churches, and the Circumfrens, who were destined to dominate Southern beliefs.

Earbuds/audiobuds

Another massive advance in nanotechnology, earbuds had progressed a long way since the days of visible objects being placed in the ear. Like the lensview, earbuds self-positioned themselves once they'd been placed on the outer ear by the user. They stretched across just above the eardrum and relayed natural sounds, as well as using built-in speakers at an atomic scale that allowed for incredibly accurate placement of sounds in 3D space.

FIDO (Fully Integrated Defence Observer)

A network of three massive quantum computer networks, FIDO's three installations were housed deep underground in three locations: Mongolia, Africa and Australia.

The decision to build the network was made at the same time as the GIA was established. The thinking being that there were some decisions best left to artificial intelligence, particularly in situations where humanity's survival might rely on having to take actions that would have negative impacts on regional populations, like when the difficult decisions to detonate nuclear bombs over London and Mongolia had been made too late to restrict the size of the target areas.

GIA (Global Intelligence Agency)

The reformed United Nations instigated the GIA to ensure that localised politics didn't interfere with global security issues, essentially taking the decisions out of the hands of politicians.

It replaced internationally focused intelligence agencies such as the CIA and MI6.

Its decisions were made with the primary focus on global outcomes.

The GIA operated in almost total secrecy. Most of its decisions were made by FIDO, preventing human sentiment from interfering in day-to-day operations. As a failsafe, a director was appointed by the Security Council with the ability to override FIDO's decisions, except for those that were deemed critical to humanity's survival.

Hypospray

The advent of nanotechnology in medicine meant there was no longer the need for traditional medicine, just hyposprays that relied on air pressure to push the microscopic pieces of technology below the surface of the skin.

Infinity Technology Corporation

The world's largest technology company, Infinity, established a campus just outside of New Haven specifically to focus on the self-replicating nanobot DNA project. The top researchers in their fields were poached early in the project's development from other tech companies or universities. Almost everyone working at the facility had a PhD in their field of expertise and were signed up to long-term contracts with water-tight non-disclosure agreements signed by every person who entered the facility.

Infinity had started out as a search engine in the later part of the twentieth century but had grown into the world's largest technology company, dominating in diverse fields.

As quantum computing began unlocking the potential of nanotechnology, Infinity extended its lead over its rivals, particularly after the British and Mongolian incidents had deeply damaged the credibility of its main rivals, Soft Corp and Mingway.

Ionia

Ionia lay on the west coast of what is now Turkey. 600 years before the beginning of the common era it was a major trading centre for the Greeks and brought together people from a vast array of cultures, all of whom had their own religious beliefs that they held to be true. As these people got together, at some stage the proposition was put forth: if we all believe our religious beliefs to be true, only one of them could be genuine, in which case they are all more than likely wrong. Thales of Miletus (640 – 546 BCE) is considered to be the first person to apply what is now our common approach to science, observing nature and using reason to find an explanation rather than applying superstition. The Ionian scientists were the first to systematically catalogue their findings and observations, establishing an approach still used by science today.

Jihadist

A generic term for hardline Islamic terrorists.

Lensview

Works hand in hand with the wristband and earbuds. The lensview was made possible by the advances in nanotechnology that resulted from quantum computing.

When placed against the eye, the lensview automatically positions itself. Its transparent structure hosts cameras and projectors that can capture everything the wearer sees and also create augmented or virtual reality scenes, projected directly onto the retina.

Like the wristband and earbuds, the lensviews have a degree of self-repairability. Although their production is so cheap that if one becomes faulty, there is virtually no cost in replacing it.

Once in place, most people leave them there permanently rather than go through the process of inserting and removing them too often, a process that can be quite time-consuming.

Removal is done by placing a finger over the eye and speaking the relevant voice command to activate its disengagement.

The lensview is powered almost solely by kinetic and quantum vibration.

Medibot

One of the most highly regarded aspects of nanotechnology had been the advent of the medibot, programmable armies of microscopic robots that carryied a database onboard of known diseases and assisted the body's immune system in dealing with them.

They did not self-repair and were often specialised to deal with particular diseases or injuries. They also helped repair damaged tissue after fractures or nerve damage and could be controlled by a surgeon if need be.

Each individual had medibots 'cultured' to match their DNA enough for the host body's immune system to accept them.

Mongolian Incident

The Mongolian incident occurred two years after the British incident.

The Mingway company was also setting out to produce self-replicating nanobots for military purposes.

Faulty workmanship in the research facilities' containment vessels led to an undetected leak. Within hours, all personnel at the campus had been contaminated and died painful deaths. Strong winds swept the technology into Ulaanbaatar, the nation's capital. By day's end, over half a million had died. A hastily called meeting of the United Nations Security Council concluded that the only possible solution was to use nuclear weapons on the capital and the lands between it and the Mingway facility 100 kms away. To be certain the technology was destroyed, a vast area downwind of the capital was also nuked.

After the Mongolian incident, a global treaty was put in place, ensuring no nation would ever again attempt to use nanobots for military purposes. Policing such a policy demanded the restructure of the UN, along with the creation of both the GIA and FIDO.

Nanobot

Nanobots were robots built at the atomic scale. The nanobots primarily talked about in this book were part of a long-term strategy employed by Infinity Technology Corporation to stay ahead of other tech companies.

The technology aimed to render medibots, wristbands, lensviews and earbuds obsolete using nanobots that bonded with the DNA within every cell, linking together in a giant network in each person's body that effectively acted as a large quantum computer that was fully aware of what was happening throughout the host body (and the host's mind). The aim was to eliminate any threat of disease and to interface with the perception centre of the brain, allowing for the same functionality of a lensview without having to physically project onto the retina. The host would also be able to interface with any other network they have access to and to have full access to them using the resources of their body's nanbot network.

Hugely controversial, the ethics had been constantly debated, while it was also recognised that whoever was the first to fully develop the technology would essentially have global control of it.

The great fear had been that a hostile nation or entity may develop the technology ahead of a nation that had signed up to the global Nano Safety Treaty.

Because of this, the GIA embedded agents at multiple levels within Infinity Technology Corporation in an effort to circumvent any possibility of their version of the technology under development falling into hostile hands.

United Nations

After the British and Mongolian incidents, the world's nations unanimously agreed that it was time to reshape the United Nations so it could act as a global government.

Under the reshaped structure, each country's representative was to be directly elected by the local population.

The Security Council had an even more fundamental change. Instead of having the five permanent members with veto powers, there were delegates for each global region: North America, South America, Europe, Africa, North Asia and Southern Asia. These delegates were elected by the representatives of the countries within those regions, with the weight of each vote reflecting the population size of the particular country. The Security Council appointed the head of the GIA and technically had veto power over military decisions from individual countries.

UNSA (United Northern States of America)

When the Confederate States chose to break away, the United States Government chose to draw a line in the sand to acknowledge the breakup within the American experiment, the name change to the United Northern States of America being emblematic of the change.

Freed from the constraints of conservative Southern voices, the new country (still embracing the original USA constitution) became a far more progressive country than its predecessor, adopting the metric system to be in step with the rest of the world, and introducing a basic wage, funded by higher taxes on the wealthy. The more progressive tax system also allowed for universal free health and education.

Wristband

Ubiquitous wearable high-powered computer and communications device. The wristband interfaced with lensviews and earbuds to create a fully immersive augmented reality experience. It could be operated using gestures on its watchface-like screen, voice commands or hand gestures. The nanotechnology at the heart of the wristband required almost no power to run and could recharge itself through kinetic movement, exposure to light and quantum vibrations.

While the wristband was an immensely powerful computer in its own right, its primary function was the connection to networks.

While there are myriad brands of wristbands in countless styles, the operating system that controlled them was almost exclusively built on a platform developed by Infinity Technology Corporation.

Probably the most important advance in nanotechnology packed into the wristband was the advent of 'self-repair' functionality. Molecular-sized robots could repair most breakages that may have occured within the wristband's technology. These robots were even able to alter the appearance and shape of the wristband depending on mood and purpose.